IN HER FOOTSTEPS

RUTH HARROW

Copyright

ISBN-13: 978-1979737074
ISBN-10: 197973707X

Contents

Prologue

I know I have made a terrible mistake; in fact, I've made lots of them. To anyone else, the signs would have been obvious. Someone else would have interpreted the warnings that have been strewn across my path in recent weeks. Someone else would have seen the red flags at every turn and run for their life. Someone else would not be in the ridiculously dangerous situation I now find myself in.

Knowing he was right behind me, I ran as fast as I could into the tiny little bathroom in the back of the shop and slammed the door hard behind me. I fumbled the flimsy metal lock shut with trembling fingers, but I don't know how long it will hold. The tiny little screws that hold the thing in place are now being forced out with each of his attempts to break the door down.

He is shouting.

I am trapped.

I'm trapped in a tiny, windowless room and the only way out is through the door he is slamming into with increased frenzy. There is no way that I will unlock the door, however. Even though I know it will be ripped from its hinges any second.

There will be a second where I will stand, shreds of wood falling around me, splinters raining down on us both as he stares at me, rage etched into every one of his features, before he drags me out.

That is the only way that I am leaving this room.

And by the way there is only a single screw holding the tiny little lock in place, I know that time is almost upon me.

1

I am going to leave him. It is not a case of *if*, it is simply a case of *when*.

I squeeze out the flannel that I have been using to try to stem the flow of blood from my bottom lip. I watch as the crimson trickle meets the clear water droplets in the bright white of the sink and they streak together to form a slow stream.

My latest injury isn't a bad one, not the worst I've ever had, anyway. But as usual, it has been inflicted the same way as all the others, by my husband, Dan.

The one thing that my husband hates the most is being disappointed. He hates that more than anything, and unfortunately, virtually everything I do disappoints him.

If I choose a film for us to watch, he won't be in the mood for it. If I select a restaurant for us to have dinner at, he will tell me the place does not have the right atmosphere. Whether it is my cooking, my outfit choice for the day, or simply the way I have chosen to wear my hair, I'm constantly at risk of hearing the same words: *You've disappointed me, Harriet.*

I'm tired of hearing these words; I have heard them for over twelve years now and don't know how much longer I can hear them for before I go mad.

By my estimations, I should have saved up enough money to leave him in around two-months. Before that time comes, however, I know I will have to endure more incidents like the one today. It was something trivial that set him off earlier – it always is.

Today we were out shopping for a new sofa, not that there is anything wrong with our current one, but Dan always likes to think he has the best of everything, no matter what the cost.

The trip was going well enough by our usual standards, and I stupidly thought that we could perhaps manage to have an amicable, outing together.

How wrong I was.

It was a bright day, unseasonably warm for mid-November. Dan and I walked along the sunny high street in our suburb this morning, before we went to the independent furniture shop. He even held my hand for most of the time. From the outside, it probably looked like we were a normal couple, happily in love; for a little while today, I could even pretend to myself that was the case.

It was only once we got back into the car after placing an order on a corner suite he chose, that I realised I had been foolish to believe that anything Dan does any more is sincere. Perhaps it never was. Perhaps he was always pretending – I don't know any more.

And despite twelve years of experience with him, I still do not feel qualified to decide.

Once we got inside the car, I reached instinctively for my seatbelt, but before my hand connected with it I felt a sudden blow to the bottom of my face. A metallic taste filled my mouth and I felt warmth spread over my chin. I lifted my hand to my lip to try to stop any more blood from spattering onto the handbag on my lap.

To the side of me, I was aware of Dan settling himself in a still, almost calm position facing forward in the driver's seat, his hands wringing slowly in his lap.

'Once again you've disappointed me, Harriet,' he said quietly, still not looking at me.

My mind whirred rapidly, images of the day flashing in my mind's eye. I had no idea what he could deem that I had done wrong at that point.

I thought of breakfast this morning. It is a fact that I took him his nine o'clock coffee in bed as I always did on a Saturday; black, with one level teaspoon of sugar just the way he liked it. Then I had gone on to prepare his pre-breakfast bagel so that it was exactly the temperature he liked to eat it and ready for nine-twenty when he finished using the bathroom.

We had then returned to the bedroom as we always did at the weekend, and if he'd had any complaints about the hour we had spent there, I would most definitely have heard them before we left the flat at eleven o'clock.

It was not like I would ever forget the right way to do any one of these things. I've learned the hard, and most definitely painful way that these tasks, however petty, must be completed in exactly the right way to avoid Dan becoming upset.

My brain struggled as it scanned through the memories. For a wild moment, I thought I had slipped on my flats instead of the brown Chelsea boots that Dan left for me in the hallway, but glancing at my footwear, I realised that was not the case.

Mentally, I surrendered and waited in tense silence for Dan to point out exactly where I had gone wrong.

I waited with bated breath, but he was in no hurry to put me out of my misery. It was as though he was drawing out the silence as if to further emphasise how upset he was.

The feeling of bitter dread rose up inside me like bile

as I stared at my shoes and waited for him to speak.

After what felt like an eternity, but was in reality closer to two-minutes, Dan took a deep breath. 'Did you get his number?' he asks, sourly.

I was still none the wiser. 'W-what do you mean?' I managed to stammer with my hand pressed against my bottom lip, which I have identified as the source of the bleeding.

He snorted, but it was obviously humourless. When Dan makes this sound, it is always a sign he is about to erupt.

'WHY do you think I am blind!' he roared abruptly, making my heart hammer faster in my chest.

I was panicking then. It is rare that he couldn't wait until we were at home before reprimanding me. On this occasion, the severity of my crime must have outweighed his need for privacy.

Although, we were not overlooked in the corner of the car park, where our car sat beneath a drooping willow tree.

'Don't treat me like I am stupid, Harriet! I saw you talking to him while I was arranging the delivery.' He finally turned to look at me then, but I remained staring at my boots. 'There I was buying a nice new piece of furniture for our home, and you are there making me look like an idiot chatting up some sales assistant!'

My heart sank, but it did not stop beating rapidly, for I realised then what he was talking about. As Dan was shown to a desk, he told me to look through the rail of hanging rugs and find one to compliment our new corner-suite. As I was doing so, a young, nervous-looking sales assistant approached me. 'What did the carpet say to the rug?' he asked, grinning at me.

For a moment I was frozen in confusion, halfway

along rummaging through the rail. 'What?'

'Don't worry – I've got you covered,' he said, waiting expectantly for a reaction.

He then looked a little awkward and shrugged casually. 'Just a little rug related humour!' He indicates the rail in front of us.

'Oh, right,' I say, catching on. 'Yes, that was a good one.' I gave a quick and, unfortunately, rather a fake-sounding laugh.

'Well, it's not the first time I've used that one.' He smiled. 'Do you need any help with anything?'

'Oh, no. I'm just looking. Thank you.'

He took this as his cue to leave and said if I needed him, he would be nearby. He then disappeared down the next aisle.

I immediately threw Dan a nervous glance to see if he had noticed me talking to someone. He was busy with papers, pen in hand, and seemed to be writing down details for the overweight and broadly-smiling salesman on the other side of the desk, and seemed not to have noticed.

It was only when I felt the impact upon settling myself in the passenger seat, I had realised I had been mistaken.

I shook my head frantically. 'No – that wasn't what happened! He was just asking me if I needed any help, that was all.'

'Really? It looked like you were both laughing your heads off to me. Everyone could hear you falling over each other laughing, it was embarrassing.' Dan often liked to exaggerate events to suit his point.

'No, he was just being friendly.'

'I could see that!'

'He was only trying to make a sale. He made a bad

joke and then left. That was all, I swear.'

Dan looked away from me and off into the distance again for a few moments. He was clearly still seething. 'Put your seatbelt on.'

On the journey home, I had been forced to press a fistful of the wispy-thin silk scarf I was wearing to my lip in an attempt to stop the flow of blood. I couldn't find any tissues. For such a small cut, it was bleeding quite profusely.

Now I stand in the bathroom, leaning on the sink for support as I console myself with the thought that this is just the latest incident in a limited number. In just a couple of months, I should have amassed enough money to leave my husband for good.

Whenever I sense Dan's mood changing now, however, I know I can get through the pain when I retreat further into my head and think of what I am keeping hidden at the bottom of our bedroom wardrobe.

2

I take the flannel away from my mouth and scrutinize my reflection in the bathroom mirror. Other than the fact my bottom lip is badly swollen with an obvious split, I don't look too bad.

My hair is still swept back in my usual French twist. The eyeliner and mascara framing my pale blue eyes is still intact, owing to the fact that I didn't shed even a single tear this time; of course, that is all down to the little wooden box I now think of every time I have to endure one of Dan's punishments. I have it hidden at the bottom of the wardrobe.

I have had the box itself for years, and for most of that time it only held childhood photographs and keepsakes, but now I have something much more important stashed beneath the nostalgic trinkets: my secret weapon against Dan. That is what gave me the strength to endure the attack today, along with many others in the past couple of months, with less of a sense of hopelessness.

I just pray that he doesn't notice my lack of obvious upset before I get to use my weapon.

Staring at my reflection in the mirror, I see how much paler than I used to be. In truth, I'm not the woman I was at all any more. I used to be confident and outgoing, with a job I loved and a great set of friends. That person is long gone, but I now have a sense of building hope that once I have made the break, I can learn to be me again.

The years of unhappy marriage have taken their toll on me, both physically and emotionally. My face is thinner, my eyes have a sad, almost sunken look to them. And although I'm still only thirty-four, there are one or two specks of grey threatening to emerge in my hair.

The cut on my lip isn't too bad, at least the bleeding has stopped now. I pick up a dark-pink lipstick from the glass shelf and gingerly apply it. Looking at the effect in the mirror, I think I have done a good job of hiding my latest injury.

If only the emotional damage was as easy to mask.

I rinse the sink and take a deep breath, before opening the bathroom door and venturing out into the hallway. I don't wander into the other rooms looking for Dan. As I approach the living room, I am aware of his voice on the other side of the front door. He is still talking to our neighbour, the woman from across the hall.

Today's incident did not go unnoticed. One person saw me as Dan half-dragged me into our flat, scarf still pressed to my mouth. We had made it in through the main door and down the hall when the woman in the only other ground floor flat emerged from behind her door.

For a split-second Dan froze; I could almost hear his mind whirring as it quickly manufactured a suitable lie.

I didn't wait for him to start making his usual excuses on this occasion. I let myself into our flat and left him to do it alone. As I slipped behind the door, I took in the woman's look of concern. She looked more animated than I had ever seen her. Gone was her usual lacklustre demeanour and she seemed strangely interested in what had happened to me.

Dan didn't disappoint. He gave a perfectly plausible story about me splitting my lip myself on the car door.

16

He put it down to my clumsiness. My supposed lack of control and care over my balance and movements is infamous amongst mine and Dan's acquaintances. They often hear from my husband about how I have slipped, tripped or simply been outright careless enough to walk into something. It never fails to amaze me, even after all this time, how he can come up with such a convincing story to cover his misdeeds so quickly. It's almost like he believes it himself. Maybe he does, and that is how he can do such horrible things to me and still live with himself.

Or perhaps he is simply genuinely insane. I just don't know any more.

All I know is I have to get away from him at the first available opportunity.

The muffled voices in the hallway continue. I wonder what he is telling her; how elaborate today's cover story is. My curiosity gets the better of me, and I press my head tentatively to the door so I can hear what they are saying.

I hear the woman talking. Her name is Sophie Wilson; I know because I once saw a letter addressed to her in the communal postbox back when she first moved in. She has a pretty nondescript accent, but I am good at guessing where people are from, and there is something particularly Surrey-like about the way she speaks.

Dan's voice reaches my ears through the door. What I hear fills me with a burning rage, but I stay still, listening. He is actually apologising to her, telling her how he can't believe, after all these years just how clumsy I am.

I can tell by the occasional noise of agreement that she is completely taken in by him.

Everyone is. I was once, too.

Dan may be a bully, liar, and manipulator, but it can't be ignored that he is charming; he is good-looking too, which seems to help. He has a broad symmetry in the features which form the basis of a handsome face, above which, he has an always-immaculate sweep of straight, dark hair. There is no denying that Dan is physically attractive. I used to think so anyway *before I realised what was underneath*. It was one of the things that I first noticed about him. Shallow, I know, and I *so* regret that now. But I know that the past can't be changed, I can only work to make the future better; I read that somewhere once. It was only recently I finally understood the true meaning of those words.

Now Sophie is speaking again. I hear her tell Dan how lucky I am to have a husband who loves me so much.

Angry, I pull my head away at this point. I can't listen any more. I feel sick. Nausea emanates from the guilt I feel for not being able to take any immediate, physical action to leave him. My finances mean it will be at least a month or two before I will be secure enough to finally make the move.

Going into the kitchen for a drink of water, I resist the urge to throw the glass at the wall in a rush of rage that suddenly rises through me. I have been so angry lately, and thoughts like this come and go all the time. I'm secure in the knowledge that I will be better once I have left this all behind though.

I have had enough of living with Dan and his constant mood swings. Had enough of living in fear; just as much, I have had enough of living in this building.

My current residence is a small, one-bedroom flat in

a Victorian conversion in Tennison Road, South Norwood. There are three other households in the building. I don't know the other people. I have never done anything more than nod or smile at them if we see them as we enter or leave the building, or when checking the post.

That's another thing I hate about this place; the post collects in a single box and residents have to sort through it in order to get their mail. I hate that, having to rifle through other people's letters, birthday cards and eBay packages just to get my post every day. I won't miss that when I'm gone.

Why the landlord couldn't put a dedicated postbox for each flat, I don't know. Perhaps it was too much trouble for him. Perhaps he simply hasn't got around to it.

Either way, I suspect it is because of the free-for-all of the communal postbox that my post often goes astray. Sometimes things I am expecting never turn up, or they eventually do materialise, but they have been carelessly resealed.

Dan was the first to notice this phenomenon. At first, I thought he was imagining things, or setting me up, trying to lead me into an argument for whatever reason.

Dan is the paranoid type, but I am not, and I have concluded that someone in the building is indeed taking my post. I'm quite certain that I have narrowed the suspects down to one particular flat too: the one across the hall with Sophie Wilson. The problem only started after she and her boyfriend moved in. I'm not entirely sure what his name is since post is addressed to flat two with many names associated with it. It took me a while to figure out what Sophie's name was for the same reason. I assume that the previous tenants didn't do a very thorough job of changing their address on everything. We still get post for the previous tenants of our flat sometimes too.

Why anybody would be interested in what I receive in the post, I cannot imagine. It is not like anyone sends me cash – I wish. And it is not like there is anything fascinating about the periodic letters I get from the bank informing me there have been changes to the terms and conditions on my account; nor anything of note about the routine letters I get from the NHS to ask me if they can screen my cervix. I have no interest in any of these things, so why would anyone else?

Dan always likes to glance over my post before I throw it out for recycling, of course. It is for this reason that I have chosen the wooden box of photographs at the bottom of my wardrobe as my hiding place for my leaving fund. I could not risk setting up a separate bank account for it, not even online. Even if I went paperless, banks always seem to find a reason to send you a letter you don't expect regarding an account. And if Dan found out I had been saving money secretly, well, it isn't worth thinking about.

Other than the possibility of a house fire, the money is safe enough. Dan would never go into my box of childhood photographs. He has seen them all before, back when we first met, and has not expressed any interest in them since.

At the moment, my *Leaving Dan Fund* is nothing to brag about, and it wouldn't get me far, but it is growing slowly and steadily. Well, a little *too* slowly, actually. I work part-time as a virtual assistant for an architect, Zack West. It isn't exactly making the most of my degree, but it is a job and the pay is reasonable, and when I first took it, I really needed the money.

I used to work as Zack's personal assistant in his office, but when he moved to Manchester to merge with another small operation, he had no room in the firm. I do pretty much the same as I did before, except for less time and money. It also means I have to work from home.

Dan was delighted when this happened.

At the time, he was highly enthusiastic about me working from home. He said it would give us the chance to spend more time together, which it did. At the time, however, I had no idea just how much I did not want that. That was before we were married, when I thought we were happy. Before I realised what he was really like.

Before he had ever hit me.

It doesn't matter now, though. I will learn from my mistakes and move on. All I need is the money. As soon as I hit my target amount, I will be gone. I will finally leave Dan behind forever.

The thought of leaving him is the only thing getting me through most days. As soon as he is out of my life, I will finally be free. Maybe I can lead a normal life again; even have friends. Friends that I don't have to constantly invent stories for to cover my frequent injuries, or have to excuse myself from social events simply because Dan decides I am not allowed to go.

I put down my empty glass and move through to the lounge, thinking of getting my MacBook out to check my work emails. It is not part of my routine to work on a Saturday, but I am at a loose end and looking for something to do. I hadn't planned on getting back from our day out shopping so soon.

No sooner have I got my laptop booted up, do I hear Dan come in through the front door. I also vaguely hear the main door to the building close, and through the open blinds, I see the figure of Sophie crossing the car park. She walks briskly and disappears around the hedge at the border of the property.

In spite of my earlier irritation, I find myself wondering what else they talked about that I didn't overhear. I am curious, but not enough to ask him about it. He would probably love that. In fact, it occurs to me that he probably even prolonged the conversation in an attempt to make me jealous.

Perhaps the way he managed to stage it right outside our front door wasn't an accident. I wonder if he actually expected me to eavesdrop, so he could be sure I heard what he was saying to her.

Then I think that sounds like the kind of paranoia Dan always spouts and I think I am being silly. Irrational.

If he was going to try to make me jealous, he would probably choose another candidate on whom to bestow his attention; it wouldn't be her. I have noticed his eye wandering many-a-time over the years, and our nearest neighbour doesn't look like the type I see him glaze over for.

Sophie is too, well... it's not that she isn't attractive. She's actually.... well, it's hard to tell what she is really. I don't actually know her. Perhaps I should, since she lives directly opposite us in the only other flat on the ground floor and she can only be a few years shy of my age.

She always looks different every time I see her go by. There is nothing unique or noteworthy about her, or her boyfriend for that matter. Often, people I see have at least one distinguishing quality, but I can't find one in either of the pair that live across the hall. It is not just the drab, wishy-washy clothes Sophie wears that seem to make her fade into the background, but also the way she acts, or rather, doesn't act. You could just lose sight of her in a crowd of people. But then again, that depends on how she has styled herself on that particular day.

It is like she doesn't have a personality. It occurs to me that this is a strange thought, but I just can't get a handle on her. And Dan aside, I am usually a good judge of character.

Or maybe I'm not, and I just think I am.

Sometimes Sophie wears glasses, but not all the time. I get the impression she doesn't actually need them. Maybe she thinks they make her look intellectual and they are merely a fashion statement. Or maybe she thinks they will help her to dissolve into the background. Whenever I have seen her coming or going I get hit with the impression she would like to blend in with the retro, paisley wallpaper adorning the hallway walls.

Or maybe she has good reason for not wanting to be seen. I have often sensed a subversive quality to her movements whenever I have seen her checking the post. And if my suspicions are correct, then she has every reason for wanting to keep a low profile.

Dan does not come to join me in the lounge. Instead, I hear the telltale sound of him locking himself in the bathroom. I know he will spend half an hour or so in there, as he always does after we have had a disagreement. What he does in there, I have no clue. In the past, I have asked him, tried to figure him out, but he hasn't ever given me a straight answer. I would assume that he locks himself away purely to sulk, but I have caught a glimpse on occasion of him clutching a little leather-bound journal.

Whatever he does, he can get on with it now for all I care – I have stopped chasing after him.

And as for exactly what they talked about, I don't care.

Dan can say whatever he wants about me after I have left. I already imagine the sort of story he will come up with. No doubt, he will weave it to suit himself, make him look like the hero.

It doesn't matter though, since I won't be around to hear it.

3

Dan has gone out. He told me he was going shopping for a new coat. I am sure he wasn't though. He often tells me he is going somewhere, and I would have no reason not to believe him, only the length of time he spends out doesn't add up.

But I don't care, I am just glad to be away from him. It would just be nice know how much time I have before he comes back so I can enjoy it more. The waiting is the worst part, holding my breath every time I hear a car outside, or movement in the building's hallway.

He seems to have mostly forgiven me for yesterday. He hasn't mentioned it since the car park, which is something at least.

Anyway, I'm pleased to be out of his company for a while. The whole building had charity donation bags delivered last week and I have wanted to thin down my collection of clothes for ages. Dan said he would be back for dinner, so that should give me plenty of time to have a thorough sort out.

Feeling optimistic, I tip every garment I own from the chest of drawers, wardrobe and storage boxes out onto the bed. For a moment it is overwhelming, but I know this task has been long overdue.

I have been gradually rearranging my clothes, changing where I keep things for a while. I have decided that when the time comes to actually pack my things, it will need to be done in a hurry. I know that I will have to stuff the empty suitcases we keep under the bed when he is not here and slip out before he gets back to find me gone. But by that point, it should hopefully be too late for him to catch up with me. That is the plan, anyway.

To speed things up on the big day, I have moved my favourite things into my chest of drawers, all tightly folded. This way, they can be packed in a hurry. Then all I have to do is grab my box of photographs and keepsakes, along with my all-important leaving fund before making my way out.

I know this way is far from ideal, but I cannot think of any other way of doing things without involving anyone else.

My relatives aren't exactly the kind of people you can turn to in a crisis. My mother visits me, but not very often, particularly since I have been married. Not that we were ever that close anyway. I think she suspects there is something wrong with Dan, but she has never said it. We don't have that kind of relationship. She is far too busy with her own life to do anything more than visit occasionally, wish me good health and tell me to keep in touch as she leaves. She isn't any good for aiding my escape.

I met Dan when I was still at Uni, young and naïve. A girl on my course had been let down on a double date and I agreed to fill in to help her out. She had bigged Dan up, made him sound like Mr. Perfect, which he was at that point. But by the time I truly realised that his endearing persona was a total facade, we had already been married for so many years.

The turnaround in his temperament was sudden. It was in the second week of our honeymoon that I first saw his true colours. We had spent the first part of our Parisian honeymoon in pure newly-wed bliss. I remember thinking that I had never been so happy.

Then one night everything changed.

We had spent the day exploring the beautiful gardens of Versailles. Having exhausted ourselves, we decided to take it easy for the evening and relax in the luxury of the hotel spa.

At least, that is what I had thought.

Dan seemed to get restless after we had dinner and told me he was going to the bar to get a drink. I said I would go with him, but he told me to go on to the spa and enjoy myself and he would join me later on, so I did.

At first, I was at a loose end, having spent the whole of the past week closely entangled with Dan. The temptation to have a massage was strong, but thought I would wait for Dan to turn up and we could perhaps have one together.

So I waited for him beside the intricately-tiled pool. After a while, I went up to our room and got out the book I had packed. I hadn't really thought I would have the chance to read it, but I was glad then that I had slipped it into my suitcase at the last second. I settled myself into one of the padded-loungers by the side of the water, surrounded by potted green palm-trees.

It wasn't long before I started looking around for Dan. I had thought he would come to join me in the spa, but other people had come and gone and he was nowhere to be seen. I slipped the napkin that I had been practising my new signature on inside the book to save my progress.

Checking the hotel bar, I expected to see him at one of the tall wooden stools, but he wasn't there. The bartender said that he hadn't even arrived.

I was worried at that point, but I caught up with him very quickly.

I returned to our hotel room and there he was, sitting on the end of the bed, elbows on knees. He had bought himself a bottle of vodka and was halfway through it when I walked in through the door, book in hand.

'There you are,' I said. 'I wondered where you got to.' I eyed the bottle warily. At that point, I had never seen Dan drink anything more than a few glasses of wine with dinner.

Dan didn't look at me at all. He just gave a snort and took a drink directly from the bottle. 'I'm surprised you even noticed I was gone,' he said quietly.

I was completely taken aback. It had been his decision to leave me on my own in the spa. Hadn't he told me to wait for him there?

'What do you mean?' I said in surprise. 'Of course, I noticed you were gone!' I climbed onto the bed behind him and wrapped my arms around his neck, kissing him playfully on the ear. I whispered playfully in his ear, 'I missed you...'

Without warning, I found myself hitting the floor with such force that I was instantly winded. It took me a few seconds where I lay on my side, dazedly watching the vodka bottle rolling away across the carpet, to realise what had happened. Even when my brain caught up, I wasn't sure if I could trust the conclusion it had come to. Not until Dan started screaming at me anyway.

'HOW COULD YOU HAVE MISSED ME!? You didn't even notice I left!'

I awkwardly scrambled into a sitting position but didn't get up, shocked to see the blind fury on Dan's blotchy face as he paced back and forth, shaking his head and muttering to himself.

I couldn't understand what was going on. That wasn't

Dan. That wasn't my husband. What had happened to the man who had refused to let go of my hand as we explored as many of the romantic restaurants in the city as possible last week? Where was the person I had woken up with that morning?

'What are you talking about? Dan, what's the matter?' I managed to gasp painfully. Clutching at my ribs, I couldn't seem to take a full breath, it hurt too much. 'You said that you wanted to have a drink at the bar! You told me that was where you were going...'

'And I did. I thought you would come and join me. But instead, you decided to lounge around by the swimming pool and read that stupid book! This is supposed to be our honeymoon. You are supposed to want to spend time with *me!*' Spit flew wildly from his mouth as he said the last part.

My brain was struggling to function properly. I wondered if I had hit my head and not realised. I actually ran my fingers over my scalp to check for an injury I might not have noticed. 'I-I do want to spend time with you! I asked the bartender, but he said you hadn't even been in the bar!'

That was the wrong thing to say.

Dan froze for a second and stared at me as if he couldn't believe that I had the audacity to answer him back. 'So now I'm a liar!? Now it is my fault, is it?' He roared with rage as he ripped the telephone from the bedside cabinet and threw it at my head with great force.

I screamed.

Whether it was the alcohol or the sheer rage he was shaking with, I don't know, but he managed to miss me entirely. Instead, the impact hit the wall above my head and when I looked behind me I saw several pieces of plaster scattered on the floor.

'Dan – please!' I begged. I actually burst into tears. 'I'm sorry! Look, it was just a misunderstanding, OK?'

Dan breathed heavily and sank with his face into his hands on the bed.

I however, sat rooted to the spot on the carpet, too afraid anything I did might set him off again. It was like I was suddenly in a room with a stranger. The man in front of me looked like my new husband, but he acted in a way I had never seen before. I was desperate to calm him down, make him act like the man I loved again. 'You are right,' I said. 'I should have come to check on you. I just thought you went down to the spa after me, that was all... Dan?'

After a few moments of tense silence, he spoke, but only to the floor. 'Why is it always me that has to chase after you?' he said, quietly. At least he wasn't shouting now. 'Sometimes it would be nice if you put the effort in. It would just show me that you cared...'

This threw me. 'I-I didn't realise that I wasn't. Oh, Dan! I'm so sorry.' I got up from the floor and sat next to him on the bed, putting my arms around him once more.

He kissed me and returned the embrace.

Although I was still confused and still shaking, some form of relief flooded me. He was behaving normally again, like the Dan I had known and loved all along.

I never quite relaxed properly after our honeymoon, however. I was always worried he might do something like that again. Nevertheless, I vowed then to pay more attention to my behaviour. I felt guilty that I had let my husband think I did not love him. It was ridiculous, since I loved him more than anything and was happier than I had ever been.

From then on, however, I went out of my way to shower him with affection, hoping this would please him enough not to have another bizarre outburst again. I devoted more of my time, more of my effort, more of my energy...

Little did I know that this was all part of the manipulation that continued for years before I realised what was happening. And of course, Dan did have more outbursts like on our honeymoon. It was at least six-months into our marriage before the next one happened. And once again, it took me completely by surprise. After that, his temper was never too far from the surface and the events became much more frequent. They did not hurt any less though. For so many years Dan did a great job of making me believe it was my fault he got so angry. I was distraught at the thought of causing all the problems in my marriage without even realising I was doing it.

Well, it will soon be Dan's turn to be distraught – when he realises I have escaped from right under his nose.

It took me a long while to realise exactly who he was, since his multi-faceted personality meant that I had no idea what I was dealing with at first, even though I know now.

As our fifth year of marriage drew to a close, I had accepted that my life was going to be different from what I had imagined. I found myself treading on eggshells all the time, watching everything I did or say, hoping to avoid another flare-up.

The thing that gets me the most is the fact I have to ask permission to do things, even the most simple of things, like letting my mother visit. The idea of me going to see her is out of the question, since Dan is too terrified of me leaving the flat alone, just in case I tried to go somewhere other than my mother's house.

So it is up to her to arrange a visit if she ever wants to see me, but Dan has that angle covered too.

He makes all sorts of excuses as to why she can't come here, using a different one each time. He will say he isn't feeling well, or he's had a hard day at work and should be allowed to relax in his own home. If I suggest seeing her on my own, it makes him angry. He will either turn to emotional blackmail, or there would be an unpleasant row waiting for me after she left.

This happened most recently when my mother sent a text last week asking to arrange her annual visit. Dan was expectedly reluctant, but seemed lethargic in his excuse-making this time. I think he was caught too off-guard.

'I just don't want people in my home when I am at work!' he said, as we sat at the table and ate breakfast that day. 'Is that an unreasonable request? I don't think so, Harriet.'

'It's not "people", it is just my mum. Your mother comes here to visit you sometimes.'

'Only because the wretched woman invites herself. And I always make sure you are here when she does.'

'Yes, I know you do.' They are never comfortable visits, Dan makes sure of it. He does it on purpose to see his mother as little as possible – the woman who spent years of her life raising him. Although, she possibly did something dreadfully wrong at some point to make him turn out the way he did. Or perhaps it was his father who I have never met that is to blame. His parents divorced when he was a child.

Not that I can talk about healthy family relations. Now I see my mother so rarely I'm pretty much dead to her.

Dan still continued talking, building himself into a rant. 'When you pay all the bills, Harriet, maybe you could be in charge of decision making and then you could let whoever you wanted into our home.'

I had to respond to that one. I fell into his trap, even with all my experience.

'You don't pay all the bills. I work too, you know that.'

'Oh yes, I'm not saying your little contribution isn't important.'

Yes, he was.

'But it wouldn't keep us afloat long would it? Do you want to pay for everything yourself, Harriet?'

I would have given him a dose of his own silent treatment then, but I can't get away with it like he does with me – he doesn't allow it. He would have just become irate and started shoving me around, blaming me for making him angry. He can give it, but he can't take it.

'No,' I said, quietly.

'Well then, maybe you should start treating me a little better. Show me some gratitude for all the effort I put in for once. You know how hard I work for you, Harriet.'

'Yes, I know you do, sweetie.' I forced myself to say. *You pathetic bully.*

He pulled me to him and I was overwhelmed as always by his strong dose of aftershave. 'I love you, sweetheart,' he said, 'but you are very hard to love when you are so argumentative. Men don't find that attractive, you know. You wouldn't find anyone else that would put up with you. I need you to try harder in the future, please. If you were more compliant, then our life would be so much better.'

33

All I said in response to this was, 'Love you too.' I always try to use as few words as possible, so it's easier to tell the lie.

It has been so hard living this way, but for the longest time, I thought it was normal. I was so young when I met Dan that I honestly didn't know any better. He told me that our marriage was just how relationships were in real life. He would tell me I was overacting if I questioned his behaviour.

Dan was the man I had married, agreed to spend the rest of my life with. I wanted my marriage to work. When he was being nice and normal, he was great, we were happy. It was just his temper that was the problem. But as time went on, anger and violence seemed to make up most of the man I lived with.

And now, I know I need to get out.

Now I am closer than ever. It is just a matter of time.

I straighten up and look at the state of the bedroom. I have managed to sort out enough clothes to fill the charity bag. But not too many as to look suspicious to Dan.

I suddenly realise I am starving and looking at the time know I have completely missed lunch. I go into the kitchen and make myself a quick sliced beef sandwich before returning to tackle the task of folding and putting away what I intend to keep.

A sudden flicker of movement outside the bedroom window makes me take in a sharp breath.

My panic is short-lived. It is simply the neighbour's black and white cat. He stands mewling at me through the double glazing, waiting to be let in.

I move over to open the window and he jumps straight through it and starts brushing himself against my legs, purring. I take out a little beef from my

34

sandwich and offer it to him, watching him gobble it down greedily.

The cat belongs to the woman in her fifties who lives in the flat upstairs. I'm sure he is well fed, but he is often keen to get into our flat for extra scraps – only when Dan is out, however. It is like he senses that my husband doesn't like cats. Dan told me once that he was allergic to them.

But I have fed George (as I've named him) in secret many times over the years and Dan seems to be completely unaffected. My aunt is allergic to cats and she knows if one has been in the room; her eyes will start to water immediately. Dan has never had any such reaction.

The conclusion I have drawn from this is that this was just another of Dan's lies. He lies constantly, I have come to realise, about everything; even things that don't seem to matter. Not just to me either, he will spin tales to anyone we meet.

He likes to give everyone the impression that he is rich and can afford anything, despite the fact he is only an environmental health officer for the council. He will often splash out on things we don't even need just because he feels like it – like the sofa yesterday, or the brand new Mercedes he determined we had to get. This is all heartbreaking for me, since I am left to use my *Leaving Dan Fund* to pay for essentials.

It is so hard trying to squirrel away money without him noticing when he is on a constant spending spree; trying to talk him out of it always leads to an argument, or worse.

I'm feeling positive as I fold the last item in my to-keep collection and slide the drawer shut. I tie the charity collection bag and take it outside. When I get back inside, I think about making myself a hot drink, but I press the cut on my lip gently and wonder if I can face it.

Before I have decided, however, I hear the main door to the house close and through the blinds, I see the woman from across the hall disappearing across the car park.

Today she is wearing her glasses. Wherever she is going, she must want to look intelligent.

I'm painfully aware I spend too much time watching people out of the window.

I really need to stop that.

A golden glow of hope rests in my chest, reminding me that soon I can start living for myself again and stop spectating the lives of others.

4

I'm feeling paranoid. I went out for my jog this morning to find the charity bag I left out yesterday has been taken. Really, I would like to put it down to petty theft, but looking out at the street, it looks like the bags from other households remain untouched. And they are not due to be collected until the end of the week.

I can't help but feel uncomfortable. I try to keep my mind from wandering over what someone could be doing with my old clothes right now. Yesterday I was more than happy to let them go, but I had intended the charity to receive them. They were supposed to be picked up and thrown together into a huge mass with everyone else's. Perfectly anonymous. I didn't expect my donation to be intercepted before then.

I rationalize that a random passer-by saw something in there that they liked too much to leave behind.

I guess I don't like the feeling of being singled out. Preferably, the thief would have stolen the entire street's worth, rather than just my own. Psychologically, that would have made me feel better.

But now that I think about it, if someone was so desperate for whatever they saw in that bag that they felt they had to steal it, then they are welcome to it.

Charity is charity, I guess.

I remind myself that I have managed to get rid of a whole load of things I would never wear if I was being honest. A few items still even had the tags on, like the purple satin blouse Dan gave me on my last birthday. These extra possessions were only going to weigh me down when I make my escape. Besides, I managed to get rid of a jacket that I hated with a passion. That one held particularly bad memories and I always try to avoid wearing it as much as possible; I fear it might subconsciously trigger Dan into red mist mode. Not that it takes much to set him off. It could be anything; I'm not sure even he knows what it is sometimes.

There was technically nothing wrong with the jacket, just the day I bought it that I had a problem with.

Dan purchased it for me about a year after we got married. I was in the changing rooms deliberating over a pair of jeans when Dan appeared behind me in the cubicle mirror. He showed me the jacket and wanted me to try it for size. I told him I would in a second, but asked him for his opinion on the jeans I was trying on first.

He told me he didn't like them and they made me look overweight and shorter. That upset me. I posed in front of the mirror at different angles, but I wasn't sure I could see what he meant.

He asked me how much longer I was going to be and was clearly getting impatient with my indecisiveness. He was eager for us to go for lunch, but he wanted me to try on the jacket quickly before we left.

'Oh, I don't know if I really like it,' I said, looking at the navy blazer he was holding out for me. 'I think I'll get all this though.' I gestured towards the other items I had already tried on.

There was a split-second where I noticed Dan's expression change in the mirror, but I didn't have time to react. The next moment, he had twisted my arm up behind my back and slammed me hard into the mirror. My breath misted against its surface with each of my rapid breaths. 'Dan! What-'

'Why can't you ever make up your fucking mind!' he

hissed at me. 'Everything always takes so long, with you doesn't it?'

He abruptly let me go, but I was too shocked to say anything. It shames me now, but all I did was burst into tears.

Dan regained his usual, pleasant composure quickly and gathered the clothes I had already tried along with the jacket he selected. 'Now, I will go and get these for you. I'm sure this jacket will fit you nicely. Why don't you change and put those jeans back on the rail, eh?'

I still said nothing.

'I'll see you in a minute then.' He smiled, kissed me briefly on the forehead and left me in the changing room, pulling the curtain shut behind him.

He often encourages me to wear blazer-jackets now; my wardrobe features many of them. Thinking about it, I wonder whether he has been trying to style me like someone else; I have no idea who. An old girlfriend perhaps? Or maybe an actress he likes. I know there was one celebrity who used to dress like that, but I can't remember her name.

Everything is about outward appearance with Dan. Maybe he thought I could be a less disappointing wife if I was to dress the way he likes on our outings together. In the end, something set him off that day in the changing rooms for reasons only he knew. It doesn't matter now though. I won't have to waste my time and energy obsessing over these things once I have left him.

I check the post mid-morning when I see the postman approaching the building. Nothing for me, but I leave Dan's single piece of mail on the kitchen table. It looks like a bank statement, but oddly there is a mistake in the address; the name is accurate, but the first line reads '*Flat 2*' instead of '*Flat 1*'. I make a mental note to tell Dan to get it corrected later.

For the rest of the day I work. After the weekend, I have the usual backlog of tasks to complete. This keeps me busy enough that I forget about my problems for a while.

By late afternoon, I decide that it is time to pick up something for dinner. Dan gets back from work at around six, and we always have dinner at around half past seven.

Dan is always in a foul mood after being at work. He hates his job. So I aim to avoid him during this period and use the excuse of getting fresh ingredients for dinner. It also gives me a chance to get some air. Working from home can make me feel very isolated sometimes. I yearn to do something that means I will have to interact with real people again.

It takes an hour to get to Aldi from our flat and back again. There are closer supermarkets, but I find the exercise helps relieve some stress.

Dan doesn't like me leaving the flat without him. The supermarket is virtually the only place mundane enough that he allows me to go un-chaperoned, just as long as I don't wear any make-up. Anywhere else is deemed too risky; I think it is because he is terrified I will meet someone else. What a joke – I feel a mess without any make-up. Dan has never accepted that I want to wear it just for myself, that I need it just so I am confident enough to step out the door and let the world see me – whether male or female.

I choose a pack of steaks, salad ingredients and a pot of double cream. I will make chocolate mousse for dessert. That should put Dan in a good mood; I have decided I should spend the remaining time I have left with Dan simply trying to placate him. Hopefully, this plan should make my remaining time as easy as possible.

When I approach the building on the way home it is just before seven and is getting dark. I immediately notice that there are no lights on in our flat and the curtains still seem to be open.

Our car is parked in the driveway making it look like Dan came home, so I can't understand why he wouldn't be in the flat.

Dan likes routine. He is obsessive about it. He wouldn't just do something in a different way one day spontaneously. This makes me worry.

Nerves bubble up in my stomach as I walk across the car park.

Dan's love of routine seems to have rubbed off on me over the years. Apart from his sudden mood swings, I always roughly know what is going to happen during each day in my life with Dan. A million different scenarios race through my mind as I fumble with the keys in our flat door and walk into the darkness.

5

The first thing that hits me is the smell of alcohol. The flat is still and quiet, but the smell that hangs in the air doesn't allow me to believe for a second that I am alone.

My heart is pounding now. Every instinct in my body tells me to run. I want to just turn around, walk out the door and get as far away as I can. But my brain tells me I can't do that.

Not yet.

Dan rarely drinks, but whenever he does it always leads him to get angry. I now associate the smell of alcohol with many episodes from the past, including our honeymoon. Now the scent of it is overpowering, making my stomach churn.

Leaving my coat and shoes on, I step forward and down the hallway tentatively, the crinkling of my plastic Aldi bag seeming excruciatingly loud in the silence.

I turn my head in either direction wondering exactly where Dan is. Is he playing a sick game of hide and seek with me? Waiting to jump out from a shadowy corner?

The kitchen is empty; safe. I put the shopping down on the worktop and tread carefully towards the living room, which is equally deserted.

Going back down the hall I pass the bathroom. The door is open and even though I haven't switched any lights on yet, I can easily see the white bathroom suite gleaming at me through the darkness with nothing between.

That leaves only the bedroom. With a faint glimmer of hope, I wonder if perhaps Dan has fallen asleep. That would explain why the whole flat is in darkness. Why else would he be in there?

I put a cautious hand on the door handle and push it down gently, wondering what is awaiting me on the other side.

The door is three-quarters of the way open when my heart plummets.

Dan is not asleep. He is sitting on the bed with his back to me, leaving me unable to see his expression. I am immediately reminded of our honeymoon. Glinting slightly in the limited light from the small window, I notice an almost-empty bottle of whisky on the bedside cabinet nearest him.

'I'm disappointed in you, Harriet,' he says, still facing the wall. His voice isn't the usual cold, flat tone I have heard on so many occasions before. Each word now shakes with anger.

As on so many occasions before however, I am at a loss as to what he thinks my crime is.

I open my mouth to ask him, but he speaks first. 'I can't believe you have been stealing from me, Harriet.'

This is the last thing I expected him to say. 'Stealing? What are you talk-'

'You do not need to lie to me any more. I know you have been planning to leave me.'

My stomach turns to ice at these words. How could he know? I try to keep my voice calm, convincing. 'Of course, I'm not planning to leave you. Why would you think that? I love you, Dan.' How plausible does that sound? I can't even pretend to myself. 'What makes you think I don't?'

'I had a letter in the post today–'

I think of the letter I left for Dan on the kitchen table.

Dan continues talking to the wall. I remain poised in the doorway.

'–The letter was from my bank, but it wasn't my account. It was a separate account I've never seen before.'

'I-I don't understand.' I cringe at my readiness to stammer.

'It is quite simple,' Dan says, managing to keep his voice low still. 'Someone other than myself set up an account in my name. That same someone has made withdrawals on that account and reached the overdraft limit. And now I have found out about it.'

'Well, have you contacted the police?' I say, moving into the room closer to him. He is simply experiencing a bank error that is nothing to do with me. I feel a little relief spread over my shoulders at the realisation that I have personally done nothing to upset him. 'If someone has done that to you, then you need to report it as soon as possible before anything else is taken.'

Dan snorts. 'I don't need to call the police. I have already found the culprit, sweetheart.' For the first time, he turns around and faces me, a look of wild fury making his would-be handsome face more ugly than I have ever seen it. 'It's you, isn't it? You did this!'

'Dan, I would never steal from you. Of course, I wouldn't! Why would I?' He has obviously worked himself up into a rage over this and I need him to see reason. Why is he always so quick to blame me?

For a second he freezes, watching me closely. Then he snatches something heavy-looking up from the floor on the other side of the bed and throws it directly at me.

I let out a yelp of surprise and dodge out of the way. Behind me, I hear glass smash and I know the object has hit the dressing table where I keep my perfume bottles. Maybe it hit the mirror and lamp too, but I don't turn around to look, because I realise with a thrill of horror what the object is: it is the box of money I have been hiding. I know this because the contents flutter to the floor as tense silence falls over Dan and me.

I open my mouth to speak, but have no idea what to say.

Dan sits on the bed and watches me, breathing heavily with anger. I know any second he is about to charge at me. He has put two and two together and come up with five. Worst of all, I have no idea how to convince him otherwise. To him, it looks like I have been caught red-handed.

'Well?' he yells. 'What do you have to say for yourself, Harriet?'

'Dan, listen!' I plead. 'I haven't opened an account in your name. It wasn't me! This is the first I have heard about this – I swear! I am as surprised as you. Honestly!'

'THEN WHAT THE HELL IS THIS!' He jumps to his feet and points to the notes strewn all over the carpet as he approaches me. His face is bright red and blotchy. His breathing is strangely erratic and I can see him visibly shaking.

I'm genuinely scared now. In our many years together I've never seen him this angry before. Dan doesn't usually yell so loud in the flat, either. He is always careful to keep his voice low enough as to not be overheard. I wonder if George's owner upstairs can hear him. Part of me hopes she can and she will call the police. I suddenly don't care about the potential repercussions – I can see the raw aggression etched into every one of Dan's features and in his body language as he draws nearer.

'Dan, look – that is my money! I save it from my salary with Zack. Believe me, I haven't stolen it from you! I wouldn't do that – you know I wouldn't.' I try, and fail, to keep my voice calm in the hope that this may rub off on Dan.

Unfortunately, it doesn't.

'I don't know what to believe any more, Harriet! There is only one reason why you wouldn't keep all that in your bank account–' he jabs at the floor with a shaking finger '-AND-THAT-IS-BECAUSE-YOU-ARE-HIDING-IT-FROM-ME!'

'No!-'

'ARE YOU PLANNING TO LEAVE ME – IS THAT IT?'

'No, Dan – please!–'

'You've met someone else, haven't you? You're planning on running off with him aren't you!?'

I turn and make an attempt out through the door, but I don't make it. Dan grabs me by the hair and slams me to the floor, winding me.

I am suddenly intoxicated by the fumes of the smashed fragrances. In the mix of chokingly strong aromas, the scent I haven't worn for years brings back shockingly vivid memories of our honeymoon.

He leans his knee on my spine and presses my face into the carpet where shards of the broken bottles lie upon the pile. The smell and bitter taste of the perfume are so strong I cough and gag.

I scream in terror and pain as I feel the sharp fragments break the skin on my cheek.

'IS THAT WHERE YOU GO?' Dan screams. 'BEFORE YOU APPEAR TO MAKE DINNER? ARE YOU COMING BACK FROM SPENDING THE DAY

WITH HIM!?'

'NO!' I scream back, trapped and helpless beneath Dan's crushing weight. 'You're wrong! Dan, I haven't done anything!' In my panic, I do not know whether it is a wave of fear or anger that rushes through me, but I suddenly feel like screaming at him. 'You're crazy! You're completely mad! Let go of me! Get off me! I HAVEN'T DONE ANYTHING!'

'LIAR!' He quickly lifts my head and slams it hard into the floor again. Even through the carpet, I feel dazed and light-headed all of a sudden, although I am aware of more sharp scratches, this time stinging my chin as more glass cuts into me.

I blink and try to stay conscious.

'WELL IT ENDS NOW!' Dan screams. 'I will put a stop to that! I am never letting you out the house on your own again – I have been too lenient with you, Harriet – and this is how you repay me! The only time you will leave the flat in future is when you are with me. Do you understand?'

I don't say anything. Images of a dim future flash before my eyes.

'ANSWER ME HARRIET!'

I am struggling to breathe with Dan's weight still pressing me into the floor, but I manage to croak out a response. 'I told you – I haven't done anything. *Please believe me, Dan!*'

'*Don't-lie-to-me!*' Dan hisses.

He slams my head against the floor again.

This time I see little bright lights whizzing around the corners of my vision.

I feel another blow to my head, but for some reason, everything seems suddenly fuzzy and I hardly feel any pain. The darkened room fades away as if I am being pulled backwards down a dark tunnel and the image dissolves into nothingness.

6

I open my eyes. For a moment, I am confused as to how I am seeing the room from such an odd angle.

Then I remember.

My head throbs. The bitter, harsh taste of perfume clings to the inside of my mouth and the back of my throat. I sit up with great difficulty, everything seems to be throbbing or stinging with pain. I feel certain something must be broken.

I am aware that my breathing is erratic now – shallow and uneven. In fact, I can't pull my lungs in properly. A sharp pain shoots through my ribs every time I try to inhale and I feel like I might suffocate.

The sound of sobbing reaches my returning consciousness, and I suddenly realise that it is coming from me – it is so unfamiliar. The noise is terrible, making everything seem worse than it is. I want to shut it out.

But it is bad, the worst it has ever been.

Easing myself up into a standing position is hard; I take my time, biting my lip to stop my whimpers from escaping me. I can't let Dan hear me. He is motionless on the bed. A closer look tells me that he is asleep. Anger bubbles in my stomach.

How dare he?

Dan has beaten me worse than ever, I'm quite certain he has even broken my ribs this time, and he has heartlessly lain down on our bed and gone to sleep.

He could have killed me and he doesn't even care. He just left me on the floor.

Other than being passed-out drunk, he is fine,

sleeping without a care in the world. But I know he will be far from contented when he awakens – I know he will be furious. A fresh wave of panic rises in my chest once more.

For a moment I consider taking the lamp that fell to the floor with the perfume bottles and hitting him over the head with it so he never wakes up. But I snap myself back to reality and it is like my brain is reawakening after a long time of being in a deep and drowsy slumber.

Suddenly everything becomes clear all in one moment. My eyes take in the cash still scattered all around the bedroom floor.

I know what I have to do.

A jolt of nerves rushes through me as I realise that the time I have been planning for so long is *now*. It is not perfect – not by a long way. It is in no way how I imagined it would happen, *but the time is now.*

I have to make my escape immediately.

7

Eighteen-Months Later

I did it. Finally, I did it – I left him. I always said I would, but now it has finally happened. It feels like I waited forever, but I am finally living a free life without him.

The first few weeks after I made the break, I couldn't quite believe it was real. After living in constant unhappiness for so many years I wasn't sure that I wasn't dreaming.

It was as though I had opened patio doors for the first time after a long dark winter and let glorious light pour down upon me. I have let sunshine into my life again. Finally, I have the opportunity to see summer once more.

For the first few months, I would awake in the morning and be convinced that I would turn and see him lying beside me. But when I did gain enough courage to open my eyes, I saw that I had really done it, it wasn't a dream.

My new career is one that I have dreamt of all my life. I can now call myself a working artist now that I have opened my own gallery here in Coventry.

I did something reckless. After I packed my tiny, little suitcase I went to Norwood Junction railway station and got on the first train that pulled in. I looked at a map of the UK on my phone and played a game of chance with myself. I blindly pointed at a random part of the map to choose my destination. Thinking about that now, it was probably the most spontaneous thing I have ever done, which is quite sad really.

I have spent too many years in the shadows and don't want to look back when it's over and have regrets at living such a pedestrian life. On the other hand, I am just glad to be living it on my own, without *him* being involved.

Yes, that is what is really important.

I selected the perfect street for my new enterprise: Stonegravel Street. A bustling, busy little road on the outskirts of the City. Just enough footfall to make it worthwhile, but without the hefty rent a city-centre shop would command. Stony Studios is doing well and is paying all my bills. I even have enough left over to treat myself now and then. Nothing much, just a nice dinner at home or some new clothes.

When I first set up shop, I wondered if I had made a mistake. I was rapidly eating into multiple credit cards just to stay afloat. I had many nights where I would spend the midnight hours staring at the bedroom ceiling, making mental calculations, making sure I was managing to balance my finances. But before long I started getting enough customers that I didn't have to worry. Sales were steady and thankfully have been ever since.

I create all the paintings myself. My work has a unique look about it. I have a style – a modern and colourful base with details picked out here and there. Some of my best-sellers have my unique style applied to forest scenes, landscapes, floral still lifes and glowing, golden wheat fields.

Many people ask me why I don't have any beach or coastal scenes. They would love to see my take on coastal scenes, they say. But I would never do coast scenes, owing to the fact I hate the beach so much. I hate the sea too, so it will never appear in my work. It would absolutely kill me to paint a beach scene.

The business certainly keeps me busy, but it is rewarding. At first, the financial side was scary. I felt like a baby deer that had found itself upon a precariously thin frozen lake and was trying to find its feet. For the first time, I was doing something on my own, with no one else behind me. That was the most frightening prospect of all. I was alone in the world. But it was also the best thing of all, because it meant that I was finally away from *him*.

He is in the past once and for all.

I now live in the flat above the shop. It's a small place, but has two decent-sized bedrooms. I set up the second bedroom as my painting studio. I didn't put any carpet down in that room, instead the wooden floorboards are covered with a large once-white sheet that catches the excess paint drops.

The flat has two doors, which I like about the place. It feels less hemmed in and it is always nice to have an extra escape route, should I need one at short notice. The back yard that contains the bins isn't overlooked, it just backs onto an alley that only the refuse collectors use. It doesn't feel all that secure at the back, but there are plenty of bolts on the back door leading to the yard. I suppose that should make me feel safer, but I think I would probably feel better if whoever put them there felt they didn't need them. It is probably just me worrying about nothing, as I am quite certain no one will find me here... almost.

The walls throughout the flat were a faded mint-green when I moved in, so when I got the chance I painted them all in cream; a blank canvas that felt much

53

more light and airy. I toyed with the idea of painting a woodland mural in the living room, but didn't think that Dave, my landlord, would be overjoyed if he saw it, so I left it plain.

This flat has a much more homely feel to it than the last place ever did. I've gradually added décor and furniture when I have been able to afford it.

Business has been doing really well for a while, so I thought I would make a new addition to my interior design. Yesterday I went into the city and found a nice thick cream-coloured rug for my bedroom. I like having something soft for my feet when I have to get out of bed in the middle of the night. Despite the fact I have intended to get a rug for ages, yesterday was the first time I have had the chance; I have been so busy since starting the gallery.

I drop the rolled-up rug down near the window, beside the bed and stand back to look objectively. I'm satisfied it will look right, but I realise I don't have any scissors to cut the binding tape.

I fetch a Stanley knife from my studio and use that instead. Even after living here for almost eighteen-months, I still don't have the bits and bobs one would collect over a lifetime of living as an independent adult. This is mainly down to the fact that I packed so light when I left. I was in such a hurry to leave that night. But I don't like to think of my previous life much any more. It helps me to avoid the nightmares if I don't dwell on the past during the day.

The only clues to my past lie in a little box underneath the bed. As I finish smoothing out the rug, my fingers disappearing in the generous pile, I lean down briefly just to check it is still there.

It is. My little box of secrets tucked safely out of

sight.

My stomach clenches with dread every time I think of it. But I cannot simply get rid of it. I might need it one day. I have fantasised many times about simply taking it outside and burning the contents, but something tells me I shouldn't. It's that little nagging voice in my head that tells me other things too. Things like:

I'm wrong.

I'm bad.

I shouldn't be doing this.

My chest tightens warningly, so I get up sharply and leave the room.

I take some deep breaths and try to calm myself down before it all gets too much. If I let my anxiety get hold of me, I will be in a state for hours. And I don't want that, I have spent too long in that condition. And besides, I need to open the gallery for ten o'clock as I do every day. That doesn't give me much time to recover.

In the kitchen, I fill a glass of water and try to stay focussed on the simple act of drinking the cool liquid.

I remind myself that only *I* know the box is there. Even if another person was to somehow get into my bedroom through the solid security bolts, they would not know what I am hiding. At least I do not have to see it, for it is hidden and safe for now.

8

By the time I open the shutters of the gallery I feel much better. I have found the best way to cope with my panic attacks is to focus on something else entirely. My art has become my life. I switch on the downlights illuminating some of my largest works on the walls and feel an instant cloak of comfort wrap itself around me.

I remind myself that this place is all mine, so long as I pay the rent, of course. But that shouldn't be a problem. I have done a good job here, I tell myself. I take a deep breath. Everything is fine.

If my family could see me now, I think they would have no choice but to be begrudgingly proud of me. Not that they would recognise me of course.

I look at my reflection in the long mirror on one of the walls.

As part of my reinvention, I dyed my hair dark red. It is worn every day swept up in an elegant twist. I have tried dying my hair before, but it never works out the way I picture beforehand in my head. It was always distorted, faded somehow like it doesn't suit my skin tone or something; I've always been left feeling like such hairstyles were meant for other women, but not for me.

This time though it's turned out exactly how I wanted it. So close in fact, that I can hardly believe I've managed to pull it off.

Old habits die hard when it comes to my dress sense, however. I live in dark jeans and heels always with a blazer jacket, topping it all off with a coordinated colourful silk scarf.

Now I only feel a hint of regret that I had not given myself this makeover sooner. I really feel like this look suits me, *like this could be the forever me*.

Perhaps it is a good thing I didn't do it sooner. My physical transformation only aided my reinvention – and my disappearance. No one from my past should recognise me now.

I think I look classy. Older. My mother wouldn't recognise me as the person I am now; neither would my sister; nor my dear ex-partner, for that matter.

It turns out that a fresh new start was exactly what I needed.

A change is as good as a rest; never have I come across a phrase I agree with more.

I wander around the shop floor and make sure everything looks right; the gallery is only small, so this doesn't take long. The shop itself is an almost perfect square and the walls are mostly covered with paintings and prints of my art. The back of the shop has a tiny room with a toilet and minuscule sink and there is another cramped room with another sink and a tiny scrap of worktop space. I had to suppress a smile when the landlord was showing me around the place; he described these rooms as a bathroom and kitchen. Still, I won't say I don't find them useful during the day when I am running the shop by myself and want a cup of coffee or a snack.

I straighten a stack of prints in one of the racks and catch sight of Sally, the broad, little woman who runs the sandwich shop across the street, putting out her boards for the day. She sees me watching her and gives me a brief smile and wave which I return before she steps back inside.

Mornings in the gallery are the hardest. I get most of

my trade in the afternoon. Much of it comes from tourists visiting the city for the day. In the morning, the few browsers are still not sure what they should spend their money on yet. By the time the afternoon and early evening rolls around, people are determinedly enthusiastic in getting a memento from their day trip.

Making friends at a printing press on the outskirts of the town was great for tapping into this trade. They give me a great deal on prints of my work and I can price it so I make a decent amount of profit on each piece. They are more affordable than the paintings themselves and are actually where most of my turnover comes from.

I knew I only needed relatively small premises – I knew I could only afford small. The rent would have been too much on a bigger unit, and unnecessary too. When I saw this place advertised I knew it was perfect, since it came with accommodation too.

I love the sense of community the street has. The street is full of charm and each shop has its own little character; Sally's Sandwiches is painted bright red; Minerva Interiors a pale purple. I wanted to be part of that, to add to it. I fell in love with the street as soon as I saw it and knew that this was the one. Once I took possession of this property, I had the peeling and neglected paintwork transformed from faded green into gleaming white.

Admittedly, the takeaway next door isn't ideal; it stays open until ten-thirty each night, but I don't notice it all that much, apart from the occasional rubbish that gets left in the gallery's doorway and odd rowdy customer, that is.

I would have much preferred to have been neighbours with the key-cutters, or even the independent pound shop further down the street. But it is how it is. The rent is good and I am turning a profit.

I have made a few friends here. I get lunch from the sandwich shop opposite the gallery and Sally is always friendly. We sometimes have a chat if we happen to cross paths at our respective closing times. She has a very motherly vibe about her, even though she is nothing like my own and is only fifteen years or so my senior. She is several inches shorter than me, with a broad face and shoulders topped with a bleached red-purple bob.

Recently she invited me out for a drink at the pub by the lakeside, but I politely declined. She looked a little disappointed but didn't press the issue. My opinion is that it's best to keep my distance; stay more anonymous.

I don't feel safe yet and wonder if I ever will.

I am just finishing my early lunchtime sandwich when I hear the tinkle of the shop bell. I look up and see that it is Andrew.

My stomach tightens in a way that is almost pleasant.

Andrew part-owns the interior decorating shop next-door to the sandwich bar. He seems to take something of a back-seat in running the place and mostly leaves his business partner to take care of the day-to-day duties. The rest of the time he works for a property maintenance company. He just drops by Minerva Interiors sometimes, to check on how things are going, I imagine.

Ever since I started the shop, he has seemed quite taken by it and pops by from time to time, although more often in recent weeks.

During his first visit, he struck up a conversation,

during which, I discovered that his parents also run an art gallery in London. He seemed genuinely excited by my paintings and was very flattering. By the time he left after our second meeting, we had arranged that I would produce work specifically for his parents to sell. The extra income has been a nice bonus.

I haven't been to visit where it is displayed, despite Andrew's many invitations. I'm never going back to London, although I will never divulge to him why.

Andrew closes the door and beams at me with his usual warm smile. He is tall, with dark blonde hair and high cheekbones. He has a natural looking tan which makes me think he spends a lot of time abroad; it also makes his almond-shaped eyes appear a more vivid shade of blue. Today he is wearing a charcoal-grey suit jacket over a dark green shirt; neither do much to hide his athletic figure.

I worry that the 'Hi,' I give him as he approaches the counter doesn't seem quite casual enough. Although despite Andrew's handsome appearance, he has a softness and warmth about him that I don't find intimidating.

'Good afternoon, Ms. Harper,' he says smoothly with his trademark smirk. 'How are things going?'

I could have changed my name. I didn't have to keep the same one I had with *him;* didn't have to let it follow me to my new life. But going back to my old moniker wouldn't allow me to be free either, since *he* knows what it is and I doubt he would suspect I would keep this one – it is the perfect double bluff.

I certainly don't want to curse this new life with *his* taint. I feel like if I even so much as think his name it would be like dropping a bottle of ink in the middle of everything. It would spread black and insidious through everything, ruining all.

From a practical point of view all my loans and credit are easily accessible, no questions asked, under the name I already had; so it really made sense to keep it to avoid complications; a wise move considering I was struggling on low funds when I arrived here.

'Fine,' I say, 'Very good actually.' I inwardly berate myself for not spending the time apart since our last meeting thinking of more interesting things to say.

'So, did you find one, then?'

'Find one of what?' I say, puzzled.

'A rug for your bedroom. You said you were thinking of getting one?' He waits for the wave of comprehension to hit me.

'Oh, yes. I did. There was a place in the city that had lots of things that would go with the room.' Honestly, I didn't expect him to remember a little throwaway comment I made in small talk. I had forgotten it myself. I had no idea he was paying such close attention.

'Ouch,' he says, placing a hand on his heart. 'Should I be offended? My shop has plenty of choice too, you know.'

'Um, yes, I know. It's just... there was a really good sale on where I got mine from.' This is a lie. I had in fact gone into Andrew's shop, but since he doesn't run the place, I was met with his business partner. And a frosty reception it was too.

She made it very obvious during my brief visit to Minerva Interiors that she does not like me. Debbie, her name is, is a thin woman, very narrow shouldered too which makes her seem smaller than me, even though we are roughly the same height. She is a couple of years older than me too; I'm guessing she must be hovering around the forty mark. I'm sure she is the other side of it, but her wispy blonde hair is such a light shade that it initially detracts years from her face.

After she ignored my friendly 'Hello,' as I walked into the shop, an uncomfortable silence fell. She then proceeded to make me very aware that she was following me around the corners of the two-floor shop, as though she was implying that I would steal something.

I'm not sure why she has taken such a dislike to me, since everyone else has been so welcoming. My suspicions tell me that she may be jealous of my friendship with Andrew. I actually think that secretly she has feelings for him. Perhaps she is working up the courage to ask him out, or perhaps he has already rejected her, I don't know. Either way, she seems to view me as a threat to her territory.

In the end, I cut my browsing short and exited as quickly as I could.

Andrew looks slightly put out but shrugs his shoulders. 'Well, if you need anything else, you know where you can get it. I can give you really decent mates-rates if you want.'

'That's very nice of you, thank you. I'll be sure to do that.' Secretly, I think that the only way I will be going back to the shop with Debbie in it is if every other home furnishing shop in Coventry burns down. And even then, I think that I would be willing to travel a bit further afield to avoid her.

'Great, I'll tell Debbie to give you a discount next time I see her.'

'No, no. You don't have to do that.' I say hurriedly.

Something in his expression belies a flash of realisation. 'You're OK with Debbie aren't you? Some women say they find her, well... a little... cold sometimes.'

I think of my visit to the shop. 'Well, maybe a little.'

He laughs. 'Don't worry about it. I think she can just come across as a bit stuck-up to some people. She's OK really. If *I* can get along with her, then I'm sure anyone can.'

'What do you mean?'

'Well, we used to be married. That's when we started the business together. But we have been divorced for just over... let's see. Two years now, already. I can't believe the time has gone so fast.' He looks thoughtful for a second.

'Right, I didn't realise.' That explains a lot. I'll bet anything the divorce wasn't her idea.

'It was an amicable split,' he insists, looking at me. It seems important to him that I know this. 'We still get along fine – better than we ever did when we were married, in fact!' He laughs again, a slight flush in his cheeks adding to his haughty look.

Andrew leans forward onto the counter. I notice he looks a little nervous now. 'Listen, Harriet... I was going to ask if you wanted to go out to lunch with me, but I see you have already eaten.' He gestures at the empty sandwich wrappings on the counter. 'So I wondered, would you like to have dinner with me this weekend instead?'

My heart is hammering almost pleasantly now, but I cannot afford to let myself get caught up in reckless excitement. I have to let him down. 'I'm sorry, Andrew. I'm... I'm really busy – with work. I have several paintings to finish for next week.'

'Oh,' he says, looking disappointed.

'I'm really sorry,' I say. And I am. In fact, I'm sure I am actually more disappointed than he is, but I know I

63

must be careful.

It is much safer for me to keep my distance.

'Listen, Andrew, it's not just that I've got paintings I have to finish – I need to get some more paint too. There is one specific shade of acrylic I need to finish a commission for a customer and I can only get it from a little craft shop just outside the city.'

'What colour do you need?'

'It's called *Naples Yellow*. Usually, I order it online, but my usual supplier told me it was out of stock at the last minute, and I haven't got enough time to make an order somewhere else. And this craft shop is great, but they have virtually the same opening hours as I do, so I will have to rush over there tomorrow evening after I shut the gallery.'

I look at his expression of concentration as he listens to my story. He nods. My heart lifts slightly; he seems to believe me.

Perhaps I could let someone in soon. In truth, I am lonely. Perhaps I could bend my rules just for Andrew. He is a nice guy after all. He is funny, interesting, handsome and even loves my art. But I have been fooled by outward appearances before. And even if Andrew is the real deal, I don't want to find that I'm not ready and end up hurting him – or myself.

'Well, perhaps we can go out another time then,' Andrew says, recovering his usual light-hearted tone and straightening up. 'When you have less going on.'

'OK, sure. I'd like that.' I return his smile as he leaves.

The door closes behind him with a tinkle. I get up on the pretence of adjusting the canvases in the window display and sneak some glances of him getting into his car before he drives away.

A flicker of movement across the street catches my attention, and I find myself staring at a window display of curtains in Minerva Interiors.

It happened so quickly I can't be certain, but I'm sure Debbie had been looking this way, watching.

No matter what Andrew says, I am convinced their split was far less amicable than he pretends.

9

I'm screaming. In my dream, I'm screaming. This time the line between asleep and awake is so thin, I'm not entirely sure I hear the sound stop before I wake up.

I am writhing in the bed sheets in the dark. Sitting up, I try to unstick them from my hot and clammy legs, but it's difficult. I finally disentangle myself and throw the duvet back, allowing the cool air to carry the heat of my nightmare away.

That was a bad one. I relived the whole thing that time.

Once again I am truly grateful that *he* isn't here with me, questioning me, criticising me for disturbing his sleep. Although not for the first time recently I feel a little cold about the fact I have woken up alone.

In the darkness, I reach out for my phone on my bedside cabinet. There aren't any street-lights in the alley, meaning my bedroom is in almost total darkness at night; I feel half-blind when I wake in the night-time hours.

I look at the screen, the brightness of it making my eyes sting in the pitch darkness; it is still only the early hours of the morning.

Groaning, I rest my still-hot face onto the now cool skin of my knees. Sleep will elude me for hours, what with the horrible images from my dream still floating around in my mind's eye.

Getting up, I switch on my bedside lamp and find my way to the kitchen without turning on any further lights and down a glass of water. I return to bed and think of the book I keep meaning to start reading; it might prove a good distraction from negative thoughts that separate me from sleep.

I pull it out of the drawer, but before I open it I let my mind drift.

When I first moved here, I stretched out on the double bed, comforted by the thought that I was alone. Now those thoughts have turned against me and I don't like finding that it is just me here. I've grown weary of it.

I retract my sprawled-out limbs and arrange myself so that I am lying on just the one side of the bed, as if leaving room for someone else. Of course, I know there isn't, but it makes it less obvious that I am alone.

For some reason, my mind indulges me in the thoughts of Andrew. I've never been to his house before, so have no idea where he lives, but I attempt to picture him wherever he is now. Thinking of him is surprisingly comforting.

I open the book and try to focus on the words, but end up reading the opening paragraph over and over without taking it in. My mind now tempts me with thoughts of what it could be like if I did decide now was a good time to move on.

*

I eventually managed to get back to sleep just after five, but I still trudge through the day tired and zombie-like.

The working day didn't do much to help either, with a slow trickle of browsers that turned into a meagre couple of sales. I love it when people ask me questions about my work or want my contact details because they know someone who would be.

But today I haven't had anything noteworthy happen,

other than some tourists asking for directions. As a result, I have ended up spending most of the day dwelling on my latest nightmare. I try not to but with nothing to distract me, I find the horrific images rising up before my eyes, even in the harsh light of day.

Even with the hustle and bustle of the street outside, I feel the terror and dread I felt in the darkness last night creeping up on me. The cold, clammy feeling manages to wrap itself around my chest before I push it down by concentrating hard on cashing up the till at closing time. In the end, I force myself to count out loud as an effective distraction, hoping that no one comes in while I am doing so.

I shut the shop for the day and focus on my next task: a trip into the city centre. I'll bank the gallery's takings and stock up with food for the weekend. Since tomorrow, I will be rushing over to the art and craft shop to get the paint I wanted, now is a good opportunity to do a shopping trip.

When I moved to the city, I had intended to get a car once I could afford it. But once I had the funds I realised that I actually didn't need one. Everything was so accessible and parking in Coventry City centre is a nightmare. I find the bus satisfactory; it gets me where I need to go at least.

After taking a seat on the packed bus and rattling down a few streets, I regret not bringing my book with me. I get my phone out and berate myself for not having my earphones in my handbag. Or maybe they are in there, I just can't see them. After several minutes of rummaging, I decide that I must have left them on the kitchen worktop in my flat and abandon the idea.

I rub clear a patch of misted-up window and look out onto the grey, rain-sodden streets. The city can look really grim when the weather is like this.

I take a deep breath and try to think of sunny days I've had, which is difficult, considering I haven't had that many. It doesn't help that the air on the bus is muggy and smells of tired-worker sweat.

My chest starts feeling tight like I can't get enough air. I look up at the window above me and wonder if I would get away with opening it on such a wet day. Just as my legs poise, thinking of making their move, a scruffy old man in a large raincoat and an overly-stuffed backpack slumps down into the seat next to me.

I shrink back into my seat and hope my stop is nearer than I think it is.

I feel slightly better once I have banked the shop's takings. But by the time I get inside the doors of Sainsbury's, I am damp and feeling shivery. Although in a way I am glad I got caught in a renewed downpour, since it refreshed me slightly from the claustrophobic bus ride. On the other hand, I caught sight of myself in one of the shop windows and I look every inch the drowned rat I feel. I reach up and try to sweep soaking stray strands back into their twist, but I don't think it helps. I just hope that I don't run into anyone I know on this trip, especially not Andrew. My stomach knots a little at the thought.

I try to remember what I need, but I can't find my shopping list. I know I am running low on the basics, so I pick up some bread.

In the milk section, there is a large woman in grey jogging bottoms and an overloaded trolley blocking access to the semi-skimmed. She has greasy hair scraped back in a tight bun and seems oblivious to the fact her children are running riot with a split bag of frozen peas.

I pick up some organic full-fat instead from the far end of the aisle and quickly move on. It is rush hour at the supermarket and it is chaos. So many people cram the aisles, dodging and weaving around each other. I dodge and weave too, but I feel clumsy and my handbag suddenly feels too big. I always come away thinking I will resort to online-delivery, but by the time I get home again I decide that I need plenty of tasks to fill my time.

Too much time alone can lead to me dwelling on unpleasant thoughts.

I pick up some salmon fillets and think I'll get some microwave quinoa to go with it, but I can't seem to find the right aisle. Everything seems to have moved around since I was here earlier this week. Or maybe I am thinking of another store.

Someone brushes past me, but I can't see who it is. Glancing around I can't see a likely candidate, everyone seems momentarily too stationary.

I finally find the pasta section, but now I am hot as well as damp and my heart is starting to hammer threateningly.

For a moment I think about abandoning my basket and coming back later, but I think that is silly. I need to learn to overcome difficult situations, not just run away from them; it is hard because that is what I have been doing my whole life.

An old man in a motorised scooter is trying to squeeze by and I have to step back between the ends of two trolleys to let him pass. He swears as someone else gets in his way, forcing him to brake sharply.

I try to find what I am looking for, but it's hard to concentrate with the squealing toddler a few metres away. His mother is red in the face and looks immensely stressed as she hastily piles her trolley with large packets of pasta twists.

I still can't find what I am looking for. I think I must look like a tourist. I feel like one.

Something forces me to glance over my shoulder and I see a young couple in their mid-twenties staring straight at me. They are standing quite still and they don't seem to be associated with any basket or trolley nearby.

I expect them to look away, but they don't. They are muttering to each other, but I can't understand what they are saying.

The woman's gaze drops, and I automatically follow it. Glancing down, I see that she is looking at my handbag hooked over my elbow. With a jolt of panic, I see that it is unzipped and the one strap is drooping slightly, exposing my phone. I tug my bag firmly onto my shoulder and press it tightly under my elbow. For a moment I think that the gallery's takings could be missing, but then I remember I have already banked them. I force myself to replay the memory in my head. Yes, I definitely did deposit them safely.

I glance back at the couple and the man jerks his head to his partner, and they both wander off and disappear at the end of the aisle.

Suddenly something cold and clammy hits my hand with some force. I gasp before I can stop myself. I look down and see one of the unruly children from the dairy section zip past me shrieking as another chases her.

In my mind, I am plunged back into my nightmare from last night. Once again, I see grey, clammy hands grabbing at me with their bloated, icy fingers. Dark water rises above my head, filling my ears, my nose, my mouth, stinging my eyes.

I am suddenly engulfed in the feeling of dread that has been stalking me all day.

My chest feels tight.

My heart is beating so hard now; I feel sure the people nearby should be able to hear it, but they seem oblivious and continue to peruse the jars of olives and pesto. The people talk to each other, oblivious; at least I think they are talking – I see their mouths moving, but cannot hear what they are saying.

It seems odd that anyone can think of something as simple as food when my whole world is slipping away. I just can't get away from the feeling of dread and grief that is suffocating me.

I clutch at my chest. My heart feels swollen like it's twice its usual size. As usual, I feel like I am having a heart attack, but know I am not.

Through the confusion of disconnected noises that echo around me, I am suddenly aware of a warm hand on my forearm, its fingers adorned with various tarnished gold rings. I turn to my right and see a woman in her sixties looking at me, her face full of concern. Like the others in the tangled mass of noise and images, her mouth is moving, but I cannot understand what she is saying.

I realise how strange I must look to the people around me. In an attempt to regain control, I shut my eyes, but it only makes things worse; I now see vividly the horrific images that haunt my night-time hours every time my eyes are closed, so I open them again.

I reach out in front of me for something to steady myself on. My cold and slippery hands find the supermarket shelf and I move to grip it tightly. I realise too late, however, that I have knocked a jar of pasta sauce from the shelf and it disappears out of my field of vision. I hear a noise that sounds like the smashing of glass and I feel pain in my foot, but my brain can't tell what is causing it and I can't bring myself to turn and look; I don't want to lose my grip and fall away into nothingness.

My sweating fingers grip the cold metal of the shelf tightly and I breathe deeply, trying to block out the chaos of the supermarket. I wish more than anything that I was back in the gallery, or in the quiet sanctuary of my flat.

I tell myself that I will be fine as long as I keep breathing. I need to calm myself down. *This will pass, but first I need to calm down.* I have no choice but to wait this out.

10

Back in the flat, my panic attack has passed and I am back to my usual self again – almost. I feel sick with shame at the thought of what happened a few hours ago. I hate it when it happens in public. People don't really understand what is happening to me. They think I am mad, or an overreacting attention seeker; but that could not be further from the truth.

I now regret stubbornly ploughing on with my pre-planned shopping trip. I should have taken notice of the warning signs that had been flashing before my eyes all day. It had all started with my nightmare; I had been foolish enough to believe I could just forget about it.

I should know by now that I am not in charge of my thoughts and feelings, or even my body any more. I should know that whenever I feel the anxiety closing its cold fingers around my chest, I am likely to fall prey to an attack. By now I should know how to control them.

I haven't always had panic attacks. I have heard of some people having them since childhood or their teens. But that's not me. For me, they started in my early twenties; one just hit me out of the blue one day. I had always been anxious, even as a child – of course, I had – ever since the day it happened. In fact, I can only remember a short period of my life where I did not live in fear. But one day I started having severe attacks that I could not ignore. They started and all of a sudden I could not function the way I used to. And amongst the other fears I had – the fear of *him* – I was living in fear of fear itself.

I know I need help.

What if the same thing happened at the gallery? I cringe at the thought of having a severe attack in front of customers, or worse, in front of Andrew. I can't let that happen – I need to take back control, just like I did when I left *him*. As long as I continue to be a slave to my anxiety, I am not really free at all, just living in the illusion of it.

I reach underneath the sofa and pull out my MacBook. When it loads, I do a quick Google search for *therapists in Coventry.*

Immediately, I am bombarded with results. I see ads for online counselling but ignore them. I have been down that road before with no success. It was just too easy to lie to the person on the other end, which obviously didn't benefit me. Speaking to someone face to face and meeting my problems head-on is the way to go. Really, I should have done it years ago.

I click on one result for a therapist named Julia Hart halfway down the page and instantly know this is the one. This woman's page lists anxiety at the top of problems she is experienced in treating.

There is a picture of her too. She has a kind face; a wild tangle of natural-looking curly dark hair surrounds a face that is lined in a friendly way, as though from smiling often. I can imagine feeling at ease with her.

I am so enthusiastic, that I pick up my phone ready to call the number on the website when I realise the practice will be well and truly shut by this time of day.

The living room has darkened around me as I have been sitting here and only now have I actually noticed. I get up and move over to the window, where I can see the last streaks of sunset are fading into the dark-blue sky visible between tiled rooftops.

I wince slightly as I walk since I cut my foot during

the incident earlier. I hardly noticed at the time. It was the balding manager of the supermarket that informed me I was bleeding, as I sat in his office begging him not to call an ambulance. In the end, he had agreed, but wouldn't let me leave before he broke open a box of plasters and sat me down with a cup of overly-sweet tea in his cramped and untidy office.

I absorb the sight of the sky for a few minutes before shutting the curtains. The beauty of it was tugging at the artist in me, but I have enough work to do already and I have resolved to make getting counselling a top priority.

Finding a scrap of paper, I jot down the number and use my phone as a paperweight ready for the next day.

First thing tomorrow morning I will call and make an appointment.

11

I'm surprisingly happy when I open the gallery the next morning, proud I did not break the promise to myself to call and make an appointment with the therapist. I managed to get through to the secretary shortly after they opened and booked a session for Tuesday. Apparently, someone else cancelled theirs, so they could fit me in at short notice.

I feel like a weight has been taken off my shoulders already. My heart feels lighter, and I have a general feeling of having everything neatly organised. To top it all off, the sun is shining brightly outside, and there are patches of bright blue sky visible through the tops of the buildings across the street.

I yawn. I'm still a little tired. Now, I wonder if my decision to substitute chamomile tea for my usual mid-morning coffee was a good idea. I take another sip and I'm sure I feel calmer than usual, but that might not necessarily be all down to the drink. Not for the first time in recent years, I feel like I am finally starting to tame my life.

Yesterday's chaos managed to temporarily take my mind off another matter, however. Today is my birthday. But since I have cut myself off from anyone from my old life, and I haven't made any close friends here, I don't expect any well-wishers.

I have never been close with my mother. Even as a very young child, even before it happened, I don't have any memories of affection from her. I used to watch as she gave my older sister love and praise and wish she would do the same for me. She told me later on that she had wanted her second child to be a son so she would have a boy and a girl; a neat set. So I always seemed to be an inconvenience for her – a *disappointment*. And later, after that awful day, I was much, much worse.

I knew then that I could never hope to see any love from her, but it didn't stop me hoping for it.

She never failed to miss an opportunity to tell me how much she hated me for what I had done. And as a child, I believed every word of it. I think I still do, and that is where my problems stem from.

My father was very much different to my mother when it came to raising children. He seemed to love me and my sister equally. Sometimes I would even get the impression that I was his favourite, but I don't know if that was true, maybe all children think that. I have no way of asking him now though since he died when I was five. He never got the opportunity to see how my mother treated me after the incident. I know he would have stopped her, stood up to her to protect me. Or maybe that is just wishful thinking. I often wonder if he too would have blamed me.

Everything would have been different if he had survived.

My mother was distraught and missed him terribly, but she has lived very comfortably from the proceeds of his will and on the back of his life insurance policy. So has my sister for that matter.

After I finished Uni I asked my mother for a small loan to set up my own art gallery, back when I first had the idea. But of course, she refused. I later found out that shortly after her rejection, she gave my sister the dream wedding she wanted at Kew Gardens so she could marry her dentist fiancée. I stopped talking to them both after that.

I still got the obligatory birthday and Christmas card before I moved, but now I don't even get those. Of course, that is my fault since I didn't mention the fact that I've changed address, but I don't see the point of telling them. What good is a token card with a cold factory-printed message inside, when the sender and recipient have endured so many years of bitterness and anger?

I haven't even seen either of them for years. I wasn't invited to the wedding; I only found out about it through a distant acquaintance from Uni. The last time I saw my mother and sister was when we bumped into each other in Westfield shopping centre in London four years ago. I don't know who was more surprised. With a horrible pang, I realised my sister was clearly far along a pregnancy and the pair were excitedly shopping for things for the new baby.

The child must be well-and-truly born by now. I can imagine my mother happily selecting a suitable school for her precious grandchild. I don't even know if it was a boy or a girl. Perhaps I should have asked at the time. I'll bet anything my mother was crossing her fingers for a little grandson to spoil; a son she never had.

If either of them saw me now, they would not recognise me. And I certainly can't let them see me; there would be too many questions and I could not answer a single one of them.

I drain the last of the chamomile tea and put my cup away in the tiny kitchen. I am perfectly content with not having any acknowledgement of my birthday. In fact, I think it is nice not to have the pressure of fixing a fake smile on my face as I receive things I know I will never use. So when I see a florist van park outside in the street, I think nothing of it. I merely wonder who is going to be on the receiving end of the large bouquet and parcel that the driver emerges with. Although, when I see him heading directly for the gallery door, my stomach plummets uncomfortably and I feel the all-too-familiar beginnings of panic.

I am aware that my body has frozen behind the counter. My mind is racing.

Nobody knows I am here. I haven't told anyone it's my birthday... Have I?

I feel a cold stab in the pit of my stomach.

Someone has found me.

I try desperately to think if I have mentioned it to someone absent-mindedly and somehow forgotten. But I'm sure I haven't – I wouldn't be that careless. I couldn't *afford* to be that careless.

The door tinkles as the delivery man walks in. He beams at me around the large bunch of pink roses as he approaches the counter.

'Good morning!' He places the gift-wrapped parcel down on the counter in front of me and hands me the flowers; I awkwardly receive them.

'If you could just sign here, please sweetheart.' He hands me an electronic pad to sign.

'It's not my birthday,' I stupidly blurt out to him as I rest the flowers down on the counter.

He shrugs. 'Someone must think it's a special occasion, love.'

I scrawl the well-practised signature I always do but see that it appears as a vague squiggle on the electronic pad as I hand it back to him.

'Cheers!' he says to me brightly as he heads back towards his van.

I immediately start rooting through the flowers, looking for a clue as to who sent them. It occurs to me that I might not find one if the bouquet is designed to be some kind of sinister message. It doesn't take me long, however before my fingers close around a card nestled in the rose heads.

I pull it out and look at it and see my name on one side. The handwriting is unfamiliar. I turn it over and read the message:

Hopefully, this little package will save you a trip – so you won't have to rush across town later. I don't want to seem too presumptuous, but maybe this leaves you free for dinner tonight???

You can text me if you are happy to join me at around eight tonight. You've got my number.

If I don't hear from you, I'll take that to mean that you wanting to buy paint was your way of letting me down gently!

Anyway, no worries either way :)
Andrew
xxXXxx

I finish reading the note with a smile on my face. A few minutes ago, my heart had been starting to pound uncomfortably, but now my chest is swelling with excitement. In spite of myself, I feel giddy and relish the butterflies that erupt in my stomach.

I eye the small parcel that came with the flowers now with keen anticipation, rather than fear, as I had a few moments ago. I tug at the curly golden ribbon, unravelling it, and tear quickly through the shiny pink paper. Inside the gift box, there are five tubes of paint in Naples Yellow, more than enough to finish the customer commission I am working on. There is also a brand new palette, and an entire set of Italian-made painting knives. I run my fingers over one of the handles; it feels expensive. I feel a little guilty that Andrew has spent too much money on all this, but I really appreciate the gesture. He has clearly made a lot of effort.

I feel my resolve to not get too involved with anyone has melted away and I know what my answer will be. I pull my phone from my jeans pocket and type a quick text:

I just got the flowers and your lovely gift :) I would be delighted to join you for dinner tonight. Eight o'clock sounds great. I'm really looking forward to it!
See you later xxxx

I put my phone down on the counter, but it is not long before I hear the buzzing of a new message:

So glad you liked it, Harriet :) Be ready and I will pick you up outside the gallery at eight.
Can't wait to see you later.
xxXXxx

*

The rest of the day passes in a kind of blur. I have a great day on the till. The warmer weather seems to have brought plenty of tourists to the city. I sell a really decent amount of prints of the local area. One man, an American, was very enthusiastic about my work and bought several originals for his relatives back home.

I drink several cups of chamomile tea throughout the afternoon. I really think it is helping to calm my nerves a little, even if it is not doing much to quell the excitable butterflies in my stomach.

Somehow these nerves are different to the dreaded panic. These nerves feel almost pleasant... almost.

I think I am handling the anticipation well. But by the time I am closing the gallery for the day, I start to feel differently. My palms are sweating as I lock up and secure the shutters.

I feel so nervous as I ascend the stairs to my flat, I actually seriously consider cancelling. I haven't been on a first date for so long. In my head, I think of all the things that could go wrong, and I am actually shaking as I try on the clothes I have pictured myself putting on all day.

To look in the only mirror in the flat, I have to go through to the studio where it is hung on the back of the door. This mirror is placed here on purpose, that way I don't accidentally catch sight of myself when I am not expecting it; I don't want my reflection to catch me off-guard – I need time to prepare myself for it. I so despise what I see.

He always wanted mirrors around; one in the bathroom, one in the bedroom and one by the front door. He actually liked to look at himself. I could never understand that.

I push closed the studio door which is usually always kept open, bracing myself as I always do to ensure that I am ready for who I see looking back at me.

Instantly, I decide that I can't wear this outfit; the jeans are far more faded than I remember and the top just doesn't look special enough.

Maybe a dress would look more formal?

Annoyingly, I don't actually know where Andrew is taking me. I curse myself for not asking him earlier. I picture Andrew getting out of his car in casual attire and his face falling when he sees me waiting for him, overdressed as if I'm expecting him to take me to an opera.

Rubbing my damp palms on my ageing jeans, I sink onto the bed. Maybe the smart thing to do would be to cancel tonight?

No, says a little stubborn voice in my head. *It is about time I had a new man in my life. I'm ready.*

An hour and a half later, I pose in the mirror with what feels like my hundredth outfit choice. Gingerly I try out different angles, making sure that I am happy with how it looks on me.

On a daily basis, I manage to put on my make-up hardly looking in the mirror at all. Actually, I've got quite good at it over the years. Foundation is easy enough, then the most subtle hint of blush that most people probably don't even notice; I don't need a mirror for that. I need to see what I'm doing with eyeliner, that's unavoidable, but I manage to do it in such a way that I can avoid looking at myself directly in the eye. I just focus on the skin directly around my lids. Unfortunately, this draws my attention to the fine lines around my eyes that aren't all that fine any more. They used to just be visible when I smiled, now I see they are a permanent fixture when I am forced to observe them so close-up.

I wonder when I'll notice them upon simply catching sight of myself in a mirror. It's a scary thought, but I think I still have a fair few years left. Although, probably less than I think. I'm in my mid-thirties now, there will only be more lines to face ahead.

Overall, I am happy with what I am wearing now. I have settled on some long black capris with a long-sleeved, fuchsia-pink top with sequin detail. Hopefully, it will cover me for wherever Andrew takes me.

I've gone for some medium-heel black shoes that aren't too fancy. I don't have to worry about heel height with Andrew since he must be at least six-foot-two; not like I always had to with *him*.

My neck feels a little bare without the usual silk scarves I've grown used to, so I put on a simple zirconia necklace to compensate.

I look at the clock and realise I still have almost an hour left before Andrew comes to pick me up. To fill the time, I busy myself carefully putting away the jumble sale of discarded clothes from the bed and floor neatly. I try to stretch out the task, making it last to prevent myself thinking too much about the ways the evening can go wrong. It works for the most part.

As I put the last pair of trousers back in the wardrobe, my hand nudges the holdall at the bottom. It is packed with some basics – clothes, underwear and wash things etc. It has been there since the first few weeks I arrived, ready to grab at a moments notice should I need to.

Just in case.

But I'm not sure now if I will ever need it. This looks like a good enough hiding place to me. I could be invisible in this bustling little street forever if it would let me – if everything stays in my favour.

When I have finished the bedroom, I grab a cereal bar from the stash I keep in the studio and devour it hungrily. I decide the sugar will do my nerves good and it will keep me going until later. While I'm in the studio, I lay out my new art equipment ready for my next painting session tomorrow.

The doorbell rings.

All thoughts of the backlog of work I have to do suddenly evaporate from my mind. I am hit with a fresh wave of nerves, and for a moment cannot remember where I left the handbag I set aside for tonight. For a moment I think that I gathered the small clutch up into the clothes I put away. Then I remember I left it hanging on the bedroom door. I swing the strap over my shoulder and hurry down the stairs. I hate it when people have to ring twice; it makes me feel under pressure.

I slow my pace as I get near the bottom steps, not wanting to look like an over-enthusiastic puppy.

A deep breath doesn't do much to help me when I open the door and see Andrew on the other side. He looks gorgeous, dressed in a dark blue shirt and immaculate black jeans. He has clearly taken extra effort to sweep his light hair back, making him look even more handsome than usual.

'Hiya,' he says. He leans in to kiss me briefly on the cheek and I get a hit of the expensive-smelling aftershave he has chosen.

'Hi,' I smile back. 'You're early.'

'Well, I didn't want to keep you waiting,' he says with a smile. 'Are you ready to go?'

I lock the door to the flat behind me and get into the passenger side of Andrew's car. He holds the door open for me and I thank him as I sit inside.

He is parked in his usual spot directly outside the gallery. For a moment, I get an insight into what it looks like from his perspective. From the outside, the little shop looks like a decent, respectable business. I still can't believe it's all mine.

Andrew sits in the driver's seat. 'So, here we are!' He gives a small laugh and I suddenly realise he's nervous. Maybe he is even as daunted by this as I am. Well, maybe not quite as much. 'Where would you like to go?

Is there anywhere you like to eat, or want to try out?'

'I'll let you decide,' I say. I haven't been to a restaurant, or out on a single social occasion since I moved here, but I don't tell Andrew that. I don't want to sound boring. 'I still feel like the new girl in the city. I bet you know where all the good places are.'

He pauses for a second. 'Well, there's one place I go quite often. They do really good food, and it's really easy-going.'

For some reason, my eyes are briefly drawn towards Minerva Interiors before I answer. 'It sounds great. If you like it, I'm sure I will.'

'Excellent!' he says heartily before he starts the engine and we set off.

I glance once more towards the dark windows of the flat above Minerva Interiors as we pass by, certain that I did not imagine the flicker of movement I registered near the kitchen window.

12

Listening to Andrew talk, I find myself at ease in his company and really, this outing doesn't feel much different from when he visits me in the gallery.

Twenty minutes later, we arrive at a pub beside the canal on the outskirts of the city: The Bluebell Inn. I can see why Andrew described the place as easy-going. As soon as I walk through the door Andrew holds open for me, I am enveloped by the warmth and cosy chatter, and feel immediately at ease. There are a variety of mismatched leather chairs surrounding rustic wooden tables, each of which, have coloured jars with flickering candles in them. The whole place is charming and feels like a quaint cottage, a far cry from the neon lights of trendy bars we drove past on the way here.

A short woman greets us with a warm broad smile. She finds us a nice table beside a fairy-light-lined window in the corner and we both order white wine before she leaves us with two menus.

The view through the window is charming. From our table, we can see a bridge going over the canal and a large burgundy narrow-boat has moored for the evening. Twilight has set in and cast everything in its dusky pink glow. To top it all off lights are starting to come on and twinkle gently in the distance.

A young waiter brings us our drinks and tells us he will return once we're ready to order food.

I glance across the table at Andrew and see him scanning his menu. I glance down at my own. Everything sounds so nice, but the butterflies in my stomach are rising again and my mouth feels so dry I wonder what I could actually manage to eat.

Suddenly, I'm hyper-aware that I have not been on a date in a very long time. I take a sip of my wine and will my stomach to stop squirming.

When the waiter returns, I decide I probably can't go wrong with the penne carbonara. It should slip down more easily than the steak and chips Andrew is ordering anyway.

The waiter leaves with our order and I look across the table at Andrew. The candlelight makes his face look softer than usual. 'This place is lovely,' I say. 'Do you often come here?'

He grins back at me. 'Is that your best chat up line?'

I blush at the cliché.

'No, seriously,' Andrew explains. 'I thought it would be a good place to talk. Better than a bar filled with students and twenty-somethings where you have to shout at each other over the loud music. You know the ones I mean, don't you?'

'Yes, they're really rowdy. That's why I only go to them on Friday nights.'

Andrew gives me a surprised glance and then his face cracks into a relieved grin as he realises I'm joking.

'You've got a wicked sense of humour, Harriet Harper. I think I'm going to have to watch you.'

Unknowingly the tension that I usually carry around in my shoulders has been eased and I feel at ease talking about how my week at Stony Studios has gone. Our food arrives and the conversation seems to flow naturally, as if we are just talking everyday business but by candlelight and not the downlights that adorn the gallery ceiling.

'And I'm working on a painting for a client at the moment that I'm really enjoying. It's really epic actually. But it needs to be just right. The lady wants it for her entrance hall.'

'That's what you needed *Naples Yellow* for?'

'Yes. Thank you for the things you bought. And for the flowers, they're really beautiful.'

'That's OK. You deserve them.'

'I improvised when it came to putting them in water though. I had to use one of my water pots in my studio since I haven't got any vases any more.'

'Any more? Since you moved to Coventry you mean?'

'That's right. I've been buying things when I've needed them so far. It's amazing what you collect over the years, but when you move house, all the little things can get lost. You know, like vases and lampshades, bedding and just general knick-knacks. Oh – and scissors. I haven't had a pair of scissors to my name since I moved to the city.'

'Well, I know what to get you for Christmas then. Sorted.' He half-smiles, but then his face turns a little more serious as he cuts his steak. 'Sounds like you moved in a bit of a hurry. You said you were from London, didn't you? Which part?'

'Yes. South Norwood.' At least that part isn't a lie.

'Bad breakup?'

'I guess you could say that.' I swallow my mouthful of pasta before I mean to. My eyes water as it slides painfully down my throat. I take a quick sip of wine.

'I didn't mean to pry.' Andrew says quickly.

'No, it's fine. Actually, I was married. It didn't work out though – obviously. He turned out to be something very different from what I thought he was.' I take another sip of wine and think inwardly of how much I'm not telling Andrew. He seems to sense that I don't want to talk about it though, as he changes the subject.

'So tell me more about your workshop,' he says, cutting into his steak. 'You said you ran it with someone else, didn't you?'

It takes me a moment to realise what he is talking about, but then I remember, with a pang of guilt, one of the untruths I told him on our first meeting. Back then I told him that I had run a workshop back in London with a fellow artist. I regret saying that now, but Andrew had taken me completely by surprise back in the first few months of me opening Stony Studios. He had expressed so much interest in my work and I wasn't prepared for it; hence the lie about the workshop.

I frantically try to remember what I told him at the time.

'Yes,' I say, making a point of finishing my mouthful of food to give me a few seconds extra thinking time. 'I started it with a friend of a friend from Uni. It was just a small sort of thing. To be honest, I was never happy with the kind of work I was doing there anyway. I found it frustrating, teaching the same class all the time. Taking people through the same motions over and over again. Nobody ever really progressed to the next level. They were all just amateurs and I wanted to be more professional. That's why I wanted my own gallery.'

'What did your friend of a friend say about that? Were they disappointed?'

I shrug and try to downplay my imaginary business partner's anguish. 'She wasn't too surprised. We never really got along with each other anyway – even when things were going well. Creative differences and all that. She wanted to focus on teaching all types of art, you know – drawing, sculpting, pottery that sort of thing. I just wanted to focus on painting. So it was only a matter of time before we went our separate ways...'

'I totally get that,' he says, nodding enthusiastically. 'It was the same thing with me and Debbie when we were married. I wanted to go in a different direction with the shop, turn it into more of a DIY and decorating store, she wanted to go down the pretty-shiny-object route. You can guess who won, eh?' He laughs.

I smile along too; he seems to have accepted my lie. I'm disappointed in a way. But then again, maybe he feels more of a connection to me if he thinks we have a similar past, even if mine isn't one-hundred-percent true. Since Andrew's invite was so spontaneous I didn't have a great deal of time to prepare for what I was going to tell him this evening. I decided from the beginning to err on the side of caution when talking about my past, tonight is no exception.

You never know how something might come back on you when you least expect it.

'Have you always lived in London?' he asks.

'Yes. I lived there all my life up until a year-and-a-half ago. Well, apart from a brief spell in my teens when I thought it would be cool to start a new life in Cornwall.'

'Cornwall?' He laughs and adopts a squint in one eye accompanied by a thick Cornish accent. 'Argghh, many an artist be wandering down to St Ives, so they do.'

A giggle bursts from me and I realise I haven't laughed properly for years. I can't even remember the last time I had anything to laugh about.

A woman with greying-blonde hair on the nearest table gives us a withering look, before returning to talking to her husband.

'Yes, I know they do,' I say. 'But it wasn't St Ives I ended up in. It was Redruth if you must know.'

Normal Andrew speaks again, 'Redruth? That's a long way to go and not make it to the seaside.'

The seaside. A wave of cold descends upon my shoulders at the thought and I try to stay in the moment. I focus on the flickering candles in their pretty glass jars and the rustic grain of the tabletop in front of me. The rest of my energy goes into trying to sound casual when I say, 'I know. I'm just not that much of a fan of the sea, really. I prefer to be inland. That's probably just the Londoner in me, though.' The level normality I hear in my voice impresses me. I just hope that Andrew doesn't press me over why I don't like the sea. To my relief, he doesn't.

'Redruth is a random neck of the woods to end up in, though. What drew you there?'

'I don't know really. It just seemed far away and exciting to my teenage self.' Mainly just far away, really. Far away from my claustrophobic family home in London. Far, far away from my mother. I thought I could be a whole new person by running away there. It turned out I couldn't. I was just the same old me.

'Oh no. There wasn't a hunky Cornish boy involved, was there?'

'No, of course not Andrew. What do you take me for?' I say in mock-offence. I'm impressed I can maintain what I imagine must be a playful smile on my face as I answer. The truth was that it wasn't a boy, but rather a man. A man in his forties. Way too old for the seventeen-year-old me. Little did I know at the time that his interest in me was limited. Even all these years later it still stings. 'No, I just thought I'd have a go at making it on my own,' I go on. 'I guess it was a teenage

93

rebellion thing.

I grew up a lot that summer. I realised how small the world really is. That I couldn't just run away from things.'

Oh, the irony. I guess I haven't really changed that much after all.

The summer evening outside has darkened to the point where I can see my slightly-distorted reflection. Before I glance at it, I feel as though my seventeen-year-old self would be looking back at me, hair dyed black with nails and heavy eyeliner to match. But all I see is mid-thirties, sensible Harriet Harper instead; it's a comforting image.

At this point, I regret not being more honest with Andrew. I really want to tell him the truth. For a wild moment, I feel like the truth might just burst out of me like that little laugh did earlier. Andrew makes me feel so comfortable in his presence, I feel like I could tell him everything and he would understand.

I take a large gulp of wine when I realise this. I can't afford to have thoughts like that.

My eyes sting again from taking such a large swallow and I don't want Andrew to again think I'm upset, so I ask him a question about his work to distract him. It works, he talks enthusiastically about a buy-to-let opportunity he is thinking about taking up.

'I think I could use some help with the decorating though,' Andrew says, finishing his meal and laying down his cutlery. 'Debbie always used to take care of it when we were married, but on my own I'm hopeless. Seriously, you should see my house. The styling is all over the place. It's not very homely, I'm just not good at matching colours and things. When I moved in, Debbie helped me out with choosing curtains and things – like

I said, it was an amicable split,' he insists in response to the surprise I thought I was doing a good job of hiding. 'We really are still friends, you know.'

'It's OK. I believe you,' setting my cutlery down too.

'You don't talk to your ex then I take it?'

'No, not at all.' I would amuse myself thinking of choosing curtains for *him,* but I already know the thought would fill me with dread and anger, not mirth. Besides, *my* ex really would not like the abode I would like to see him in. *A six-by-eight cell would be too good*, I think. 'But I can understand how civilised people might still be civil with each other,' I say.

'Anyway, she chose these lime-green floral curtains for the bedroom and similar ones for the lounge, but in orange. They really aren't my thing – at the time I thought she might have chosen those out of spite – but she still seemed to be acting normally around me, so I don't think that was it. Anyway, I thought maybe you could help me out. You know – having an artists eye and all?

'Decorate your house?'

'Well, I meant this flat – that's if I get it. It's an auction, so there's no guarantee. And Dave – you know which Dave I mean?'

'You mean my landlord?'

'That's the one. He already owns half of Stonegravel Street – including Minerva Interiors and Debbie's flat above – but he's planning on bidding on this flat on Everard Road and he seems really keen on it. But even if I don't win the auction, I'd still love it if you could do something with my house. That's if you want to, of course?' He looks at me hopefully.

'OK, I can help out if you want. But don't you part-own an interior design shop?'

95

'I know, I know – it's terrible. But really that is Debbie's thing, not mine. I just used to run it with her. Whenever I suggest I want to do my place up, she makes suggestions, but I get the feeling they are along the lines of the curtains – done just to get at me a bit. Seriously, it really needs work doing to it. I still have the wallpaper up from the previous owners, and I'm sure they last decorated in the eighties.'

I snort.

'I keep meaning to do something with it, but other things keep cropping up–' He counts items on his fingers. '–Work, going for a drink with my mates, Facebook notifications, the Great British Bake Off. You know what it's like.'

I laugh. 'Procrastinator. Not that I would expect anything else from a property maintenance officer. You're probably just in the habit. Aren't you basically paid to delegate jobs to other people?'

'Cheeky! Well, it's not like I haven't tried. I mean, I even went to B&Q a few years ago and bought a pot of magnolia paint – inspired, I know – but I didn't get around to using it. It's probably gone off by now, it was so long ago. Can paint go off?'

'Yes, it can.' I sip my wine. 'I'll come and see what I can do if you like. But I'm no expert. I've only ever done up my flat you know though.'

'I'm sure what you've done with it is great. Maybe you'll let me see it sometime.' Andrew gives me a cheeky smile, which I find myself returning, and raises his wine glass. 'To interior decorating.'

I raise mine and clink it against his. 'To interior decorating.'

We order a satisfyingly large salted caramel sundae with two spoons for dessert.

'Oh, I know one thing you need to get for your own flat before you do anything else though,' he says taking a heaped spoonful.

'What is that?'

'You need to get yourself a vase. And you know where you can get a great one from don't you?'

'It wouldn't be Minerva interiors would it, by any chance?'

'You got me,' he says putting his free hand on his heart.

'Yes, I'll take a look next week,' I assure him with a smile.

Although, I still have no intention of setting foot in that shop ever again.

13

I've always wanted to be an artist. When I was young, I thought of nothing else. Whenever everything became too much at home I would retreat to my bedroom and reach for my sketch pad and pencils; that was all I had back then. My mother was never the arty-type, she never even encouraged us to paint as small children. Personally, I like to think I inherit my gift from my father's side of the family. Honestly, I don't think any of his relatives were arty either, but I like to think it anyway.

I had originally wanted to study art at Uni, but my mother kicked up such a fuss about it she managed to steer me away. She wanted me to pursue something more reliable and was keen for me to follow in my sister's footsteps by opting for law. We had a major argument where she told me that pursuing a career in art was a waste of time. In the end, I graduated with a graphic design degree – a strange kind of compromise which made neither of us happy.

Working to the strict requirements set down by a client was something I loathed. I longed to do my own thing, create an image that brings people joy, last forever. I didn't want the result of my working life to be pieces that people either ignore or bin as soon as it lands on their doorstep.

It was before I went to Uni that I met Richard when I was just seventeen. It's really strange, but I can't even remember his surname now. Usually, I have a good head for names and facts. Come to think of it, I can't even remember his address either, which is really weird.

The conclusion I have come to is that I am not unable to remember – I just don't want to. I remember reading somewhere once that trauma can cause you to forget things. My brain must not work properly though, or be selective in what it chooses to remember. I certainly can't forget other traumas so readily.

Perhaps my mind just doesn't deem Richard important enough. I met him online one summer. That was back when people were even more clueless about the dangers of the internet. Well, I was certainly clueless anyway – perfect prey for a predatory parasite like him.

We started talking online one day in a public chat room, he quickly invited me to a private one. We started chatting every night through our computers. I was so isolated from my family, my school peers, everyone, and I was really lonely. What he said to me seemed really sincere, I was totally taken in. He told me he was lonely too, that his wife had left him for another man and he just wanted someone to talk to. Then he confessed how he'd unexpectedly fallen for me through our conversations and wanted to meet up. He invited me to stay at his cottage in Cornwall. By that point, I was so trusting of him that I didn't question his intentions. I told him I wanted to be with him too and the next day I packed a holdall, left a note for my mother and got on a train.

Looking back, I think he had only intended to take my virginity, but I was so desperate not to go back to my suffocating home in Surrey with my mother and sister I must have seemed like too good an opportunity to pass up.

I ended up staying with Richard in his cottage for almost six-months. while he was at work I would occupy myself with my sketchbook. The local town and countryside provided the perfect place to draw on location. I liked it best when he wasn't there.

It didn't last very long though, whatever we had together. It wasn't long before I found he was chatting up other girls my age, and another that was only fourteen. Fourteen sounded like a child compared to my own mature, grand old age of seventeen. I realised then what a mistake I had made. A mistake many young girls make, especially when their mother has abandoned them, shut them out and left them to their own devices.

I was forced to go home. I never saw or heard from Richard again. Not that I wanted to, but what got me was that he never even called me to see where I'd gone. I guess a missing suitcase and an absence of my things was a clear message enough.

In truth, I didn't really like him that much. I just wanted to think that I was finally doing something right. I felt all grown up, and I thought I was, for once, in control of a situation.

How wrong I was.

When I got back, my mother was furious with me. It took me by surprise how much she shouted. It was almost as if she cared, but really, I think she was just angry that I'd embarrassed her in front of her friends, the neighbours, my college. I can't imagine what she told them to explain my absence.

I'd run away from my education, having missed my exams I'd completely messed up my A-levels. She forced me to go to university the next year – a year later than I should have done.

I often wonder if I had gone to Uni a year earlier,

when I was supposed to, whether I still would have met *him*. I often fantasise that I don't. In my fantasies we don't cross paths, he finds himself another woman to put up with him instead. My whole life would have been different.

Still, it's looking much better now. *Everything is all right now.* If I don't tell myself that, I risk spending the whole day feeling awful, low and in a slump I can't escape.

After graduating, the few casual friends I did make settled into their new jobs. Another went off travelling, but I started painting – I adored it. I got my own place after leaving the halls of residence – a small, damp studio apartment. I didn't have a job, but I worked out that if I sold even just one painting a week, I could keep myself afloat.

I would get up in the morning before I even dressed and return to my canvas from the night before. The only reason I abandoned a piece the previous night was because my eyes had become so dry and tired that I was forced to put down my paintbrush in the early hours. I loved how I could be entirely engrossed in a painting, lose myself in it. Hours and hours would pass by and I would not even miss them. I loved the freedom, too. I was free to choose my own subjects, colours, moods.

That period in my life was the first time I had felt some happiness. I had also started dating *him* by that point, but he was OK back then. He was nice to me and I liked him back. That was before I found out what he was, it might have even been before he had accepted it himself, but I can't say for sure.

What excited me the most was earning money from doing what I loved. The problem was, my paintings weren't earning me any money back then. The main issue being the lack of an outlet to sell my work from. What I had needed more than anything was a location or premises of my own for people to browse and buy from. But since my mother rejected my suggestion of a loan, that was out of the question.

People bought a painting here and there, a friend of a friend, a couple of sales on eBay for a pittance, but nothing solid. I didn't have a real outlet for my art.

Within ten-months I was broke. If it wasn't for *him,* I would have been homeless. My dream would have actually made me homeless. That's the point when we moved in together.

At the time I thought he was helping me, and I think I should have felt gratitude, but I didn't. All I felt was resentment towards him. Although he didn't say it outright, I could sense the infuriating "I told you so" attitude. It was overwhelming.

I always thought that when I got myself back on my feet again I would get rid of him straight away. But the months turned into years and I never found the definitive point that I could say that I got myself together. And so only now can I say that I am rid of him for good. My lifetime of failure and shame with him is not gone, but at least it's behind me.

Today I am happier than I can ever remember being. My date with Andrew went really well. I actually really enjoyed myself. I don't have a memory of having a good time like I did last night. Apart from when I'm painting like I am now, of course, but that's different.

I'm sitting at my easel in the studio, working on the custom request painting for the client I told Andrew about last night.

I love woodland scenes. This one has the glow that all my paintings have to them and today all the colours

102

seem even brighter than usual. This one owes its lighting to a haze of morning sunshine reaching through the tree trunks.

It's a kind of three-dimensional project. At first, there were only two paintings, but my client, Mrs. Hopkins, loved them so much she wants another piece.

Before I started, she insisted I had to go to her house see where the paintings would be hung once they are finished. The first two are views in either direction on the outskirts of a forest at sunrise and now face each other in the large entrance hall. She and her husband don't have any children, seeming instead to focus their energy on filling their large, suburban house full of shiny trinkets. Every time I see her, she flounces forward to give me a single air-kiss on one cheek. She introduced herself by her title and surname, making it clear I was to address her like that and never by her first. That would be too informal. She is the kind of person that sweeps around and gives orders. I always feel like an insignificant servant when in her presence, waiting to be directed as to how I can improve her palace. She always gushes with compliments whenever I finish a piece for her though, so I don't mind that much.

This third piece I work on now is a view straight into the forest. I'm really excited about seeing the final result.

When it is finished, I'll add the finishing highlights of Naples Yellow to add an almost firefly-style light effect to it. That is my favourite part of the whole process – adding the finishing touches.

I've spent more time than I meant to on this painting, but I feel it is going to be worth it. It's taken every evening of a week so far to get to this stage and I would say another week should see it finished.

I stand up and stretch. Even with my padded, leather stool I still find long stretches of painting make me stiff all over. I decide I should probably have some lunch since I missed breakfast this morning.

Just then, my phone buzzes. I pick it up and unlock it to read a text from Andrew.

Good morning beautiful :) Hope you enjoyed yourself as much as I did last night. I had a really great time. Can't stop smiling today! I picked up some accounts from Debbie this morning and she asked what was up with me! Looking forward to our coffee this afternoon. Can't wait to see you later ;) xxXXxx

I can't keep the smile from my face as I read, and re-read Andrew's text. When he drove me home last night, we arranged to go out again today. In the car outside my flat, he leaned over as we said our goodbyes and gave me a brief, gentle kiss on the lips. I took it to mean that he'd had a good time and was sincere about wanting to see me again; I'm glad I hadn't misread it.

I just wonder what he told Debbie though, the last thing I want is to end up the talk of the street.

14

The rest of Sunday passes in a wonderful haze. Andrew meets and greets me with the same kind of kiss we parted with last night. Then we find a charming little coffee shop in the outskirts of the city, before going for a walk to while the rest of the afternoon away.

I find that Andrew talks more about himself than he did on our first date. He tells me more about his childhood, how his parents moved around a lot in his teens and how he struggled to fit in. I tell him I know how he feels, that I can relate to what he's saying. Just like on our first date, we have a wonderful time. Before parting, Andrew asks me out to dinner on Friday night and I delightfully accept, trying to keep myself from grinning too much.

Monday usually feels like a huge relief to be back in the gallery after a day off alone. But since I had some company yesterday, opening the shutters this morning is a much different experience. This must be what it's like to be a normal person, free of crippling fears.

I feel almost like I'm in a happy cloud and nothing can touch me. For a little while, I actually wonder if I even need my therapist appointment tomorrow at all. I feel brighter and more positive than I have done in years. At lunchtime, I actually bring up the number for the therapist on my phone and my finger even hovers over the call button.

But then reality hits me, and I realise that a few days of happiness should not rule such an important decision. So I dismiss the call screen and slip my phone back into my pocket.

Tuesday is upon me before I am even ready for it. Today is the day of the appointment. It seems almost laughable that I had my phone in my hand ready to cancel. I wonder if it was an attempt by my subconscious to sabotage me, trying to make sure I don't give away any secrets.

I got an appointment much sooner than I expected. I haven't had time to prepare my thoughts, prepare what to say. *What if I slip up?*

The few days I have had since booking have been unexpectedly taken up with Andrew, and yesterday I was just so busy at the gallery, then later in my studio that I didn't get the chance to think.

Now I'm angry with myself. Why haven't I given something so important more thought? I feel like a naughty little schoolgirl who hasn't done her homework.

I wipe my damp palms on my jeans and make a concerted effort not to bite my nails. I don't want the therapist to think I'm a nervous wreck; even though I am, I still don't want her to think it. They're trained to pick up on things like that.

I consider cancelling and making an appointment for next week instead. But then I remember the cancellation fee for not giving at least twenty-four hours notice. I can't really afford to throw money away like that.

I feel my heart give its usual nervous flutter. My anxiety levels are back at the level I have been used to for so long. It's almost a relief in a way. Feeling happy, even just for a day or two felt strange and so unlike the version of me I'm familiar with that it was almost unnerving.

I have a steady stream of visitors and a handful of sales to keep me busy and the morning disappears faster than I would have liked it to.

Just as I'm about to pop out to Sally's Sandwiches to pick up lunch, I get a lovely text from Andrew that lifts my spirits a little.

Hello gorgeous! Hope you are having a wonderful day :) Mine's been really boring so far. This week is really dragging! Missing you loads. Can't wait to see you this weekend xxXXxx

I can't help but smile at his message. For a few moments I get a little perspective on things and I manage to push my fears to the back of my mind where I wish they would stay. I flip my 'Back in Five Minutes' sign on the door around feeling a little more in control of everything.

I take my time as I cross the road and walk towards Sally's Sandwiches. Now that I have set foot outside, I have stepped outside myself a little and I can appreciate the day more. The sky visible around the tops of the buildings is a bright, beautiful blue and there isn't a cloud in sight. I have the urge to grab my painting things and go and paint on location somewhere.

The sun is in full blaze, making everything look more colourful. Every car parked on the street gleams brightly back at me.

A young woman in a pretty pink, floral summer dress walks past me, glued to her smartphone. I feel dull in my plain dark blues and greys when it's such a nice day. But it's not as if I have the confidence to choose anything different from what I am used to.

I pass the sandwich shop window where I can see a

busy queue of customers has already formed. Sally glances across at me as she is handing change to a trio of builders and gives me a beaming smile, which I return. As I approach the open doorway, I stand aside to let the builders out. They bustle past with their white paper packages of food and the shortest and broadest of them gives me an enthusiastic 'Cheers love,' as he passes.

Before I take another step forward, however, a collection of bright colours catch my eye from the window of Minerva Interiors next-door. My gaze is drawn towards the window display, and I immediately realise it has changed since I last noticed it.

My feet seem to carry me automatically away from the threshold of the sandwich shop. I drift almost dreamlike along the pavement so I end up directly in front of Minerva Interiors.

I feel my stomach drop horribly as I peer through the glass.

The window display isn't the usual selection of cushions, curtains, and lamps. Today there is nothing but a collection of beautifully coloured canvases in a variety of shapes and sizes. Each image is arranged on its own easel, just like the ones in my shop window. And just like the ones in my shop window, they all depict a similar subject matter; there are a couple of what are clearly Coventry City scenes, as well as a few generic cityscapes and some woodland scenes too. With another unpleasant jolt, I notice a pair of seascapes beside the centre easel.

I gape stupidly at the display. The window-setting has clearly been set up to emulate my own, with the woodland paintings on the left, and the cityscapes as the main focus in the middle. Beach scenes are set on the right, where in my window some more abstract still lifes are featured. Debbie has clearly had difficulty finding anything to emulate these images, so filled the void with something more random.

At least I think it's random. There surely isn't any way she could know I hate the seaside. I try to scan back through the things I've said to her, or in her presence. I realise we've never really spoken anything more than 'Hi,' or 'How are you?' and she once asked 'Are you settling in OK?' back when I first moved here. Everything she has said to me in the past was always accompanied by a fake smile.

As my eyes grow accustomed to the sight, more uncomfortable details leap out at me. My heart sinks as I take in the prices, set almost exactly below the range in my shop. I also notice the sign that has been placed beneath the centre of the display.

Original canvases – best in town.
Support a genuinely talented local artist. Come in
and take a peek!
We won't be beaten on price!

The loud diesel engine of a white van outside Sally's Sandwiches snaps me back to the here and now. Suddenly I am aware that I am still standing outside Debbie's shop. I feel like I have foolishly walked right into a trap that has been lain, ready and waiting for me.

I scurry back across the road at a much brisker pace than I approached a few minutes ago. Silently, I pray that Debbie hasn't seen that I have noticed her display. It won't be so much fun for her if she does not know I've seen it.

But she must expect me to see it at some point; I live

and work almost directly opposite. There is *no way* I wouldn't have seen it eventually. *But of course, that must be the point*, I think.

Debbie isn't really interested in stealing my customers, she is clearly only trying to send me a message. And it has certainly got through all right: she doesn't like my relationship with Andrew. I just don't know what to do about it.

What does she expect me to do? End things with him to please her? She needs to grow up. Andrew seems like the kind of guy who would bend over backwards to keep someone happy. Perhaps she had him catering to her every whim, treading on eggshells to keep her happy. Maybe that's what she's used to. Well, *I* won't be doing that, that's for sure.

I risk a glance across the street to where the window display is now immediately obvious. Why haven't I noticed it before? How long has it even been like that? I'm sure it wasn't there yesterday...

It's only been a few days since I went out with Andrew on Saturday night, so Debbie hasn't had much time to get everything together.

But maybe it wasn't the date that triggered this act of revenge. I remember the large bouquet of pink roses Andrew sent me – not at all subtle.

Then, according to the text Andrew sent me yesterday, it sounds like he might have outright told Debbie personally that we went out together. Although, I suspect she was watching from her flat as we left together.

I cringe all over, feeling heat spread up my neck at the thought of her seeing us return on Saturday night when Andrew leaned over to kiss me. But I have no idea if she did see us or not. Surely, even if we were seen leaving together, Debbie didn't sit beside the window, keeping a vigil in the dark for our return...

Even though I don't want to, I look again outside to Minerva Interiors. Debbie must certainly have been riled badly to have done this. There is nothing accidental about the way the display is set up, right down to the last detail.

I have a mental image of her rushing around, her waxy cheeks set in grim determination as her bony hands are busy, acquiring all the necessary items, putting so much energy into getting everything ready. This causes another pang of upset in me: the effort that Debbie has spent just to hurt me.

Well, it's worked, I grudgingly admit to myself. She's really hit me right where it hurts – in the work I take so much pride in. I feel a slight lump forming in my throat. I bite my lip and take a deep breath in an attempt to stop myself from crying.

The last thing I need is for Debbie to get wind of how much she has unsettled me.

15

A few minutes later, my staring out the window is interrupted when I hear the doorbell tinkle, as a couple of middle-aged tourists in matching sun hats stroll in. For some reason, they look curiously at something on the door as they walk in.

I quickly turn my back, as I call what I hope to be a cheery-sounding 'Hello,' and pretend to be looking for something under the counter.

While the pair wander into a corner to look at some canvases featuring Coventry Cathedral, I crouch down and wipe my face gingerly on my jacket sleeve, trying not to smudge my make-up. I curse myself for not wearing water-proof mascara every day as standard. Not that I have ever needed it before; I'm not one to cry usually. I just let things cut me and I bleed deep inside, but I very rarely let it flow to the surface.

For the rest of the day, I try to continue working as normal, even though it feels like one of the hardest days of my life. I force my face to remain placid, but more than once I feel my eyes prickle with very unwelcome tears.

Now and then I catch a glimpse of the paintings across the road. It's the strangest thing, but I've never noticed how visible Minerva Interiors is from the gallery before this afternoon. Before lunchtime, the interior design shop was just something over the road, just another shop in the row of terraces. But now it seems to be the focus of the street, almost like the centrepiece. Now I can't help but glance across at the malevolently glinting jewel in the crown of Stonegravel

Street more often than I would like to.

I feel shaken and weak, as though the shock has drained all the energy from my limbs. It's just before three o'clock when I realise that I forgot all about my usual lunchtime sandwich from Sally. My stomach burns with hunger at this thought, as though it too has become aware of the missed food.

All afternoon I try to convince myself that people would still rather prefer to buy art from a dedicated gallery, rather than an interior design shop, especially when they are so close to each other. Although, unsettlingly, I see people look at Debbie's canvases throughout the day; a few even stop to properly peruse.

I also try to convince myself that people aren't bypassing my shop more than usual too. Apart from the tourist couple that came in earlier, no one else comes in all afternoon. Although Tuesday is my slowest day, I can't help but feel paranoid when I see several people look as though they are coming towards the door, only to move away again at the last moment.

I look at the time on my phone; it's just coming up to four o'clock now. This morning I had been dreading my therapy appointment. Now, however, it is a relief to shut up shop for the day and get out of the glass windows of the gallery where I feel like I am on show for the whole world to see.

Although, I'm sure I'll be closely scrutinised by the therapist.

When I have tilled up and am locking the door, I discover my 'Back in Five Minutes' sign is still up. I curse myself inwardly. No wonder people weren't coming in this afternoon. If Debbie hadn't stressed me so much, that wouldn't have happened. I wonder how much trade that silly mistake has cost me.

113

I don't have time to ponder, however, and I hurry up the stairs to my flat to get ready for my appointment.

Since the therapy office is not that far from here, I'll be walking. A good half hour walk should calm me down a bit, clear my head. I find public transport flusters me and I want to make a good first impression. I don't want to appear more of a mess than I am.

I put a piece of bread in the toaster, thinking I should eat something to keep me going until I get back. While I'm waiting, I change from my heels to some black and white Sketchers, my favourite for walking in.

I get my phone out and set up the Maps app with the address of the therapist. Now the prospect of actually talking to someone about everything seems very real.

Too real. Now I'm really scared.

My heart is hammering badly. I put my phone down on the worktop with slippery hands.

The toaster pops up and even though I know I would feel better afterwards, I realise I'm in no state to eat anything; my mouth is the driest I've ever known it, and I feel physically sick.

I throw the slice of toast in the bin. I think I might actually throw up if I try to force it down.

It has never been my intention to tell the therapist the truth – not the full truth anyway. I was going to give a slightly alternative version of events. Leave bits out – the most incriminating bits anyway.

But I haven't properly prepared for this, not at all. I would have thought about it more this afternoon, but Debbie unwittingly managed to put a stop to that.

According to the Maps app on my phone, the walk should take twenty-eight minutes. But I decide I will set off early and take my time.

If I take a slow stroll I can think more carefully

about what I am going to say during my appointment.
Make sure I get my story straight.

16

Walking to the therapist's office was a great idea. I feel much more calm and together than I did an hour ago. It feels almost as though I have simply walked away from my afternoon woes.

The therapist, it turns out, works from a large, nineteen-thirties house conversion. My childhood dentist was the same. I bet it annoys the neighbours to have people coming and going all the time, day in, day out.

Having arrived with ten minutes to spare, I sit in the large waiting room, alone apart from the receptionist who is busy typing away behind her desk, receiving phone calls. I didn't realise up until now, but my appointment is probably the last of the day.

It's not hard to ignore the old copies of Cosmopolitan and Take-a-Break with their peeling, tattered covers set upon the round table in the middle of the room. Instead, I again go through my story in my head.

At a few minutes past six, the door to the left of the reception desk opens and a middle-aged couple moves swiftly out, both looking surly.

A minute passes by before the door opens again and a woman appears. She is dressed in various shades of blue, with a flowing, knee-length skirt over dark-honey legs. 'Harriet Harper?' she calls.

'Hello, I'm Julia,' she says warmly as I approach, reaching out to engage me in a firm handshake. She has a soft, soothing voice. I feel instantly at ease in her presence. Reassured. I wonder if this is something that comes naturally to her, or if she had to practise.

The therapy office doesn't feature the classic leather-studded couch as I had pictured. There isn't an artificial plant, or a vast bookshelf of psychological literature either.

'Please take a seat,' Julia says, closing the door behind her.

'Thank you.' I settle myself onto a well-worn leather sofa with an assortment of colourful, mismatched cushions. It's surprisingly comfortable.

The room itself is quite large and airy; it has a very homely feel to it. The walls are painted in a modern grey and there are shiny trinkets dotted here and there, on the window-ledge and on a desk in the corner. Also on the desk, are a collection of photo frames set with the images facing outwards towards the room. I can see Julia featured in every picture, with what I assume are her two golden-haired children. A boy and a girl; a perfect set.

Julia herself has dark brown hair, set in wild, tangled-looking curls; I assume her children inherit their fair locks from their father, although I can't see him in any of the photos.

Julia settles herself down on the squashy leather armchair opposite me. She smiles broadly without showing her teeth, as she opens a large purple notebook with a floral gold pattern on the cover.

Her eyes crinkle around the edges with her smile, making the crows feet around her eyes deepen dramatically and giving her face an almost mask-like appearance.

'OK, Harriet. I think we'll start by confirming why you've sought therapy today. I understand you've been suffering from anxiety issues for a while. Is that correct?'

117

'Yes. That's right. It's really quite bad. I've been suffering from severe anxiety for a long time. But the main reason I need help is because of the panic attacks. They are the worst part.'

I pause to allow Julia to respond, but she just nods her head slightly and says nothing and I feel compelled to continue.

'I've been getting them for a few years now,' I go on. 'But they seem to be getting worse. I mean, not just more frequent, but also more severe.'

She nods gently again and waits for me to continue. At the back of my mind, I'm vaguely aware that Julia wants me to keep talking to see what comes out of my mouth. A classic psychological trick. Even though I'm aware of this, I find social convention drawing more words from me involuntarily. I'm talking nervously, with quickened pace, just to fill the void.

'When I have an attack, it's like the whole world just stops. I can't breathe and I feel like I'm... like I'm going to die. Everything just feels so... well – so out of control. Like I am falling and I won't ever get back up again.'

I'm slightly breathless as I finish, but I feel a little better already just by saying all this out loud to someone. *Don't say too much*, a little voice in my head warns. *Keep it professional.*

'I see,' she says softly. 'And has there been a specific incident recently that has really troubled you? Something that has really made you sit up and think that this can't go on any more. Like a really bad attack, perhaps?'

'Yes. It happened in the supermarket last week. It was awful. I've never had a really severe panic attack in public before.'

'All right, I'll bet that wasn't fun for you. Often people are at their wits' end before they seek help,' Julia says, scribbling a few notes in the open notebook on her lap. 'OK, Harriet. Most patients walk in here thinking that therapy sessions are something of a magic bullet. That they can be cured of their problems just by *me* talking to *them*, when really it's the other way around. So to get a better picture of your situation, I'll ask you a few questions. They'll help me get a better idea of what is going on in your life.'

Questions. I thought there would be questions. 'That's fine,' I say brightly, squeezing out what I'm sure is a calm smile.

'How about you tell me a little bit what your relationship with your family is like.'

'It's fine, I guess. We haven't had a great deal of contact recently though.' I try to downplay it. 'Just the odd Christmas and birthday card.' Which I don't get any more. 'We're all very busy with work, you see – our own lives.' I'm sure my sister is very busy with her own life since she had a baby. 'People drift apart. You know how it is.'

Non-existent would be a more accurate description of our relationship, but Julia doesn't need all the details. They're not important.

She seems to disagree, however, as she makes a note here. 'What about growing up? Would you say your relationship with your parents was good?'

Before I answer, I straighten the straps on my handbag. I find I can't look Julia in the eye at this point. I just need a moment to compose myself. 'I guess it was probably about average,' I lie. 'I never felt that close to my mother, especially when I got older. I would say I got on better with my father, really.'

119

'Are you still close with your father?' she asks

I open my mouth to respond but find I can't say it. I can't tell her he's dead. So I simply answer with an awkward 'No,' and leave it at that.

'Why would you say that is, Harriet?' she presses gently.

'Um, no reason really... Listen, I thought this would be more about the here and now to be honest. I thought you would show me some tricks or something to stop my panic attacks – not a magic bullet – I mean, I understand you want to get a background picture of me and everything. But really, it's not my family that is causing the problem.'

'Mmm,' she says thoughtfully. 'Well, it's just that – like you say – I do want to get an overall picture of who you are and what you've been through.'

What I've been through? Have I given something away without realising it? What have I done? I am suddenly aware of my breath catching a little in my chest. I take a deep breath as subtly as I can, hoping Julia doesn't notice.

'Actually, my parents got divorced,' I invent. 'They split up when I was five. It wasn't a friendly parting. My mother cheated on my father. He was really hurt by what she'd done, and he kind of drifted away from us all eventually.' I say this with such a matter-of-fact air, that even I'm impressed. The phrase, 'compulsive liar' springs to mind. Is that what I am?

'And you don't have any contact with him at all?'

'No. None at all. I don't really speak much with my mother either if you must know. Or my sister.'

'For the same reasons?'

'Yes.'

'Even your sister? Wouldn't you say she was a third

120

party in the breakup of your parent's marriage?'

'Yes, she had nothing to do with it. But she took my mother's side.'

Julia pauses and taps her pen on her notebook thoughtfully, the shadow of a frown crossing her lined forehead. 'Obviously, I don't know you, Harriet. So I can only build up a picture of what might be causing your problems from what you tell me. So it's important to be open, and honest.'

Open and honest? Does she know I haven't been entirely truthful? *Of course, she does*. She's trained to pick up on unconscious tells. She must have seen something in my body language. At this point, I'm tempted to just get up and rush through the door.

Julia asks me about partners. I tell her that I was married, but I split up with my husband because we wanted different things and grew apart. I mention I'm dating now. She chews the inside of her mouth while she is listening and I wonder if she suffers from stress too. Or maybe because it is her last appointment of the day her mind is wandering.

I wonder if she is even really listening. Her ears might just prick up at certain phrases and she has pre-programmed responses prepared in her memory banks. At this thought, I find my woes of saying too much melt away slightly.

A cynical voice in my head jumps to action immediately. *A sneaky trick,* it warns. *Don't let your guard down*.

Julia looks at me curiously for a moment. 'Do you have any problems sleeping, Harriet?'

'I have difficulty getting to sleep. But, I guess everyone has that from time to time.'

'Would you say you have difficulty falling asleep

121

often?'

'Yes, usually every night. But I drink coffee in the day, so that might be the issue there.'

She writes a note with another frown. I try to make out what she is writing, but I can't. I don't know what I said to warrant a note at this point.

'What time do you have your last coffee?'

'I just have a couple of cups in the morning to wake me up. Probably around ten to eleven.'

She makes another note. 'Do you ever wake up in the night?'

'Sometimes, if...'

'If you have a nightmare?' she finishes for me.

I nod.

'How often do you have nightmares?'

'It's hard to say... I probably have one at least once a week.'

She quickly notes this down. *Is that too often?* I have no idea what a normal person's night-time quota of torment should be.

'And what do you dream about, Harriet? Is it different each time, or is it the same sort of subject?'

I fiddle with my bag strap again. Should I tell her? Should I divulge the fact that it's the same dream over and over again, with only slight variations?

As I try to decide how to answer, I glance across at the clock on Julia's desk. It's six minutes past six already. I had no idea so much time had passed. My session was only supposed to be an hour long.

'I didn't realise that was the time,' I say, nodding towards the clock. 'I have someone picking me up and I don't want to keep them waiting too long.'

Julia glances over at the clock too. 'Oh, of course,' she says. There is notable disappointment in her voice.

122

I feel a bit guilty, like I've cheated her out of a real treat.

'We will pick this up again next time,' she says, laying her open notebook on her desk in the corner. 'In the meantime, I want you to start a journal for me. Every time you start to feel the anxiety building, I want you to write down the date and time and what you were doing before it started. Also, if you could put a score out of ten, depending on how stressed you feel, that would be super.'

I promise to do so and thank her. She shakes my hand again and I make an appointment for next Tuesday with the tired-looking receptionist, who is already gathering her things ready to leave.

*

Later on in bed, I think about how the therapy session went. Overall I think it wasn't too bad. I feel silly for getting so worked up over it, but I guess it's just in my nature to get anxious about things – that's why I went to Julia in the first place.

Thinking of the questions about my family, I still am unable to see how they are relevant now. I left them behind years ago; emotionally, even earlier.

It is undeniable that I miss my father dreadfully from time to time. My recurring prayer is that he can't see me now...

Rolling onto my back, I watch car headlights glide across the ceiling in the dark. As far as my anxiety problems are concerned, I still don't feel as though I've made any progress. It's not that I expected to be cured after just one session, though. I'm proud to say I'm not one of those who thinks of therapy as the "magic bullet" Julia described.

I know there is a lot of work still to do, and it's going to be hard to face it all. That's partly the reason I've put off therapy for so long – my reluctance to face the music.

My soul has been scarred by a whole lifetime of horrors. I know they won't be so easily dispelled in the space of one day.

17

I think it is the mere idea that I am getting some professional help for my anxiety now that spurs me through the rest of the week. I feel calmer and happier, despite what happened with Debbie on Tuesday. Of course, it helps when Andrew visits me at Friday lunchtime.

The first thing I see is a large bunch of flowers moving towards me outside the gallery window. I think it is a florist delivery again until I spot Andrew's car parked in the street.

I wonder what Debbie will make of this if she sees Andrew moving this way with a massive bouquet. My question doesn't remain unanswered for long, however, as I spot her in her shop window, peering across at the gallery with a very stony look on her face. Not that I care or anything, in fact, I can't stop grinning, even after Andrew leaves again when we finish the picnic-lunch he brought. I put the flowers in a new vase (happily purchased in a home décor shop on the other side of the city) and leave them next to me near the till so I can see them while I work.

Andrew thought it was important that we have lunch together since we won't be going out on Saturday. It's his great-uncle's funeral and although I was invited, he thought it might be a bit awkward for me if I go with him. He anticipates the event to take up his whole day, what with catching up with relatives he hasn't seen for years and such. I was in agreement and we made arrangements to go out on Sunday instead. I don't mind, it will give me chance to catch up with some painting I need to do.

It turns out to be a fantastic day for takings, one of my best ever, and I am glad I have the whole of Saturday evening ahead of me to get to work on replenishing my stock. Andrew has the property auction to go this evening, but he sends me a lovely text afterwards to tell me he won and to wish me goodnight:

Hi sweetheart! Managed to bag the flat – at not much over the guide price too! A few of the regulars weren't here :) Their loss! It will take a while for everything to go through, but get your thinking cap on as to how we can decorate. When I eventually get the keys, I'll give you a grand tour if you like :) See you soon gorgeous xxXXxx

*

Once I have shut the shop for the day on Saturday afternoon I eat a simple dinner before I settle myself in my studio to paint. I still get excited every time I sit in front of my easel.

It takes me a few minutes to settle on my next subject. I arrange some magazine clippings from a breakfast cereal advert out on my little table; the lighting and colours struck me so much, as they were so similar to my own, that I knew I had to work from these images.

I get to work straight away and before I know it, the room is darkening around me and I realise I need to shut the curtains for the evening and switch to lamplight.

I get up and start to pull the curtains to a close. As I do so, I see Debbie's tiny, purple Peugeot pull in across the street. I don't know why, but I continue to watch her

126

for a few moments instead of minding my own business.

When she gets out of her vehicle, the thing that immediately strikes me is the fact that she is dressed entirely in black – a far cry from her usual vivid red and purple paisley prints she usually drowns herself in. Her shoulder length, blonde hair is pulled back in an elegant bun, rather than being allowed to flow and bounce around her face. Although, I see some strands have escaped, giving her the look of someone who has spent a tiring day out somewhere. Still at the window, I watch as her car lights flash in response to the click of her key fob. She turns and unlocks the door to her flat.

I hurry to finish closing the curtains. Although it's dark and I don't think I'm visible, I don't want her to see me looking.

I switch the lights on and sit back down at my easel feeling somewhat unsettled. I usually have no interest in what my neighbours do – *like I have the time*. But I can't shake the suspicion that Debbie has been to the funeral of Andrew's great-uncle today.

I don't know why this would trouble me. Andrew and Debbie were married, after all, she would be well acquainted with his relatives. And Andrew said it was an amicable split, so there probably wouldn't have been any falling-outs.

And after all, Andrew invited me to go with him, I just refused. Was I supposed to do that? Maybe I should have gone; established myself as part of his circle.

Even though I have never met Andrew's parents and have only ever spoken with them over the phone to discuss my work, I have built up a strong mental image of them.

They are both very well-spoken, especially his

father, and sound to be well into their sixties. I can picture Andrew's parents at the wake, muttering to other faceless relations about how much of a shame it is that Andrew and Debbie split up. I see these relations shaking hands and clapping each other on the shoulder as they leave the grand house (which I imagine Andrew's parents live in) and suggesting how nice it would be if the pair could reconcile.

Sitting alone in my studio, I find myself feeling the first unwelcome stirrings of hot jealousy. Now I start to doubt my decision to turn down Andrew's invite.

But did he really invite me, though? He was trying to downplay the whole thing. He was leading me towards a definite 'No,' I think. But then, why ask me at all? Why even mention it?

I run my fingers through my hair and sigh. This is one of those situations where a life-manual would be useful; a large book full of dating etiquette and the reasoning behind the things that men do.

I mentally shake myself and tell myself that it is *me* Andrew is dating, not Debbie. She had her shot and it ended in divorce, which was her idea too according to what Andrew has told me.

Debbie was probably only there today for the friends she made within Andrew's family, she was maybe even close with the deceased himself for all I know.

What really surprises me now is how strong my feelings are about this. I hadn't realised up until this point how much I like Andrew. That thought really scares me. I thought I was doing a good job of keeping everyone at arm's length. But somehow, he has sneaked through my defences without me realising it.

The underlying fear that I have been mentally dodging comes rushing to the forefront of my mind and

I can't ignore it. The one that makes me worry I am making a big mistake by participating in a relationship again.

What if I am making the same errors I have done in the past?

My logical side tells me that things are different this time. *Andrew is all right,* I think. He isn't like *him* at all. This is a completely different situation.

18

The sunlight pours against my closed curtains on Sunday morning, illuminating the damask design and waking me up.

A quick bagel with cream cheese serves as breakfast before I get dressed. I opt for a white shirt tucked loosely into dark blue jeans. I guiltily switch the flat, golden pumps I had set aside last night for some cream heels. Since I know I'm going to be standing and walking for most of the day, my feet wince in anticipation, but I think the extra glamour is worth it for Andrew.

Andrew picks me up at ten and we drive to Coombe Abbey Park where we spend the morning strolling around the beautiful woodlands and talking about our week. I leave out any mention of seeing a therapist. Andrew doesn't need to know anything about that.

The surroundings are lovely. I feel a great sense of freedom walking in such open scenery after living and working in such a small street in the city all week.

Andrew is overjoyed that he managed to win the flat at the property auction on Friday night and is very excited about the prospect of doing it up. He talks animatedly about everything that needs doing to it before we get started on the interior design aspect.

For lunch, we have a delightful afternoon tea in the beautiful restaurant at Coombe Abbey hotel. I am taken with the grand, period stone building of the hotel.

'This place is beautiful,' I say, over a Red-Leicester and spiced pear chutney finger sandwich.

'It is, isn't it? My Mum and Dad used to bring me

here when I was little. We used to stay at the hotel on our way to visit relatives.' Andrew looks dreamily out at the sunny grounds through the window.

I think about asking him about how the funeral went yesterday, but feel it isn't the right time. I don't want to burst his happy bubble.

'There are a lot of happy memories for me here, playing in the woodlands,' Andrew goes on. 'I haven't seen this place for years. It's nice to be back.'

'It would be a beautiful place to stay. What are the rooms like?'

'Really nice,' Andrew says earnestly, setting down his coffee. 'They're done out all traditional and proper. I didn't really appreciate it when I was a kid so much, but I would now. We could stay if you like? I mean – not tonight,' he says hurriedly. 'I just meant – you know – sometime in the future...'

'Yes. I'd like that.' We haven't explored the physical side of our relationship yet, and we catch each other's eyes and exchange nervous laughs.

Afterwards, we go out to explore the ornate and sprawling hotel grounds. The heat from the sun pours down on us as we stroll beside the hedge maze, and we both take off our jackets; always the gentleman, Andrew offers to carry them for us.

We walk further through the picturesque grounds, and it's not long before my impractical footwear starts a fresh attack on my feet. Now I regret switching my shoes. Heels are fine when I sit behind the counter all day, but wandering around a park for hours is a different story.

'Hey,' Andrew says, juggling a folding visitor map and the coats. 'Shall we see if we can find where I used

131

to go and play when I was little? I used to find other children who were staying at the hotel and we would play this game where one of us would stand on this massive tree stump and the others would sneak up on him and try to make him jump.'

I smile sarcastically. 'Wow, that sounds like endless hours of fun right there.'

'Erm, excuse me, it's great fun when you're eight, I'll have you know.' Andrew is clearly struggling to navigate the map and carry our coats at the same time.

'Here,' I say, taking the burden from him. 'I'll be in charge of coats. You be in charge of maps. Deal?'

'Deal,' he agrees, handing them over. A mischievous smile spreads across his handsome cheeks. 'Hey, I've got a hand free now,' he says. 'Do you want to hold it?' He winks at me cheekily.

'Go on then,' I say. I reach out and put my hand in his, feeling a new wave of butterflies.

With the help of the map, we eventually find the place where Andrew described playing as a child, but we find that the old tree stump has gone, to be replaced by a roughly-carved wooden sculpture instead.

'Never mind. At least you still have your memories.'

A sudden buzzing comes from the coats draped over my arm. Since my phone is in my jeans pocket, I know it's not mine. 'Hey, Andrew. I think you have a phone call.'

'Hang on a sec.' He slips his hand into his jacket pocket and pulls out his phone. One glance at the screen and his expression turns suddenly more business-like than it has been all day. 'It's Debbie,' he says, frowning. 'Do you mind if I just answer it? Sorry. She only usually calls on a Sunday if it's something important.'

'Sure, no problem. I don't mind.' Although, for some reason, I just have the feeling that Debbie knows Andrew and I are on a date. Maybe he told her at the funeral yesterday.

Andrew moves a few metres away and wanders automatically around a large redwood tree as he talks. The phone call lasts no more than thirty-seconds and he is back by my side again. Looking puzzled, he slips his phone back into his jacket pocket.

'Is everything all right?' I ask.

'Yep, everything is fine. She just wanted to know if I was OK for her to make a large order of cinema box lights. It's really weird, she never usually asks me for permission on stuff like that. She usually just goes ahead and does it on her own. I'd be damned if I tried to stop her.'

'Maybe she wants you to take a more active role in the business?'

'Nah, she likes making all the decisions. Besides, we only get along in small doses before we start rowing with each other. She knows that.'

I feel the buzzing of another phone call coming again from Andrew's pocket. 'Your phone is vibrating again,' I say, proffering his jacket towards him.

He takes his phone and looks at the screen with a slight flicker of annoyance. 'It's Debbie again. I can't imagine what she wants this time. What's up with her today?'

He rejects the call, but this time he slips his phone back into his jeans pocket.

We resume holding hands as we venture back the way we came. We have only gone a handful of paces, however when I distinctly hear the two short buzzes of a text message.

With a trace of a grimace, Andrew pulls his phone back out again and looks at the screen.

Even though I am walking side-by-side with him, the bright sunlight and the angle I'm at deny me the opportunity to see the content of the message.

Nor does Andrew feel like sharing, it seems. He puts his phone back into his pocket and begins to reminisce about his dreamy childhood again as we retrace our footsteps, savouring the fresh air and freedom of the park.

Later on, we visit the gift shop and Andrew buys me a mug with the image of Coombe Abbey on it as a souvenir. Then we walk back to the car park, discussing where we should go for dinner. Andrew suggests a new Indian restaurant he has wanted to try for ages as we get into his stiflingly warm car.

'It sounds nice.' I settle myself into the leather seat and opening my passenger window. 'You can't go wrong with curry after a long day in the countryside–'

I trail off as I hear the unmistakable sound of Andrew's phone buzzing with another phone call; in the quiet, still air of the car, there's no disguising it.

Andrew quickly rejects the call. 'Harriet, I'm so sorry. Debbie doesn't usually harass me like this. Do you mind if I just send her a quick text? She must think I'm on my own today, even though I told her yesterday at the funeral that I was busy. She must not have taken it in.'

So he isn't hiding the fact that Debbie went to the funeral. That's good news, I suppose, although he could have been more careful not to mention his plans for today to her. Tact and diplomacy. I might have to mention it to him subtly. Or maybe I shouldn't, as we're all adults, and it's a free country.

134

Debbie seems to be under the impression that she left a 'Do not touch' sign around Andrew's neck. And if any woman should ignore the sign, then she takes it as a personal slight; someone moving in on her territory; an enemy force to be subdued. She needs to grow up.

'No problem,' I say. 'I don't mind.' Which is a total lie, but I won't say it, even if it's for no other reason than to make sure it doesn't get back to Debbie that she got to me – again.

'Don't worry, it'll only take me a minute. Then we'll get going.' Andrew taps out a text quickly; apologetically. He keeps his tone light and breezy, but I'm sure I can see a faint red flush spread from his neck to his cheeks. I am forcibly reminded of who else I've seen with the same visible, creeping rouge and I look out the window quickly, afraid to recall the memory.

The window is open all the way, but there isn't a breeze from where we are in the car park. I'm anxious to get going again so the stale cabin atmosphere can be replenished by a cool kiss of fresh air.

Instead, I sit with my back damp against the leather seat. My feet are throbbing in multiple places, and now I severely regret not having stuck with my original idea of pretty pumps.

Andrew is still tapping away, so I glance away from him and out of the passenger window to give him a little privacy; I don't want him to think I'm reading his message. Instead, I let my arm trail out of the open window, the metal of the door hot against my skin. The tops of my arms enjoy the faintest whisper of cool air. Idly, I watch some passers-by through the open window.

A cluster of people pass by on the way back to their cars. An elderly couple, and a large group of Japanese tourists, a few of which are armed with heavy-looking photography equipment.

I assume most people will be doing the same as us, leaving the park for the day and be on their way to dinner.

I see a young child; a little blonde-haired boy, half-hopping, half skipping into the car park from the path. A short, dark-haired man pushing a buggy approaches swiftly from behind him, looking stressed. I can't see much of the baby inside from this angle, I can just make out the fact that it is adorned in every possible way in soft pink. The wheels of the buggy crunch loudly over the rough ground of the car park as they draw nearer. 'Finchley!' the man calls out, sounding fatigued. 'Don't run off. You must hold mummy's hand, now.'

With surprising obedience for such a hyperactive-looking urchin, the child turns around and runs past the father and swiftly attaches himself to the extended hand of a slender, brunette woman.

My eyes travel from the child to the mother.

Everything seems suddenly strange, as though it's happening almost in slow motion. My brain rapidly feeds me details of the woman, but in the wrong order. The first thing I process are the seemingly overly-narrow knees; odd for a taller-than-average woman and made especially visible by her bare legs and tan riding boots.

The next thing I see is her shoulders – they look too square. It doesn't help that she has chosen to wear a tight, sleeveless dress; it only seems to accentuate the problem. My mind focusses on these details as though it's trying to delay me looking at the woman's face.

But I do look, and there is no way I can prepare

myself for it.

I freeze in horror.

A jolt of recognition rushes through me as I realise who the woman is: she is my sister.

Even though I haven't seen Amy for several years, I can see straight away she hasn't changed much. Her hair is longer than the last time I saw her. Her flowing beachy waves rest just past those angular shoulders that are so much like my mother's.

The rest of her looks just the same as the last time I saw her. Her perfect tan is, well, perfect. Motherhood doesn't seem to have affected her ability to get to the salon for regular top-ups of her golden glow.

I sit pressed to my seat, too afraid to move an inch. My heart has suddenly ramped up and is pounding so hard I think Andrew might hear it.

I try to distract myself from my rising panic any way I can. Hastily, I glance around, attempting to focus on other people in the car park, but they've all disappeared.

The little family are just metres away from the bonnet of Andrew's Audi. I don't dare retract my arm, for fear of drawing a glance in this direction. It is possible the husband might recognise me. I've never met him of course, but I suspect he has seen pictures of me when looking through our family snaps, as he is bound to have done.

My mouth has gone horribly dry and I can't swallow. I sit and silently hope that none of them looks this way.

There is a shiny, red Range Rover parked next to us; for a horrible second, Amy seems to be leading the way directly towards it. She disappears in the gap on the other side of it and when I hear a car door open, I breathe a half-sigh of relief that she seems to be getting into the silver saloon I can just about see through the window of the neighbouring car.

It is far from safe though. One glance through the four-by-four's windows and she might spot me. I sit as still as a gazelle that has suddenly become aware of a creeping lion and pray that they leave quickly.

Please don't look this way. Please don't look over here. Just go!

The terror is so strong and has erupted so suddenly in me, that I feel I might genuinely be sick. I am so worried that I clamp my lips together tight and fold my arms across my stomach as discreetly as I can.

How long does it take to fold a pushchair up? Just strap the baby in and leave. What is taking so long?

The fear is agony, making the minutes drag out into little eternities. My sister is apparently putting the little boy in the car first.

I can still see the pushchair and the husband. I can't for the life of me remember what his name is; I think it is Gareth, or Graham or something like that. Anyway, he has parked the pushchair a little way from the back of their car, has unclipped the baby and is holding it to him, evidently letting the warm summer air cool the baby's bare legs after it has been confined to a pushchair for so long.

The husband – maybe he is a Gary? – wanders mindlessly in small circles a little way from their car – too far from it in my opinion. My paranoid mind wonders if my sister has actually seen me. Maybe she told Gregory who I am already.

If Amy got even the vaguest whiff of the fact that I didn't want to talk to her, she would make a beeline for me. She would make a determined point of engaging Andrew and I in idle chit-chat; I know her too well to suspect otherwise.

I can't let her see me now. *Not like this.*

Then there would be the introductions. My stomach turns over horribly at the thought of that. But that is surely inevitable and is only seconds away from happening if they don't strap their brat into their car and *get-the-hell-out-of-here* now.

Or maybe we could quickly leave? What is Andrew playing at? How long does it take to send a text to your ex-wife who has no business harassing you, when she knows full well you are on a date?

I see the husband slip between the two cars now. It is possible he is a Gerald. A minute later, he starts folding up the pushchair, although he seems in no hurry to do it.

I have a fleeting image of both our vehicles attempting to leave the car park at the same time.

A fresh wave of panic washes over me. My chest seems to lock, and I can't draw breaths in normally any more.

I close my eyes and through the open window, I hear what I hope to be a final door slam before departure.

It's an agonising wait before I hear the roar of the ignition and crunching of tyres on gravel.

I dare to open my eyes and see the back of their car – a sleek silver Jaguar – as they pull out and turn. The vague silhouette of the boy is in the back, sipping a carton of juice.

The car pulls away, compressing the ground below and causing small clouds of pale dust to rise in its wake. The sound of the engine dies away and then it is quiet again in the car park.

At first, I can't believe they have really gone. It is a few seconds before I realise I am virtually holding my breath.

I exhale in relief.

I cringe inwardly at the thought of almost running into my sister. We were so close – too close. If Andrew and I had come back to the car a minute or two later I would have been faced with the prospect of direct engagement.

But we did avoid her, I remind myself. *Everything is all right*.

But everything was very nearly not all right. For a few minutes, my whole life was on a knife-edge. And my sister was completely oblivious to the fact that just for a few moments she held my life in her hands.

19

The background sounds seem to come back to me like they had been switched off without me even realising. Now there is nothing but distant tourist chatter, and even more distant birdsong.

I'm aware that I'm covered in more of a mist of sweat than I should be. But I managed to avoid throwing up, which is something to be proud of, considering the situation that I was facing mere moments ago.

The last I heard, Amy was living in Northampton. She probably still lives there as far as I know. There would be no reason for her to move, not when she already has her perfect life. She probably lives in the biggest house they can afford. She's got her two children – a little boy and girl – the perfect set. Her ideal, little family have just enjoyed a wonderful day out. Now they're probably off to some family-friendly restaurant, probably one with an indoor soft-play area, for pizza and chicken nuggets, or whatever it is that kids eat these days.

'There,' Andrew says, awkwardly straightening his leg within the confines of the driver's seat so he can put his phone away.

His voice snaps my consciousness back into the car.

'That should be taken care of now. I'm so sorry about that. Debbie doesn't usually behave that way. She must be having a bad day or something. Someone probably has ticked her off.' He glances at me. 'Harriet? Are you all right?'

'What? Erm, I'm fine.' I try to force a smile out, but it feels more like a grimace.

'You look very pale all of a sudden. Are you feeling all right?'

'Yes, I'm fine. It's just a bit warm in the car, that's all.'

He seems unconvinced but immediately pushes his control to open the other windows in the back of the car, which does absolutely nothing to tempt the summer breeze inside. 'Listen, don't worry about Debbie. She's harmless enough. I've put my phone on silent now, I'm not going to answer it again, I swear. I'll have to have a word with her...'

'Oh please don't do that,' I beg, feeling mortified. For a moment, my Amy woes get pushed to the back of my mind.

'Why not?'

'It'll just sound really patronising if you "have a word" with her. It might make her more upset.'

Andrew laughs. 'She's not upset. Debbie used to do this before we got divorced. She hasn't been like this for years. It's really weird – it's like I've just slipped back into the last months of my marriage. There must be something else up with her, I'll find out what's getting her knickers in a twist later.'

'I don't think she likes the fact that we're dating,' I say quietly, looking out the window.

'What? That's nuts. She doesn't mind, I'm telling you. She left me remember?'

'Well, that doesn't mean anything! She might have just been calling your bluff and it backfired on her.'

Andrew looks thoughtful for a second. Then I see the look of dawning comprehension on his face, as though this thought had never occurred to him before. 'Nah, that's not it,' he says finally, as though to himself, more than me.

'Anyway,' I say. 'Just promise me you won't have a

"talk" with her about this. I would just carry on as normal. She'll probably calm down, or forget or something eventually.'

Andrew still looks thoughtful, but he agrees. 'Yeah, all right. I promise.'

We go to the Indian restaurant as we planned. The food is delicious and I can't fault a thing. An hour or two earlier, I would have really enjoyed myself.

But now I find myself trying to force my consciousness from the deep chasm of thought I've fallen into, and back into the moment. But it's so hard. All I can think about is the narrow escape I had in the car park.

Just a few minutes either way would have made a stressful situation into a disastrous one. It was just pure chance that Amy didn't look my way.

The smile I plant upon my face makes it ache and I find my eyes have a glazed feel to them. I try my best to stop it showing, but Andrew seems to sense there is something wrong.

He is under the impression that my problem is Debbie. I wish it was. Cowardly, I allow him to go on thinking that his ex-wife is the source of my disquiet. I certainly can't tell him what really perturbed me.

When the evening is finished Andrew drops me off as usual at home and we kiss in parting, just as before. He still seems worried that he has upset me. 'Listen, I'm really sorry about earlier,' he says again. 'I'll just keep my phone on silent in future.'

'Don't worry about it,' I say. 'I really have had a good time today. It's been lovely.' This seems to lift his spirits a little and he seems more at ease as he drives away.

I had intended to run upstairs as soon as I got inside and watch out the window to make sure he doesn't stop

143

off at Debbie's flat on his way home. Although I was worried he might attempt to talk to her about today, creeping thoughts and niggling doubts crept their way in throughout the evening, and I'm so preoccupied that I've forgotten all about it by the time I get home.

I feel exhausted; emotionally drained. My feet are really pounding, and I want nothing more than to sink into a hot bath with a large glass of wine. But I know if I do, then I will get caught up thinking for hours until the water goes cold and my toes crinkle.

Besides, I have to finish the forest painting for my client. Today is the last day I can finish it so that it has time to dry.

Even though it's already past eight o'clock, I make myself some coffee. I put a pod in the machine and wait, trying to gear myself up for the evening's work ahead.

I eventually settle into my studio, having convinced myself that it's just the finishing touches I have to complete. This is my favourite bit, I remind myself, adding the final splashes of colour and lighting effects. It's like making a cake – the baking has already been done and I am left to add the fun decorations, making it look extra pretty.

I try my best to focus on my painting, to block out thoughts of what would have happened if Amy had seen me earlier.

In an attempt to further motivate myself as I work, I envisage Mrs. Hopkins's face when she sees the final piece. I'm so happy with it, I can't wait for her to see it too. I can just imagine her brimming with delight like she did with the other two pieces in the collection.

It's just past midnight when I finally put my brushes down for the night having finished the painting. Despite how tired I am, it's worked out much better than I had imagined.

I will leave it on the easel to dry overnight. Tomorrow, when I'm not so exhausted, I'll photograph it for my portfolio. And on Tuesday, I'll package it ready to send off to its new home.

I try to assess how tired I am and wonder if I could have that bath now. I ache all over from the day's excursion and from sitting at my easel for hours. Thinking that I'm so tired I should be asleep in a matter of minutes, I decide against it.

An hour and a half of tossing and turning later, I regret my decision. I tell myself the coffee was a bad idea, but I know the real source of my disturbance.

As soon as I lay down and closed my eyes, the images of the day came washing over me, like they were waiting in a film reel in the dark and my eyelids meeting was the cue for someone to press play.

I can't stop seeing the narrow-miss with my sister. It plays over and over again on repeat. The background has faded away and the small family have centre-stage. I see the little blonde boy running, he turns almost in slow motion, every move feeling deliberate and lengthy as he finds the outstretched hand of his mother.

I forgot Amy lived in Northampton. That's not a million miles away from here. Why didn't this occur to me when I was planning my escape, playing Russian Roulette on the map? I thought anywhere away from London would be safe enough.

Clearly, I was wrong.

I make a mental note not to visit such family-friendly places within the region in the future, especially not with Andrew.

The terror of almost colliding with my sister was far

worse today than I expected. I think I might have preferred to have seen *him*, than Amy. Although maybe not quite – I might say they are equally dreaded if I had to rate them, each would score a 'ten' in my anxiety journal.

I'm safe here though, I tell my rising nerves. My sister would have no reason to venture too close to where I live and work.

And besides, even if she had looked in my direction today, would she have recognised me? I have changed so much, I think a momentary glance wouldn't cause enough recognition to warrant further scrutiny. There are times when I do not recognise myself.

I look at the clock, it's past two am, but I know sleep will continue to elude me for hours.

Today was a very near miss. My stomach still squirms uncomfortably every time I see my sister mere metres away in my mind's eye.

She would have given the game away. She would have ruined everything.

20

I wonder how many times a person can have the same nightmare and not go mad.

I'm so tired on Monday morning that I feel like I'm only managing to exist by drinking coffee after coffee. I eventually stopped clock-watching last night sometime after five am, so all-in-all I only ended up getting three hours of sleep. My limbs are so fatigued it's like they are making themselves weak out of pure protest, refusing to right themselves until I take a nap.

I had the same old nightmare again. The one about the beach; the one that has haunted my nights for years. I can pretend anything to myself during my waking hours, but at night when my subconscious lets its guard down I am open to any manner of fear and phobia. It's just that in my mind there is so much horror, really too much for one person to endure; the unwanted products of my subconscious simply reflect that. I can never shake that looping nightmare, always see the same sequence of events. It always starts and ends on that beach, just with slight variations here and there.

I sink into the stool behind the counter. While I'm not serving customers, I might as well rest. Even my heart feels weary, like it's straining to keep me going today.

My gaze falls upon the pile of post I stashed under the counter this morning. I might as well make the most of not having any customers and open it. I have a credit card statement and some junk mail offering me the chance to win a Caribbean holiday. The envelope is printed with a full-colour photograph of a woman lying in a hammock surrounded by endless white sand and crystal clear water.

Dread swarms into my insides immediately. I screw up the envelope, trying not to look at it and stuff it firmly to the bottom of the bin in the kitchen.

Most people like pretty beaches and the sparkling sea. Not me. I see happy couples hand-in-hand perusing travel-agent windows, or I see ads pop-up online and have to avert my attention or click something else just to block them out.

Just the sound of the sea is enough to tie my stomach in knots. Footage of even the gentlest of tides can instil waves of dread in me in seconds. It happens mostly when I watch television. If I don't change channel or focus all my energy on blocking out the thoughts, then my mind wanders.

And before I know it I'm drowning in bad memories, hearing panicked shouts, sobbing and screams.

As the morning drags on I fantasise about going to bed and sinking into a blissful, dreamless sleep. But I can't just leave the shop, not today anyway.

Towards the end of last week, I mentioned to Sally I needed to get someone to run the shop on Tuesday afternoons for a while. I didn't say it was because I was seeing a therapist, I just told her I'm making regular visits to a spa. 'It's all right for some!' she said, jovially in response. She then launched into a pitch for her son's girlfriend, Bethany, who is looking for work in the summer holidays before Uni. Sally spoke most earnestly about how much experience she's had already of shop work. I told her I'd be happy to consider her and arranged for her to drop by this afternoon to see how I run the gallery.

Although Tuesday is my slowest day, it is still worth my while paying for some cover and avoiding closing.

148

Not only is there the potential lost revenue, it also doesn't look very professional to simply shut the gallery at random times. I don't want people to dismiss Stony Studios as a hobby business, something I do for fun and I'm not serious about.

At lunchtime, Andrew surprises me by bringing in an indoor picnic. He still seems to think he has upset me. I can't correct him by telling the truth, but I try my best to reassure him.

He brings roasted red pepper and lentil soup and a packet of ham sandwiches which he has had cut into heart shapes.

'The bloke serving me didn't half give me a funny look when I requested that,' he says.

'I'm not surprised.' I can't help but grin. It's nice to embrace a real smile; it lifts the tension in my shoulders and I feel instantly a little brighter.

Bethany shows up at one o'clock ready to be shown the ropes. She doesn't seem overly interested in the shop. Rather, she seems quite bored and spends much of the time on her phone, but is competent and polite enough with customers. Smiling at the right times, engaging in a little small talk and she seems sincere enough. She can handle the technical side of transactions without me having to show her, something I struggled with when I first started.

'You certainly know your way around the till,' I say.

'Oh, yeah. It's, like, just the same as in Sally's shop – and in Debbie's.'

'You've worked in Debbie's shop?'

'Only for a bit. That was my first ever job. I worked at Sally's for a bit too, but it's, like, really stressful in there at lunchtimes.'

'Yes, it does get busy. My shop doesn't ever have that

149

many people in it. Most people that come in just browse and we get a sale every so often. And not that many on a Tuesday. Do you think you'll be all right with that?'

'Yeah, no worries.'

*

I wake up early on Tuesday morning from an unsettling nightmare which involved me missing my therapy appointment. In my dream, I had managed to miss a bus, and then somehow ended up getting on a train to Leeds by mistake. Only then I was trapped in the railway station because I hadn't purchased a ticket for Leeds, and for some reason, I couldn't find my handbag. The train conductor led me to a small, claustrophobic room with unfriendly security guards and then my sister showed up to pay for my ticket. All the while, I was having a major panic attack and no one noticed.

It is a relief to be awake and secure in the knowledge that I am walking to Julia's practice later.

I'd had my usual, recurring nightmare too of course, but I'd woken in the early hours and then gone back to sleep with less fuss than usual. The second nightmare was just a bonus. It was almost nice to have a different subject to dream about, just for a change. After all – a change is as good as a rest.

Now that the paint is thoroughly dry, I can wrap up the canvas for Mrs. Hopkins.

I make myself some coffee and lovingly package the painting in a great deal of foam wrap before sealing with much brown paper and packing tape.

I leave the precious package behind the counter in the gallery, so all Bethany has to do is hand it over when the courier arrives later.

Looking objectively from her point of view – you can't miss such a large parcel; even if she somehow manages to forget when I tell her, she will be left in no doubt as to what it is when the courier comes to pick it up.

I manage to beat the daily lunchtime rush in Sally's Sandwiches and order a tuna salad baguette.

'Hiya hun!' Sally booms enthusiastically as I cross the threshold. 'Didn't see you yesterday. Thought you'd lost your appetite.'

'Oh, someone brought me lunch,' I mutter.

'Yes, I thought I saw Andrew's car.' She chuckles and gives me a cheeky wink. 'Bethany should be with you soon,' she says.

'Great. She was really good yesterday,' I say, accepting my change.

'Oh, she's a lovely lass, Beth. You'll have no problems with her, I tell you.'

Even though my appointment is less of an unknown this time around, I can't stop my nerves from prickling as time ticks away more quickly than usual. Luckily Bethany does not leave me to stew for too long and she arrives on time, or near enough anyway.

'OK,' I say, swinging my handbag over my shoulder, walking shoes on and ready to go. 'You remember how we did everything yesterday?'

'Yep,' Bethany confirms, settling herself on the stool behind the counter.

'And don't forget, someone from the courier service will come out and pick up the parcel next to you.' I point, just in case she was confused over which five-foot package I meant. 'Just make sure they pick it up, it's all arranged.'

151

She gives it a casual half-glance. 'OK. You already told me this, Mrs. Harper.'

'Yes, I'm just making sure you understand,' I say, blushing slightly. I hope she doesn't feel too patronised. 'I should be back no later than four. You've got my mobile number. You can call me at any time if you have any questions. I'm going to have it on silent, but check it regularly and I'll call back as soon as I can. I see you have your phone with you–' I gesture at the Samsung Galaxy that has already appeared in Bethany's hands '– but there is also the landline – just in case you can't get a signal or something.'

'OK, no worries.' She smiles at me reassuringly.

I look at the time on my phone. I need to get going, or I really will be late, even if I don't end up in Leeds.

The niggling feeling that I have forgotten something won't let me go. I have one last look around the gallery, as though a visual reminder might just jump out at me now, but it doesn't. I say goodbye to Bethany and set off on my way.

21

It's a good thing I left when I did because I arrive with only a few minutes to spare. Julia welcomes me with the same warmth as the first session that puts me quickly at ease.

'Come in Harriet. Please take a seat.'

'Thank you.'

I hand over the journal she advised me to keep in the last session, the one with times of attacks and what I was doing just before. It's not all that complete. I couldn't mention the incident with Amy for starters. So for that particular feeling of anxiety, I have simply put that my boyfriend was texting his ex-wife. I've put the other incident with Debbie in too, when she started selling paintings like mine – that was a bad day. Plus I've listed a handful of other occasions where panic has come out of nowhere, seemingly without provocation.

Julia takes a few moments to read it. There is nothing but the turning of pages and the ticking of the desk clock to fill the silence.

She has gone for a deep purple skirt today. Still flowing, but with a floral print and plain plum cardigan to match. She has even got little dangling, bead earrings in the same shade.

She obviously pays a lot of attention to detail. I must always be careful of what I say here. Always think ahead, be careful not to say something seemingly innocuous that could unravel everything I've worked for.

I'm Harriet Harper, successful artist. I'd be almost average if I had never murdered anyone.

Julia looks up at me from my diary. 'I see you have some problems in the evening quite often. There is a recurring theme going on there, I think. Quite a few episodes seem to have happened when you are – it says here – taking a bath? Why do you think that is?'

'My mind drifts when I'm in there. I think I have problems when I start thinking too much. I prefer it when I'm working and I'm really busy because then I can push out bad thoughts.'

'Bad thoughts?'

'Well, I just meant... thoughts that aren't very nice. Stuff that everyone thinks about. Like worrying if my business is doing OK. Or, how I would pay the bills if something happened. Or, am I eating right, or doing enough exercise.' *Or, what would happen if I ever get caught?*

'Or, how is your relationship going?' Julia offers. 'You're with a new partner at the moment, aren't you? It might still seem like early days, but how would you say that's going?'

'Fine, I guess. We haven't been seeing each other that long. But things are good.'

'But you say he texted his ex-wife while he was with you?'

'Yes, but I don't mind. There was just a small business matter she wanted to talk to him about.'

'On a Sunday?' Julia seems sceptical. 'You've given that moment an eight out of ten in your diary. That's quite high, isn't it? You must have felt upset about it at the time.'

'Yes, well, no – not really.' I should have just left Sunday out of the diary. Why didn't I just leave it out? Seeing Amy caused me so much anxiety, I felt I couldn't really avoid mentioning it. She was within metres of me. If she had glanced my way, that would have been it.

Andrew was right beside me too – I feel physically sick at the thought. *What if he had found out what I have done?* That would be the worst thing. And it was mere luck that I didn't get exposed on Sunday.

Amy would have relished the opportunity to spite me if she had seen one, she always has. She has always blamed me for what happened that day, just like Mother did.

If I looked even remotely happy, then Amy would have loved to step in and spread some poison – even though she hasn't spoken to me for years, even though I am finally happy. Or almost happy, anyway.

I know I should be more content – I am living the life I have always dreamed of – almost.

I didn't ever imagine living like this, but apart from the perpetual anxiety, everything is sort of all right.

It really doesn't matter exactly what I jot down in my journal anyway. It is not important what causes my panic, despite what Julia says. I just need to get through these therapy sessions so I can find out how to cure it.

Julia turns to a blank page in her own notebook, smoothing it down unnecessarily. 'I get the feeling that you push things down a lot, Harriet. Instead of confronting a problem face on, as some others do, you tend to do the opposite. Uncomfortable thoughts and feelings – things that can hurt you – you push them away and try to ignore them. The problem with this habit is that these thoughts and feelings never really "go away". You are simply ushering them to the back of your mind, and they come back at you in the form of anxiety and panic, often at times when you are not expecting it. Would you agree?'

'Yes.' For some reason, I struggle to say just the one simple word. It should be easy, but it takes a great deal of effort.

'You say it's easy for you to throw yourself into work, to take your mind off things. But I think it might be dangerous for you to continue to bury your head in the sand.'

Sand. The image of that beach comes into my mind's eye. Unexpectedly in the comfort and security of Julia's bright and homely space, I feel flooded with cold panic. A band of bright sunlight still illuminates the wall behind Julia, but suddenly the room seems to have darkened a shade. I take a deep breath to steady myself – I can't lose control here. The fear that everything might just tumble out if I descend into panic ripples over my skin.

Julia gives me a sympathetic look and slow nod. 'I know it can seem like a scary prospect – to finally face what's been troubling you all these years. But if you don't, you won't have the ability to stand up to your panic attacks. You need to have the strength to say: "This will not happen to me any more. I am not a victim."'

She's right, I'm not a victim. I'm more of a perpetrator. 'All right,' I say. 'So how do I do that?'

'Harriet, I want you to practice something called mindfulness. That is where you force yourself to take notice of things around you and make sure you experience a moment, instead of merely being a bystander. The key is to be focussed on everyday things around you. Take when you are in the bath, for instance. You need to be aware – be *mindful* – of the environment you are in – the feel of the bubbles, the temperature of the water, the colour of the shampoo bottle. These things should ground you and keep your mind in the moment and not dwelling on the past, or fretting about the future. Just for now, whenever you feel your nerves getting to you, practice this technique. It won't be easy at first. It takes much more bravery to face your fears than to simply hide from them.'

I leave my session with Julia feeling much more satisfied than when I left the first. I feel like I have actually learned something useful, like I am finally getting somewhere.

On my way back to the shop I practice mindfulness. Leaving Julia's street, I focus on the hanging baskets of the neighbour's houses. I take note of the colourful flowers, and how they wave and dance in the brisk, cool breeze. I take note of how blue the sky is and few the clouds are that scuttle across it. The summer wind lifts the tiny hairs on my face, and I am aware of how my hand grips the tough leather handles of my shoulder bag.

At the end of the street, I remember I need to check my phone and set it back to vibrate. I meant to check it periodically for messages, but the session went so fast I didn't get the chance. I pull it out of my bag and feel a wave of dread wash over me.

There is a missed call and voicemail from Sally.

Fumbling with my phone, I listen to the message, straining to hear it over the sound of the wind and passing cars. I'm pressing it to my ear painfully hard, but all I can hear is some rustling and a couple of clicks before the message ends.

I play the message again, but can't make anything of it. Why is Sally trying to call me? Is there something wrong at the gallery?

Calling Bethany is no good either, as she does not answer her phone. I try again, but still no answer. On the third attempt, I go straight through to her voicemail. She's turned her phone off. *Why has she turned her phone off?*

The only number I have for Sally is for the sandwich shop. It rings through time after time. I take the phone away from my head to look at the clock in the corner of the screen – it's only ten past three – Sally doesn't close until four. Why isn't she answering the phone? Why couldn't she leave me a proper message?

What the hell is going on?

My heart races erratically in my chest. In an instant, I forget all about mindfulness and can only picture horrible scenarios going on at my shop. My first thought is that it has burned down, but I tell myself I'm being ridiculous – there isn't anything that would likely cause a fire in the shop. Then I consider the possibility that Bethany has wandered off somewhere and the place has been robbed, stripped bare. Sally is calling me to tell me, since Bethany is too ashamed, or still oblivious to the fact to tell me herself.

My blood runs cold at the thought – so many irreplaceable hours of work all lost.

I need to get back to the gallery – fast. If I had any numbers for the local taxi service, I would call one right now, but I don't have any stored on my phone, nor do I have internet access without wifi. I start jogging back the way I walked here, trying to rack my brain, thinking if I saw any bus stops along the way; I can't

158

recall any.

My breathing is coming in short rasps that strain my lungs, but it is not because I'm running.

A few streets away I consider calling Andrew. But he will be at work, and even if he did drive over here to come and get me, it would take just as long as if I walked – maybe even longer.

I switch between jogging and walking, alternating only when I can't bear to do the other any longer. I can hardly breathe. The sound of each laboured breath inside my head makes everything feel a hundred times worse.

By the time I round the corner of Stonegravel Street, I have pictured so many horrific scenarios in my head I honestly don't know what to expect.

I'm sweating and shaking. Strands of my hair are sticking to my face. My handbag swings annoyingly, hitting against me on every other stride. The pink silk scarf I carefully chose for today is bunched up roughly in my damp palm, the ends flapping wildly in the wind as I trot quickly along the pavement.

The gallery looms into view in the distance and I am surprised, albeit relieved to find that it still appears to be in one piece. There are no broken windows or any other signs of visible damage. From here the window display looks intact. As an added bonus, there are no emergency vehicles in sight.

I've considered so many possibilities on the way here. I'm prepared for anything.

Or at least – I think I am.

I rush up to the door and immediately notice the 'Back in Five Minutes' sign is facing outwards. I get a snapshot of the shop through the glass door – everything looks just the same as I left it. With trembling arms, I push myself against it. The bell tinkles loudly above my head.

The sound causes the woman behind the counter to look up as I enter, gliding towards her in shock.

The woman is not Bethany, it's not even Sally – it is Debbie.

'What are you doing here?' I blurt out stupidly, bewildered.

Debbie looks me up and down, taking in my flushed cheeks and bedraggled appearance. Her green eyes are so pale that her pupils seem to pop. She gives me a horrible smile that looks more like a grimace. 'Sally said she needed someone to cover this place for her.' She jerks her head at the walls with a disgusted look on her face, almost like she has unwittingly been put in charge of a home for flea-bitten, unwanted dogs with rabies.

'Where's Bethany?' I demand.

'Her mother's been taken ill. She's epileptic, you know. Beth went to the hospital to see her.' She speaks slowly, calmly, as though we are friends discussing something boring over a cup of tea.

My brain seems to be struggling to make sense of it all. Debbie isn't helping me either. She seems quite content to sit behind the counter – my counter – and watch my sweating wreck of myself slowly piecing everything together. 'So – so where is Sally? Has she gone to the hospital too? Why isn't she answering her phone?'

Debbie looks deliberately confused, as though pretending to decipher a tricky crossword puzzle. 'She isn't answering her phone? I don't know why she wouldn't answer her phone. Maybe she is too busy to deal with unimportant phone calls. She's still working.'

She nods her head towards the glass door where I can just about make out the figure of Sally bustling around behind the counter in the sandwich shop.

Is she is right there then why hadn't she answered her phone? Or left a proper message?

'But why are *you* here? Don't you have a shop to run too?'

'It's my day off. Sally asked me nicely though, so I helped her out. I employ someone to run my shop for me on Tuesdays and Saturdays. You know – someone *reliable*. Beth is a nice girl and everything, but I wouldn't trust her to make so much as a cup of tea. She worked in my shop last year and she was terrible. She turned up late – if she even turned up at all. And she couldn't handle deliveries at all. I just had to get rid of her.' Debbie gets up and slips around the front of the counter as she talks, moving towards the door. 'Maybe you should be more careful who you hand your business over to before you go running off to the spa. But I suppose you want to make some attempt to look your best if you've got a date coming up...'

At the door, she turns. 'Oh, I almost forgot. Here.' She reaches into her pocket with her thin hand and throws my keys so far past me, there is no chance of me catching them. They hit the front of the counter so hard they make a loud clatter that reverberates through the wood and they fall to the laminate floor with a clink.

161

22

The door closes shut behind Debbie and I am left alone in the gallery. I can feel rage boiling inside me. Now I am shaking – not from fear, or from a frantic jog – but from pure anger.

How could Sally do this to me? I thought she was my friend. How could she sell me a dud like Bethany? The girl had worked in her shop too, she must have known how unreliable she was. But then, today was an exceptional circumstance; Bethany's mother had been taken to hospital. Although, the fact that Debbie declared Bethany so unreliable, totally discredits the story about her mother being taken ill. Is it even true? My instinct tells me not to believe it.

The tinkle of the bell startles me. Some German tourists walk in, talking excitedly to each other in their native language. I suddenly realise I'm still standing in the same spot Debbie left me.

There is still an hour and a half trading left; I need to calm down.

I slip away to the kitchen in the back, looking for somewhere out of sight to put my handbag until closing time.

Something crunches beneath the sole of my walking shoe.

I look down – there are shards of china all over the floor. I withdraw my foot, bewildered. The white pieces look luminescent in the gloom of the kitchen.

I start gingerly picking up the pieces with my bare hands. I suddenly notice one fragment has the image of a period building on it – it's Coombe Abbey. This is the mug that Andrew bought for me on Sunday; it has been smashed all over the floor. Not just shattered either – but left in pieces for me to clear up myself.

I hate myself for feeling the hot sting of tears in my eyes. I blink them away furiously.

It was Debbie, I think. This was definitely no accident.

How dare she? The gallery is *my* business. How dare she just come in and create an incursion on my space like this? Sitting behind the counter like she is too good for the place. How could Sally let her in? Can't she tell Debbie hates me?

Or maybe she can. And since they are both such good friends they decided to play a horrible little trick on me. They don't realise how much this affected me. They don't realise the terror and panic that coursed through my veins as I ran here from seeing Julia. They are oblivious to the fact I felt like I was having a genuine heart attack, feeling as though every ragged breath I took could be my last.

I bet they are both putting their heads together and having a little laugh about it now. Commending each other on a job well done.

How dare they.

Before I even realise what I'm doing, I've dropped my handbag and am marching towards the gallery entrance. Reaching out, I pull the door open so hard the 'Open' sign flaps chaotically and falls to the floor. I don't stop to pick it up. I'm so enraged that I don't even stop to look for traffic, warranting a prolonged beep from a BMW driver who has to slow down for me.

Sally has already put up her 'Closed' sign and is shutting shop for the day. I glimpse a snapshot of her wiping down the counter-top while Debbie sits at the nearest table with a takeaway cup of coffee before I push the door open.

Sally looks up as I sweep inside. 'Hiya hun,' she says, by way of her usual greeting.

'Don't "hiya hun" me!' I snap, furious. My voice has an edge to it I haven't heard in a long time; it unsettles me and I hate it, but I am powerless to stop more words from tumbling from my mouth. 'What did you think you were doing? Why did you sell me Bethany as a "great little worker?". You told me she was "as reliable as the day is long". And she's about as enthusiastic as a vegetarian at a barbecue!'

Sally looks genuinely shocked. She stops her cleaning of the counter, still in mid-stroke, cloth in hand and stares at me. She shakes her head vaguely as though unusually lost for words. 'Now hang on just a second, Harriet. Beth – she had to go and see her mum. She's not well, you see.'

She looks at her seated friend for some reassurance. 'I thought Debbie explained all this to you already?'

Once again, I have the feeling that I have been led into one of Debbie's traps.

Debbie avoids looking in my direction. Instead, she keeps her gaze either directed towards Sally or on her coffee cup. She acts as though I am not there.

'Oh yes, she told me the story you both concocted about why your son's girlfriend couldn't be bothered to complete a measly hour of work. No wonder she can't keep a job down!'

Sally still looks genuinely shocked. She is looking at me like she hasn't ever seen me before, weighing me up as though to assess how irate I can get. Most people don't see me get angry. Only very few people in the world have seen that, but I've left them all behind.

164

'Harriet,' Sally says, with a pleading note in her voice as though it will cause me to come to my senses. 'There's really no need to get upset, now. You don't want to go saying things like that. I can get Bethany to call you if you like. Or when she's up to it, I can get her mum, Jan, to call you if you want? To tell you herself. Would you like that?'

I pause. I don't think she is calling my bluff. She seems to be telling the truth. But still, this was all handled incorrectly. 'You can't just put a random person in her place though. It's not right without my permission. Especially *her*.'

Debbie shoots Sally a meaningful look, almost subversively, as though she thinks I can't see her.

As soon as I say the words, I regret them. To admit in front of Debbie that I acknowledge her as a problem feels like admitting defeat. But I *need* Sally to understand why she shouldn't have enlisted Debbie for the task.

'I did try to call you, but I didn't get an answer and I had customers to serve–'

'–One phone call and a rustle on a two-second voicemail message isn't really trying hard enough,' I tell her firmly.

Sally ploughs on, as though she didn't hear me, folding her arms resolutely. 'Debbie had some free time this afternoon – and luckily so – or we would have been forced to close the gallery. I think you should be pleased she was there!'

'Well, I'm not pleased. She is the worst person you could have chosen to replace Bethany. She hates me!' I avoid mentioning the broken gift from Andrew. It would just sound pathetic and school-yardy to complain about a broken mug to two fully-grown women, despite the fact one of them childishly broke it in the first place.

Debbie shakes her head and takes a sip of her coffee. 'Maybe you should just drop the money off, Harriet and then leave. You're getting very worked up. You're upsetting Sally, too.' She gives her friend a simpering look. 'This won't be doing your blood-pressure any good, will it? Maybe you should sit down, Sally hun?'

Sally shakes her head dismissively and does not move. She fiddles nervously with her apron strings which are tied loosely in a bow around her plump waist.

I ignore Debbie's cringeworthy attempt to overplay the situation. 'What money are you talking about?' I ask, bewildered.

'Beth's payment for today's work,' Debbie explains. She is still avoiding eye contact with me, which must be difficult considering the holes I am boring into her with my own.

I force out a humourless laugh that doesn't even sound like me. 'Today's work? If you think I'm paying that girl for twenty minutes of sitting in my shop and playing on her smartphone, then you will be waiting for a very long time!'

Sally and Debbie exchange glances. Sally looks mortified, but Debbie is putting on an overly sombre face that barely conceals her glee at watching this scene play out.

I want nothing more than to get out of Sally's Sandwiches; the walls seem so much closer than they did on every other occasion I have been in here, and the atmosphere is poisonous. But I still have another bone to pick. 'And another thing while I'm here,' I say, still riding on my high horse. 'Why was my sign the wrong way around on the gallery door? Hoping to drive customers elsewhere are you?'

Debbie answers quickly. 'It was already like that when I got there. I assume you left it that way.'

Sally wades in, clearly hoping to defuse the situation. 'Well, maybe Beth did it before she left, eh?'

Debbie pipes up again, now looking at me for the first time since I walked in. 'No, Beth didn't. The sign was already like that. You leave it like that quite often, Harriet. It's almost like you want your customers to pass you by. I suppose I should probably thank you for sending them my way, though with that little sign of yours.'

Tears sting my eyes. I try to blink them away so that neither of them notice. I shake my head. 'Why did you suddenly decide to start selling paintings the same as mine, anyway? I know what you are doing – I'm not stupid – I just think that you are for being so childish. Well, I have some bad news for you, Debbie – I am not someone who can be easily bullied. I was once, but not any more, I promise. If you want to play silly little games, then fine. But I'm not going to change my behaviour one inch because of what you do!'

Debbie recoils sharply like I have hit a raw nerve. 'I can sell whatever I want in my shop, thank you very much! Those paintings were freely available to buy in various outlets around the city. Maybe it is *you* who should be careful of what you sell. It's not exactly an original idea to paint pictures of the city now is it? Maybe you're the one that has been ripping off other people! Don't you know it's not nice to steal other people's things!'

167

Her subtext is loud and clear, but I'm not sure Sally hears it.

I am upset with myself for acknowledging her window display of canvases. I am even more upset that she can see how much it got to me.

I open my mouth to retort, but Sally cuts across me, speaking quietly but firmly.

'–I think you should leave my shop now, Harriet.'

She leaves me in no doubt that our exchange is over. She is not comfortable with me being in her shop – her territory – any more.

Despite having been here for over eighteen-months, I still feel like the new girl on the block. Everyone else was here before me, long established, all old friends. I'm the odd one out. The one that can be expended, pushed out anytime the going gets tough.

The zeitgeist of my school days creeps around my neck and sends shivers down my spine. I'm plunged into a bad memory – I'm suddenly fifteen again and starting yet another new school. I'd been kicked out of the last one for writing poetry all over my mock GCSE papers instead of answering the questions. Starting again so late in the school system meant I was never going to be accepted. That is exactly what is happening here now.

I open my mouth to say something, but I don't have the words. I turn and walk straight out the door, aware the tense silence behind me will erupt the moment I am out on the street.

The tourists have gone by the time I get back to the gallery. I've never been pleased to see the place empty before. But now I hurriedly grab my keys and lock up as fast as I can.

My breathing is frantic and loud inside my head and

my chest is restricted. My lungs try desperately, but can't pull in any more air.

I hurry inside my flat and shut it firmly, sliding across every lock, bolt and chain. I never want to go outside again.

I run upstairs, shakily pulling off my jacket as I go. At the top, I kick off my shoes and head straight for the bathroom. My shaking fingers slide the door lock across and I step into the shower, fully clothed.

I want to wash the day off me. The water needs to cleanse me of Debbie's snide and sneering features. I can't get the image of Sally's round, horrified face out of my mind.

The warm water seeps through my clothes, making me feel oddly numb. Within seconds, the fabrics are clinging to me, making my huddled form feel heavy. I sink down, leaning against the wall for support, any ounce of security. But the white tiles of the shower cubicle are cold and unforgiving – just like the two women across the road would be.

I've made a real mess today. I have to live and work opposite Sally. And what would Debbie do next in response to this latest exchange? Probably start selling her canvases on a market stall outside the gallery.

I wasn't supposed to get this involved with other people. Moving here was supposed to be a fresh start. I was supposed to blend in, be invisible.

Now I'm tangled up, caught in the consciousness of the street.

My wall of defence won't hold up any longer and a sob of misery escapes me, followed by another.

No one will hear me over the sound of the water, even though now more than ever I want there to be someone here. Someone to put their arms around me, to comfort me. But I'm alone now. I let my tears flow, blending in unison with the warm water raining down upon my head.

I let the water run until my sobs subside. Sitting huddled in my little frosted-glass cubicle, I'm safe from Sally and Debbie. They can't see me, although I can see them. My mind won't let me forget. I see the scene replayed over and over again. I'm glad the water rushes loudly over my ears, for I'm certain if I allowed myself to be aware, I would surely feel them burning.

What would Julia say about this? I think I definitely need to mark today down in my anxiety journal. But explaining this to Julia might be tricky. How can I justify myself? After all, Debbie was only behind the counter in my shop. She had no right to be there, of course. She deliberately broke the mug Andrew gave me, but other than that, no real harm has been done.

I try to practice mindfulness. Deliberately, I make myself aware of the water raining down on my head, my neck. I focus on how the water feels colder down here than it did when I was standing. More than ever, I am aware of how my shoulders tense uncomfortably as I shiver.

I would like to focus on a glass of wine. Or maybe a whole bottle.

I turn the shower off. Soaking wet, I pad along to the kitchen and get a bottle of red wine and a glass before returning to the shower and resuming my seat on the cubicle floor.

One glass should be enough to calm my nerves, then I'll get out of these wet clothes and sort myself out.

The wine tastes so good and sweet on my tongue. I suddenly realise I haven't eaten since my early lunch and my stomach growls; that was hours ago. The light now coming in through the bathroom window has the unmistakable deep glow of a summer evening.

The wine disappears from my glass quickly, running so easily down my throat that I can already feel warmth spreading in my fingers.

I pour myself another and drink it almost as quickly as the first.

I feel more relaxed after two glasses, and decide to have a third to help me sleep – I will certainly need it. Sleep is all I want now; I want to close my eyes and forget the debacle that today has been.

One step forward in therapy, two steps back in everything else. It is as though something doesn't like the idea of me not feeling desperately anxious all the time. Perhaps a vengeful spirit...

A chill runs through me at the thought of that and it has nothing to do with the wet, cold clothes clinging to my form. I'm suddenly desperate for warmth. Reaching up, I turn the shower back on.

I bask in the heat as the water washes over me, my skin tingling as the blood returns to it, making me feel alive again.

23

The first thing I am aware of the next day is the intense throbbing of a severe headache. The next thing I notice is that the bed is extremely damp – more than just nightmare-sweat-damp too – but actually sodden. For a second, I can't remember why; then it all comes back to me in a rush of colours and negative energy. I groan into my pillow. For a few moments, it was like yesterday had been erased, now it might as well be daubed all over the walls of my bedroom in red paint.

I feel sick. Hot and sick and damp.

I drag myself out of bed, feeling nauseated by the pain in my head and hobble towards the bathroom. I open the door and step into a cold puddle. Shocked, I look down. There are large pools of water all over the linoleum where the old floorboards underneath are uneven. I grab a towel and lay it down to soak up the worst of the deluge. The empty wine bottle is still sitting upright in the shower, along with the empty glass.

I use the toilet and as I am washing my hands I look in the mirror. I'm startled to see how much of a mess I look. My eyes are red and puffy and are underlined with very dark circles. My hair is tousled, wiry and clings together messily at the ends.

I pull my hair up into a bun and I peel the damp clothes from me with difficulty, wrapping my old blue dressing gown around myself instead. Now that I'm not damp, I feel slightly better, but I can't think straight because of the pounding in my head – I need some painkillers before I do anything else.

The carpet is wet all the way from the bathroom to the kitchen. I can see the trail of dark patches and carefully tread around them. Did I really make this much mess?

Drinking so much on an empty stomach was a bad idea. Although, to my credit, it looks as if I tried to make myself something to eat; in the kitchen, the frying pan is out and still in position on the electric hob, complete with a dry and hardened toasted cheese sandwich. An empty packet of Cathedral City is strewn on the worktop next to the cooker and a bottle of ketchup waits beside it in earnest, ready and waiting.

It looks like I abandoned my late-night snack without even so much as a bite. I'm truly thankful I somehow had the presence of mind to switch the stove off. The sight of the stale food turns my stomach and I have to turn away quickly. I get myself a glass of water and some paracetamol and sink down on the sofa.

My phone is on the coffee table. I pick it up and look at the time – it's past half-eleven. I've really overslept – I need to get myself sorted out.

Just as I am about to get up to get ready, I notice a new text message notification on the screen. The message was sent at 08:24 am – it's from Andrew:

Hi Harriet :) Have only just got your text – I keep my phone switched off overnight. Am on my way to work. You were certainly up late last night! Trouble sleeping? Sorry to hear you had a such a bad day. Hope everything is OK now. Will try to pop into the gallery later so we can have lunch and a chat if you like? See you later xxXXxx

My heart sinks. What did I tell him? I feel an

uncomfortable flutter at the thought of mentioning the incident yesterday.

I note Andrew uses my name, instead of his usual term of endearment. Not a good sign. But maybe he was just in a hurry on his way to work?

A vague, blurry image floats to the forefront of my mind of myself lying on the sofa with my phone in my hand, tapping out a text to Andrew. I scroll up the conversation, wondering what the hell I wrote. There was a text sent from my phone at 02:14 am:

Hello Andy!! xx It's really nice to hear from someone who doesn't hate me :) Had a really shitty day myself actually – I want you here so badly it hurts. Sorry your back aches – I give a great massage that would put a smile on your face. Wish you were here xxxxxx

Staring at the screen, I find myself gritting my teeth. I'm cringing so badly I hardly appreciate the fact that I didn't mention Debbie or Sally. I called him "Andy" – he hates that – that was one of the first things he told me. Why would I even think to call him that? Is that the pathetic attempt by my drunken-self to be playful? I shudder. It doesn't even sound like the sort of thing I would do.

In my message, it sounds like I'm responding to a text from Andrew, but I don't remember getting one. I scroll up again and see another text above mine sent at 21:58 pm. It doesn't seem at all familiar; I feel like I've never even read it before:

Hi Beautiful :) Hope you've had a better day than mine. It's been a hard day's work here. Had to stay late at the office with a mega backlog of paperwork and my

back is killing me. I missed seeing you today.
Goodnight and sleep well sweetheart xxXXxx

I put my head in my hands. It could be worse. It could definitely be a *lot* worse. For instance, I could have told him that I'm a nutcase who yelled at her neighbours yesterday over a relatively minor misunderstanding.

I could have told him all sorts of things I shouldn't have. I could have told him absolutely anything...

A wave of cold fear sobers me more than anything else. I vow never to let myself drink so much again.

Mentally, I brace myself for getting ready; it's going to feel like an uphill struggle since I am virtually as low as I can possibly get right now. I will need plenty of concealer under my eyes, that's for sure.

Time is marching on though – the gallery is still shut and I've lost half a day's takings already. Besides, I need to make myself look presentable for when Andrew arrives with lunch and if I don't get a move on he will be turning up to an empty shop, wondering why the shutters are still up so late in the day.

When I go back to the bedroom to get some clean clothes I freeze.

The rug beside the bed has been disrupted; it is ruffled and one corner is curled over. I feel a tingle of nerves run down my spine. Glancing under the bed, I see that the little box looks undisturbed. Perhaps it was me that upset the rug last night, that's all.

Nobody could have been in here while I was asleep, could they? I surely would have woken up... Then again, I am astonished that I managed to sleep through while being soaking wet.

Half an hour later I'm showered and clean, and a

175

fresh layer of make-up hides most of what could belie last-night. I still look a little puffy around my eyes, but no one should notice unless they are looking too closely.

Through the gallery window, I can just about make out the figure of Sally in her shop serving customers. She is busy with the lunchtime rush and I don't notice her look in my direction once. The inside of Minerva Interiors is as uninviting and dark as always; I assume Debbie is in there somewhere, lurking.

I wonder if she ever takes a disliking to random customers that annoy her for some reason. Andrew said that some other people have found her cold too; I wonder who they were and what they did to warrant Debbie's unwanted loathing.

I treat myself to an emergency KitKat I've been keeping behind the counter to keep me going until Andrew gets here. If ever there was a time for chocolate, it is now.

The bell above the door tinkles as someone walks in. 'Aha – caught in the act!'

I look around – it's Andrew.

I stow the half-finished chocolate under the counter, with a guilty smile. 'I was just having a snack.'

Andrew kisses me and places packages of Chinese takeaway on the counter. 'It looks like you need one, Harriet. You look a bit peaky. Are you feeling all right?'

'Yes, I'm fine.' I broaden my smile and shrug my shoulders. 'I'm just a bit tired, that's all.'

Andrew fetches his usual stool from the kitchen and places it on the opposite side of the counter. He takes a seat and starts unpacking the boxes of food. 'Yes, I thought you were burning the midnight oil – and then some. It was past two when you texted me.' His face is full of concern. 'What were you doing up at that hour in the middle of the week? Has something happened?'

'No, nothing's happened. I just thought I would stay up and catch up on some work.' I pray that he doesn't find out about yesterday, but I'm sure he will as soon as he sees Debbie.

Andrew looks unconvinced as he separates his chopsticks. 'Well, I thought there might have been a death in the family or something.' He closely studies my face for a reaction. 'But maybe that might just be on my mind because of my great-uncle passing recently. I just thought you look like you've been crying, that's all.'

'Nope,' I answer, carefully focussing on winding some noodles around my chopsticks. 'My eyes tend to look a bit different if I'm tired.'

'Yeah, I get that too sometimes. Not that often though. I mean, I'm dedicated to my work and all, but I don't stay up until two o'clock in the morning doing it.'

'Well, you must not love your work as much as me then do you?' I force out a laugh, but it sounds so fake I wish I hadn't.

Andrew notices too. 'You know, Harriet,' he says slowly and carefully, as though he already knows he is wading into dangerous waters, 'you never mention your family. Are your parents still around?'

I take a large sip of my plastic cup of Shloer, and determinedly keep my movements casual, my body language neutral. 'They are divorced,' I say simply. 'My father moved to Edinburgh and my mother still lives in London where I grew up. I have a sister too, she lives in Northampton with her husband and two children.' *And we were so close to them a few days ago, we could hear their voices. But they didn't see us, I didn't dare even say a quick 'Hello.' I couldn't risk it, you see.*

177

Andrew's face looks suddenly playful for some reason. 'I didn't realise you were *Aunty Harriet!*'

I didn't fully realise it until very recently too. 'Yes, I am. But don't go calling me that, OK? It makes me sound like I'm fifty and carry a bag of knitting wherever I go.'

Andrew laughs. 'Aww, that's a shame, I could do with a new jumper for the autumn.'

I give him a look.

'OK, OK I promise not to call you *Aunty Harriet*. It does suit you though...'

I playfully slap at his arm, but he is too quick for me and dodges the movement, laughing. 'So what are their names?' he asks, recovering and returning to his food.

'Whose names?'

'Your nieces or nephews?'

'Oh – right.' Some heat rises to my cheeks. 'Well, actually it's a niece and nephew.' At least I think it is, but my sister would have to be mad to dress a baby boy in that much pink. 'The eldest is a boy. He is three, his name is Finchley. And the girl is just a baby, her name's Emmaline,' I invent. The name comes to me so easily because I thought of it years ago; it is the name I would give to my daughter if I were to have one.

'So no falling out's then? No family feuds I should know about?' He grins at me and I do my best to smile back.

'Nope. Just the usual family stuff, you know. We catch up every now and then. It's just hard to keep in touch with family when you grow up. When you're an adult, you've got so much going on with work and stuff. There's always something that needs to be done. I just struggle to find the time. It's not like I've struck them off my Christmas card list or anything.'

178

Except I *have.*

'Good. I'm glad I'm not getting in the middle of World War Three or anything by going out with you.'

'Well excuse me, but you don't *have* to get in the middle of anything,' I joke.

'Yes, I do. I think you would be worth it, anyway,' Andrew replies smoothly, taking my hand in his spare one. He raises his white plastic cup in a toast and I raise mine, letting them touch briefly before drinking.

'Hey, you should be having your drink in your new mug,' he says. 'I couldn't see it in the kitchen. You said you were going to use it when you're working in here during the day.'

'Um, yes, I was using it, but it kind of got broken.'

'Oh.'

'I'm really sorry Andrew, it was an accident.' I can't tell him Debbie did it because that would raise awkward questions about yesterday. I have to take the bullet on this occasion and let Andrew think I was so careless with his thoughtful gift.

He shrugs. 'Never mind, eh. It was only a mug. Accidents happen.'

We eat our food and Andrew tells me he has a training day his boss is pressuring him into going to on Saturday; he will be away on Friday night too because he has to drive up to Scotland for it. But we arrange that I will visit his flat on Sunday to see what I would suggest he do with the décor.

With something to look forward to, I find the rest of the day much easier to face.

From under the counter, I get an envelope and put some money inside for Bethany's few hours of work. I slip an extra twenty in too. I want to make amends with Sally and she surely would appreciate this gesture.

179

Other than the last time I saw her, she has been nothing but warm and friendly towards me.

After all, the whole thing was a misunderstanding. Debbie did no harm, really. I counted the money in the till – it looks like somebody made at least one sale that afternoon, and there wasn't any cash missing, so at least one of them did something right. So no damage done.

I can apologise, give Sally the money to pass on to Bethany and this whole thing should be smoothed over. I just need to catch Sally at a good time.

Finding the right moment might be tricky; I want to make sure Debbie is well clear of Sally's Sandwiches when I make my visit.

24

My moment comes in just a few days time, it seems. I'm having a reasonable day for takings on Friday, I sell many prints anyway. At lunchtime, I pick at a dry ham sandwich I packed for myself, and contemplate the uninspiring packet of biscuits I keep in the kitchen. I haven't been back to Sally's shop yet. The right time to approach her for a chat is not when she is busy serving customers in the lunchtime rush.

Later on in the afternoon, my mind wanders as trade slows down. I think of the painting I have sent to Mrs. Hopkins, wondering if she has hung it yet. I'm not sure if she does it herself, or if her husband is the resident DIY expert of the house and handles those jobs; all those little things that I have to handle myself now that I'm living alone again. Maybe if I ever move in with Andrew he would take care of things like that for us.

Perhaps my happy client has it already sitting proudly on her wall and she is taking a few days to admire it before she tells me how much she loves it. She always shows so much enthusiasm towards my work, it's really good to hear nice comments when I have laboured over a painting. For me, it's the best part of a piece – watching the reactions from people when they see it. It's a compliment in itself when people walk in off the street, just because they are attracted to something they have seen in my window. But it's also nice to hear it too.

Mrs. Hopkins can always be relied upon to say flattering things. I just wonder when I will hear her views on the third piece in the forest set. The waiting for a response reminds me of when I used to sell my work on eBay; sending off a parcel and hoping it arrives intact, hoping the person is happy with it. You aren't there to see their reaction, so you just hope they like it. Then their feedback acknowledges their receipt of the item. Mrs. Hopkins has always given me ecstatic praise as soon as she has ripped off the brown paper and bubble wrap. I just wonder what is taking her so long this time.

I glance out of the window. It is a hot day and a strong heat haze is visible far down the end of the street. It blurs the parking restriction signs and makes me think I should be somewhere else making the most of the weather. I'm guessing that is where my potential customers are. It isn't really the weather for browsing shops. Bright blue cloudless skies suggest it is more of a picnic-in-the-park kind of day.

Across the road, Sally is shutting her shop for the day. She turns around her 'Open' sign and starts wiping down surfaces.

I look next door at Minerva Interiors. It looks like Debbie has shut early for the day. Not only that, but her car is gone. How long has it been like that for? I didn't even see her leave. Now is as good a time as any to approach Sally. Without Debbie hanging around, Sally should be alone in her shop, leaving the two of us free to talk without being interrupted.

I grab the envelope from the till and grip it tightly. I just know this will win Sally over and things will be set virtually as they were before. She is old-fashioned and appreciates good, honest gestures like this one. I hurry across the street, taken aback by how much hotter it is outside than in the gallery.

'Now is not a good time Harriet,' Sally says before

the door has even shut behind me. 'I'm in a hurry. I've got an appointment.' Even though there isn't a nasty curl around the edges of her words, she is short and brisk and doesn't look in my direction. I notice she only takes little glances at me as she bustles about at high speed, wiping tables and discarding waste food.

'An appointment?'

'Yes. My cat hasn't been well lately, I'm taking him to see a vet.'

I can tell she is lying.

She glances at me and something about her seems to melt slightly. She sighs. 'Perhaps we can talk about it some other time, Harriet. I really am in a hurry.' She glances nervously beyond me and through the window.

'Of course. I didn't realise you were in a rush. I'll come back tomorrow.' I turn to leave, envelope still in hand and feeling put out. My visit hasn't gone the way I'd imagined and it feels very anticlimactic. 'Well, good luck with the vet.'

Sally gives me a strange look.

I cringe inwardly. *Good luck with the vet?* Who even says that? Well, maybe she will appreciate the sentiment later.

The gallery phone is ringing when I get back. I pick it up and Mrs. Hopkins's sing-song voice greets me.

Finally, I think. I had been wondering when I was going to hear from her. She must have just been getting used to the new piece hanging on her wall, trying it out at different angles or positions or something.

I pick up the pen on my counter and start doodling on the notepad next to the phone. It is a habit. I always have to do something with my hands when I am on the phone.

'Yes, I'm very well too, thank you,' I say, smiling a

smile that she can only hear, but not see via the phone line. 'So what can I do for you? I assume you're calling about the new painting?'

'Yes, Harriet sweetie. I *am* calling about the third piece in the woodland collection. The piece you said would be finished this week and would arrive on Wednesday?'

'Yes, it was collected on Tuesday afternoon and was sent by special next day delivery. You will have received it on Wednesday.'

'Yes, I remember you *did* say it would arrive on Wednesday, dearest. But I had someone wait in all day and nothing turned up.'

I stop doodling, the pen frozen in mid swirling-spiral.

My mind goes blank. All white and empty, aside from one black fact in the middle: Mrs. Hopkins does not have the painting.

How can it not be there? It was sent on Tuesday and it's now Friday. Has it become stuck in transit?

I come up with reasons why the painting hasn't reached my client yet. Mrs. Hopkins is reassured by the fact I have an online tracking number for the parcel and when I tell her that she should get it soon. I apologise sincerely and theorize that the courier must be having an issue and I will contact them immediately to find out what is going on.

'You know what delivery companies are like,' I say. 'It's probably sitting in some warehouse somewhere because the delivery driver's satnav took him to the wrong place. It will be something silly like that, I'm sure.' I try to inject another smile into my voice as I speak, but not sure this one is audible. 'Thank you for being patient while I sort this out. This hasn't happened

184

to me before. I will look into it to see what's going on. OK, Mrs. Hopkins. Speak to you soon. Bye.'

I put the phone down.

Something doesn't feel right. I can't understand how the parcel hasn't reached Mrs. Hopkins yet. I ordered special, next day delivery. Where has it gone to? I packaged it so carefully and painstakingly on Tuesday morning. I can see an image of myself clearly in my memory; I was awake early and had the painting wrapped and ready by eight am, so it was ready to send on Tuesday afternoon.

But I *did not* hand it over for collection on Tuesday afternoon. I asked Bethany to do it. But Bethany had presumably already left, she wasn't there at the courier pick up time – Debbie was.

I break out in an instant cold sweat. I stand, wringing my hands and trying to imagine what happened on Tuesday afternoon while Debbie was in the gallery. She must have handed the painting over to the couriers, what else could she have done when they turned up? There must just be a mistake or something with the courier's side of things, a processing error on one of their computers or something like that, that's all.

A simple Google search brings up the courier's phone number on my phone. I hastily call as soon as it appears on the screen and find myself listening to an 'out of hours' message. I will have to try again tomorrow.

Although, do I really believe the parcel has gone astray after being picked up by the courier?

I know deep down in my heart that isn't the case. But it doesn't stop me from spending the next half hour tearing the counter apart looking for a collection receipt from the courier. Whenever I have sent a painting with

185

them in the past, they always gave me a receipt as confirmation of pick up. It will be a little scrap of paper with a package ID and tracking number.

I pull out boxes of pins and paper clips; Blu Tack and masking tape; bills and receipts; spare change and empty cereal bar wrappers; brochures for my work at Burton-Hughes Galleries (the gallery Andrew's parents own).

A half-empty Graze snack box topples from a shelf, spilling cashew nuts and raisins all over the floor, but it doesn't stop me rummaging through a stack of magazines, shaking them sideways one by one.

The courier was here on Tuesday and picked up the package. They *must have* handed over a receipt to Debbie.

What would she have done with it?

Maybe she put it in the back of the shop? For starters, I know she was definitely snooping around in at least the kitchen when she broke my mug.

It doesn't take long to search the tiny little kitchen area – or the toilet – which admittedly was clutching at straws. But I'm desperate and Debbie seems to like playing games. Maybe she thought it would be funny to hide the ticket from me.

But if all that has happened is that she has hidden the receipt, then that would mean that the package *was* picked up, which is good news. But if it was picked up, then where on earth has it gone to?

I consider all the things Debbie could have done with the parcel.

She could have obscured the address and replaced it with another, maybe even her own? That wouldn't have been hard and would only have taken a few moments to orchestrate, I keep the things that would be necessary to

186

do such a thing behind the counter; blank paper, pens, sticky tape. She could have simply grabbed some and written a quick address to affix over that of Mrs. Hopkins if she had wanted. It wouldn't even have been difficult.

After half an hour of rummaging to no avail, I come to one conclusion: the receipt is not here. The painting must never have been picked up by the courier.

My heart plummets, feeling as though it settles somewhere in my stomach. I know the piece is lost. And along with it, hours of hard work and creativity have gone down the drain.

I open the till and pick up the envelope of money I had set aside to give to Sally – the woman who left Debbie alone in my shop. For a moment, I stare at it, realising with sickening dread just how much she has cost me.

I don't hesitate for a second before emptying the cash back into the till.

For a goodwill gesture to work, there needs to be some goodwill involved, and there definitely is none to be had here.

25

I haven't been practising any mindfulness since leaving the therapy session on Tuesday afternoon. That technique was great when I had a clear head and no stress to distract me. But when fear and nightmares are crashing in on me from every angle, it turns a relatively simple task into a near-impossible one. Maybe Julia missed out a vital bit of information. Perhaps that is how she operates. It took two sessions to be offered the technique of mindfulness in the first place, then perhaps in the third session I will learn how to properly implement it. But then there will be another stepping stone to curing my anxiety completely, so I will need another session. Maybe it's like collecting hobby magazines with something attached to them, like getting a piece of a puzzle in each issue. I need to collect the whole set before I can put the answer together.

Even though I promised myself to watch how much I drink, I find myself collapsing on the sofa and cracking open a new bottle of wine as soon as I get into my flat. I sit and drink, unaware of the fading light around me as the evening draws on.

Today has been a nightmare. A piece of art I've been working on for weeks has disappeared into nothingness. So many hours of painstaking work, dedication and love have been destroyed – or so I think. In truth, I have no idea where the painting is, or what has happened to it. I just know that Debbie is responsible.

The familiar pressure builds in my chest. I know the

feeling so well it's almost like meeting with an old friend, except this acquaintance is most unwelcome.

I realise I should do something more constructive than dive further into the bottle of wine, seeking oblivion, even though that option is very tempting right now.

One thing I can do is write in my anxiety journal. Losing the package is definitely a source of great stress. I would label it a 'nine' for sure. It is all I can think about. I know I won't sleep tonight.

Every few minutes I am fighting off an overwhelming feeling of dread that threatens to drown me. Yet, I still would not give it a 'ten'. That number is reserved only for incidents like in the supermarket.

I go to write in my anxiety journal, but I struggle to find it. During a good twenty-minutes of searching, I actually convince myself that Debbie got into my flat too and she found and stole my log. Oh, she would have had a great time with that. I have actually referenced her in it by name on multiple occasions. Not only would she have got a great laugh herself, but she would also show it to Sally in the case of proving what a headcase I am.

But before I drive myself completely insane, I manage to locate it. It was stuffed in one of my bedside drawers. At first, I thought this odd, since that was not where I left it. Upon opening it to start writing, however, I realise that I made an entry on Tuesday night after my bottle of wine; it is a very angry entry that goes into far too much detail about how distraught I am with Sally, Debbie and Bethany. I rant on for a whole A4 page about how much they have upset me and how awful I felt rushing back to find out what was happening.

189

The words are gorged dark and deep into the page, and into those beneath it too. I rip out many sheets of paper and resolve to rewrite the entry in a way that doesn't make me look insane.

My pen hovers over the paper, thinking of what I should write about today's incident.

I freeze; I can hear a noise coming from down the hallway. A clinking, rattling sound and some faint banging.

What the hell is that?

Even though I don't recognise the sound, the hairs on the back of my neck are standing. I force myself to stand up on unwilling legs and creep out quietly into the hallway. It is dark in here, apart from the tiny bit of dusky light coming from the semi-circles of frosted glass on the back door.

The noise has stopped. I pause in the hallway, turning my head this way and that, trying to decide where the sound had been coming from.

A few seconds pass, and I start to decide that maybe it has stopped, or was just the flat next door – but then I see it.

The back door handle is pulled down. Someone is on the other side, turning it. The faint banging starts again and I realise that is the sound of the person pressing their weight against the door, trying to force it open.

I try to suppress my shriek by clapping my hand over my mouth, but I only half-stifle it.

Suddenly the door handle is released.

There is silence.

Even though I can't see them, I know the person is frozen too, thinking of their next move in a split-second, just as I think of mine.

I do the only thing I can think of and flick on the

light switch next to me. The bare bulb illuminates the hallway brightly and I wonder if the person outside can see it through the frosted glass.

My question is answered almost immediately as I hear rapid, heavy footsteps on the concrete staircase outside.

They're leaving.

I stand breathing heavily in the same spot, clutching the bedroom doorway for support, listening to the footsteps quickly fade. My reasoning breaks through my trance and I rush back into the bedroom and frantically pull back the net curtains. Even standing on tiptoes I can't see anyone out in the backyard, or in the alley. The person has gone already.

I go back to the hallway and stare at the door. A chill runs through me at the thought of someone trying to get into my home while I am in it.

26

I have an uncomfortable night of tossing and turning. I eventually manage to nod off, but it is past four am when I finally slip into a sweaty, disturbed slumber.

Nor does my mind get to escape so easily. For all of my meagre few hours of sleep, I feel as though every moment is filled with mental torment. I dream of the usual beach, and of my sister again. I dream of Debbie and Sally with their heads together, staring at me maliciously as I run around frantic, trying to find my missing painting.

The only way I could give myself some semblance of peace last night was to barricade the door with a chair. I'd even set a saucepan filled with glass beads upon it so that if someone tried to get in again, the racket would at least wake me so I can get out the front door in time.

As soon as I woke up this morning, I peered out of the bedroom and down the hall to check my makeshift alarm was still in place. To my relief, everything looks just the same as I left it last night.

I make a mental note to invest in something a little more heavy-duty in terms of security measures.

To make myself feel more secure last night, I had fallen asleep with my phone in my hand. I had wanted to call Andrew last night, but he was away at his training event. I check the screen now and am relieved that even with the wine I had not taken it upon myself to send any more silly texts to him.

I re-read the goodnight text I sent to him just before ten; even in the harsh light of day, it seems all right.

There wasn't a response last night though, and I still haven't had one this morning, which is weird.

Andrew had mentioned getting limited phone reception in the area where he is staying, however. Perhaps I was mistaken when I thought that only applied to calls and not texts.

The doubt that Andrew got my text and is simply ignoring me nags from the dark recesses of my mind.

He is probably just busy, I tell myself. *Or he could still be asleep or have his phone off.*

I think I might just be in the habit of being overprotective of my heart, though, since I was mistreated for so long in the not-so-distant past. I know I need to recognise the warning signs that something is wrong before it is too late; I should be an expert at reading the signals.

As for whoever tried to break into my home, I have no idea. It's not like I have any valuable possessions; only my MacBook, but nobody knows I own one, or where I keep it. It's not like I go flashing it around or anything.

All night I told myself that the person trying to gain entry was nothing more than a simple burglar. Nothing personal. The alleyway has always seemed overly dark and sinister looking at night. Nothing overlooks that dark passage, and there aren't any street lights. I don't have a car parked outside, and the lights were off; that is an open invitation for an opportunistic thief, is it not?

No, I'm sure I would know if it was someone coming after me personally.

If they really were after me, they wouldn't have stopped when I switched on the light.

Despite the lack of sleep I've had, I've woken early and I have a few hours before I need to open up shop for the day. I make myself some marmalade on toast and sit on the sofa in my dressing gown to write in my anxiety journal. I've got some real catching up to do. I rewrite the incident with the gallery staffing on Tuesday, then I note the nightmare of the missing painting. On top of that, I condense the terror of someone trying to break into my home into a few lines in my journal. I rate the last one a 'ten'. I think that's fair. Who wouldn't?

Even in the light of day, I'm still shaken. The sugar from the marmalade is helping. I suppose I should probably report an attempted break-in to the police, but I won't do that. I just know it will be a tremendous hassle without any gain.

My phone buzzes with a reply from Andrew at long last. He says he is sorry for missing my text last night, but he has only just received it. He says he is having a really boring time and misses me. I send him a quick reply to concur that I look forward to seeing him soon too.

I feel a little better after writing in my journal, somewhat unclogged, like my diary is really a silent friend I have shared my problems with. A problem shared is a problem halved, right?

The next thing I do is call the courier as soon as their office opens for the day. Since my request is not a straightforward one, I am passed from person to person within the office. They all seem bemused as to why I do not know if my own parcel was picked up or not. I find myself having to repeat my story to each different voice on the end of the phone.

'I've already explained this,' I say, telling my version of events for the fourth time to a young man who sounds no more than twenty. 'A member of staff was supposed to hand it over, but I'm not sure if they did or not.'

'Because they were off sick?' he asks.

'Well, yes – sort of. But someone else was covering for her. Look, it doesn't matter who was there. I left the parcel in the shop before I left. There was definitely someone running my shop at the courier pick up time. When I got back, the parcel was gone.'

'And you think your employee stole it?' He catches on quickly. 'Sounds like you've got staffing issues.'

'Yes, I'm aware.' My face flushes. I hope he can't hear my gritted teeth down the line. 'Listen, I just want to know what happened to my parcel. Was it picked up by your company or not?'

'Well, we've asked around, right. But we're not one-hundred-percent on who took that end of Coventry that day.'

I sigh. This is getting me nowhere.

'I'll keep asking around the office – oh, hang on a sec – Eric!'

I hear muffled talking on the end of the line, then the man starts talking to me again. 'Hello, you still there, Mrs. Harmen?'

'Mrs. Harper,' I correct. 'Yes, I'm still here.'

'Right, one of our drivers just came in – he says he did pick-ups in your area on Tuesday.'

'And?' I prompt.

'Well he says he went to the pick up address – Stony Studios, isn't it? – but there wasn't any parcel. The woman in the shop told him there had been a mistake, and that the shop owner was going to deliver the item to the customer herself.'

I'm stunned into silence.

'Hello – you still there?'

'Um... yes. Thank you. You've been really helpful.' I put the phone down.

That sly bitch.

27

Later on, it is another slowish day in the gallery, unusual for a Saturday. At first, I am paranoid that my sales could be walking across the street to Minerva Interiors, but a few glances over there and I conclude that this is not the case. Trade seems slow over the road too I'm pleased to note. Most people are most likely still off enjoying the nice weather, and home improvements are not the top of their priority list.

My time is not wasted, however. I look under the counter for something to write with. As I rummage, my hand makes contact with the spare set of keys I keep for the flat.

But that is not right.

I pull them out and examine them. There are just two silver keys on a single keyring, exactly as the landlord handed them over – one for the front door and one for the back.

What is strange is that I always keep them securely in the till. Why are they under the counter?

Did I move them when I was searching for the courier receipt? Or did I take them out of the till prior to leaving Bethany in charge? I don't remember doing either.

Why would I take them from the till where they were safer? Did Debbie or Bethany move them? I feel horribly violated when I think of either of them going into my flat while I was away that afternoon. Surely they wouldn't have done such a thing...

Trying not to think of either of the two women entering my flat, I pull out some blank paper and a pen from under the counter and start writing. I make a comprehensive list of all the things Debbie could have done with my painting.

At the top of my list is the possibility that she could have hidden it on her premises – it is only across the road, after all. Although not ideal, that option does seem like the lesser of all the evils. At least my work could still be intact if that is the case.

But how would I know? Is Debbie keeping it in her flat? Or perhaps stashed in her shop? For a crazy moment, I think that perhaps she is selling it in her window display of canvases, and I actually move over to the glass frontage of the gallery and peer across the street, but I don't see anything – just the same display that was there last week. I didn't really expect to, that would be too blatant even for Debbie.

She might be paying me far too much attention than she should, but she isn't stupid. She is far too sneaky for that.

I continue with my list, writing down every eventuality, marking each one with a bullet-point. I write down options that don't include deliberate sabotage on Debbie's part too. These involve Bethany being the mastermind behind the whole thing. It is possible that she could have taken the package and lied to Debbie, but I don't think it's likely.

I look at my list. Of all the points I write down, one theme joins most possibilities: Debbie most likely moved the painting to her premises. If I want to ever see it again, then that is where I need to start. I just don't know what I am going to do about it.

Calling the police without solid evidence is risky. I could end up drawing unwanted attention to myself for no reason. I don't even know if the painting is still there, or if it even was in the first place. At the moment though it is all I have to go on.

At lunchtime, I'm partway through my home-made chicken salad sandwich when a young couple, both with very long hair and many colourful wristbands, take a liking to one of my golden meadow scenes. They pay me great compliments about it and we chat for a while. They tell me about their plans to tour Europe now that they have graduated. Despite the strong smell of weed coming from the pair, I start to think I have made a sale, but when they realise the price of the piece they can't wait to leave.

I screw up the empty foil from my sandwich into a ball and lean back on my stool, aiming for the bin in the kitchen.

Inevitably, I miss. I sigh and pick up the crinkled silver ball, dropping it into the bin that I haven't emptied for a while; it is almost overflowing. My 'Back in Five Minutes' sign sits at the top of the rubbish; I discarded it first thing this morning. Since I have no plans to pop across the road to Sally's Sandwiches for lunch any more, I have no need for it. Underneath that there are various packets from previous meals, including mine and Andrew's recent takeaway lunch.

A thought occurs to me: it is collection day for our street's commercial bins on Monday.

If Debbie has stolen my painting, she might have destroyed it and disposed of the evidence in one of her bins at the back of her shop – possibility number two on my list.

I need to check Debbie's bin before it gets collected. That only leaves me with today and tomorrow to do it, as it's Saturday today. Didn't Debbie say she isn't in the shop on a Saturday? I'm sure she said that, whether it was true or not is another matter. Now that I think about it though, she went to the funeral of Andrew's great-uncle on a Saturday.

I go to the window and look out at the street again. Her little car is not there. I wonder if I could sneak down the alley that leads around the back of the shops and get into the yard of Minerva Interiors. The rear layout of the buildings on that side of the street is just the same as the ones of my row. I remember seeing the satellite view on Google Maps when I was thinking about setting up the gallery, doing my due diligence on the area. The yards over the road are just the same as mine, and they are not overlooked by any surrounding buildings.

Last night someone managed to get into my yard, up the stairs to my flat and attempt a break in without being seen. I could be in and out of Debbie's yard without anybody seeing me, I'm sure of it. I'm really careful. I know all about hiding in plain sight.

28

A little nagging voice in my head tells me I should wait until tomorrow to do this. On a Sunday Minerva Interiors will be shut, although there's a fifty-fifty chance that Debbie could stay in for the day and not leave at all. Some weeks I see Debbie leaving, dressed in her Sunday best; I'm guessing she goes to church, which makes me laugh. My mother is a churchgoer too.

But I can't gamble this opportunity on the chance that Debbie will go out tomorrow, plus I am due to see Andrew. At the moment, her shop will be open for a couple more hours with a part-time worker half-heartedly running the place. But logically, this is the best time to venture into the yard across the road and not be caught.

At first, I considered the dead of night, but I would not have been able to see anything either and would have required a torch. That surely would attract attention from Debbie's flat, or one of her neighbours. A professional couple live above Sally's Sandwiches. I have never spoken to them, and if either happened to glance outside and see me rummaging through a bin in the middle of the night, I don't think they would understand.

I shut the gallery and lock up for the day. Trade has been slow anyway. On Monday I will have to reshuffle my window display, freshen things up a bit and get things back on track. Right now though I have only one mission.

I've thought about it thoroughly. Minerva Interiors doesn't get deliveries on Saturdays; there would be nothing to unpack today, therefore, no reason to venture out to the bins with waste packaging.

I haven't noticed Debbie's car at all this morning, or this afternoon, so I'm assuming she has popped out somewhere for the day. Perhaps to Cannon Park Shopping Centre for a weekend spending spree, probably eating out for lunch too. I have seen her unloading bags of brand new clothes from her car on several occasions since I've lived here. Yes, that's probably what she is doing today. I guess since she split with Andrew she has to fill her spare time with something, even if that is materialistic and unfulfilling. Not that I can talk, I have many garments in my wardrobe still with their tags on; the thrill of the chase was over as soon as I had made the purchases.

Anyway, it is unlikely Debbie would stay out all day without going home for dinner. Or if she does eat out then that is great, it just means I will have even more time to get out of there. Not that it should take long to find out what I want to know.

I walk down to the end of the street, before crossing and striding purposefully towards the beginning of the alley. I'm glad I was sensible today and put my bronze pumps on – I just couldn't bear the thought of forcing my feet into heels for a whole working day. Not today, I'm not at all in the mood. I'm even more glad now since my feet hardly make any sound as I step over bottle tops and broken glass, looking for the yard of Minerva Interiors.

The buildings all look the same from here, with hardly any distinction between each of them. I'm not sure which one is which. They are all brick-built and look rather shabby from the back. It all looks damp and here and there weeds poke through the mortar. The alley is strewn with decomposing litter in varying stages. A Walkers crisp packet that has faded almost completely to white rustles beneath my step.

I count each shop as I go along to get my bearings, but am not entirely sure how many along Debbie's shop is anyway. I pass a crumbling outbuilding and suddenly know this is the right place. Over the mossy, brick wall I see the top-half of a wooden door is painted a pale purple, matching the frontage of the interior design shop.

As I approach my mark, I feel a little like I'm creeping. I stand up straight and make a deliberate effort to look as though I am meant to be here. Looking sneaky is a sure way to attract suspicion. As long as I look like I belong, no one will pay me any attention. Besides, it's not like I am really doing anything wrong. I would draw the line at breaking and entering, but looking through someone's rubbish isn't really a crime – not when something has been stolen from me anyway. I'll leave everything as I found it and only take something if it already belongs to me.

The wide wheelie-bin rests against the wall in the alley. I move towards it and lift the lid tentatively. There are a lot of flattened cardboard boxes and various scraps of ripped up paper in here, along with giant cardboard tubes and some small decorative boxes that have been scuffed and damaged around the edges; this is all just waste from the shop. No painting, no sign even of the wooden frame it was stretched over. All that is in here is paper and cardboard.

Debbie's general waste bin must be in the yard; that is surely a better hiding place for something more contraband. Taking a casual glance around me, I move closer to the yard.

The old wooden gate isn't locked, but the squeak and clatter it makes as I open it seems too loud in the quiet of the alley. Another subtle half-glance around tells me the coast is clear.

There are so many bins crowding the small yard. I open each one methodically, but I don't find anything that shouldn't be there. Not one single thing is out of place, apart from some cardboard in the general waste bin that could have been recycled. Not exactly a smoking gun, unless I was an eager environmental officer looking for petty violations.

Disappointed, I go back through the gate, shutting it as quietly as I can behind me. I take a step back the way I came, intending to go home, but then I stop.

I don't know why I do it, but I lift the lid of the large wheelie bin again and peer inside; it's all still just used packaging and ripped up invoices. I don't know what I was expecting – maybe to see something I hadn't noticed before. I close the lid again, but before I turn to leave, something in one of the windows above the shop catches my eye – the figure of a woman staring down at me. I can't see her face, but I quickly get the impression of wispy-blonde hair as I duck down behind the wall.

It's Debbie.

My mind buzzes.

Why the hell is she at home?

How long has she been watching me?

I lose my balance as I crouch and have to put my hand out to steady myself. Immediately, I recoil; I have put my palm in something cold and wet that I can't even identify – something black and slimy.

I swear under my breath. Hurriedly, I wipe my hand on the brick wall, right next to where someone has written '*Bazza is a twat*' in black marker pen.

I don't know what to do. She must have seen me, but I can't just stand up again.

Why did I have to come here?

I'm no more knowledgeable than I was an hour ago, and now Debbie has seen me snooping around her yard. As if she would have left the evidence on her premises. What was I thinking? Debbie is not that stupid – I already knew that.

I can't stay crouched behind the wall, Debbie could already be coming downstairs to burst through the door any moment. I need to get out of here.

Awkwardly and keeping low, I hurry back along the alley. My side bumps against the wall every few steps, causing clumps of moss to detach from the brickwork and fall.

It is a circuitous route home for me, as I plan to approach my flat from the alleyway at the back of the gallery. The last thing I need is for Debbie to see me go in through my front door, further cementing the fact that I have just arrived home from her premises.

I exit the Minerva Interiors alleyway and cross the road on the corner of Stonegravel Street. As I cross, I look back towards Debbie's shop – her little Peugeot is still not there. Odd, since she never goes anywhere without driving, even if it's just a few minutes down the road. Her car is small and super-economical, so she probably thinks nothing of nipping around everywhere in it. She is one of those people that treat their car as a bike, hopping in and out and running errands all the time. She is never to be seen without her car. So why would she be at home without it? She must have put it through an MOT, or be getting it serviced, perhaps.

After all, I definitely saw Debbie at the window, watching me.

Didn't I?

Although it was really only a figure with Debbie's hair colour, and I only saw it for a split-second before I hid, I'm sure I couldn't have imagined such a thing. Unless... unless I was so worried about Debbie coming back that my brain projected the image of her into the window.

But she *must* have been there. I may have been through a lot, but I'm not the kind of person who imagines things. But now I think of it, I don't have a solid mental picture of her through the glass.

How strange, since I was so sure of the fact just a few minutes ago.

I make a mental note to leave this incident out of my anxiety journal.

29

I tug at the shiny golden ribbon that has been carefully tied up in a bow; it slides away in one satisfying movement. Lifting the lid of the silver gift box, I glimpse the gloss of a white, porcelain mug with a purple band, nestled amongst pink tissue paper. Pulling the mug out of its box, I read the text.

Aunty Harriet
KEEP CALM AND CARRY ON KNITTING

'It's to replace the broken Coombe Abbey one,' Andrew explains. 'I found this website, where you can personalise the message. Do you like it? It's not too on the nose is it?'

I plant a wide smile firmly on my face. 'No it's lovely,' I say. 'I mean it's outrageous, but it's still really thoughtful.'

On any other day, a reminder of my sister and her children would be most unwelcome. However, after staying up all night worrying about yesterday's fresh debacle with Debbie, it is almost refreshing to experience a wrench of stress about something else for a change. Well, almost.

'You don't need to buy me gifts all the time, you know,' I say.

'I know. I just like doing it.'

I smile. 'Then you're a great boyfriend to have.'

'You could do a lot worse.' As he gives me one of his trademark winks, I see new speckles of little freckles on the more delicate skin around his eyes that I haven't noticed before. In fact, now that I look closely, I'm sure Andrew looks a little more tanned than he was a few days ago. Perhaps part of his training day was held outside? He didn't mention that it was, actually, he was reluctant to talk about his training day at all, explaining he didn't want to bore me.

I'm at Andrew's house – a modern-build, two-bedroom semi in the suburbs of Allesley. The house itself is nice enough, but Andrew was right about needing to re-decorate. Most walls are covered with fading wallpaper of various designs. No two rooms share the same paper either. The only exception being the living room which, oddly, shares its covering with a walk-in closet on the landing upstairs. The paint-work on the banisters and skirting boards is streaked with brush strokes and chipped in places.

We sit on his cream-leather sofa in the living room, surrounded by an assortment of cushions that is reminiscent of Julia's therapy couch. However, Andrew's cushions haven't been chosen to deliberately conflict with each other in an aesthetically pleasing way – they seem to simply be a random collection. When Andrew caught me looking at them, he explained that they were part of a box of items that Debbie threw together for him during the divorce. 'Some of them were in the sun lounge, some from the living room and these two–' he indicates a lime green cushion and a faux fur one with a broken zip '–were defective stock from the shop which Debbie let me have. Quite generous of her really.' He laughs. 'Would you like a drink?'

'I'd love one. Coffee would be great, if you've got it,' I say, even though I can clearly see a Nescafé Dolce Gusto machine through the open kitchen door.

'One coffee, coming up. You can try out your new mug then – Aunty Harriet.' He disappears into the kitchen.

I sigh playfully. 'What did I say about calling me that?' I call after him.

He pops his head around the doorway and screws his face up in mock-concentration. 'You said, "Andrew, please keep calling me that, it's my favourite term of endearment."' He disappears again.

Later, we sip our drinks as rain patters against the window outside and I suggest the colour schemes that would work well for the house. I find some Pinterest examples to show Andrew on his iPad.

'I mean, you can go for something really neutral like light grey,' I explain, showing him a Pin depicting a perfectly immaculate lounge. 'I've seen grey and silver around a lot. I think it's the new magnolia. Or, if you want something more colourful, then dark blue is really popular right now.' I set down my empty *Aunty Harriet* cup on the coffee table and look around the living room. 'That could really work in this room, I think. You have this light-coloured sofa, so it shouldn't become too dark in here. What do you think?' I look around at Andrew, but his bright blue eyes are focused on me, rather than the walls or the iPad.

'What is it?' I ask, noticing how the flecks of colour in his irises seem more obvious with the gloomy grey light filtering in from outside.

'You look really tired, Harriet. Did you have trouble sleeping again last night?'

'A little,' I shrug, trying to sound casual, as though I hadn't lain awake until the early hours, trying to stave off waves of negative thoughts. In the end, I opened a new bottle of wine to help me relax and I don't even remember actually falling asleep. 'I should probably cut down on caffeine, or something. I do drink a lot of coffee.' I lift up my empty coffee mug, shaking my head and slapping my wrist in mock-dismay. 'So, what did you think about colours? Would you like to see some colour in here?' I ask to distract him from the subject of my insomnia.

He nods. 'Navy blue sounds like a good idea. So, how is everything going with the gallery? Trade been good?'

'Yes, it's been OK.' *Although it would have been much better if your ex-wife hadn't been taking up so much of my mental energy that I can't properly focus on running my business.* The displays have become stagnant and I need to re-jig things, paint some fresh works to attract new customers.

I don't want to admit the possibility that Minerva Interiors has stolen business from me by selling canvases like mine. Although, if I'm honest with myself, it is unlikely that Debbie's introduction of a new product range has gone without consequence. I wonder if Andrew has even been to the shop and noticed what she has done yet.

'So what do you think?' Andrew says, snapping me from my reverie. He looks at me expectedly. 'Does it sound like a good idea?'

I look at him blankly.

He nods to himself, setting his mug down on the table. 'I thought you weren't listening. Your eyes had that glazed over look.'

'Sorry,' I say. 'Like you said, I think I must be tired. Tell me again.'

'I was just saying, maybe you should host an exhibition one evening. Get some interest in the gallery from some new people.'

'An exhibition? You know how small my shop is, don't you?'

He shakes his head. 'It's not that small. And anyway, it doesn't matter. I've been to these things before in many outlets of all shapes and sizes. You don't have to own a museum or warehouse to host an open evening. Events like that can really help the artist take off, make a real name for themselves.'

'I don't want to make a name for myself,' I say, without thinking.

Andrew suddenly looks at me confused. 'What do you mean?'

'Well.... I just meant that – that I don't want to be mega famous or anything – that is not why I paint. The gallery has been doing fine for ages now. It's just these past couple of weeks. I just need to have a shuffle around, get some new work in, that's all.'

'These past few weeks, eh?' He puts the iPad down and moves along the sofa to sit close beside me, putting his arm around my shoulders as he does so. 'I'm not keeping you from your work now am I, Harriet Harper?'

Suddenly I hate Andrew calling me that. I don't want any trace of my old life anywhere near me right now. I don't want any evidence of what I had before, with *him*. But I know I will never be free of his taint in so many ways, no matter what I do. The thought makes me want to be closer to Andrew all of a sudden. I lean closer to him and press my lips against his.

He kisses me back keenly, and quickly we are kissing in a way that we haven't before – eagerly and yet somehow tenderly at the same time.

Outside, the summer rain beats down heavier and

211

louder, but I hardly notice. I only appreciate the warmth of Andrew's hand as he takes mine and leads me upstairs.

30

Andrew drops me off at my flat on Monday morning. He kisses me enthusiastically before I get out of the car and neither of us can stop smiling.

He drives off with the haste of someone who spent too long in the shower with his girlfriend and is now cutting it fine if he wants to get to work on time.

I let myself into my flat and think of getting ready for my working day too. There is over an hour before I have to open though, so I'm not in much of a hurry. When I get to the landing at the top of the stairs I stop dead.

My makeshift alarm has been disrupted.

I see the saucepan of shiny, red beads has been upset and is now lying on its side, the contents scattered like little droplets of blood all over the carpet.

My heart rate is rapidly escalating against my ribs and I can feel my blood surging in my head. Then I realise that my nerves are getting the better of me without reason – it must have been me that caused my alarm to go off.

When I came back from Debbie's yard on Saturday evening, I went down the alley and tried to get in through the back door of the flat. I stupidly forgot that I had barricaded it and genuinely couldn't figure out why the door was jammed. For a few minutes, I even got it into my head that someone had managed to get inside and had locked me out, which now that I think about it, is even more ridiculous than I realised at the time.

I was forced to go back down the alley and through the front door instead. When you are trying to hide from your neighbours across the street it is not a good time to have your back door jammed.

A thought occurred to me, however, as I passed the key-cutters a few doors down from the gallery that day. What if either Debbie, Bethany or even Sally got a copy of my keys that day? It would have been easy enough. They could have been there and back within ten minutes.

I told myself that I was being too paranoid. Why would they want to get into my shop, or my home whenever they wanted?

I don't know if Debbie saw me get into my flat on Saturday. I just held my head up high and went inside as quickly as possible, without making it look like I was rushing. Not that I care so much now; I have the last twenty-four hours with Andrew to think about if I need cheering up.

I clear up the glass beads and put the chair back in the kitchen where it belongs; it was more of a hindrance than a help, and the attempted break-in was probably just a one-off. It is still a good idea to avoid keeping the keys in the door, but I cross purchasing a security light and dummy CCTV camera from my mental to-do list. I was scared at the time, but I might have been overreacting.

Whoever the would-be intruder was, they ran away as soon as they realised someone was inside. The chair was just in the way inside my small hallway anyway. What if I had needed to get in or out in a real emergency?

In the kitchen, I make myself some coffee. Andrew already made me some this morning, but I can never stop at just one cup usually. Maybe I really should give up caffeine. My mind wanders to the box of chamomile tea that lies abandoned in the gallery kitchen with a twinge of guilt. Maybe I'll make the swap tomorrow. At the moment though I need caffeine just to get through the day.

Settling myself on the sofa, I put down my new mug on the coffee table. I can't decide whether to use it for my drinks in the gallery or leave it up here. Leaving it in the flat would mean I see it less, but then Andrew will notice that I am using it more if it is at work with me, earning me more brownie points. I lean forward and turn it round until the handle is angled towards me, so I don't have to see the text.

Just then I notice a scrap of paper beneath the low table. From my seat, I can see angry black letters written jaggedly on the lines. Bemused, I reach down and smooth it out with my fingers.

I recognise the writing from my anxiety journal. This is the page I wrote the day Bethany abandoned the shop. But it can't be because I threw that page away. Anyway, this is just part of the page; just a small scrap with jagged edges, clearly torn from the original piece. The paper has been ripped unevenly, traces of other words visible along the rough edges, but someone has clearly taken an interest in one particular sentence, making it the focus. Now only one line is legible and it reads:

DEBBIE IS A SPITEFUL BITCH.

I feel unnerved. I'm sure I threw the whole page away. How did it end up underneath the table? I look around for other bits of paper, but there is nothing.

I look back at the sentence. The words seem to gleam back at me ominously before I screw up the

215

paper and stuff it firmly into the bin.

I'm sure I threw the page away already. I search my memories for an image of me dropping the journal entry into the bin, but I can't find it. Did I really throw it away, or did I just think I did? I remember tearing the page from the journal, but I can't recall what I did with it after that.

Even though my instinct tells me otherwise, I suppose I must have neglected to discard it.

I did have a little to drink on Saturday night, but it was only to calm me down a bit. Was it really enough to cause me to start rummaging through my own rubbish?

31

I have an odd morning at work. Customers come and go as usual and turnover is decent, but I have something really weird happen when I go for a quick snack.

Mid-morning I go through to the shop kitchen with the thought of indulging in some coffee and biscuits. I have a shock, however, when I reach out to fill the kettle and realise it is not there.

It is the strangest thing.

For a few minutes, I am utterly bewildered. I quickly scour the cupboards and even briefly wander around the shop floor looking for where the kettle could have gone, but I can't find it anywhere. The same goes for the biscuits – the little kitchen is empty apart from some old plastic food boxes that were left by the previous occupant.

Did I move the kettle? Maybe it stopped working and I threw it away? And maybe I ate the biscuits absent-mindedly. I can't remember doing either of those things, however... But that must have been what happened. Even if someone had been in here for whatever reason, they surely wouldn't steal a cheap Argos kettle and a half-eaten packet of digestives. There would be no reason to do such a thing – unless they wanted to frighten me, but they surely could think of a better way to intimidate someone than that...

I'm unnerved for the rest of the morning. Then

later, just before lunch, I glance across the street and notice another strange scenario; Debbie talking to a very scruffy-looking man with prematurely grey hair. My best guess is that he is homeless. His clothes are overly baggy and very obviously faded; as I look more closely I can see a few holes in his threadbare trousers in places too.

She seems determined to keep her distance from him. I don't pay the pair much attention and am about to look away when I see Debbie point this way, towards the gallery.

What the hell?

Why would she be gesturing this way? Was she really pointing, or was it more that she was shooing him away?

All of a sudden the exchange seems to be over and the man slouches off down the street, taking large strides with an odd limp. I take in his broad face and excessive squint before he disappears from view.

Andrew texts me to tell me he has to work through his lunch break, so we can't eat together.

Instead, I am surprised when he sends a pink bouquet of roses to me, brightening up my afternoon and taking my mind a little off this morning.

After I shut the gallery for the day I rush upstairs to shower and get changed in anticipation of Andrew coming over to my flat for dinner. I only have minutes to spare when he arrives, bringing with him some Italian restaurant food and two bottles of wine.

'I wasn't sure if you wanted Prosecco or red wine.' he says. 'Prosecco is fine,' I say, wrapping my arms around his neck and kissing him.

I take the batteries out of the smoke alarms and light some candles for some ambience. The food is all delicious.

I have hardly set down my fork after finishing my baked cheesecake when Andrew takes my hand and asks me to dance. It's quite a strange gesture since there isn't any music and not much space in the open plan living room-kitchen. Nevertheless, I humour him and we sway around the room, with him spinning me around once every so often. He pulls me closer to him as we rotate slowly on the spot.

'You know, I think you need an early night, Harriet,' Andrew whispers softly in my ear, making the hairs on my neck lift pleasantly.

I lift my head and we kiss, deep and slow and it isn't long before I lead him along the hallway to my bedroom.

Afterwards, as we lie in bed, I show Andrew the sketchbook I keep in the bedside drawer. Andrew holds the book and I rest my head on his shoulder, flipping through the concept drawings of works I haven't mapped out in paint yet. He listens raptly and I am overcome with a new wonderment that anyone could be so genuinely interested in something I've done.

We lie that way for hours talking. I can hear the steady rhythm of Andrew's heart beating loudly against my ear. Gradually the conversation becomes more sparse as we both start drifting towards sleep.

'We should go away somewhere,' Andrew suggests dreamily, snapping me back into the room suddenly. 'I know somewhere you'll love that has great scenery – Pelistry Bay in the Scilly Isles. My parents took me there once – the beaches are so beautiful and the water

219

is really clear down there. You could get some really nice work out of it, add some seascapes to your portfolio... And, you know, we could make the most of the trip too.' He plants a kiss on my forehead, blissfully unaware that he has said anything that would cause the sensation of sudden pressure on my chest, reversing my slowing heart rate.

Everything was so perfect. I had felt normal for an entire evening. *Why did he have to mention a beach?*

I feel like I'm cursed; like there is something that won't let me forget, ever.

'What's wrong?' Andrew asks me, turning his head to study my face.

I open my mouth to say 'I'm fine', but my heart won't let me; I feel like to tell another lie would shatter it into pieces.

'Harriet, what is it?'

I take a deep breath. 'Nothing,' I say, feeling my heart sink behind my ribs. *I'm such a coward.*

'If you think it's too soon, we don't have to go anywhere, I just thought–'

'No, I would love to go somewhere with you.' I kiss his chest. 'But I prefer more inland scenes for my work. You might have noticed that by now. I don't really like the sea.'

'Oh, I remember. Like in Cornwall, you made it as far as Redruth, but didn't make it to the coast.' There is a pause, and I can almost hear his mind whirring, almost hear the inevitable words forming at the base of his tongue. 'Why don't you like the sea?' he asks.

'I just don't.'

Andrew seems to sense that I don't want to talk about it and doesn't press the subject, instead he changes it.

He talks about a cottage his parents own in the Lake

District. 'They rent it out all year round, and it's usually fully booked in the summer, but they said I can have it anytime I want. Maybe we could go there instead? The views are beautiful and you get really great sunsets – and there are plenty of places to sketch too. I could even dust off my Nikon SLR too. It's really quiet out there, no traffic or anything. You would like it, I'm sure.'

'It sounds perfect.'

32

I stand on the wet sand. The sunshine is glorious, illuminating the sea and making it look a bright turquoise. The sand is a white sheet, providing a barrier from the sea by wrapping itself around the grassy land.

My father takes my hand and mine feels so small in comparison. We easily jump together over the wave that sweeps towards us. It wets the bottom of my pink sundress, so Daddy picks me up and quickly hoists me onto his shoulders, making a whooshing noise as he does so for my amusement so that I shriek and giggle with glee.

I feel like the highest person in the world on his shoulders and we wade out deeper until the water reaches Daddy's waist. Everything is great, even though the sun has gone behind the clouds and everything is cast in a grey luminescence. For a few moments, everything is wonderful.

The next thing I know is that I am falling.

Water shoots painfully up my nose and fills my ears. My bare shoulder grazes painfully against pebbles half-buried in the sand.

I surface and splash around frantically.

What is happening?

I can't see anything because my eyes sting and burn when I open them. After a few moments, I feel my toes brush against something hard and gritty and I stand up.

I can't see Daddy anywhere. Wading back out of the water, I feel heavy as my wet dress clings to me. I call out for him, but he doesn't answer. There is nothing but the sound of the waves. They sound loud and scary now that I am alone.

Another wave rushes towards me and I suddenly make out the shape of a hand. Then I see Daddy's white shirt beneath the water and I can see his hair now too, floating dark and ethereal beneath the surface.

'Daddy!' I shout, but he doesn't move. He floats oddly, moving back and forth with each new wave.

I don't know what to do. My fingernails dig into my palms, but the pain feels distant, disconnected from me.

I know there is something wrong with Daddy, but why isn't he moving even a little bit? Why won't he get up?

I don't understand.

My feet sink into the wet sand. I wait for Daddy to get back up, but he doesn't. And part of me knows he won't ever get back up again, but I stand and wait anyway because I don't know what else to do; I cry and watch, horrified as the tide pushes and pulls my father's body relentlessly.

I am screaming. Suddenly I am aware of being very hot – too hot – and damp too. I feel like my little pink dress is clinging to me again, but as I snatch at it I realise it is just a tangle of bed sheets.

Then I see my father's hand reach out for me.

No wait, it is Andrew's hand.

It's dark. I'm in my bedroom. Andrew is here with me. I can see his bare torso in the dark. He reaches out and grasps my shoulders. As my eyes adjust to the darkness, I see his face looks terrified.

'Harriet! Harriet – what's the matter!?'

My mouth opens to speak, but it doesn't form any words. I'm still breathing rapidly as though I have been running and there are tears wetting my cheeks. I hope Andrew can't see me too well.

'Were you dreaming? I think you've just had a nightmare. Just calm down. You're safe, OK?' Andrew pulls me into a hug; it's awkward because the bed sheets are still sticking to my legs. I appreciate how cool the skin of his chest feels against my hot and clammy cheek.

Andrew strokes my hair soothingly. 'Everything is all right now, Harriet.'

But everything is not all right.

I close my eyes, even though I know I will be faced again with the images from my dream, just as I have done so many times before.

The image of the beach floats forward and fills my mind's eye. The sea laps malevolently towards me with its grisly cargo. I am once more that little girl, terrified and alone on the shore.

I could have run that day; I could have found help from an adult nearby – if only I could have commanded my body to do so – but I stood frozen; my mind locked in fear and horror.

Even in my dreams since then, I am unable to take control. I can't change my actions and am forced to observe them with the full realisation of what is happening, of what will happen next.

In my waking daydreams, I see myself run to get help. Often there is someone not too far away, as there must have been on that hot mid-summer day in July 1988. I shout for help and drag the hands of a kind middle-aged couple to where my father is. The man is strong and doesn't hesitate to dive in and drag my father back to safety while the woman wraps her arms around me, comforting me. Sometimes there is CPR, sometimes my father simply splutters and coughs onto the sand and doesn't need any help to breathe. Then my mother appears. She screams his name and frantically pulls him into a hug and kisses him, thankful he is OK.

In reality, that is not what happened.

An ambling elderly man with his two grandchildren walked by and saw my father's body being jostled around by the waves like a weighted balloon. He turned his head this way and that shouting for help. I don't know whether it was because there was no one else around, or he just felt so compelled to do something that he couldn't wait, but he ran straight into the waves himself. Moments later he dragged my father onto the stability of the sand and I think he knew immediately it was too late. Looking back, that man must have been in his eighties. Yet, he still somehow found the strength to burst into action and pull a well-built, six-foot-two man to safety. I still wonder if I had forced myself to take such action, whether I could have found the strength out of nowhere too. Don't people say that they are suddenly endowed with such vigour in those situations? Maybe I was supposed to? Maybe that was why things happened as they did, and I was forced to be the only witness? That could have been my moment to be a hero...

But I did nothing. If it was some kind of test, I failed.

I just stood there. A pathetic five-year-old crying hysterically for her Daddy and yet being so useless to him at the same time.

My mother appeared as the man was pulling him from the water, limp and pale apart from the blue around his mouth. She screamed his name, introducing me to an electric jolt of terror that I would relive in my nightmares to this day. There was such a primal note in the noise she made that caused the hairs on my scalp to lift. It hardly even sounded like her voice, it was like she was using a different part of her throat to make the sound – the guttural part that is usually reserved for women in childbirth.

I had to clap my hands over my ears to block it out. I remember doing that clearly. That was a mistake, because then all I could hear was the chorus of the sea rushing in my ears, just like when Daddy lifted a shell earlier in the day and told me that was what the sound was. Not that it seemed like the same day when he told me that, but it must have been.

When I let my hands drop, I could hear my sister shrieking. 'She was just standing there! Mummy – why was she just standing there doing nothing!?'

I wanted to shout and correct her. I *wasn't* simply doing nothing. I was willing with all my might for him to get back up again, to re-appear and be all right, for someone to come and help him... someone... anyone... anything to make him get back up again.

But again, I just stood there and remained silent. I'll never forget the way my mother looked at me then. She seemed to tower above me, looking at me like she couldn't believe I could do something so terrible – like I had pushed him into the water and held him down myself. Her eyes were full of tears and there was such anger and hatred in her face that I was sure I was about to get a smack. I even braced myself for it, but then she turned away.

I caught her looking at me like that several times for years afterwards. That was all she would do, just look at me and never say anything. She only spoke to me after that day when she had to, even as an adult. Especially as an adult.

It wasn't just because she had shut down her feelings and become emotionally withdrawn or anything like that either. She still had love for my sister, showering her with praise and gifts just as she had before – even more so in fact – now that she wasn't wasting her love on me.

It probably didn't help that Amy was always my mother's favourite anyway. They were both girly-girls and I was born a tom-boy. They had always liked doing the same things. Just as I had always liked being Daddy's favourite, spending hours in the garden looking for insects and going fishing together, just the two of us. It is what makes the whole thing so ironic, that it was my fault. He was gone because of me. Mother always resented me for taking him away from her, for killing him.

Going back to school it seemed strange that the other children could engage themselves in such trivial games. I was suddenly much older.

Just two-months before, I was one of them, part of the group, joining in without a care in the world. From the position I regularly took up underneath a withered tree on the edge of the stone playground, I could clearly see they were just the same as ever, indulging themselves in thoughtless activities.

But I was not the same. I was something different. Dirty. Contaminated. A murderer.

A little girl that took a devoted husband and father away from a family couldn't possibly know how to engage in a mindless game of tag and pretend nothing had happened.

The other children sensed it too. Any friends I'd had before the holidays made a beeline towards me at first like nothing was wrong, but one by one they gradually drifted away.

The same thing happened in secondary school. On the outside, I must have looked like everyone else. Whatever it was that I had done before, whatever it was that had made me 'normal' had gone. I don't know what it was, even now looking back, but it was absent and eventually, the others stopped trying to talk to me. They must have just thought I was a broken child, probably from a broken home.

The truth was that it was broken, just not exactly in the way that they might have imagined. It was all because of me. And I, myself, was more broken than anyone could have expected.

33

Andrew must think I'm mad. I can't believe he is even still talking to me after he saw me going to pieces last night. I haven't been like that in front of anyone before, not even in all the time I was with *him*. Only when I have been alone, have I openly let the tears flow.

Of course, I had the nightmares when I was with *him*, but he used to roll over and mutter into his pillow about being woken up and how I should "get over it". I used to turn over and face the other way, biting into my pillow and sobbing myself back to sleep.

Andrew did a good job of consoling me. We lay together for a long time and he held me with my head on his shoulder as he stroked my back. I found it helped to calm me down and I managed to fall back to sleep after a while.

He did ask me what I dreamed about though.

I told him I suffer from bad nightmares, but I couldn't describe what they contained. Like with Julia, I didn't divulge the content of the dream, or the fact that I have the same one constantly. I wanted to tell Andrew the truth so badly it scared me. I felt so close to him last night that the lies I am carrying around with me felt like a barrier, a shield stopping me from connecting to him completely.

What stopped me from telling the truth was the thought that I wouldn't know where to stop. Do I tell him everything? If I told him about my childhood, would I then tell Andrew about *him*? Would the story of my life justify remaining in such an unhealthy relationship for so long? Would Andrew understand why I have done what I have done? Somehow I'm sceptical.

He really wanted us to have lunch together today, but I told him I have to shut the gallery early because I have a dental appointment. I couldn't tell him about my therapy sessions. Having violent nightmares is one thing, admitting you see a therapist is another. I don't want him to think I'm completely touched in the head.

*

Julia is a little late seeing me in. When she opens the door, a teenage girl with bleached-black hair and matching nails storms out, leaving her red-faced mother to trail embarrassedly out after her.

When I see the girl, I can't help but be reminded of myself.

I wonder what their story is. I know it can't be very much the same as mine. It wouldn't have occurred to my mother to have taken me to therapy, she always said it was her that needed it, not me. In her mind, she was the victim.

She left me pretty much to my own devices after that summer. Gave up on me. She probably barely even noticed when I left to move in with Richard in Cornwall.

For years afterwards, I thought that perhaps things could have been different if I tried perhaps talking to my mother, tried to explain to her that it wasn't my fault.

I know now that there wouldn't have been any point though. I was in my mid-twenties before I realised exactly why my mother had acted the way she did. I came across an article online that talked about

Narcissistic Personality Disorder and I immediately recognised her in the list of traits; she had a constant demand to be the centre of attention, relentlessly favoured my sister over me, belittled me constantly, made me feel worthless, a waste of space. She was always unaware that I had feelings. Whenever something happened, it was always my fault and my mother was the victim. It was always about her.

She was the protagonist in our tragic family story. She never really thought about other people. That is why she could so easily blame me without considering that I was just a child; too weak and too stupid to have done anything to save my father. So maybe I shouldn't continue to blame her. She might not have been able to help it.

Julia looks over my anxiety journal. Her eyes seem to linger on the centre of the book and she runs her fingers down it. For a few moments I worry that she will ask about the missing pages, but she doesn't.

'I see you've had quite a few nightmares this past week, Harriet,' Julia notes, her soft voice seemingly expressing deep concern. 'Can you tell me what you were dreaming about? This wouldn't happen to be a recurring theme, would it?

The tone of her voice instantly relaxes me, but my nerves quickly tingle and the tension immediately spreads through to my stomach by the thought of discussing my nightmares.

I can't do it. I can't spill the secrets I have been carrying with me my whole life. I've never even come close to discussing it with anyone. Even last night when Andrew tried to get me to open up, I couldn't do it.

If I couldn't share the information with him, then I certainly can't do it with Julia. She is a relative stranger to me. This is only her job, she doesn't really care. I can imagine she would jot down the juicy details in her notebook and she would keep them to herself for a while; patient confidentiality and all that.

But then I picture her at a psychology conference or something in the future, catching up with her old colleagues and peers from Uni. I can see her discussing the case of a patient she had once: the little girl that killed her father. 'Well, now she is crippled by anxiety,' she says to her eager listeners. 'Now she can't get through the day without falling apart in some way.' Some of them nod and shake their heads, listening raptly. Some of them have even heard the story. It was all over the newspapers at the time, both in Torquay and in London. I think it might have even been national news, but I'm not sure; I have never had the courage to look it up.

From a journalist's perspective, it was solid gold. One of those tragic stories that people apparently love to devour – fine to read about, absorbing an overview of the most horrific details is a wonderful way to pass a few minutes, just as long as it never happens to them.

It was such a stupid accident. There wasn't a freak wave or a rogue, poisonous creature, or the sea rushing in before we noticed and cutting us off on a sandbank. It was just my father's body giving up on him, betraying him at a bad moment. No one even knew he had a heart problem before that day.

If we had delayed going into the water by a few minutes, then he would have been fine. If we had spent longer at the restaurant at lunch, then everything would have worked out all right, he would have collapsed with plenty of people around, my mother included. If my sister hadn't wanted an ice cream and stayed behind

232

with my mother. If, if, if – the list goes on.

My sleepless hours are tortured with the thoughts of what could have been done differently to produce a happier outcome. Maybe in a parallel universe where we did follow another path, I now wouldn't have to endure a wave of shame and dread every time I see or hear about the sea.

I shake my head. 'I don't think the subject of the dream matters that much,' I say to a sceptical Julia. 'The most useful thing would be to find a way to stop the anxiety. I tried mindfulness, but it's just so hard to do when I can't even breathe properly.'

She surveys me for a few moments, biting the end of her pen. 'I understand, Harriet,' she says softly. She adjusts her books and switches her crossed legs over. 'But based on our sessions together, I think perhaps there is a root cause that all your anxiety stems from. The best course of action is to focus on setting up a treatment plan now that we have a clear fix on your diagnosis.'

'Diagnosis? I don't understand? I already know that I get panic attacks that are caused by an anxiety disorder.' Using the term 'anxiety disorder' must make me sound a little more knowledgeable. I am talking her language. It shows Julia that I have done my research. I know what I am talking about, Dr. Google told me.

'Yes, that is true, Harriet. But I don't think yours to be a simple case of things getting on top of you. I think there is more at play here–'

Panic fills me, even as I sit on my comfortable sofa amongst the colourful scatter cushions in my safe and homely therapy room. Is Julia about to label me with some other mental illness too?

That is not what I came here for. Does she think me

schizophrenic? Or is she going to declare me as having a personality disorder? She wouldn't be the first. Not that my mother was ever qualified to make such assumptions.

'–I don't believe you are suffering from the same type of anxiety as some of my other patients who simply feel the build-up of pressure from everyday stresses and worries. It is my belief, Harriet, that you are suffering from Post Traumatic Stress Disorder. That can develop in response to a single event–'

Alarm bells go off inside my head. I realise I can't do it; I can't tell her the truth. I want to run for the door. I'm not ready to go through this – I never will be.

'–Or can arise as the result of prolonged exposure to something traumatic. So you see, your anxiety disorder has most likely developed from living with PTSD for so long without getting help.'

I burst into tears. I actually burst out into sobs so quickly it startles me. It happens so suddenly I can't do a thing to hide it. I feel like Julia has unblocked something. Perhaps this is a psychological trick she had up her sleeve. Or maybe it is just the pressure of being in a psychiatrist's office – I thought I could deal with it and I can't.

Julia hands me a box of tissues from her desk. I can see through blurred eyes that she has multiple boxes on her desk. Perhaps for other people who crumbled under the strain.

Now I am one of them.

My sobbing subsides enough for Julia to continue. 'From what you have told me,' Julia goes on, delicately, 'You suffer from frequent nightmares. In my experience, that usually means that people are dreaming of the same or very similar things. Would you say that is true, Harriet?'

I wish she would stop calling me 'Harriet'.

I can't stop crying enough to say anything audible, so I nod my head. Why can't I stop crying? I need to pull myself together.

Julia doesn't look phased, she must have seen this many times before. At least she thinks she has, she doesn't quite know the full story. I just pray that I can regain enough composure so everything doesn't all come spilling out of me; the years of deceit; years of poisonous lies.

Dangerous lies.

Illegal lies.

My sobs subside and I determinedly wipe my eyes with a clump of tissues, disregarding my carefully applied make-up totally. I know that ship has sailed; I can feel the hot trails running down my cheeks and I know they are watery-black.

Julia's voice floats across the room to me. 'Do you think you could tell me what you dream about, Harriet?'

I *really* wish she would stop calling me 'Harriet'. It is not even my name – I stole it from a woman in my old building who lived across the hall from me – just like I stole the money to set up Stony Studios.

My name is Sophie, and I am not just a little girl who killed her father – I am an identity thief.

34

Harriet Harper was one of the easiest marks I've had. She was a mess – she had the perfect life, but she didn't even notice, she was so self-absorbed. She had a great life with her husband Dan. He really loved her, you could tell.

I saw her come into the building the week before I left. She'd had some silly accident and Dan was virtually falling over himself to help her into their flat. Not that she cared, she seemed to take it for granted. She even seemed to resent him for helping her, with his arm wrapped tightly around her, supporting her. She just scarpered as soon as she saw me, didn't even say 'Hello.' I can't say I wasn't a little hurt by that little snub.

Dan stuck around in the hallway and explained what had happened. He was always very friendly and polite, quite a charmer actually. Apparently, she had caught her lip on the edge of their car door. Dan had immediately sprung into action and applied pressure to it to stop the bleeding. It was lucky he was there really.

Harriet was more than just a mark to me though. Despite her aloofness, I admired her. I actually wanted to be her. In particular, I adored her style. Whenever she was out with Dan, she always wore such stylish clothes. Usually always topped with a blazer jacket with her hair swept up into a neat twist, looking immaculate, glamorous even.

She dressed much more casually when Dan wasn't around, always taking the opportunity to go make-up free and adorned in baggy clothes when she was alone.

It was like she was sticking two fingers up to the image-obsessed world and saying 'I don't care'. I loved that about her; I thought she was really cool; it told me she had an inner rebel like me, but she had the confidence to show it more than I.

One day she was careless enough to throw out some of her old clothes in one of those charity collection bags. I say 'old', but they weren't really. Some things, like her navy blazer jacket, looked like they had hardly even been worn – and she was just throwing it out.

She was so ungrateful for the life she had; dismissive of a devoted husband who loved her, supported her and took care of her. When he wasn't working he went with her everywhere, always made sure she rarely had to go out alone like I did. Not that I wanted to go out with *him* much anyway, especially towards the end.

Late one night, I saw her leaving with a single suitcase. I had heard her and Dan arguing earlier in the evening when I was cooking dinner; by 'cooking', I mean I was basically defrosting a frozen pizza – that was all *he* ever wanted to eat.

I saw Dan a few days later and he confirmed my suspicions. Not directly, of course. He told me Harriet had gone to stay with her mother for a while. That was clearly code for 'she has left me'. He didn't need to spell it out. He was putting on a brave face, but he was clearly mortified that he had been dumped so unceremoniously after years of marriage.

So that was it. She just walked out and left him in the middle of the night, couldn't even wait until morning. Dan was the perfect husband – polite, charming, good looking with a good job and Harriet just walked away and left him.

It surprised me how much that struck me.

I thought if she could just walk away from the perfect man, then what the hell was I doing staying with *him*?

I knew that night I had to leave. *This is my moment*, I thought. A fresh start suddenly seemed not only possible, but a great idea. I suddenly had the confidence to do it. If Harriet could just trash her blessed marriage, then I certainly could do away with *him*.

Follow in her footsteps.

That wasn't the only reason I left though. If Harriet had left the building for good, then it would look strange if post with her name on was still being delivered six-months or a year down the line. That was if Dan saw it though – it was my job to get to the postbox before anyone else in the building. The postbox was communal, it was like the landlord wanted people to take the mail of others as if it was designed that way on purpose. It was just so easy. No rummaging through postboxes at the end of long countryside driveways and no pretending to just be stepping out of the gate of a property just to casually intercept the postman.

It was simple, just as long as I got to the post on time. I always did, except for one day in the week before I left where I missed the post. The postman must have arrived when I nipped to the toilet briefly.

It was stupid; I should have checked, even if I had only spent less than two minutes in the bathroom. Especially since *he* was expecting a statement from one of the accounts in Dan's name.

It has now been over eighteen-months since I left Tennison Road; I know I should be able to even think *his* name – my darling, ex-other-half – Nick.

He was the biggest mistake of my life. If only I had

never met him, things could have been so different. I know I wouldn't be deliriously happy, but he was just the cherry on top of my already messed-up life.

I met Nick when I was at Uni. One night, towards the end of our first year, I went to a house-party with a girl on my course. Nick was one of her elder brother's friends and seemed to make a sort of beeline for me.

I can't say it was love at first sight, not for me anyway. He didn't exactly stand out from the crowd with his mousy brown hair and scrawny physique. I hadn't even noticed him at all until he introduced himself. But I guess that is what allowed him so much success, the fact that he was so ordinary he didn't stand out one bit.

We started dating from that night on. He seemed keen on me; he took an interest back then. Other than my brief escapade in Cornwall, he was the only other boyfriend I'd had.

He always had money to spend, taking us out to nice restaurants and on weekends away. I couldn't figure out how he was financing it all at first since he didn't have a job. At the time, I just assumed his parents were supporting him and didn't question it too much. I only discovered the truth after we'd moved in together.

That time in my life is another where I wished I could go back and move in a different direction. I fantasise about being able to travel back and take control of the nineteen-year-old me. I want to shout at myself and steer the young and stupid version of Sophie away from the bad path she is about to take.

But I can't. The damage has been done.

Nick spent years living from the profits of his illicit business. I suppose I was already an accessory just because I lived with him. Although I was the one that found a stable income. I went out and got a real job while Nick continued to do what he did. The truth was, I stayed because I thought I loved him; I thought I could change him. I stuck with him, thinking eventually he would find a career of his own.

Nick's money was inconsistent. Some years I think he would have been better off actually using his business-studies degree and working full-time in a proper job. Not that the thought would have occurred to him.

If he was smart, then he wouldn't have been doing something like that to start with. But then what does that make me, for staying with him for so long and eventually participating in it all?

A year before we moved to Tennison Road, I lost my steady job as an administrator for a small building firm. The business folded and was forced to shut down. They didn't even pay me for the last month, which left me in a tricky situation. That was when it happened – I got involved with Nick's shady dealings, more than just being a knowing bystander and hoping he would stop.

The first time, I assumed the identity of a woman that resided in a large, secluded house in Addington, not a million miles from where we lived. The place was so large and concealed that the postbox at the end of the driveway was nowhere near visible from any of the windows.

I almost chickened out when it came to actually raiding the box, but Nick swooped in and gathered the contents smoothly. At that point, I realised he had a dog lead swinging from his wrist. He had thought of everything; if anyone saw us, it would have looked like we were simply some dog-walkers out for a countryside-stroll and our dog had scampered off ahead somewhere.

Nick told me it was a great haul; a gas bill and an early fortieth-birthday card. The sender of the card had helpfully written '*not to be opened until 29th April*' upon the envelope; the card and envelope had unwittingly given us the full name and date of birth of the lady of the house. The utility bill too was crucial as proof of identity for opening accounts and gaining documents.

That was how it started for me, from there I got drawn in deeper, snatching more identities unbeknownst to their owners and always with Nick at my side, encouraging me, egging me on. 'Just one more,' he would say. 'Please Soph, just one more time. Don't let us down – we *really* need the money.'

I felt trapped and I didn't know how to stop. For the longest time, I was convinced I needed him. To rent in London definitely required more than one income. I know now I should have moved somewhere else, found another job, gone it alone. Looking back, it is easy to say what I should have done. The trouble was, I was weak and I'd already fallen down financially once when living alone. I was scared of it happening again.

I heard once that elephants kept in captivity are trained from an early age not to try to escape. If they are chained to a heavy stake as infants and are unable to move, they believe they can't break free. So when they grow bigger, they can be attached to so little as a cocktail stick and they don't even try to break away because they already believe they can't.

I was like those elephants – stuck in such a rut I thought I could never break free. I would probably have stayed there too, had Harriet not shown me how easy it was to walk away. The way she just slipped away from Dan shook me and I was inspired by her bravery.

241

I stuck with Harriet's identity because I admired her so much. Even though we had hardly shared more than a 'Hello,' I really felt a connection with her. I had never seen the other people whose names and dates of birth I had assumed, not on a daily basis like with her.

Not only that, but Nick would never suspect that I would keep Harriet's name, never in a million years. So he would have no way of finding me, not that I expect him to try, but if he ever got caught I wouldn't put it past him not to drag me down with him. He has always been the petty and spiteful sort.

When he came back to an empty flat that day he probably just assumed I'd gone straight. He would never think that Harriet Harper would start a new life in another part of the country, on her own, without him.

I feel tugs of guilt all the time for taking money in Harriet's name. It prickles me at night when I can't sleep; in the day when I feel anxious and I don't have the energy to block out negative thoughts. However, I don't think she would even notice what has happened; she should be able to live mostly unaffected.

Harriet and Dan never had financial woes. They were never short of money and were always making big purchases. Their credit scores were fine. Well, they were back then anyway. I have been paying back the loan for starting the gallery religiously – I've put it first. I want to do things right this time, if not entirely legitimately. The last thing I want is to mess up Harriet's life, or draw attention to myself.

As for Nick, well, I think he may have exhausted Dan's credit by now and moved on long ago. There is no way to tell; I haven't seen him in years, not since I left. I walked out Harriet style – I packed light, just a suitcase and a holdall and didn't even say goodbye.

All in all, I took less than Harriet and Dan paid for the brand new Mercedes they bought after we moved in.

The real Harriet should be fine, wherever she is. Oblivious to who I am.

I wasn't ever greedy like Nick, so Harriet will never find out what I have done.

I know how to be careful. I know how to avoid getting caught. The plan was to hide in plain sight, pretend to be someone else forever. Keep my head down, lie low.

But I'm involved now. I've made friends – enemies. I'm known to the community. People know me as Harriet Harper.

My heart hammers erratically and I feel instantly dizzy. Back home inside my flat, I press my back against the hallway wall and slide down it.

I've got a boyfriend – that was never supposed to happen.

I've become involved; I'm so well established here. A real business revolves around me, a real life.

I don't want to admit it to myself too, but *I've fallen in love*.

But none of it is real. Andrew is dating someone fake. I've told him so many lies, he is smitten with a character I've created, not me. He doesn't even know my real birthday...

I feel sick. I roughly pull my blazer – no, *Harriet's* blazer – off and throw it aside. The cold sweat covering my skin all over makes me shiver through my thin blouse. I wrap my arms around my knees and curl up, trying to give myself some comfort, but sitting here alone there isn't any to be had.

What have I done?

I'm committed. Stuck. Trapped.

I don't know what I am going to do.

I like the person I've become as Harriet, but she isn't real. I've made such a mess of things. I can't run, not again. It's too late to start over now. By my age, I should be established for real. I should be thinking of marriage, I should be planning a pregnancy or already raising children, not dreaming up a new place to hide.

I'm tired of hiding – I'm sick of it.

I'm sick of Sophie. I wish I could just scrub her out for good and never have to see her again.

I want her gone forever.

35

I can't deal with anything at the moment. Facing even the most basic things feels like a huge task. I'm so glad, now more than ever, that I only have the one hidden mirror. I wouldn't be able to risk catching sight of Sophie. I just cannot handle the rush of dread and loathing I would experience. There would be no bracing myself for it; I just don't have the strength to put up the usual front to stop the image of her crushing me.

I can't escape her though. No matter how hard I try, she lives and breathes in me. She is in my blood, rooted to the core of my mind.

I may have taken another woman's name, her clothes, her style, her very identity, but I know I can never really leave myself behind.

If I were to see myself in the mirror now. I look too much like me without make-up on. All I would see is Sophie looking back, the little girl who killed her father. I would hear her mother screaming at her for taking away her husband; for killing him. The school counsellor told me it wasn't true, but I knew he was lying. His reassurances and look of concern were too overplayed to be real.

It is now Friday. After my appointment with Julia on Tuesday I came home to my flat and have stayed there since. I was thankful to Andrew for bringing with him an extra bottle of wine when we last had dinner together. I sank myself into glass after glass and disappeared into oblivion for a while on Tuesday evening; it got me through the night at least.

Wednesday was a little more tricky. I didn't open the gallery at all. I just stayed up here and hid. It was a hard day because I didn't have any way of distracting myself from all my fears and doubts. Inevitably, I fell prey to a major panic attack; I even had a few aftershocks too.

Thursday was exactly the same, except the tone of Andrew's texts got a little more concerned. I sent a single response to all of his messages; I told him that I have a stomach bug and he should avoid visiting me. His reply was immediate:

Oh you poor thing, you should have said sooner! I hope you didn't get ill from anything I brought you – I'm fine though, so you can't have. Let me come over and look after you. I can take the rest of the day off here, no one will miss me in the office this afternoon xxXxx

I quickly texted back, telling him it was very contagious and that he shouldn't see me. There was a ten-minute pause before his next text.

Are you really ill? This isn't because of what happened on Monday night, is it? Everyone has nightmares, Harriet. You can talk to me about it if you want xxXxx

I know I need to do something about the Andrew situation, but I just can't. There would be questions I just can't answer. Not just that, but I don't want the agony of letting him go. Right now it is far easier to hide.

Today I have broken the monotony slightly. On my way out of Julia's office on Tuesday I made an

246

appointment for today; Julia had wanted me to start cognitive behavioural therapy for my PTSD. I already knew I had no intention of keeping it however, and today I plan to cancel it.

I have fallen foul of the twenty-four-hour cancellation policy, so I will still be charged for the session, but I don't care. It is worth every penny for Julia to not find out what is really wrong with me.

There is *no way* I am stepping foot in her office again. I came so close to telling Julia the truth, not just about my father, but telling her everything, finally letting it all go. *So close.* The therapy room was so safe and warm, and Julia's voice so comforting that I could almost feel the words bubbling up inside me.

That was so dangerous, it makes me sweat just thinking about it.

I am forced to use the gallery landline to make the call to Julia's secretary since my phone battery is completely dead – so dead I can't even make a call while it is charging. Last night I stayed up until the early hours, browsing the internet, following whims and leads I should leave well enough alone. I ended up looking up people from my past on Facebook. I searched for my mother, my sister and Nick.

At one point, I even tried to look for Richard, my Cornwall fling; I shouldn't have gone down that road.

Of all the people I used to know, my sister was the only one I managed to find. I set up a fake Facebook profile in a random name so I could access hers. She would never guess it was me – I didn't even upload a photo. On her timeline, she has various pictures of her and her perfect family. I follow lead after lead and somehow end up on her husband's LinkedIn profile. His name is Gary; *I knew it was something like that.*

Luckily my phone battery died before I could read every feedback comment in his and Amy's shared eBay account.

I leave my phone on charge and go downstairs into the gallery.

I cancel the appointment and put the phone back down on the counter, but I jump out of my skin when I see a figure approaching the gallery door. The shutters are down on the windows, but I had to roll up the one on the front door to get in. The 'Closed' sign is facing outwards, so they should get the idea, but the figure of a woman steps right up to look in through the door.

I shrink against the wall behind the counter, hoping to remain invisible. It is then that I recognise the woman – it is Mrs. Hopkins.

She puts her face so close to the glass I see her breath mist up the surface. She cups her hands around her face and presses closer, peering in. I think it is sufficiently dark in here that she shouldn't see me.

After a couple of minutes that seem like much longer, she turns around and walks away again.

I let go of a breath I didn't realise I was holding. I'd forgotten about her and the debacle of the missing painting. As if I need anything else to worry about.

36

My stomach growls with hunger, but I have virtually run out of food. I haven't done a proper shop for ages and this morning I ate the last bit of stale bread; I toasted it in an attempt to counteract the mould. My refrigerator is empty, apart from some blackening lettuce and half a jar of marmalade.

It is Saturday now and I still have not left the house. Downstairs, the gallery remains still, dark and untouched. I know I need to pull myself together for the sake of the business.

This morning, I have dressed on three separate occasions ready to go and start the working day, but have frozen each time. I can't apply my make-up because I can't stand to catch a glimpse of myself in the mirror. I don't want to run the risk of seeing so much as a cheekbone of mine or a regrowing root of Sophie-coloured hair.

I know I should do something constructive. I try to paint. I need to redo the piece for Mrs. Hopkins, since I can't find the original. The first painting took so much work and energy, I feel like a colossal task sits before me to recreate it and I know it will not be the same, even if I do.

I try several times to sit at my easel and start working on a blank canvas, but I don't get any further than getting all my paints ready and setting everything up. I can't seem to find the energy to get started.

By evening, I am more determined. The sky outside has dulled to a dark grey by now and the room is dark and gloomy. I flick on my lamp and pick up my paintbrush on my third attempt.

I try practising mindfulness to block out all the horrible thoughts that make my insides squirm. Instead of looking at the blank, white canvas in front of me I close my eyes. Gripping my paintbrush tightly, I feel the rough wooden texture of the handle with my thumb. The sound of the bustling, weekend traffic on the road outside reaches my ears, as does the gentle pattering of rain against the window. The chemical smell of turpentine and acrylic paints surrounds me, filling my senses.

I hear a crash outside.

My eyes snap open and I look through the open studio door. What the hell was that noise? It was close – I'm sure it came from the yard. I rest my paintbrush on my easel and creep out into the dark hallway to listen.

Silence.

Maybe I imagined it, or it was the takeaway next door.

I hear scraping and a strange shuffling sound.

A rush of panic flows through me when I remember the shuffling noise I heard when someone was trying to force their way through the back door. However, this time the sound is too far away to be just the other side of the door, but it isn't much farther.

It is definitely coming from the yard.

I'm scared – I don't know what to do. I shift my weight back and forth from one foot to the other and wring my hands. Calling the police isn't really an option, and besides, by the time they arrived the person would probably be gone.

I creep unnecessarily quietly into the bedroom – the intruder wouldn't be able to hear me from outside – and pull back the nets to look out the window. The yard itself isn't visible from this angle – but I register that the gate is wide open. Even standing on my tiptoes the bedroom window is so high I can barely even see the yard wall. It doesn't help that it is a foggy, grey day with drizzling rain falling, spattering the window.

I run into my studio and grab my little painting stool, setting it down in the bedroom and stepping onto it to look outside.

More of the yard comes into sight now, just the bottom half nearest the alley-side wall, but it is better than before. I can get more of an idea of what is going on.

It is far worse than I thought.

In the scrap of yard I can see, rubbish is strewn everywhere – old tubes of paint, silver takeaway containers, used tampons, tissues and crisp packets are tossed all over the place. Someone is going through my bin. Who would do such a thing?

Debbie, I think. *This must be Debbie's doing.* She must have seen me break into her yard, and this is her petty idea of revenge. She must think that because the gallery has been shut for days I am not here. Perhaps she thinks I have gone away on holiday?

Well, she is about to get the shock of her life – I am not going to stand for this.

I forget all about not wanting to face anyone. Rage takes over and all I can think of is telling Debbie what I think of her. Snatching up my keys from the kitchen, I race to the back door, unlocking it as quickly as I can.

It occurs to me that I am making way too much noise, but I want to get to Debbie before she has the chance to get away – I want to catch her right in the act.

I slide across the bolts and the chain, flip on the hallway light and slip quickly outside onto the concrete steps. The light from the doorway illuminates a rough rectangle of rain in front of me and for a second I can't see beyond it. I hear heavy, scuffling footsteps and then the gate bangs with great force.

Frantically, I blink and my eyes lock onto a dark figure rapidly bombing out of sight as they fade into the gloom of the alley.

37

I stand rooted to the top of the steps in shock. I had been so sure that I was about to come face to face with Debbie, but I was mistaken. The figure I just saw was definitely a man. The heavy footsteps and broad build have left me in no doubt that they didn't belong to a woman.

I'm bewildered. I look over the railings at the mess that covers the ground below. There is literally rubbish everywhere – like someone has taken my wheelie bin and tipped the contents out, creating a tremendous mess.

A chill runs down my spine. Out here I feel exposed and unsafe. The misty rain dampens my hair. I hurry back inside and slide across every bolt and every lock securely.

In the hall again I stop, deep in thought.

I had thought I was safe here. Why has someone made a deliberate effort to get into my yard? Who the hell was it? And why were they going through my rubbish? Does someone suspect I am not who I say I am?

I'm unnerved, but at the same time, something is tugging at the back of my mind. Somehow this all has overtones of Debbie. It can't just be a coincidence that someone has gone through my bin the way I did behind Minerva Interiors less than a week ago. She must be behind it somehow, perhaps even putting one of her friends up to it or something.

A memory rushes to the forefront of my mind and I suddenly realise what was nagging at me – I saw

Debbie talking to a scruffy-looking man not that long ago. Now that I force myself to picture him, the more it seems to fit and I realise he could be the same figure I saw just now.

I remember now, she was pointing him in my direction – towards the gallery. At the time, I thought she could have been shooing him away, but now I realise she wasn't – *she was giving him instructions.*

Debbie thinks she is so smart, hiring a tramp to do her dirty work for her. I wonder if he was the same person who tried to break into the flat. *I bet he was.* That was the day after I argued with Debbie and Sally. *Now everything makes sense.* The pair might even be in it together, gone halves. Not that it would cost them much. By the look of the vagrant man, I would say he would have done anything for a sandwich.

The difference is that I had good reason to search the bins belonging to Minerva Interiors, and I did not leave colossal disarray behind. This has just been done to spite me. Why else would someone throw my rubbish everywhere?

How dare Debbie do this to me.

She needs to mind her own business. She is going to leave me alone and that starts now.

I look at the time on the microwave – it is coming up to five-thirty. Debbie will be shutting the shop any minute now. I rush through to the hallway and am at the top of the stairs with my hand on the bannister when I remember that it is Saturday. I pause. Debbie has Saturdays off.

I go back through to the lounge and look out the window. Debbie's little purple car is parked in the street, she must be either in the shop or in her flat.

That is good enough for me.

I hurry across the road towards the front door of Debbie's flat. On the way, the door of Minerva Interiors opens and a woman I often see behind the counter on a Saturday strolls out. I note that she saunters down the street without locking up, meaning that someone else is doing it for her.

I glance in through the window and see Debbie busy tilling up for the day.

I pull open the door and stride in.

My eyes take a moment to adjust. There are so many drapes and curtains at the windows, Minerva Interiors seems dark, even in contrast to the grey gloom of this afternoon. The shop is lit only with artificial lights; downlights and the various light fittings and lamps for sale. In any other environment, it would be cosy; in Debbie's shop, it seems only fake and dull.

'We are closed!' Debbie calls out flatly without looking up.

'I don't want to buy anything,' I spit coldly.

Her head snaps up at the sound of my voice, and she appraises me like she usually does, as though she is a lion eyeing up its next meal.

'What the hell did you think you were doing?' I demand, eyeing her with similar dislike. I don't skirt around the point of my visit. There isn't any point. She must know why I am here.

'What are you talking about now? Are you here to accuse me of something else this time, Harriet?'

'I don't remember being on first name terms with you – and don't play games! You know what you have done. Why did you have someone go through my rubbish?'

She does a good job of looking surprised, but her face quickly twists into pure hate. 'Gone through your rubbish, eh? Nobody in their right mind would go through someone else's bin. Although, having said that, I have seen a bit of that about recently.' Her eyes shine with malice.

'I wouldn't have had to go through your bins if you hadn't stolen from me!'

'I have no idea what you are talking about. You want to be careful who you go shouting at, especially when you go accusing people of things! Coming over here all the time, shouting at me and Sally. Don't you know you're not supposed to be over here?' She suddenly adopts a patronising tone, as though I am stupid and she is spelling something simple out for me. 'Your shop is on the *other* side of the road,' she explains. 'Why don't you stay there, eh?'

'I'm well aware of where my shop is, thanks. And don't you dare tell me what I should and shouldn't do!'

She bristles like she has been stung. 'You've got no right coming into my shop and shouting at me. I haven't done anything wrong!'

'Like hell, you haven't! It's not like you have committed theft and criminal damage, or anything, is it?'

My heart pounds irregularly. The fog of dread in my chest intensifies, feeling as though I have missed a step on the stairs, but it doesn't go away. Why am I here in this situation again? In someone else's shop, shouting at them, when all I want to do is find a quiet corner and hide until I feel nothing.

Debbie glares back at me. 'I'm *barring* you! Yes, that's right! I'll have words with Sally too and make sure she does the same. And if you ever dare to set foot in my shop again – I will call the police!'

I'm quite breathless now and speaking is really difficult. Each word costs so much effort. 'You don't need to ban me – I never want to set foot in your shop again. I'd like to never have to speak to *you* a-again – but you keep insisting on m-meddling in my private business!'

This is bad. I haven't stuttered since I was fifteen.

Debbie scoffs. 'Do you think you're so important that I care what you do? You really do think a lot of yourself, don't you Harriet? Just because you think you can paint, doesn't make you any better than us *ordinary folk*!'

'I don't think I'm better than anyone. Although I'm nowhere near as pathetic as you. You won't even admit that you stole the painting when you were in the gallery. I know you did it, Debbie!'

She looks at me and a twisted smile appears on her face. '*Prove it*,' she hisses.

'You evil cow,' I whisper breathlessly. 'I spent ages on that piece. What did you do with it?' I know I shouldn't let my guard slip, but I just want to know where it went so badly. It is driving me mad. Even if she has destroyed it, I want to know; I need some closure.

She pauses, eyeing me with a malevolent grimace. It is clear she couldn't be enjoying torturing me more. 'Not that I know what "piece" you are talking about, but I would suggest giving up hope of ever finding whatever it is you are looking for. Lost things have a way of disappearing for good, you know.'

I can hardly breathe now. White sparks move in front of my eyes and I feel the world twist and give me a threatening jolt like I am about to collapse.

My arm reaches out for something to hold onto to steady myself, but I have the familiar feeling of it colliding with something. I hear a thud and a dull

257

smash. Even through the fog of panic that surrounds my head, I can make out the leafy top of a golden pineapple surrounded by other broken pieces on the floor.

'I'm s-sorry,' I manage to say, but Debbie is shouting at me and I can only make out the words 'now', 'criminal' and 'damage'.

I need to get out of here. My body needs oxygen. My heart needs to stop racing or I think I might actually die.

38

I step out into the rain again and take a deep breath. The cool water on my face is refreshing, steadying. It is far less claustrophobic out here. Instead of running straight back into my hidey-hole of a flat I set of briskly intending to go for a walk around the block. I need to clear my head.

It is nice to be outside after being cooped up for days. I walk quickly away from the street, but once I round the corner I slow down again. A block away, I pass a dog-grooming shop and reach the corner where there is a convenience store.

Really I could do with some chocolate, but I don't have my purse with me. I don't even have my phone. Common sense tells me I should probably turn back, but I don't want to lock myself up in the tiny little flat just yet. Nor do I want to see the gallery, the business I have worked so hard to build up, shut and abandoned-looking. My feet carry me on down the main road and onto a street lined with new-build breeze-block houses that have already run shabby with dark streaks running down the paintwork.

It has been years since I yelled at anyone like I just did with Debbie. Of course, Nick and I argued, but I hardly had the energy to participate properly. I just let his words roll over me most of the time until he blew himself out.

It was my mother that saw the worst of me. She was privy to the outbursts that went far beyond those of a normal teenage tantrum. My sister was often there too, on the sidelines spectating. Sometimes I would scream at her too if she happened to be around. The pair of them were unanimously against me in the family house. They had always blamed me for the day my father died. They had each other – were together – them against me, always. A bond forged in hate is much stronger than one created in love.

The look of shock and outrage on Debbie's face just now was the perfect mirror of my mother's.

Why did I have to lose control like that?

Losing my temper was a mistake. The breakage was an accident of course and I apologised. Although I could hardly get the words out and I'm not sure she even understood me, but the sentiment must be obvious. Either way, I can't let anything like this happen again. One more incident and Debbie might start involving the police.

I will have to make sure I never go near her again.

My pace slows to a gentle walk now that I am far enough away from everything and attempt to practice mindfulness. I try to focus on anything I can to ease the tightness in my chest and lower my heart rate back to normal.

A car behind me turns onto the street, but I'm so busy trying to breathe deeply and slowly that I hardly notice it, until I am aware that it is slowing down.

For a second, I think Debbie has called the police and they are attempting to locate me. Even though I'm strongly tempted, I don't dare look behind me.

Then I hear someone call out. 'Harriet!'

I freeze and turn around. It's Andrew.

'Andrew!' I gasp, exasperatedly, and some relief. 'You scared me half to death! *What are you doing here?*'

'What are *you* doing here, more like? Do you know

260

someone in this area?' He glances around as if to see a welcoming party at one of the houses. 'I was just on my way over to see you and I saw you turn down here. I brought you some goodies.' He indicates a wicker basket on the passenger seat, inside of which, I can see packets of crackers, biscuits and cartons of soup. 'Are you still feeling unwell?'

I open my mouth, but I'm not sure what to tell him. Did he really see me turn onto this street? I have a suspicion that he has followed me from the flat.

'You look like you've got some decent colour in your cheeks,' he said, peering at me. 'You don't look too bad, actually.'

'Thanks,' I say sarcastically.

'Standing out in the rain isn't doing you any good, though. Why aren't you getting in the car? Come on, hop in.' He reaches across and opens the passenger door for me, moving the basket to the back seat.

I have no choice but to accept. My damp clothes cling to my form and I shiver at experiencing the sudden shelter of Andrew's car. I didn't realise how cold I was.

'You look half frozen,' Andrew says, looking at me up close.

Now I am hyper-aware that I have no make-up on and haven't showered for days. 'I'm fine. I just thought I should get some exercise. I haven't been out for a few days.'

'You look like you could do with a good meal, you know,' Andrew says softly, grasping my hand.

Back in my flat, I take a shower, put on some clean clothes and a little make-up, while Andrew makes us something to eat.

'You haven't even got any bread,' he says as he

261

checks each cupboard. 'I would have brought some if I had known. You should have called me.'

'I know, I'm sorry,' I say, sitting down at the kitchen table and taking in some of the soup he has served. As soon as I am aware of how good the hot liquid tastes I realise I'm ravenous and start eating enthusiastically.

Andrew sits down and joins me. 'I tried to bring you some things a few days ago,' he says slowly, watching my face for a reaction. 'But all the lights were off and you didn't answer the doorbell – or my calls. Were you actually here?'

I stop eating. That night I was here, of course, but I was lost in bad thoughts, wondering what the hell I should do; in no condition to face Andrew. 'Of course, I was here. Where else would I be? I was just asleep probably. Or I might have had my earphones in. Listening to music can help take my mind off things sometimes.'

'Hmm.' He doesn't seem to believe me. 'Is there something you're not telling me, Harriet?'

The warmth from the soup seems to dissipate in my stomach very quickly; it might as well have turned to ice. I close my eyes for a few seconds and take a deep breath. Is this a time for confessions?

'Like what?' I ask quietly.

He shrugs, but still studies my face. 'Is there someone else, for instance?'

'No! Of course not. I'm not cheating on you if that is what you're asking. I wouldn't ever do that.'

I suspect Nick cheated on me a few times over the years and I wouldn't wish it on anyone. Just be honest or leave, that is my motto.

'But there is something though, isn't there? *Please* talk to me, Harriet.' He takes my hand across the table and gives it a reassuring squeeze. His hand is so warm and comforting that I can feel words I never dreamed of saying to anyone start to rise up from deep inside me.

I scan Andrew's face. He looks so genuinely worried about me, I could almost fall for it. I could tell him everything, but I know I shouldn't. I have no idea how he would react. He could call the police. Honestly, he probably should. I bite back the words and blink away some tears, wiping my eyes.

'You are right,' I say, taking a sip of the orange juice Andrew brought. 'I haven't been honest with you... A lot has been going on here – with the gallery – with me, that I haven't told you.'

Then I do it – I confess everything that has been happening over the past weeks with Debbie. I tell him about the missing painting, about her selling art to rival my own; I mention the argument with Sally and Debbie and the hit trade has taken, along with the incursion on my yard earlier. When it comes to mentioning the attempted break-in, I steer around it; I'm not entirely convinced that Debbie was behind that one and I'm not sure how to categorise it myself yet. Plus I don't want to worry him too much.

Andrew puts his face into his hands and groans. 'Oh for goodness' sake, Harriet. Why didn't you mention any of this at the time?'

I shrug, adjusting my spoon so it sits neatly in my empty bowl. 'I don't know. I guess I wanted to try to forget about the day-to-day things when I'm with you. I have to think about all this stuff all the time as it is. Besides, I didn't want you to worry, or feel you have to get involved.'

'But I *am* involved, and I want to be. You are my girlfriend.' He shakes his head. 'Maybe you have just

263

misunderstood. Maybe Debbie didn't do it deliberately. She might not have known what she was doing. Although, I don't remember her mentioning she bought in any canvases. We have never stocked them because they take up too much space. We have always just sold prints and poster-type pictures in frames, never canvases before.'

'Well, you do now.' I get up and lead him over to the window, pointing to where the window display is visible from the lounge.

'Oh, Harriet. I didn't know she had done this. I hadn't even noticed – and I've been driving past the whole time.' He shakes his head. 'You are right. They are all the exact same subjects you paint too... Why would she do that?'

I shrug. 'I told you, I don't think she likes the idea of us being together.'

'That is crazy... I'm really going to have a word with her this time.'

'Please don't. You might make things worse.'

'Worse? You said that the gallery has been losing takings? We need to get that sorted.'

'Yes, I know. But I don't know if I'm losing trade across the road. Hardly anyone has looked at the window really. It is just the stress of everything combined more than anything. It has stopped me from focussing on my own window displays and making the same effort I used to.'

He nods. 'Yes, we need to get you back on track. I can help you with that.' He turns away from the window and faces me. 'Remember I mentioned that you could host an exhibition at the gallery?'

'Yes... but I don't know about that at the moment. I just don't think it is the right time.'

'The right time? It is the *perfect* time. The business needs a boost – this could be a great way to get people interested in your work. Sell some pieces you have had hanging around for a while – pardon the pun.' He winks, finding his usual smile.

'I don't know,' I say slowly. 'I don't know if I'll have time. I still have to redo that painting for my client. She is still waiting for it.'

'Come on, now you are just making excuses. Don't be shy, Harriet. You've got no reason to be shy. You're a grown woman with an exceptional talent. I've loved your work ever since I first saw it. You deserve to be successful. Get some credit for all your hard work for once.'

I am still hesitant.

'You don't have to do any selling or anything,' he goes on, earnestly. 'Just be there, make an appearance. Have a glass of wine. If you don't want to be the focus, then let your work speak for itself. I can talk to people if you want.' He smirks and snakes his arms around my waist. 'I can pretend to be your agent if you like – answer questions, stuff like that. I've been to loads of these things before, I've seen how they work. The artist always sells loads of stuff and gets repeat customers too. Come on, Harriet, what do you say?'

My finances could really use a boost and Andrew seems to really believe in this idea. I trust his judgement. 'All right. I'll do it.'

'Great!' Andrew says, kissing me. 'I'll help you to arrange everything, don't worry. Just leave it to me. It will be fun, I promise.'

'All right, but if it doesn't work out it is your fault. And if it is a roaring success, then I will have to claim all the credit, you know.'

He laughs. 'All right. It's a deal.' He pulls me tighter and plants a kiss on my forehead. 'But, Harriet, I want you to talk to me in the future if there is anything bothering you. Don't just hide away and throw a wobbler on me, all right?'

'OK, I'll behave myself in future.'

'And don't worry about Debbie. I think we both need to have a little chat–'

I open my mouth to speak.

' –I know what you're going to say. But she needs to be set straight, don't you think? You don't know her like I do, she is harmless really. I'll just have a word with her. What is the worst that could happen?'

39

Over the next week, Andrew and I are very busy arranging the exhibition. The date is set for next Saturday. While it doesn't leave us with a great deal of time to organise everything, it does mean that I am keeping my mind occupied and as a result, I'm sleeping better at night. Although, Andrew is helping with that too since he has stayed over at my place virtually every night.

Julia had said that I should take the time to do things I enjoy. Well, I love painting; it is my life. It feels great to be throwing myself back at the gallery with new enthusiasm. Andrew's pep talk really helped me, I feel like I couldn't do any of this without his support.

I don't notice any strange happenings over the next week, either. Maybe it is a good sign. Maybe things are going to be better from now on.

In an effort to boost my income, Andrew helps me set up a Google Places listing for the gallery one night. He sits with my MacBook on the sofa. I place my hands on his shoulders and read the screen over them. 'Is it a good idea to have my mobile number on there too?' I say. 'Maybe you should just stick with the gallery landline and leave it at that.'

'Oh no, I've done that deliberately. Clients with more money like to be able to talk on the phone, and if they have your mobile they can reach you anytime.'

'That is what I am afraid of.' I love my work, but it is nice at the end of the day to have some time away from it.

'Trust me, you can get some bigger commissions this way.'

The day of the exhibition comes around faster than I can anticipate. I wake early on Saturday morning with nerves writhing uncomfortably in my stomach. The room is still dark. I turn my head to the side; Andrew is still fast asleep, breathing heavily. We stayed up until past midnight last night rearranging the gallery ready for tonight. I have painted two new pieces in the last few days, and they now hang downstairs waiting to be seen by the eyes of the public.

By the time dusk falls I start to feel a severe case of nerves. I feel oddly outside myself and at the same time, I am very aware that my heart rate isn't right and my palms are sweating. I wish I hadn't eaten so much for dinner, as my stomach churns uncomfortably now and I fear I may lose its contents. I'm half-ready to run to the toilet in the back of the shop if I need to.

The gallery glows warm and brighter than usual with some extra lighting, courtesy of Andrew; I am guessing he got them from his shop, therefore I assume that Debbie knows that I'm hosting an exhibition by now. That would probably give her more fuel to tell everyone that I think a lot of myself, but I don't care. This evening is for the gallery, not me. My profits need a boost and Andrew thinks it is a good idea. In spite of myself, I find I trust him, even though my natural instinct tells me to pull away.

I'm not entirely satisfied with my outfit choice. I'm wearing some formal black trousers with a satin blouse in deep wine – one of the things I got from Harriet's charity donation bag. While I usually feel more comfortable in this type of clothing, I can't help but think that this is more of a cocktail dress kind of

268

occasion; I just don't know for sure, and Andrew wasn't much help either. He has told me how much money he estimates the artists make at these things, what kind of food and drink is served, and many other anecdotes, but he can't for the life of him seem to recall what people generally wear. 'Just go for smart casual,' he said. 'You can't go wrong with that.'

At the time, I was glad he made this suggestion, because I really am more of a trousers kind of girl, and I was also able to slip my phone into the pocket. It is rare that I receive phone calls on my mobile, but I feel lost without it nearby.

I smooth down the front of my blouse unnecessarily, feeling I should have put in more effort with my appearance. I've even stuck with my standard, everyday up-do because I don't feel right having it any other way – I feel too much like Sophie when I wear it in any other style.

Before I have too much longer to worry about my attire, I start to see unfamiliar cars pulling up in the street outside. It is not long before my little gallery is full of people, all strangers, and there are different types of people compared to the typical customer I get in the gallery. I mostly rely on tourists for my trade. Now there are all sorts of people walking in. Some of them glance in my direction as they walk in, as though appraising me as much as the art on the walls. I notice the women's eyes linger on me longer, looking me up and down. I feel even more self-conscious about what I am wearing, but try my best to stand up straight and act confident, as though I haven't noticed.

A smartly-dressed man in his thirties strikes up a conversation with me about one of my meadow scenes. He wears a navy suit with a pink shirt underneath and his hair is set neatly, but the immaculate-businessman image is offset with a double-stud lip piercing. 'I really love your style,' he says. 'It is so refreshing to find an amateur artist that isn't all about painting coastal perspectives.'

'Thank you,' I say, uncomfortably. I'm not sure whether his use of the word 'amateur' was intended to be an affront or not; it doesn't seem to be, however, as he buys the piece anyway.

Handling the transaction is just like an ordinary, daytime sale in the gallery.

My nerves have subsided a little now that I am in the swing of things. This really isn't that bad. I feel silly for getting myself so worked up over this evening.

I'm initially spurred on by making a sale, but no one else attempts to talk to me for a while. To me, randomly approaching people would feel too much like the hard sell.

I agreed to let Andrew take charge of doing the talking as my representative. He seemed very confident he knows how these things work and I trust him, but it is leaving me standing around a lot, feeling a little awkward on the sidelines.

Although I know the less attention I get, the better, I can't help but wonder if most people wandering around even know that I am the artist.

I check my phone just for something to do, to make it look like I am not just standing around twiddling my thumbs. I've had it on silent and the first thing I notice is that I have had two missed calls and a text message from an unknown number. The message reads:

Hello Harriet,

Sorry to bother you at the weekend. I am just following up on an incident that was reported to me a few days ago. Debbie (one of your neighbours from across the street) tells me that you two had an altercation last week, during which, some property on her premises was broken. Would like to check in and hear your side of the story. Please call me back when you get the chance. Thanks, Dave.

My face burns and my stomach clenches. So Debbie ran off to my landlord to tell on me. Not only is that petty and infuriating, it is also on a new level of low. The landlord could kick me out if Debbie makes out I am causing trouble and damaging property. I bet her story was a much different version of events to what actually happened. *Is she trying to get me evicted now?*

Distracted, I store the contact in my phone almost on autopilot. The calls and messages were from an unrecognised number – Dave must have a new phone. I slip my phone back into my pocket and look around for Andrew. He is engrossed in animated conversation with a white-haired couple in front of a wide cityscape.

The night wears on without me hardly noticing. Since seeing the text, I feel as though I have been drawn out of the crowded room and my mind is somewhere else, my body remaining behind to look the part. I don't need to be stressed out any more right now. I pull out my phone and re-read the message a couple of times. One line jumps out at me in particular: "*...I am just following up on an incident that was reported to me a few days ago...*"

A few days ago? Why did Debbie wait so long before telling tales about me? If she was that upset, why not do it straight away? *Unless...*

271

I glance across the room to Andrew, who is still deep in talk with the couple who now look like they are preparing to make a purchase. I scan his face from a distance and wonder if he has had a talk with Debbie without telling me. Perhaps he chose the middle of the week to do it? Is that what set her off? But he can't have done; we have both been so busy. There wouldn't have been time...

I see a couple of familiar faces emerge from the crowd. A handful of people who have bought from me before all appear over the next half-hour to say 'Hello,' and wish me luck with the evening. Andrew was in charge of advertising and I don't know what he did to get word around, but it seems he has done a very thorough job.

I happen to glance across the room and see Mrs. Hopkins coming towards me.

'Hello Harriet, sweetie,' she says, eyeing me with a certain scrutiny I have not seen her use before.

'Oh, hi Mrs. Hopkins. I didn't see you.'

'No, I've only just got here,' she replies stiffly. 'I heard you were hosting an event and I just thought I would pop in, see how you are doing.'

She doesn't have to say it. I know why she is here. I am suddenly deeply ashamed that I have not spoken to her since telling her the painting had gone missing and I would look into it. Red-faced, I explain to her that there was a problem with the courier service and that they lost the package. She makes a big show of looking deeply annoyed when I tell her this, but she accepts my sincerest apologies and my insistence that I am in the process of recreating the painting.

'It should be ready in two weeks time.'

She scoffs. 'Really Harriet, sweetie. I would have

272

thought that the final piece in my collection should have been your number one priority considering you were so careless with the original.'

A stab of irritation strikes my insides.

I open my mouth to respond, but she quickly takes a glass of champagne and wanders off, striking up a conversation with a pair of women in the corner.

I have always thought of Mrs. Hopkins as pompous and over the top, but essentially a fun character. Now it is impossible to ignore how much she reminds me of my mother. Her snootiness and overdone displeasure with me make the resemblance hard to ignore.

At around eight-thirty, Andrew moves in my direction with a plate of nibbles which he proffers forward.

'No, thank you,' I say.

'Suit yourself,' he says cheerily. 'You are missing out though – those Antipasti canapés are delicious. Are you having a nice time? Hey, I saw you make a sale earlier!'

'Yes, I did. Listen, Andrew, I had a text from Dave. Debbie told him about what happened last Saturday – when I accidentally broke something in the shop. I think she might have made it sound worse than it was – like I did it deliberately, even.'

His face falls and he pauses for a moment. 'Right. Well, not to worry – I will have a word with Dave next week when I get the chance. Me and him are friendly, we go out for a drink now and then. He'll be all right.'

'You didn't talk to Debbie, did you? You said you wouldn't.' I've been gently nagging him all week to avoid having a patronising talk about our relationship with her, and I thought I had finally managed to get rid to agree.

He avoids looking me in the eye. 'I don't think I said

273

that. I'm going to get some more food. Be back in a second.'

I sigh and watch him disappear into the little kitchen.

Just then, my attention is drawn through the glass window and out onto the street. My stomach turns to ice when I see Debbie's face floating around outside. She walks past the window slowly as though in a casual manner, but her eyes take in everything in the room. She appears not to notice me, however, and she disappears down the street and out of sight. I don't have long to stress out about her, though.

I turn my head to the entrance where a thin, sharp-looking woman in her early-forties strolls in casually. She takes in the scene differently than anyone else this evening. As though she is weighing up the whole event, rather than looking for a way to participate in it. She hovers in the doorway for a second, before a younger man in his mid-twenties walks in behind her. He has the same look of not wanting to join in about him, except that it is more apparent in his body language. Another thing that immediately differentiates him from the rest of the crowd is the large-lensed camera hanging from a thick black strap around his neck.

I feel like I have just been plunged into very cold water.

The young man picks up his camera and moves to take a shot of the room at large.

I duck slightly behind a pair of short-haired women who look like they could be sisters. I'm aware that they ruffle slightly and give me a strange look, but I ignore them and pretend to be straightening my trouser hem.

When I think it is safe, I keep my head down and move towards the back of the gallery. When I make it level with the counter, I put my hand to my head, pretending to check my hair is still neatly in place and at the same time covering my face a little.

I turn and can see the door leading through to the kitchen and toilet. I make my way over to it when I hear someone address me.

'You must be Harriet.'

I spin around. It is the woman that came in with the photographer. She grasps my hand with hers and gives me a very firm and enthusiastic handshake. 'I'm Natalie. I'm from Coventry Weekly News.'

I freeze. 'Oh – no. I'm not the artist, I'm afraid.'

'Oh really?' She looks thoroughly disappointed and snaps her head around, peering around the room. 'Well, do you know which one she is, then?'

'Um... no, I don't. But her representative is around, I think. I'll see if I can find him for you if you like?'

She smiles broadly back at me, exposing teeth that seem overly bright against her dark lipstick. 'That would be lovely, thanks.'

I slip away just as the photographer arrives at her side. Once in the kitchen, I take a deep breath, safe in the darkness in the back of the shop.

There is a tray of champagne glasses in here waiting to be served. I take one and sip it. I regret that the sting of the bubbles stop me from downing the whole thing in one go.

Andrew's voice makes me jump out of my skin. 'Harriet?'

I gasp and a little champagne goes down the wrong way, making me cough and my eyes water.

The half of Andrew's face that is lit up looks puzzled. 'What are you doing in here in the dark? I've got the local paper out here, they want to meet you, take some photographs for an article.'

275

'Well, they don't need me for that. This thing is really about my art, not me. All my paintings are out there, aren't they? Maybe they could just take some photos of those instead?'

'Don't be silly. Come on Harriet, you are not *that* shy.' He takes hold of my hand to lead me out of the kitchen.

'No. I really don't want my photo taken.' I pull back firmly, standing my ground.

He stops and looks at me. I see a flash of something run across his face, but I can't tell what it is. 'Well, OK then. You don't have to if you don't want to. I just thought it would be a good idea. Come back out here though when you're ready, eh?'

I spend a good twenty-minutes hiding in the kitchen area before I re-emerge. By the time I come out, the press-pair are gone.

It is past eleven o'clock when everyone has gone and Andrew and I clear up the gallery, collecting champagne glasses and crumb-covered plates. He informs me that he made a solid handful of sales on some original canvases. He also tells me that he spoke to a solicitor that wants a custom piece for his office.

I till up and count the money from this evening. Something isn't right. 'Andrew, there is too much here.' I turn to him. 'What else did you sell?'

'Nothing. Just the paintings I told you about.' He gives me a sneaky little look over his shoulder as he takes the extra lighting features down. 'I put a little extra on some price tags,' he says.

I look around at the cards under the paintings nearest me. They display different prices than I had set. How could I not have noticed? 'Andrew, I didn't want you to do that. Isn't that a bit dishonest? I didn't even realise.'

276

'Don't be daft. People expect to pay a higher price at these kind of events. You were selling yourself short anyway. Don't worry about it.' He bins some disposable plates and eyes me cautiously for a few moments. 'Hey, listen. I'm sorry about inviting the press without telling you. I just thought it would be some good exposure for the gallery. I didn't mean to put you on the spot or anything.'

'Oh that. No, don't worry. I'm just a little camera shy, that's all.'

Better an understatement than the truth. Andrew can never know what I have done.

I care too much about him now to risk losing him; I'm so aware of never having felt like this about anyone else before.

While it may not be ideal to keep up a false pretence, I convince myself it is for the best. I don't see any other path to a future with him by side.

Now in this moment, I am almost overwhelmed by the awareness that I will do anything to make sure Andrew never finds out who I really am.

No matter what.

40

Dan

You think you have won, don't you Harriet? You
think you have managed to get away from me. These
past nineteen-months have been hard for me. I might
even call them the hardest of my life. Suddenly being
forced to live without you took its toll on me, I'll admit.

Without warning, you weren't there to satisfy me,
Harriet. I don't just mean cooking and looking after the
flat, either. Of course, I had other women take care of
my basic needs while you weren't here – that is nothing
new. But other women can't fulfil me like you did.

It took years for you to learn how to behave the way
I wanted; years for you to realise how you must obey
me, respect me. It took you so long to finally fall into
line. *But you were worth it*. I know I will ever find
another woman like you and I'm not motivated to try –
it is *you* I want. No one else will do.

Some things I regret now – like the night you left.
You forced me to hurt you so badly I thought you were
dead. You didn't move and I was worried I had gone too
far. At first, I was angry with you for passing out on me
like that. You went still and quiet before I had even
finished with you; you had made me so angry and I still
had so much more in me.

You left me most *disappointed*.

But what hurt the most, my sweetness, was when I
woke up and you weren't there. I expected breakfast
and profuse apologies; I wanted my morning coffee and
you desperate to make amends for what you had done;

278

wanted to make up properly, in bed.

Stealing from me, Harriet, that is a low I wouldn't have expected from you. I knew you were slipping away from me gradually, I had felt it for months before, but I never thought you would actually rob me. When I found you were gone, your suitcase and possessions too, I was very displeased. There are no words to describe how upset I was.

Devastated, would be close.

You humiliated me, Harriet. The neighbour from across the hall asked me where you had gone to and I told her that you went to stay with your mother for a while. She knew I was lying, I could tell. I should have given her something for her nosiness, she would have deserved it. She had no right to pry into our private affairs. She paid too much attention to us if you ask me.

I have spent so much time trying to find you. When you first left, I searched everywhere. For some time, I even suspected you went running off to your mother – I know, that is a ridiculous thought. She pretty much left you to it when you married me, didn't she? It was prudent to explore all possibilities, though.

I was so desperate to get you back.

Once six-months had passed, I stopped searching so frantically, was forced to ease off a little. Work were on my case, because I had missed so many days, and I turned up late so often that I was threatened with the sack.

So I reined myself in, always keeping a watchful eye on anything that could lead me to you. I continued to follow your family, your employer, your colleagues, but less often. Zack Edwards was my priority. You always seemed to have a soft spot for him. I was convinced for a long time that you must have been seeing him behind my back and that was who you had run off with.

But I was wrong.

Little did I know that he or anyone you used to know wouldn't be what gave your location away.

I set up a Google Alert to be notified of anything online that contains your name. I have had a few disappointments though. Unfortunately you share the name 'Harriet Harper' with some other people in the world.

Whenever anything gets posted online that contains your name, I get an email with a link.

I have scanned Facebook periodically too, just in case. I have an account with a fake name and photograph I lifted from someone else's profile. You would never have seen me coming. But you were too smart for that. I didn't think you would be stupid enough to splash yourself over social media when you were trying so hard to hide – but I had to check, just in case. I couldn't sleep for the first few weeks after you had gone and it was a late-night whim to check Facebook.

I was *beside myself.* You did that to me.

I bet you would call it obsession, you were always trying to label me, but I call it love. We made vows, Harriet. I expected you to stick to them.

I did consider the possibility that you would have gone back to your maiden name. But I just knew that you wouldn't. I knew that if you have gone to these lengths to get away from me, you would want to stay hidden. And using your maiden name would seem too predictable, wouldn't it? You knew that I would search for you by that name first. Very clever. Of course, I set up an alert for that too, just in case.

But seeing how your family name was more rare, I

280

haven't had any of those results appear in my emails at all. Just as well really, I'm not sure I could face any more disappointment.

But I am not disappointed now, Harriet. Do you know why? It is because I have found you. That's right, you sly bitch, I know where you are now.

This morning my inbox lit up with a new alert. As soon as I saw your name alongside 'artist' and 'exhibition' I just knew that it was you. It was an article on a newspaper site, Coventry Weekly News, entitled: *Talented Local Artist Harriet Harper Hosts Successful Exhibition*.

You see, I don't forget, Harriet. I remember you were studying art at Uni when we met. You've had that worthless art degree the whole time we were together and you never made use of it.

What a waste of time that was. Back then, you were always surrounded by those ridiculous arty types on your course. Jokers with their hair swept at ridiculous angles, their clothes torn just for the sake of it. It was hard for me to approach you at first, but I managed to prise you away and eventually they all stopped talking to you, didn't they? I made sure of it. You didn't need *them*, sweetheart, you only needed me.

I must have read the article thirty times or more since this morning. I haven't gone into work. Probably, I should have called in sick, but I just can't stop scrolling down the page, re-reading the details. They jump out at me like they are marked with little red bullet-points.

Your "representative" is featured more heavily than you. Strange. He seems to be quite an admirer of yours, though. I'm not stupid – I bet he is more than that. Even if he isn't, I bet you fancy him, don't you? He

281

practically falls over himself trying to compliment you in the article. "...*Harriet has so much talent... I fell in love with her work the moment I saw it...*" What a drip. He doesn't deserve your attention.

I'm so hurt that you decided to throw away our marriage like you did. It doesn't matter now though because today I am happier than I have been in a long time. I am going to put things right.

You may have run, Harriet, but you can't hide. Not from me – you must have known that.

You've slipped up. That streak of pride that I thought I had crushed seems to have regrown to full size. You just couldn't resist showing off, could you?

I wonder if you even realise yet what you have done. You will soon enough.

41

Since the exhibition I have been so busy, painting virtually every night.

It is now Sunday, over a whole week since we hosted the open-evening and I am taking advantage of the fact that the gallery is shut for the whole day to get some serious work done.

Right now I am seated on one of the benches in the ruins of the old cathedral and paint. As I sit in the open-air, I capture the angles and dark curves of the building's grand Gothic architecture. I add my own twist of bright colours and dramatic lighting. It is not hard to see why these scenes are some of my most popular; the tourists love them.

I haven't painted on location since I moved here, so today is something of a novelty for me.

The weather is delightful. Bright and sunny with some white-billowing clouds lined with silver. It is not humid or overwhelmingly hot so I know I can easily sit here for a good few hours.

Andrew dropped me off with my new travel-easel and equipment this afternoon. He had to go back home and do some household chores. Although at first, he had wanted to stay and watch how I work, I told him he would be bored and I wouldn't be able to concentrate.

He reluctantly left to tackle a pile of washing and ironing that he has been putting off while staying over at my flat this past week. We arranged that he would come and pick me up at five to take me back home. That should give me long enough to make some headway on this piece. I can always finish off details at home from memory.

I feel like a great weight has been lifted off me since I did the exhibition. For a few days, I was worried about the press that Andrew had invited. I eagerly pounced on the finished article when Andrew showed me it on his iPad. The event coverage consisted of nothing more than an online article, and it turned out they had failed in getting a snap of me in the end.

That was a major relief.

They featured a photograph of the outside of the gallery and included a flattering shot of Andrew further down the page. The article focusses mainly on my art, dropping a few basic details like my name and age, not going into detail about the person behind the canvas, which is how I like it.

It was a close one that night, but it has all worked out OK.

The whole open-gallery thing was Andrew's idea and I feel like it has brought us closer together. Now that I have confided in him about my troubles with his ex-wife and the business, I feel that some barriers have evaporated and we are now a more solid couple. Now it is more 'us against the world' than it was before, despite the secrets I still hold back from him.

I just wish I wasn't so busy this week so I could spend more time with him. After the success of last Saturday night, he had suggested we go away for a couple of weeks to his parent's cottage to celebrate, but I just have too much to catch up on work-wise. In the end, we agreed to arrange a get-away for next month instead.

The sheer volume of work I have been doing for the gallery stocks has left me little time to do much else. Unfortunately, that meant putting Mrs. Hopkins's painting on hold for a while. Although now it is not just a blank canvas – but an outline – a faint sketch on the white, which isn't so bad. I really need to get to that when I get some free time. But admittedly, I have been busy with Andrew some nights too and I haven't had the chance. It wasn't like I could run an empty shop, so I made replenishing the gallery the first priority. Finishing, or rather starting, Mrs. Hopkins's painting is the very next thing on my to-do list.

I resolve to start it tomorrow, as soon as I finish work.

42

Dan

You have changed the way you move, Harriet.

You may have lost weight, you may be holding yourself differently, but I still know it's you.

Even from this distance at the end of the road, and even in the rear-view mirror I still recognise the shade of your hair – like fire.

Your step says that you do not know I'm watching you. You walk as though you think you are getting away with it, with leaving me... humiliating me.

You don't turn around, so I can't see your face, but I know there is a smug look upon it. I can imagine the subtle look of satisfaction spread across your cheeks at thinking you have won.

You won't get away with it much longer, Harriet – I promise.

My hands are shaking so badly I have to grip the steering wheel to steady myself. I can't afford to lose control.

Not yet.

I watch you put the shutters up on your shop and unlock the door to the flat beside it. So you live right above your precious little enterprise? Quite convenient really. I should probably torch the whole place while you are sleeping. Throw a can of petrol through the window.

Yes, it would probably wake you. You always slept so lightly. Almost as though you were keeping one eye open and on me. But that is perfect, I don't want you to go and slip away peacefully in your sleep.

You won't find me doing anything sneaky like that, Harriet. I'm not like you. I want – no – I *need* to see the look on your face up close. I want to see the fear, the defeat in your eyes when you realise that I have won – that I have found you.

I want you to know that it was me that got you in the end.

43

Dan

The next day I follow you. It was so lucky that I did not miss you – I just caught sight of your new beau from the news article shutting the car door for you. What a gentleman. You know, I must say he doesn't look as good as his picture. The photographer must have caught him at a good angle that night.

I suppose you like when he does that sort of thing for you, don't you, sweetheart? Makes you think you are special, worthy of someone's careful attention, even though you are nothing but a backstabbing whore.

You always did think you were someone important didn't you, Harriet? You thought you were too good for me, always. Whenever you were with me, I could always feel that you wanted to be with someone else. I tried my best to make sure you knew your place, but you would never stay there, in mind and spirit at least.

Your sweetheart gets into the vehicle himself and drives the pair of you somewhere. I notice he is tall. My paltry height was never enough for you, was it Harriet? I saw you practically swooning over the postman when he delivered an Amazon parcel to you one day. You thought you were out of my sight, didn't you? Well, you weren't – *I caught you at it.* He must have been at least six-four. More like it wasn't it?

What really got me about that was that you never said a word about my measly five-nine bothering you, didn't have the decency *to say it to my face*. You chose to show me how much it mattered to you by flirting with any man that exceeded me. Spiteful, Harriet.

My car is different than you knew, a grey BMW. I keep an overly generous distance as I proceed, however, just in case.

You two lovebirds seemed to be off to the city centre together for the day. I had visions of myself mingling in with the crowds in the background and seeing you in the open air when we are not separated by the hush of a windscreen. But I don't get the chance. Your "representative" drops you off near the cathedral. I see a flash of red hair, up in that style I always adored when you were with me before you disappear into a crowd of tourists.

It is nice to see that you haven't changed your hair, although I am upset that you wear it like that for him.

I think my memory of you Harriet is a little rose-tinted, however. In my head you are always the picture of loveliness; whenever I have thought of you over the last eighteen-months, your frame is more elegant and slender, your knees are more slight. They say absence makes the heart grow fonder, don't they, sweetheart? But I'm not sure I can that say that is the case with you.

For a moment, I am disappointed that I am not parked closer, or in a different position, or that I did not get here a few seconds sooner. Here, the angle is all wrong and I lose sight of you quickly.

Too quickly. I would have liked to have seen more of you, even if it was just a longer glimpse. But then I decide that it is better this way. I don't want you to know I'm here yet, then I wouldn't get the chance to cause you the kind of pain that you have caused me.

Your new man – Andrew, isn't it? – pulls away and

drives off again. I do the same, never letting his black Audi out of my sight.

So I will have to make a vow to see you soon. Your new boyfriend seems so important to you that I know I cannot miss an opportunity to say hello to him alone.

44

I think my work here is complete. I look at my finished canvas and feel a sense of pride that I have done a good job today. It is nice when a picture goes exactly the way I had envisioned in my head. The day has clouded over somewhat, but it is so warm that I am still as comfortable as if I were at home in my studio.

The number of tourists wandering around taking pictures has diminished slightly over the last twenty-minutes. Looking at the time on my phone, I feel a swoop in the pit of my stomach when I see that it is 16:57 – I've got three minutes to get to the meeting point where Andrew is picking me up.

Hastily, I pack away my things and don't properly put them back in their designated sections of my holdall. They are stashed away quickly; I will sort them out properly when I get home. I don't want to keep Andrew waiting on double yellows.

Folding my easel is tricky; one of the wing-nuts is stuck. I curse myself for winding it up too tightly. After a few minutes of struggling I get the thing down and fold it for carrying under my arm.

Now that I have a still-wet canvas to carry in addition to my other things, I am forced to take a slower-than-desired pace back to the pick-up point. My heart pounds and the tension rises in my torso. I try to convince myself to stay calm. In just a few minutes, I will be within sight of Andrew.

I make it back to Priory Street a little later than I expected. Oddly, as I descend the wide stone steps I don't see any sign of Andrew's car anywhere.

Maybe he saw a traffic warden coming and was forced to do a loop around the block?

I look up and down the narrow street. He isn't here. Lowering my easel, I pull out my phone from my pocket. The time is now 17:07. We arranged to meet at five, it is not like I am really that late or anything.

I give Andrew ten minutes to turn up, but he doesn't. Wandering further down the road, I check for his car stopped behind a boarding coach of students.

Where is he? He has always been punctual so far in our relationship, he makes a big deal about it. Lateness is one of his pet peeves.

I call his mobile. It rings, but he doesn't answer. I leave a few minutes, in case Andrew is driving, and then I try again, but the same thing happens – it rings through to the answering machine. I don't leave a voicemail though; I always think that a text is faster.

Quickly, I tap out a message.

Hi Sweetie. I'm waiting for you like we arranged – near the steps on Priory Street. I was a couple of minutes late – sorry! I promise I will make it up to you later when we get back to my place :) See you soon xxxx

The text is sent and I wait expectantly for a response. Now, I stand exactly where Andrew dropped me off earlier; the University entrance stands opposite, the entrance to the cathedral behind me. I'm right by one of the large circular boulders that line both sides of the road. If Andrew drives past, he will definitely see me.

Ten more minutes pass with me checking my phone compulsively every thirty seconds or so.

I call again, and again I hear the monotonous voice

292

of the answering machine.

I am really panicking now. Even in the heat of the warm summer day, my hands are cold and feeling clammy. All sorts of thoughts are running through my mind.

What if Andrew has had an accident? He could have dropped me off earlier and then a lorry could have smashed right into him. I wouldn't know...

I slump down onto the steps and look at the time. Andrew is now over forty-minutes late, so completely out of character for him. It occurs to me that he might have been here on time earlier, but then left again because I was late.

Is it possible he takes time-keeping more seriously than I thought? Maybe he has left me here on purpose to teach me a lesson? I haven't seen a dark side of Andrew's character yet, but he must have one. Everyone does. Is his alter-ego the reason Debbie divorced him? She must have had a good reason; Andrew is usually so nice.

The patterns of the water feature across the road repeat on a loop, and by now I know exactly the effect that will come next.

I am annoyed with myself now for allowing myself to become stranded with all my painting gear. I don't have the energy to drag all this stuff onto a bus and have to squeeze past people with the bulk of my easel; the mere thought makes my stomach squeeze.

I look up and down the street. There are still plenty of people milling about here and there. I get up and stop a middle-aged man in a dark suit and ask him if he knows the number for a local taxi.

He takes several paces past me before he stops. I actually think he was going to pretend he hadn't heard my question. He might have caught sight of the cumbersome load set upon the ground around me however and changed his mind.

I call for a taxi and as I wait for it to arrive, I look around me constantly for any sign of Andrew.

I don't know what to think. I am so anxious and on-edge. The panic surges through my body like poison. It feels worse now because I haven't experienced it for a week or so. My body hits me with a fresh wave of stress, reminding me of what it can do.

45

I'm quite pissed-off by the time that I get back into my flat. Not only did I get abandoned in the middle of the city with all my stuff, but the taxi driver didn't offer any help to get my equipment in and out of his car. He just sat in his cabin and waited for me to do it all. I'm sure customer service used to be better.

Once inside my flat, I feel a slight breath of relief just at the fact I am in my own space again. As soon as I reach the top of the stairs, sweating and flushed from lugging everything around, I drop everything and go through each room in turn. I don't know what I am expecting to find; I thought there might somehow be some sign of Andrew. On Friday I had a key cut for him; he had seemed pleased, even telling me he would return the gesture, so where is he now?

My heart pounds as I move from room to room. A sinking feeling descends upon me, I can tell my personal space has been invaded.

Someone has been in here while I was out.

What if it was Debbie? She would have seen us leaving earlier and known the place was empty.

Looking around, I can't immediately see anything out of place. I feel under the sofa for my MacBook and get a fright when it isn't there. Although seconds later I spot it on the kitchen worktop; Andrew must have left it there earlier.

Items in the kitchen aren't where I remember leaving them earlier either; although I didn't make a note of how the room looked when we went out. Andrew had made us breakfast and lunch, so maybe he left things in a different order than I usually would.

I would like to think I am imagining it, but the feeling of disquiet running down my spine says otherwise.

I pour myself a glass of wine, take a large gulp and collapse onto the sofa with my eyes shut.

I don't know what to do. What the hell has happened to my boyfriend? He has never done anything like this before. Should I call the police? Don't they have a twenty-four-hour rule before they can look into it or something like that?

Wearily, I check my phone for what feels like the hundredth time, expecting to find no new updates.

My heart leaps when I see that I have a new message. It immediately sinks again when I see that it is not from Andrew – it is from Dave, my landlord.

I toss my phone onto the coffee table in annoyance. I had thought I was going to get a message from Andrew. Whatever Dave wants, he can wait.

I rest the back of my head against the sofa and shut my eyes again. I almost immediately open them when I remember something Andrew said to me about Dave last week: *"Me and him are friendly, we go out for a drink every now and then."*

Maybe Dave is sending me a message about Andrew? Suddenly, I feel terrified. What if something *has* happened to him?

I snatch up my phone from the table and hurriedly tap on the message to read it.

Hello Harriet,
I had a chat with Debbie earlier. She tells me you had a private party on the shop premises outside of business hours. I'm told that it lasted late into the night

last Saturday, causing disruption. Debbie complained
that there were cars coming and going frequently and
she lost her parking spot as well as being disturbed by
the noise. I'm also told that there was alcohol served. I
can't allow that on my property without the proper
licence, I'm afraid. You could face a VERY serious fine
for such activity, even if it is just a one-off. I need to
discuss that with you further. I am also still waiting for
you to call me back about the damage that occurred to
property within Minerva Interiors the week before too.
We really need to have a talk. Please call me back.
Dave.

I let out a groan of rage and throw my phone onto
the table so hard it leaves deep marks in the pale
veneer. I'm so sick of Debbie and her meddling. She
must really be trying to get me evicted. My eyes fill up
with tears, stinging and blurring my vision.

That wretched woman. Why can't she just leave me
alone?

It sounds like Andrew didn't talk to Dave even
though he said he would. Was he just too busy and
forgot?

I want to talk to him so badly right now. I call his
phone again but get the answering machine. This time I
listen to the whole message that the woman with the
toneless voice relays and wait for the beep.

'Andrew? Look I don't know what has happened to
you. Why won't you answer your phone? Please just
call me back when you get this...'

As I hang up, I'm annoyed with my wavering voice
for sounding so lost in my message. It was such a
mistake to get involved with anyone.

After I finish my wine, I pour another glass. The

edge needs to be rounded off my nerves. My hands shake. I should probably eat something, but I've completely lost any appetite I had earlier.

As I look back at Dave's text, another surge of anger rushes to my head. The exhibition was just a quiet affair. It certainly didn't create the kind of disruption Debbie is talking about and she did not lose her parking space at all – her little car was positioned in the street the whole time. And it is nonsense that she was "disturbed by the noise" – the takeaway next door bothers me virtually every night, but I don't go running to Dave about it. I regularly see drunks staggering around, ordering kebabs late into the night and urinating up my shop shutters. Sometimes I even find myself having to clear up their disgusting rubbish from in front of the gallery before I can even start work in the morning. For Debbie to complain about that is utter rubbish. Surely Dave must see that?

In his text, he says that he spoke with Debbie "earlier". Weird. The exhibition was last weekend, why has Debbie only just complained to him today?

As for alcohol consumption on business premises without a licence. Why didn't Andrew think of that? The champagne had been his idea, after all. I thought he knew what he was doing... Unless they are both in it together, I think. Him and Debbie. What if today was me being dumped? What if he has gone back to her? And Andrew has devised a scheme to get me out of the street, out of the area...

That is ridiculous, I think. That can only be the wine talking.

It is strange though.

Why would Debbie wait so long to complain about me again? Unless...

I have a penny-drop moment and something clicks into place. Debbie complained to the landlord about me last time only *after* I suspect Andrew had spoken to her.

Andrew must have seen Debbie today or at least spoken to her over the phone.

That is the only explanation.

46

The near-oblivion of sleep eludes me until past five am. Then I am awoken two hours later by a noise outside. Quickly, I get up and scurry through to the living-room window. When I see that it is a bread delivery for Sally's Sandwiches, I am absolutely furious.

I rush back into the bedroom and grab my phone, but the screen is black – the battery has gone dead. I groan and go back through to the lounge to plug it in, fumbling with the power button and will it uselessly to load faster. *Come on. Come on. Why does it take so long?*

I rub my eyes. I'm so tired; I could not sleep last night until I had finished almost the whole bottle of wine. I felt like it wouldn't be so bad if I left a little liquid in the bottom; my headache says otherwise though.

All night I kept flitting between the idea of calling the police and then chickening out again at the last second. I would pick up my phone, and a few times I even dialled the number, but I was too scared. I'm too much of a coward to risk exposing myself.

There would be questions. I would have to tell them who I am, but what if I made a mistake, or they realised I was lying? One thing could lead to another and my whole life could become unravelled.

I thought of calling Andrew's parents. But I knew I wouldn't do that. I don't even know if they are aware that Andrew and I have been dating.

At one in the morning, after much wine, I called the

number for a taxi again. Someone answered, but when they asked me where I wanted to go, I ended the call.

I wanted to go to Andrew's house and knock on the door, ring the doorbell until he answered me. But I couldn't do it. I chickened out of that too. What if he has dumped me? I was a wreck by that point and couldn't face the prospect of being rejected like that. It reminded me of Cornwall, of Richard and how he moved onto other girls without even saying anything to me. No wonder I needed so much to drink before I could sleep.

I drank a little more and at two am, I actually went out into the street and walked up and down, trying to see into Debbie's flat. It was all dark, of course, by that time. I don't know what I expected. Did I really think Andrew was in there with her, the pair of them watching me struggle home alone with all my equipment and laughing?

Despite my intoxication, I was strong-willed enough to go back inside without pressing my thumb repeatedly on Debbie's doorbell. For some reason, I now clearly remember thinking last night: *I mustn't set Debbie off. If I go near her again she would make another complaint.*

My phone finally loads and for a second I see no notifications. Then I suddenly get the buzz of a new voicemail from an unknown mobile number.

My hands shake slightly as I listen to the message; I press the phone so painfully hard against my ear that it makes it burn.

'Hello, Harriet. This is Judith Hughes, here. I'm calling to tell you that Andrew was admitted to hospital last night. I have only been informed myself this morning. I have to say it is quite a shock... most unexpected... Well, I know you would want to be notified of his malady. The doctors have told me he is in a stable condition, but still very serious. So perhaps you could give me a call back when you get this message. Goodbye for now.'

As soon as I hear the voice of Andrew's mother my stomach feels like it drops so low it could go through the floor and I fear the worst.

Through my horror, I hear the words "stable condition" and it seeps into my consciousness. He is alive. It is "very serious", but he is still alive. That makes it sound like he is very badly injured. *What the hell happened to him yesterday?* He must have been in an accident, after all.

I feel thoroughly sick and disgusted with myself for allowing my mind to drift into disloyal territory; I had started thinking he had left me, gone back to Debbie, or was teaching me a lesson for being a few minutes late. How could I even think that? *There must be something really wrong with my brain.*

I call Judith and she informs me there has been no change in Andrew's condition. She has been at the hospital since this morning and she asks if I can leave work to arrange a visit. There is a pleading note I have never heard in her voice before.

'Of course, I can,' I say, without even thinking about it. 'I haven't opened the gallery yet. I'll be there as soon as I can.'

The bus journey to Clifford Bridge Road Hospital seems to take forever. All the time I can hear Judith's words in my ears like I am still on the phone to her. Her voice lacked the authority and stability it had the last time I spoke to her. That alone would have been enough to scare me. The fact that her son is in such a serious condition makes my heart sink dreadfully.

*

I approach the harassed looking receptionist on the front desk. 'Hello, I'm here to see Andrew Hughes,' I tell her. Even just this far into the building I am hit with the smell of hospital cleaning fluids. 'He was admitted here last night. Could you tell me which ward he is on, please?'

'Are you family?'

'Well, no. Not technically. I'm his girlfriend–'

'Harriet?' A voice behind me has me whirling around.

A tall man in his sixties approaches me from down a corridor. He takes hold of my icy, clammy hand and shakes it firmly. 'Hello, I'm Charles, Andrew's father. It is nice to finally meet you in person.'

'Yes... likewise.' Automatically, I search his face for a resemblance to Andrew, but other than his height I can't see any.

Charles leads me down corridor after corridor, up in the lift and pushes open large double doors for us. As we walk, he gives me a rundown of everything his wife already told me on the phone; that the doctors have stabilised Andrew, are keeping him unconscious for now, and that there has been no change in his condition since Judith initially called me this morning.

We finally reach a ward and Charles opens the door for me and follows me inside. There is much more hush in here compared to the rest of the hospital. Some beds I pass are occupied; some have their curtains drawn. I avert my gaze and try to focus on the floor, on making my footsteps quieter on the shiny surface.

An older woman with greying-blonde hair emerges from the end of the ward and she moves swiftly towards us. Without uttering a word, she pulls me into a tight hug. At this, I find my eyes welling up with unexpected tears. I bite my lip to stop myself from crumbling completely. I was fine all the way here; I think the reality has just hit me.

Judith came at me from a funny angle, so I can do nothing but pat her on the back awkwardly until she releases me.

'You must be Harriet,' she says, stepping back with a sniff. She dabs at her eyes and I try to blink mine clear. 'Andrew told me you two had become close. Thank you for coming here so soon.'

'Of course. I had to come and see him.' Then, because I don't know what else to say, I ask, 'How is he?' I feel stupid before the words have fully left my mouth. Luckily Andrew's mother seems to understand and she simply tells me there has been no change.

I follow the pair to a bed near the end of the ward, my feet moving automatically, as though I have no choice but to move them. As we draw near, my eyes fall upon an intimidating web of wires and machinery. Tangles of cables and pipes and softly beeping equipment surround the bed, and at the top, some pipes snake into a mass of red and purple.

A gasp escapes me before I can stop it. It is a horrible sound and I hate myself for making it – I just wasn't prepared. Beside me, Judith lets out a sob and puts her hand to her mouth.

I can hardly recognise Andrew. One side of his face is completely swollen and discoloured. The bruising on the other side looks mild in comparison, but it at least allows him to be identifiable as the man I have known for the past nineteen-months. An oxygen mask covers the lower half of his face, and now my senses are a

304

little more adjusted to the scene, I notice that a machine seems to be breathing for him.

It is hard to find an area of Andrew that is not covered in bruising or cuts. Even his hands bear signs of damage, the knuckles are bright red and grazed.

Judith takes a seat beside her son and strokes his left arm gently; his right is hidden inside a large white cast.

No one says anything for a while. It is quiet, except for the rhythmic beeping of the machinery and the hiss of the breathing apparatus. Andrew's mother occupies the seat beside his bed, but I hover awkwardly at the end of it. Charles stands behind his wife and rests his hands on her shoulders. I feel like I am outside the family grief, looking in. I feel like if Judith yelled at me in this moment to get out, she would have every right. But she doesn't. She just looks desperately at her son; now and then she wipes a tear away from her cheek.

I feel very weak and wispy. I try to press my feet hard against the pale and polished floor in an attempt to ground myself. Everything feels so unreal. Like I am wandering around the halls of a dream, or rather, a nightmare.

It just doesn't seem to fit. Now that my eyes grow accustomed to his injuries, they just don't seem right. I voice my confusion out loud, my voice sounding too harsh in the delicate quiet of the room. 'How could a car accident do this much damage to him?'

Charles looks up at me, his face pale and a look of confusion upon it. 'Car accident? No, we didn't say he was in a car accident. Did we, dear?' He looks down at his wife.

Judith looks at me bleary-eyed. 'Oh, I'm ever so sorry, Harriet. I haven't told you, have I? What must you think of me? No, Andrew hasn't had an accident.

305

Someone...' Her voice falters. 'Someone did this to him.'

The words sink into my skull like needles, but their meaning seems to remain caught in my scalp. 'Someone did this deliberately? You mean he was attacked?'

Judith nods and puts her hand to her mouth, turning her head away from me. Her husband squeezes her shoulders tightly. He keeps his face steely and solid, staring at the wall, as though worried he might cry too.

'I couldn't understand what had happened to him,' I say, more to myself than Judith or Charles. 'He was supposed to meet me on Sunday, but he never showed up. I couldn't understand why. Where was he when it happened? Was he mugged?'

Charles shakes his head. 'He was attacked at home,' he says stiffly. 'A neighbour saw him lying on the floor through the patio doors and called an ambulance. It was lucky he was seen. The doctors said it was close, but he was brought in just in time.'

Judith gives another sob and tries to stifle another. It is like she thinks that if she falls apart now, she will never be able to pull herself together again. That is the way I feel right now anyway.

'I just don't understand why someone would do this. If someone wanted to burgle him, they didn't have to hurt him so badly. Who would do a thing like this?'

Charles takes a deep breath. 'That is what the police are going to investigate.' He glances over his shoulder at the ward door. 'Speaking of which, it looks like they are back again.'

I glance over my shoulder too and see a man in a suit approaching us.

Every muscle in my body locks stiff. I am rooted to the spot. And even if I could move – we are at the end

306

of the ward – there isn't any way out.

47

Judith seems to have regained control over herself and is able to speak again. 'This is Harriet Harper,' she says to the new arrival. 'She is Andrew's partner.'

He nods his head towards me in greeting. 'I know this is a difficult time for you, Ms. Harper, but do you mind if we have a little chat? We will step outside for a few minutes. It shouldn't take long.'

Even though he isn't in uniform, there is no doubt that he is police.

I nod, unable to speak; my mouth is so dry. I try to swallow my beating heart, but it remains stubbornly in my throat.

I am once again following my feet without thinking. This time they take me from the ward to the stark seating area just outside.

He gestures for me to sit down, but I tell him I would prefer to stand. 'My name is Detective Constable Clarke,' the officer says, as we fall into position opposite each other beside some hard-looking chairs. As we stand to face each other, I am glad that he is only an inch or two taller than me.

My hands automatically move together in the way they do when I am about to start wringing them, but I manage to stop myself at the last second. D.C. Clarke sees this though and I can almost see him etching it into his memory for later.

He has acne around his lower cheeks. I try to avoid staring at it. A girl in high school had it the same way; it used to make me so angry that no one would ever let her forget it.

'This is nothing to worry about, Ms. Harper,' D.C. Clarke continues. 'I just need to ask you a few questions – build up a clear picture of what happened on Sunday afternoon.'

'OK, that's fine.' But it is not fine. I don't think I have ever been less fine in my entire life. I hope the colour of my face isn't too obvious in the flat hospital light.

He asks me some basic questions and I fill in the blanks with times and details. I tell them that Andrew had been staying over at my flat and that he went home to do some housework while I painted in the city centre. If nothing else, I think bitterly, being in one spot in a very public place gives me a perfect alibi. Not that I need one; it would have taken someone much stronger than me to inflict those injuries on Andrew, or someone filled with much more anger...

'You didn't make any calls, though?' D.C. Clarke presses. 'Didn't call Mr. Hughes's parents or anyone else he knew to try to find out where he had gone to?'

'No – like I told you, I called his mobile lots of times, but there was no answer. I just kept getting the voicemail message.' He jots this down and looks up from his notepad for me to continue.

I know I need to play it down, my relationship with Andrew. I need to be a nothing to the police. A nobody, not even worth a second glance.

'We... well we hadn't been dating for that long... I wasn't sure what had happened to him.' I fear with every word I utter, I might be making myself more than completely insignificant. 'I–I thought maybe he didn't want to see me, or something. We were supposed to meet at five, and I was a few minutes late. I thought maybe he had got annoyed and left without me.'

More scribbling. 'I see. How late were you?' He stares at me, pen poised.

'I don't know, just a few minutes...'

His pen waits for further details.

'Maybe seven minutes,' I say.

His voice takes on an incredulous tone, with a look on his face to match. 'So you thought that because you were four minutes late, your boyfriend decided not to pick you up and drove home without you?'

My face burns. I chastised myself for having that thought last night and all the way here on the bus. It sounds even more ridiculous to hear it said out loud.

'No,' I say, quietly. 'Well, it was just a thought. But, no I didn't think it later on – when he still wouldn't answer his phone.'

He taps his pen on his notepad distractedly. 'Did you and Mr. Hughes argue that day? Have any kind of falling out?'

'No. Of course not. Everything was fine–' My voice breaks.

'Take your time,' D.C. Clarke says, with surprising compassion. His voice doesn't seem to match his features. I think his mouth is too small for such a broad face.

I take a deep breath. 'We spent the morning together yesterday. Andrew was supposed to meet me, but he never turned up. I had no idea what had happened to him. I called his mobile loads of times – but it just kept going through to the answering machine. I just... I just didn't know what to do.'

'And can you think of anyone who would want to hurt your boyfriend? Anyone at all, no matter how significant they may seem?'

I shake my head. 'I thought someone had tried to

310

burgle him. Maybe he tried to stop them, and that is how he got like this?'

'To be honest, Ms. Harper, it doesn't look like that is the case at the moment. Like I said, we just need to get an idea of what happened yesterday. Does anyone immediately spring to mind?'

I try to avoid looking at the officer's cheeks; instead, I stare a poster on the wall.

Who would want to hurt Andrew? And in the middle of the day, in his own home? Only someone who is crazy, or thinking purely of drug money, perhaps.

I shrug, dabbing the corners of my eyes with my fingertips. 'He has loads of friends and he's popular with lots of people at work too. I can't imagine Andrew making an enemy of anyone.'

But then I think of one person who may wish him harm. One person he may have recently made an enemy of.

One person who could not simply let him go.

48

I feel utterly flat like I have been drained. Ever since I spoke to the police officer yesterday, I have been unable to think of anything else. Panic attacks come and go with more frequency than they ever have. During a particularly bad episode near midnight, I felt like calling Julia up and begging for help. I had my phone in my hand, and I still had her mobile number stored in my contacts. What stopped me, in the end, was the fear I couldn't catch my breath long enough to speak.

This morning I realise that I wouldn't have got an answer anyway; Julia wouldn't be on hand to answer phone calls twenty-four hours a day.

Besides, I had already given up on therapy. I could never go through with the kind of treatment Julia told me I needed. I just can't be honest enough. Not officially anyway.

In my dressing gown, I make coffee in a daze. Everything seems so unreal still; my surroundings look so normal, so familiar, but it is like the world beyond them has stopped spinning. I put the television back on again in the background in an attempt to make things feel normal. I had it on all last night to coax me into sleep on the sofa.

I could never have expected anything like this to happen. Andrew is the most decent man I have met in my adult life. I can't imagine him falling so fowl of anyone. The police will have to come to the conclusion that a random stranger did this to him, that it was the handiwork of some desperate drug-addict looking to fund their next fix. No sane person would ever cause another so much damage.

And yet D.C. Clarke seemed quite sure that this wasn't just a case of a burglary gone wrong...

When I sink onto the sofa with strong coffee in my *Aunty Harriet* mug, I make no attempt to hide the slogan. I wrap my hands around it, weaving my fingers through the handle and savouring the warmth.

Just forty-eight hours ago, Andrew and I sat here together, feeding each other toast and happily making plans for the day. That seems so long ago now.

A noise from outside startles me and has me jumping up to look out of the window. I feel my eyes darken when I see that it is Debbie, opening her shop for the day.

Did Andrew go and see her on Sunday? Would Debbie have been the last person to have spoken to him before the attack? What did she do, let him go home and have someone follow him there?

I watch her disappear inside Minerva Interiors and wonder if she even knows what has happened to Andrew. If she hasn't had a part in his condition, then she might still be oblivious.

It is all so bizarre that I don't know what to think. When I press my face into my hands, all I can see is the image that has troubled me all night – the one of Andrew lying unconscious in hospital, his mother stifling her grief by his side as if the worst has already happened.

I'm so tired. I just need all this to go away so I can rest and come back at it with a clear head. Or better still, to wake up and for this to all have been a harrowing nightmare.

My eyes fall onto the half-empty bottle of wine on

the coffee table. On the way back from the hospital, I picked up a couple of bottles of red from the local convenience store. There was no point in pretending that I could have just come home and not been beside myself. I needed something to calm me down – something stronger than chamomile tea. The man behind the counter could tell from my pale face and wiry hair that I wasn't planning to host a dinner party; the look on his face said it all.

I feel like I don't have the energy to open up the gallery today, but the prospect of sitting up in the flat alone all day frightens me more. Last night seemed to drag on forever; I need a change of scenery.

I pull myself together and open up. To an ignorant eye, it would look like any other day. I try to fill my time with as many tasks as I can.

I am helped out initially by a phone call. My heart sinks when I answer and I realise it is Mrs. Hopkins. She is checking up progress of her custom piece. I still have not developed it any further than the basic sketch. With my insides squirming, I tell her that it is going very well and she should be able to pick up the finished piece on Friday. When I put the phone down, I am annoyed that I have given myself such a short deadline. But she has been waiting so long for this painting; she was getting very impatient on the phone and I couldn't bear to tell her it was going to take any longer.

I will have to push myself and do it tonight, I think. As soon as I get into the flat after closing, I will get started. Maybe if I force myself to concentrate on something else I might feel better.

I really wish it wasn't a Tuesday. I could do with more people coming and going, even asking me mundane questions to keep me distracted. After my difficult phone call first thing, I have little else to do.

I sit on my seat behind the counter before lunch and look wistfully through the large glass windows. Outside, the sun shines down on the street, making everything look brighter. People wander past in shorts and loose t-shirts; pretty summer dresses and colourful blouses. Envy rises in me when I consider that all they have to worry about is trivial nonsense like which flavour ice-cream to opt for and which restaurant they will choose for dinner...

I won't be doing any of those things for a while; won't have my boyfriend by my side; won't wake up with someone that cares for me. I might well not even get to do them at all this year, or the next...

For the first time, I consider the fact that Andrew might not survive. What if he never leaves that hospital bed? Never breathes on his own again? His face never returning to its natural, handsome state?

I screw up my face and try to force down the storm of anguish that comes howling from my mouth. I try hard, but it is too strong, too stubborn, too raw for me to squash down. Uncontrollable sobs make my shoulders shake and I am truly grateful now that I am alone in the shop.

There is no way I can stand behind this counter for the rest of the day. I close up as soon as my tears ebb enough to allow me to see what I am doing.

I plan on jumping in the shower and trying to scrub this latest misery from my skin. Maybe I'll take some wine in with me too. It is far too early though and I'll definitely need some later to help me sleep. I don't want to be forced to buy more and face the condescending looks the local shop staff might give me. Maybe I will look for another store nearby, just in case I need it.

I open the door to my flat and pick up the post that lays upon the carpet.

It looks like I have been bestowed a generous handful of junk mail again by the postman. I stand by the recycle bin in the kitchen and quickly tear open envelopes. I have a water bill, a generic broadband promotion, a supermarket leaflet and a blank envelope I assume will be an ad for a local service.

Last Christmas, a local gardener sent out Christmas cards to everyone in the area with his contact details inside. I thought it was quite creative at the time, but the business-owner, or whoever was in charge of marketing, should have done their research and skipped our street because we don't have anything more than weedy paved yards.

I tear open the blank envelope and a thrill of dread shoots through me as I take in the message printed on a single sheet of white paper. Two lines, in plain Times New Roman, reads:

You stupid, fucking bitch. I bet you wish you had never gone near him now, don't you?

What are you going to do now, Harriet?

My hands start to shake. My numb fingertips moisten against the paper.

All thoughts of starting the client painting go out of my head, to be replaced by a sheer rush of anxiety until it is all I can think about.

The paper flutters to the floor and I sink against the wall, struggling for air. My chest won't expand far enough for me to breathe right. I feel dizzy, in danger of slipping away into nothingness.

316

My fingers run through my hair and I grip until it hurts.

I need to feel pain – something – anything other than absolute terror; something other than pure panic.

49

Harriet

I think I am finally safe. It has been at least eighteen-months since I left Dan. Since I moved to the South Coast I still have not heard so much as a whisper from my ex-husband. Working as a chambermaid in one of Brighton's seafront hotels, the money isn't great, but it is steady. The best part is that it is behind the scenes, in the shadows. Out of sight and safely hidden. Dan would never think to look here.

Not that he hasn't tried.

I ditched my phone when I left. I had long suspected that Dan had installed a tracking app to keep an eye on me.

Only my mother has the number for my new phone. She told me Dan had been following her, my old employer too. He had obviously been searching for me for over six-months after I left.

And I am under no illusion that he has given up.

My mother sounded worried when I first spoke to her after leaving Dan. She offered me help, but I refused it. Not that I wasn't tempted, but it was so important for me to stand proudly on my own two feet after so long living in fear on my knees.

My biggest worry now is that I have grown too complacent. The only way Dan's attention would be drawn this way though, is if something about me gets posted online, but that shouldn't be an issue. Dan didn't ever allow me to have any social media accounts anyway, so I didn't have the hassle of deleting any.

I just have to be careful of what my colleagues post

online. I've kept my distance from people here, and haven't made friends as such, but there have been near misses; like the staff Christmas party photo that someone posted to Facebook last year.

I think I got away with that one though. I explained to the girl that posted it that I didn't like having my photo taken. She looked confused, but took the picture down.

A Google alert is set up to send me an email anytime my name is mentioned online, just in case anything slips through the net. And that Christmas photo didn't show up in my inbox, so I'm sure I got away with it.

I know Dan knows about this trick, so I want to be alerted straight away if anything shows up to give me time to get away.

When I get a new alert in my inbox this morning, I get the familiar feeling of dread and I click to open the email with numb fingers.

Sweet relief washes over me when I see that it is simply a news article about some artist in the West Midlands. *Not me, thank God.* She just shares the same name – not unusual – I have had several false alerts in my emails.

For a few moments, I get caught up in reading the article. It states that this Harriet Harper has set up a successful art gallery and recently hosted an exhibition. That is nice.

I have an art degree, not that I have ever used it. Looking back, it was probably a waste of time. That is what Dan always told me, anyway.

Maybe now that I have built up my savings a little I can think of a career change. This article mentions how this woman had always wanted to follow her dream of becoming a professional artist and one day just did it.

Reading the article, I am lost in thought about how I would love to do the same thing.

But as I read further, I notice strange coincidences pop out at me. This woman not only shares my name, and my exact age, but the article even mentions that she has an art degree too.

Small world.

I close my emails and look out the window where a seagull glides past, ready to start attacking the bins outside. I frown at the sea, but I am not really looking at it. Something is niggling at me.

When I left Dan in such a hurry, I was lower on funds than I wanted, so I applied for a credit card; something I have never done before. My thought was that it would tide me over until I built my savings back up again.

But during the application process, I was told that my credit score was a little low, and that I would have to pay a higher rate of interest than advertised. I argued that I had never had a credit card before. They didn't believe me; they probably get that all the time. In the end, I ended up paying more to borrow on the card. It was a good thing in a way though, because although frustrating, it forced me not to overspend.

I checked out my credit file afterwards and noticed there were multiple entries I did not recognise. I suspected Dan when I saw them – since some of them were even taken out while we were still together. It must have been him – he had access to my personal information; he knew my name, my date of birth and he probably received my post for a while after I left. He could easily have used those things as proof of ID. I didn't set up a postal redirect because I was so afraid it could be traced back to me; instead, I just shut down my accounts and started new ones.

Dan could easily have applied for things in my name. It would be a new low for him, granted, but I know he would have been livid with me for slipping away from right under his nose.

I didn't risk reporting Dan to the police for fear of giving my location away. Unless he was sent to prison for life, then I would never feel safe. And after all, I've only lost points on my credit score, no big deal. It could be worse – I could have lost my life...

But now I am not so sure it *was* Dan. Many of the creditors listed in my file were smaller companies and many of them were based in the West Midlands. Did Dan move to another part of the country straight away after I had gone? I can't imagine him just leaving his job like that...

I remember the night I left – the night Dan accused me of setting up a bank account in his name. I still think that was odd. Did the perpetrator do the same for me too? That would explain everything. I wonder if the person behind it knew that their actions almost got me killed...

I frown as I try to remember the most recent item recorded on my credit file. Now that I think about it, that was from Coventry Savings and Loans. The Harriet in the article was based in Coventry. Is that merely a coincidence?

I move over to the window and look out at the day. What was a sunny afternoon has now blown out towards the horizon. There is now just an opening in the clouds, and the sun beams down on a strip of sea far away, making it appear bright turquoise when everything around it looks grey.

What if Dan has seen this article too?

I am sure that he must have done, sure he would have received the email just like me this morning. He must have seen all the strange coincidences too – only to him, they would not have been coincidences. What if he thinks that it is me the article is talking about? Even I had to re-read the text several times to make sure I hadn't misread it.

I know Dan. I remember with a horrible rush of fear and dread what he used to do when something happened he didn't like. My leaving him would have enraged him more than I care to imagine. I'm just thankful I managed to get out before he regained consciousness that night.

He would have been seething, desperately searching for me any way he could. I know he followed people I knew. My mother told me he had been parked outside her house, trailing her whenever he could.

If Dan has read the article, he could be moving into action already.

I open my emails back up. The alert was sent at 10:34 this morning. Today is Thursday; would Dan take the day off work to travel to Coventry? It is now almost three o'clock in the afternoon. He could already be there if he saw the email earlier.

If he turns up at this gallery thinking this woman is me, there is no telling what he would do. The last time I made him angry, and I was there to face the consequences, he almost killed me. I close my eyes tightly and try not to think about that night... the night when I thought Dan was going to beat me to death; when I thought I was never going to get up again.

Dan is irrational. Crazy. He can jump to a conclusion even if it is miles away.

What if he turns up in Coventry and realises this

woman isn't me but suspects she is somehow connected? He doesn't think logically when he gets into a rage.

There is no reasoning with him.

50

This time I really thought I might die. Everything I have been through lately, followed rapidly by everything I have ever been through, came crashing in on me in an instant. I couldn't breathe.

Even now, where I have taken refuge in the calm emptiness of the bathroom, I still feel weak and shaken.

Every breath I take is tentative, leaning against the cold tiles of the wall, wondering if my lungs will pull in enough air to prevent me from suffocating.

Through the frosted glass of the bathroom window I see a dark figure moving around outside in the alley, or maybe it is in the yard next door. From here I can't tell. Between the darkness of the passageway at the back and the goldfish bowl of the shop front, I feel like there is always someone around, lurking, feel as though I am always being watched.

I pick up my glass of wine from the side of the bath and take a sip. The worst has passed, but I still am far from being calm.

I think of the note that I crumpled up and stuffed into the bin.

How can Debbie do this? It must have been her, after all. Who else would do such a thing?

She must be mad and be trying to drive me insane too. How could she send that note after what has happened to Andrew?

I am in two minds whether I should fish it out of the bin and show the police, or leave it where it is and try to forget about it. It might help catch whoever attacked Andrew; on the other hand, it might simply draw further attention towards me and that is the last thing I need right now.

In the quiet of the bathroom, a slamming of a car door snaps my attention back to the here and now. As has become my habit lately, I scurry through to the living room and sneak a look outside. A police car is parked outside Minerva Interiors, the occupants getting back inside.

I swear under my breath. *How long have they been there?*

I berate myself for not seeing them sooner. Debbie stands outside her shop, watching as the vehicle pulls away and disappears at the end of the road. She pauses for a moment and I am surprised to see a Debbie I have never seen before. Her face is pale, even under her make-up, and the lines around her mouth seem more obvious as she chews the inside of her cheek, making her appear suddenly older.

Without warning, she looks across at the gallery and then straight up at me.

I slip behind the curtain. I'm certain she could not have seen me through the net curtains, but I still feel a thrill as though I have been caught doing something naughty.

I move my head slowly forward and chance a cautionary glance out of the window. Debbie has gone.

Returning to the sofa with my drink, I am disappointed to see so little left in the glass. I turn it around and around idly on the coffee table, thinking.

Something niggles me about the way Debbie looked. Her pallid face looked strained, in shock even. Perhaps the police visit really was the first she had heard of Andrew's condition? She opened the shop as always and was going about her daily business as though nothing had happened, after all.

Is she really that cold, or did she genuinely not have a clue?

I am itching to know what was said and annoyed that I didn't get to survey the visit through the window. The gallery would have been the best place to watch from. Why couldn't I have kept myself more together earlier and stayed open?

They must suspect Debbie of having involvement in the attack on Andrew. There would be no other reason for them to come here, surely. I mentioned to the police officer at the hospital that Andrew is still in touch with his ex-wife, that he may have even visited her on Sunday, but I didn't mention any of the things she had done to us. I had to bite my lip to keep them all in. But it seems as though they have put two and two together themselves. Maybe I gave something away in my body language and D.C. Clarke picked up on it?

For a good twenty minutes, I let myself believe that Debbie is the centre of the police investigation. Then reality hits me like a wave of cold water and I am drenched in a sudden influx of fears and doubts.

It occurs to me that the police talking to Debbie isn't a good thing – not at all. What if they had come to ask her about me, not her ex-husband? They may have been scouting the street, looking for someone who knows me.

What if she spoke about me from her narrow-minded perspective? She could tell them I have a bad temper – OK, it might not be an untruth, but it certainly wouldn't look good in the present circumstances.

What about the incident Sally witnessed too? Two words against one, they would surely corroborate, make me sound as disruptive as possible.

Our altercations might not have been bad enough to push Debbie to call the police before, but if they come knocking on her door, she might seize the opportunity with both of her bony hands.

She might even make a formal complaint.

I can't stand to face the police a second time – I have too much to lose.

Why did I allow myself to get so involved with people here? I've made such a big mistake.

51

The force of another panic attack tears through me for well over an hour at its worst. Two major attacks and it is barely six in the evening.

I am left weak and shaken and desperately craving something comforting. My sweet tooth demands satisfaction, but I don't think anything in the flat would suffice. I rummage through the cupboards, looking inside with disappointment.

The only thing I can make is a cheese sandwich, but I'm starving so I take it. I find some onion chutney that I have been avoiding. It has been lurking in the back of the fridge for some time, but I smear some onto the bread; it is the only thing I have that can give me anything close to the sugar rush I crave.

I put on the television for some background noise and sit down to eat my unappetising dinner. After a while, I get so tired of hearing ludicrous celebrity reality nonsense that I mute it, leaving the brightly-tanned characters to keep me company in silence.

It is getting dark now and the only light comes from the television. I know I should put on a light, but I quite like it like this in a way. My attention can more easily be drawn to the screen, and it's much easier to ignore the fact that I am alone.

I can almost distract myself from what a horrible mess I am in.

My phone lights up and vibrates with a phone call, making me jump. I snatch it up, thinking it will be news from the hospital.

It isn't. It is Dave.

I groan. I have completely forgotten to call or text him back. He probably thinks I am ignoring him.

Well, I sort of am at the moment. I put my phone delicately back down on the coffee table, afraid to touch the screen and accidentally accept his call. Like I can deal with any of that right now.

I want to pretend to be someone else. I want someone else's inane, everyday problems, not to be in this situation.

I loved being Harriet when everything was going well. The comfort I derived from being her has all but slipped away.

I didn't mean to make such a mess of everything.

My phone buzzes with a text.

Hi Ms. Harper, I seem to be having trouble getting hold of you. I've popped by the gallery a few times, but you never seem to be open. Is everything all right? I heard the gallery takings have dropped. If you are having financial difficulties, as your landlord, I really need to know! We can't bury our heads in the sand over this, we would need to take some grown-up action. Really need an answer this time, please.

Please call me back ASAP! Dave.

My eyes blur with tears, making reading the end of the message difficult. I am no longer Harriet, I am 'Ms. Harper'. For starters, that is a bad sign.

And how does he know my turnover has dipped? Surely Andrew didn't tell him that? Maybe he did speak to Dave after all? He might have tried to use that in my defence over the breakage incident with Debbie.

I re-read the message. Dave's meaning could not be clearer when he says that we need to take some "grown-up action". My bottom lip trembles; I take a deep breath I will myself not to cry. It sounds like he doesn't think I can keep paying my rent.

With a fresh wave of panic, it occurs to me that my lease will be coming up for renewal soon. My home and livelihood could be felled in one cut. I really need to sort this out. The sensible thing to do would be to call him back immediately and talk to him like a "grown-up".

But I don't.

I swipe away the messaging app and slide my phone under a cushion so I can't see it.

I feel like a naughty child trying in vain to hide evidence of some wrongdoing. My insides squirm with guilt when I think of how I have left the gallery closed and shut-down looking several times lately.

I vow to sort the situation out tomorrow when it is daytime and not a single drop of alcohol can influence my decision. That gives me all night to decide what to say, make a good case.

I can call from the gallery phone and speak to Dave properly. It will look better if I call from my business number; it might help to assure him the place is doing fine and I haven't been forced to shut it due to poor trade. Yes, that is what I will do tomorrow morning.

I skip through the channels and try to find something to watch, something I could really focus on to take my mind off things for a while, but I can't. Everything available is either mind-numbing or reminds me too vividly of reality. I come back around to the beginning again and skip quickly past Holby City, trying not to look at it.

I should probably have gone to the hospital this evening to see Andrew. Even though he is

330

unconscious, he might still be able to sense I am there. Besides, I feel the need to show Judith and Charles some support. It is what Andrew would want and I should do that. I should do a lot of things. My eyes prickle and I swallow down tears – I don't want to see him if he might die. I can't bear it.

My cushion starts vibrating. Is Dave really determined to talk to me tonight? I pull my phone out and look at the screen.

It is a mobile number I do not recognise.

My finger hovers over the answer button, but I stop and slide my phone back onto the coffee table.

I have had a couple of unknown numbers call me since Andrew put up the Google Places listing for the gallery.

Last week, when I was feeling positive about the business and my future, I would have probably answered it. Perhaps I can give them a callback tomorrow, right after I have finished speaking to Dave.

I let the call ring through and my phone goes still and quiet again.

I finally switch the television off and am just about to go and get that book that I have been avoiding for ages from my bedside drawer, when my phone lights up with another call.

It is the same unknown mobile number.

Well, they certainly are persistent. I look at the time in the corner of the screen; it is past eight-thirty. Surely they can't expect me to take a work call in the evening?

Why wasn't I more firm last week? Wasn't it common sense not to allow my personal number to be available online to anyone who looks up the gallery?

People shouldn't be allowed to harass me twenty-four hours a day. If some snooty architect wants to order a custom piece of art at four in the morning, should they expect me to answer it?

I'm definitely switching my phone off tonight when I go to bed.

My phone stops ringing and the room suddenly seems very dark without its overly-bright glow. It takes my eyes a few seconds to adjust. Closing the curtains, I switch on the lamps, heading to the bedroom to go and fetch my book.

I pause at the studio door and look into the dark room. With other lights on in the flat, this room looks neglected. Even the white sheet covering the floor looks white and ghostly in the darkness. I feel the pangs of conscience, as I know I should probably work on Mrs. Hopkins's painting, but tonight I want a rest.

I need to forget everything for a while, or I think I might actually go mad. If the call was anything important they would leave a message like Judith did.

The renewed buzzing of my phone brings me out of my reverie and I realise I am still leaning in the studio doorway.

I swear under my breath and go back into the lounge to look at the phone screen – a third call from the same number.

Who the hell do they think they are? I don't care how important they deem themselves, or what kind of budget they have, I'm not going to answer now just out of protest.

I reject the call in a flare of temper. Calling more aggressively isn't going to make me suddenly answer my phone.

I quickly regret my hasty action when a cold doubt

sinks into my chest.

What if it is Charles trying to give me an update on Andrew? I don't have his number stored, although I'm sure I would recognise it if I saw it.

Wouldn't I? He might be calling on behalf of his wife, maybe there is something wrong with her phone... She might have spent too long at the hospital and the battery has run down... or the news is so horrible that Judith is simply incapable of relaying it herself...

I don't dare call the number back, just in case it is work-related, I can't handle a call like that now. Although I don't think I can handle a call with bad news from the hospital, I need to know if it is...

I spend the next hour rummaging through the counter in Stony Studios searching for Charles's number. I'm sure I have it somewhere. Why didn't I just store it when I had the chance?

I pull out drawers and rifle through papers, getting deja vu from when I searched fruitlessly for the courier receipt. I screw up my eyes, pinching the bridge of my nose and try to go back to that day in my mind. Did I see his number then? I can't recall that.

What if Debbie saw the contact details of Andrew's parents when she was in here that afternoon and threw them away?

Maybe I am being too paranoid now. I know I need to stop obsessing over that woman so much. Really, I would be happy if I never had to think of her again.

For whatever reason, I feel like I won't find Andrew's father's number here. Perhaps it was me that moved it or discarded it absent-mindedly.

A sudden flash of inspiration has me straightening up and reaching for the phone on the counter. I'm so stupid – Charles's mobile *is* in here. I check it against the number on my phone screen. They are definitely different. Of course, that doesn't dispel the possibility that he could have changed his number since–

A sudden noise from the back startles me. I freeze and turn my head towards the little dark kitchen area.

I am certain I can hear other noises too – a faint tapping or banging, but my heart pounds so loudly too; I am not sure my hearing is reliable over the sound of it coupled with the rushing of blood in my ears.

But I can feel it, rather than seeing or hearing; Instinctively, I know someone is out there in my yard.

I'm so scared that I do nothing but hurriedly switch off my torch and rush out the front door onto the street. I roll down the shutters in record time and hurry into my flat. Sliding across every lock swiftly, I press my back against the wall in the dark.

I breathe heavily, ashamed by how terrified I am. Some distorted voices suddenly float out of nowhere in the darkness and I actually gasp out loud. For a split-second, I believe that there is actually someone inside the flat I have just thoroughly bolted myself into.

I am angry when I realise it is just some drunken pedestrians on the pavement outside, most likely leaving the takeaway with a disgusting late-night meal.

In my pocket, my phone vibrates with a new call, making me jump.

I take a shuddering breath and know it will take more than just deep breathing to make it through the night.

52

Harriet

After seeing the news article about the other Harriet Harper, the successful artist, I managed to carry on with my daily routine. I won't pretend my insides haven't ached with guilt the whole time.

For almost a week, I went to work as normal and tried my best to act as if nothing is wrong.

My colleagues kept asking me if I was OK. They told me I seemed "distant" or "even more stressed out than normal". Obeying my rule of never confiding anything in them, I told them that I was fine.

I haven't told anyone about the other Harriet Harper; that I have tried to ignore thoughts of what could have happened, or could be happening to her as I go about what has become my daily routine of never-ending washing and ironing at the hotel.

During my lunch-break yesterday, I found myself imagining with horror what could happen if Dan catches up with the other Harriet and allows his simmering anger to boil over into an eruption. At that moment, my manager came into the staff room and told me I looked terrible.

'Thanks,' I said. He asked me if I was having personal problems at home and suggested that maybe I should take my annual holiday time, as it was due to expire anyway.

I didn't feel like spending a couple of weeks at home alone, but I agreed; I don't want to face constant questions and end up breaking down and divulging my life history to anyone.

Having some time and space to think led me to one conclusion: I should make contact with the other Harriet. I don't necessarily even have to tell her who I am. I can call and pretend to be one of Dan's work colleagues; I could tell her I have noticed Dan using his work computer to obsessively look her up.

There is no need for her to know who is calling. Although, if the suspicions that have also been keeping me awake at night are correct, she might already know exactly who I am.

I am so torn over what to do, but I know I should definitely attempt to talk to her, warn her.

Last night I tried calling her. Her mobile number is listed on the Google Places ad for Stony Studios.

The number seemed to be active – it rang through several times at least – but I didn't get an answer. The fourth time I called, the phone had been switched off. Strange, considering it was listed as a business number. Is that how she deals with customers? But I guess it was late, or she was busy. I hoped it wasn't because Dan was there. My mind kept dreaming up horrible scenarios, including the possibility that Dan had already got to her and has her phone.

But surely I would have heard if something had happened. I still have that Google Alert set up and there have been no further news articles with her name in – I have been checking several times a day.

I could have texted or emailed, but I had no idea how to word what I had to say without it sounding odd.

I wanted to talk to her on the phone, to have made her understand. She would have heard how genuinely worried I am.

But I knew I wouldn't be able to do that – I hate the

thought of pretending to be someone I'm not.

There is another reason I don't want the conversation to be one-sided. Having a real conversation with her would allow me to perhaps glean some details about who she is, and why there are so many coincidences between us...

This morning I wait until Stony Studios is open. I have the opening times according to Google Places displayed on my laptop screen. As long as they are correct, the woman should be in there and running the shop by now.

This time I call the landline number. It rings and goes through to the answering machine. I try again but am left listening to the monotonous answering machine message and nothing else. Perhaps she is busy with a customer.

I wait impatiently and call again just before lunch. Nothing.

Doesn't this woman ever answer her phone?

I slam my laptop shut and delete the outgoing calls from my phone. I don't want to see them. This was a mistake. I don't want to think of it again.

Later on in the afternoon, I change my mind and hurriedly bring up the gallery details on my laptop again. I dial Harriet's mobile number, but it goes straight through to the answering machine.

What if she is unable to answer the phone?

I try the landline several more times, leaving ten minute gaps between each call.

I look at the Street View of the front of the little shop. It is only a small place, wherever the phone is, she must surely be able to hear it.

Unless she is lying dead in a back room...

When I call the landline again, it starts ringing and I

337

feel a jolt of nerves, thinking she must answer it this time.

The phone cuts off mid-ring. Now all I hear is silence.

53

Harriet

All night I was deliberating over what to do. I haven't got anywhere by trying to call this woman on the phone. I try to pretend to myself that she might have taken some time off, gone on holiday perhaps, but I don't think so somehow. I just get the feeling something else is going on; I just hope it is not what I suspect.

My satnav app informs me I still have twenty-yards until my destination, but I switch it off. I am close enough.

I had to come here. What other choice did I have?

I have been beside myself with worry. I have Googled her name – my name – constantly, trying to bring up any fresh news results. My internet browsing history is littered with visits to local press websites, including the one that published the first article, but to no avail.

There hasn't been anything posted about this woman, nor have there been any horrible incidents in the street at all, as far as I can tell.

I was going mad going through the continuous cycle of checking and waiting. I had to come here and find out for myself what is going on.

I have had my phone in my hand ready to call the police so many times over the past week. Each time my crippling fear stopped me.

If I get the police involved, Dan might find out where I am. I might have to face him, even if it was just

339

in a court. I don't ever want to see him again.

I can't deal with a messy investigation that goes on forever. How long would Dan be sent to prison for? He would only bide his time and find me again when he got out.

If remaining far away from Dan means hiding in the shadows my entire life, then so be it.

Now that I am positioned on Stonegravel Street in the harsh light of day I start to panic.

I shouldn't have come here in person. What am I doing? What if Dan is here already?

My damp fingers grip the steering wheel tightly. I could just turn around and drive away now. I could pretend I was never here. My insides writhe guiltily again and I know my mind will not let me rest until I know.

I have to do this. I need to know what is happening here. I want to know who this woman is – I need to know she is safe.

I turn the engine off. Through the windscreen, I can see Stony Studios further down the road.

Looking around, I scan carefully for any sign of Dan. I have no idea if he still has our old car, he might have changed it since then. He would know I would always have an eye open every time I walk down a street, looking out for it. I still panic every time I see the same model until I check the licence plate and driver and realise it is a false alarm.

After a few moments, I deem it safe. Dan could be driving anything now, but he would never choose to drive a Purple Peugeot 107, or a white transit van.

With my hands in my pockets and trying to look casual, I wander down the pavement until I am standing right outside the gallery. It looks just like its photo

340

online, except that the shutters are down and the place looks like it has been closed all day. According to the opening times, the place should be well and truly open for business by now.

I step around some discarded takeaway trays and peer in through the little holes in the red shutters. Everything is dark in there, no sign of anyone at all. The counter looks a mess, there are papers and bits of stationery strewn all over it.

I huff out loud when I see the phone cord lying on top of the chaos, pulled out from the empty socket on the wall. So that is why the phone stopped mid-ring. Someone with the keys must have been around yesterday.

I wonder why they pulled the phone out of the socket? I was a little persistent with my calls, but they wouldn't be able to hear it unless they were in the shop... Or somewhere above it...

I step back and look up. There is a flat above the shop. Is it possible Harriet lives up there?

I give the doorbell a ring.

No answer. I didn't really have high hopes. She probably doesn't even live there. I try again anyway, thinking whoever does might at least know where I can find her, but there is no sign of life.

Glancing around, I see there aren't any cars parked outside. I would be inclined to say there wasn't anyone in, but all the curtains are drawn.

There is a sandwich shop over the road. The woman behind the counter is serving a customer, but she keeps her eyes trained over here. Does she think I'm trying to break in? I probably look conspicuous.

It isn't even a few moments before I realise another set of eyes is upon me but from the interior-design shop next door. The woman over there peers at me too, making no attempt to even pretend to look busy like her neighbour.

Friendly locals, I think sarcastically. I would have maybe gone over there and bought something, asking casually about the shop across the street, but neither of the two women looks approachable.

I'll have to try again tomorrow, maybe then I will have more luck.

Unless something terrible has already happened here.

54

I woke up so late this morning, I didn't think there was much point in opening. Actually, that's not true – I just couldn't face it. I am a mess and no amount of showering and make-up will hide it. Not today.

I hardly slept at all. Not unusual, but today it was almost twelve pm before I woke up. I think a noise from downstairs disturbed me, but once I was awake I couldn't hear anything.

If I had rushed to get ready then I might have been able to open the gallery for a few hours in the afternoon, but I did not see the point. Even a generous application of perfume wouldn't cover the smell of alcohol, and serving customers like that is worse than not opening at all. I caught a whiff of it myself and knew I couldn't go out – even if I could get motivated.

My headache pounds relentlessly and I feel thoroughly sick, although that might be from the amount of wine I drank last night. Ashamedly I pick up the empty bottle from my bedroom floor and drop it into the waste bin without looking at it. I should probably put it in the glass recycling, but I don't want to risk anyone seeing it.

I stuff the bottle down with the rest of the waste, trying to hide it. The bin really needs emptying, but I haven't got around to it. The smell of rotting rubbish wafts up into my face, making my nausea worse. I gag and rush to the bathroom.

Later, I take some paracetamol and force some toast down myself. My dry mouth struggles and I have to sip water just to swallow properly.

I need to sort myself out. I need to stop drinking.

There is no real way to get away from my problems when they surround me at every turn.

I stay in the flat for the rest of the day and try to let my headache ease. Even with the painkillers, it still makes me feel queasy.

Downstairs, the phone rings every now and then in the gallery. If my suspicions are correct, it is Mrs. Hopkins asking for an update on her painting. She was very impatient when I last spoke to her. Little does she know, the painting is still nothing but a sketch in my studio.

Annoyingly, I told her it would be ready on Friday. That only leaves me today and tomorrow to get it finished so it can dry in time. There is no way I could get it finished for a Friday pick up now. Maybe if I really got down to it, I could have it ready for Saturday. Yes, I'll do that. Just for my sanity, I know I should do something constructive today; something to take my mind from the fact that I should be visiting the hospital.

I need to get back on track – I can still do this.

I set everything up in the studio and try my best to get into the flow of the painting. It doesn't go very well to start with; the colours seem murkier than I remember them being. The trees seem still and lifeless like they are dead. Maybe that is because that is how I feel at the moment. Empty and hollow and waiting for some new energy to revive me that may never come.

The phone rings again downstairs.

The sound is louder in here; there isn't any carpet to muffle the noise and each ring is distractingly loud through the bare floorboards of the quiet studio.

I will have to switch it off – I can't think. It makes my stomach twinge with nerves every time I hear a new

344

call. I don't like to be under pressure like that. There used to be a time when I could shut everything out by painting, now that is not the case.

Downstairs, the gallery is still a mess from when I was searching for Charles's phone number. There are papers and receipts all over the counter, along with boxes of spilled paper-clips and drawing pins everywhere. It really needs tidying up, but I'll have to do it tomorrow.

At the moment, re-doing that painting is my priority. I hate having to make excuses and I am already on my last chance with her. I really need it to be done so I don't have to think about it any more. Really, I wish I had never accepted the third commission from Mrs. Hopkins in the first place.

The phone starts ringing again as I walk behind the counter. With satisfaction, I pull the phone cable from its socket and drop it onto a pile of papers.

The call cuts off mid-ring and there is silence in the gallery.

55

The next day I wake up at a more reasonable time and get to work in the studio.

I keep the curtains closed so nobody knows I am here. It makes me feel safer, even though the person I most want to run from is myself. I can enjoy some peace and quiet for a while so I can get some good work in. Today is my last chance to finish this piece, or I'm sure I will have to say goodbye to the money for it.

Settling down in my studio after lunch, I look at the canvas with fresh eyes. The painting doesn't look right at all. I thought I had maybe been staring at it too long, but now I sit down again I see it has gone quite awry. The colours are dull and I haven't managed to capture the glow the first one had. The highlights that are yet to be added won't even save it.

Perhaps it is time to consult the photograph I took of the original on my phone. I look around for it, but can't see it anywhere. As I wander into the hall, the doorbell rings.

I quickly shrink back into the studio doorway. I'm sure they couldn't see my feet from the front door, though.

It must be Dave, annoyed that he didn't get an answer to his last message. He has every right to be.

I'm so annoyed that I haven't dealt with that yet, but I can't answer the door now. How can I? Look at the state of me.

After I used the toilet earlier, I caught sight of myself in the mirror and was shocked. Dark circles underlined my eyes and my cheeks had a sallow quality I have not seen before.

I haven't been taking time to cook proper meals for myself, so I think I have lost a little weight. While I would usually think of that as good news, at the moment it does nothing to improve my image – it just makes me look wasted and unkempt, making the lines on my face seem more obvious. I feel like a plant that has been kept from the sun; a promising seedling that has been starved of warmth and light from a young age, that time has managed to develop into a weak imitation of maturity.

My dishevelled appearance won't do my case any good. Dave might think I am drowning my sorrows because business is bad; I can't afford to let him think that.

I don't dare go near the window and look out in case I get caught. The other day, I couldn't shake the feeling that Debbie could see me, even if it was just my shadow through the nets.

He must have gone by now though. I am just about to step back into the hall when the doorbell rings again.

I wonder if he knows I am in here. Where else would I be? Andrew is in hospital still, and I already told Dave long ago that I don't have any family.

I wait twenty minutes, and then when I think it is safe, I go to the living room window and pull back the curtain a little to peer out. I can't see Dave's car anywhere; he must have gone.

I'm aware I need to get in touch with him – I don't want him terminating my lease. To buy myself some time, I will send him a message and arrange to meet up. I'll see if he can pop into the gallery on Saturday.

That gives me a few days to sort myself out. I'll cook some real food tonight and smarten myself up again. I will open the gallery tomorrow on time and make it look like it is doing well.

I just need to send Dave a quick text in the meantime, but first I need to find my phone.

Searching every conceivable place in the kitchen and the living room is fruitless. In the bedroom, I ransack my bedside drawers and even shake my pillows. I check the studio, even though I am confident I wasn't in there last night. I lift up the sheet covering the floor and smooth out the creases, just in case they conceal anything.

Going back to the kitchen, I rummage in the cupboards, peer behind the bin, the gap under the microwave, places where I know my phone can't be, but I check anyway because I don't know where else to look.

I go down to open the gallery shutters, planning to use the landline to call my phone, all the time trying my best to ignore Debbie and Sally. They are both in their customer slump of the day and stare at me shamelessly through their respective windows. I turn my head and angle myself away to stop them seeing how bad I look, but I think they have already taken in my neglected appearance.

That will give them something to gossip about later.

I get a shock when I put my keys in the shutter padlock and realise it is already open.

What the hell?

I move to unlock the front door, but that is unlocked too.

Did I leave it like that? I walk in and look around. Nothing looks out of place. I am virtually holding my breath when I venture into the back rooms, but there is nothing untoward there either.

But why was the front door unlocked? Has someone been in here?

I rush to the till and check inside. Recklessly, I hadn't banked the cash after the last time I opened for business, but the money is still untouched. I gather it up quickly and slip it into an envelope, keeping one eye on the door.

Maybe it was Dave. He might have come in here and had a look around after he rung the doorbell earlier.

I didn't hear him though, and I was working right above in the studio...

I try to ignore the suspicion that it was Debbie with her stolen keys.

But was it either of them? I try to think back to yesterday when I unplugged the phone. Did I even lock up after that?

I command my brain to bring up the memory of my keys in either of the locks, but I can't access it. Does that mean I left the shop unlocked all night? I can't even say for sure.

I may or may not have left my business open overnight, and now I have lost my phone.

I need to start paying serious attention to what I'm doing.

The gallery phone is cordless, but I don't know if the signal will reach far enough to allow me to call from the flat. After reconnecting the phone cable, I call first from behind the counter, just in case I left my phone down here without realising.

I wait for a dial tone and strain my ears, ready to hear the buzz nearby. I press the receiver to my ear but get my default answering machine message.

I swear. My phone is switched off.

56

Most of the evening is spent tearing the gallery and flat apart looking for my phone. The conclusion I come to is that it isn't in either property. Now that I think of it, I don't think I had it at all yesterday. I was asleep for half the day and the other half I tried to shut everything out while I worked.

A wave of shame washes over me when I can't remember the last time I even had it. But I know I received the text from Dave on Tuesday – so I definitely must have had my phone on me then.

Another memory comes to me – of my hand sliding it under the cushion on the sofa. I was drinking, then I had some calls from an unknown number...

Now I remember – I had it in the gallery... But then I definitely took it back upstairs with me, because it rang in my pocket with the same unknown number again.

Then I started having another panic attack. I know I had some more to drink then, but I can't remember much after that.

I groan and sink down onto one of my sofa pads that I tossed onto the floor. Just in case I missed it earlier, I run my hand along the inner sides of the sofa and along the back too. Like earlier, I cringe at the number of crumbs and unidentifiable bits there are but don't feel my fingers grip around anything else.

I need my phone – I feel lost without it – like my whole life is on there. I often find myself reaching for it in the day whenever I need to check anything, to read my messages or view notifications. Plus I have all the private messages sent between me and Andrew; I cringe at the thought of anyone else reading those.

What if I have had more correspondence from Andrew's parents or the hospital? A strong dose of self-reproach comes my way for trying to shut everything out, pretending it hadn't happened. I know Andrew would not have done the same if the tables were turned...

And what if Dave has sent me another message? Maybe that was why he rang the doorbell today? He could have tried sending a text, but not received a reply again. Maybe he came to serve me eviction papers earlier...

And there are my photos too – the only evidence I have of Mrs. Hopkins's painting was on my phone in the form of the photograph I took before I packaged it. My photographs aren't backed up anywhere either.

Although... did I even photograph the painting at all? I'm even doubting that now.

I was so busy worrying about Bethany making sure the courier made the pick-up and stressing out about my therapy appointment. Did I even remember to take a photo? I try to remember, but I seem to have mental fog when it comes to thinking of that morning. There was so much stress later on that day...

Did I do it or not? I can't say for sure either way now. There is only one way to know whether I am losing my mind or not, and that is to *find my phone right away.*

I rack my brains and try to think exactly what I did with it, but I keep coming back empty.

I'm scared to think it, but I suspect I may have ventured outside on Tuesday night. I don't have any memory of doing any such thing, but it is the only explanation. Was I so out of it that I could have gone for a wander outside somewhere for a late-night walk and dropped my phone? It doesn't sound like me at all, but that could be said for many other things I have done lately.

I get a sudden thrill of shame. I wonder if that was why Debbie and Sally were both staring at me earlier.

Did I do something to them? Did I make another scene? Damn, what if they told the police?

I check my handbag for any sign of what I might have done that night, but can't find anything. Counting how much money is in my purse doesn't help me since I can't remember how much I had to start with. I should have paid more attention.

The room has darkened at some point during my search. I think it might be time to switch some lights on.

Before I flick the living room lamps on, I get up and go over to the window; my last chance to survey the street before I blow my cover by lighting up the room.

I look across at Debbie's flat, the net-less windows of which are fully illuminated already, glowing brightly in the dark; it looks almost cosy. She is bustling around in the kitchen, cooking. I am confident she cannot see me over here in the dark.

I am just about to shut the curtain again when something catches my eye down in the street. A dark figure moves at the edge of my vision and I look down just as a man turns and moves to the end of the road before disappearing around the corner.

I don't know why, but I get the sense he was looking up here just moments before.

Watching.

57

I feel the hairs on my neck stand up. The man, whoever he was, was looking up at my flat, I am sure of it. He can't have been watching me though, I had only just gone to the window and pulled the curtain back. It was more like he had been surveying the property itself. Who the hell was he?

I tell myself that it was probably just Dave, but I don't believe it for a second. I can't see his car anywhere for one thing. Why wouldn't he be parked in the street? There are plenty of available spaces.

For another few minutes, I watch out of the window, but the stranger does not return.

I am unnerved, even though I cannot say specifically why.

I attempt to settle down in the studio, but my nerves tingle unpleasantly and I feel too on-edge as if I am about to run a race that I am desperate not to lose.

Now more than ever, I need something to calm me down. In the kitchen, I think of making some chamomile tea, but I know it is not strong enough. The tea helps me mellow out a little, but it won't stop a panic attack.

What if that man is something to do with Debbie? What if he was the one who went through my bins? He could have been the one who attacked Andrew too. Was that done on Debbie's orders? Or have I become far too paranoid?

I really wish I had my phone with me. Earlier, I tested the gallery landline up here, but it just lost signal halfway up the stairs.

I open the refrigerator instead. The bright light makes my eyes hurt after being in the dim lamplight of the studio. The last of the wine is lying on its side on the bottom glass shelf. I hesitate.

I pick up the cold bottle, the condensation makes my fingers slip against the cold glass. I am craving oblivion but am torn between that desire and wanting to stay alert, in case something happens. What if the man came back and tried to break in here when I am under the influence? I would have a better chance if I was able to be more alert; my reaction time would be faster if nothing else.

I make a decision.

I open the bottle and tip the remaining liquid down the sink.

58

Even though I have only just woken up, my heart is pounding as though I have been running. I analyse my mind a few minutes ago. Was I dreaming?

In the darkness, I reach out for my phone and after a few seconds of sleepy fumbling, I realise I won't find it. Judging by the limited amount of light, I'm guessing it must be somewhere around four am; at least I got a couple of hours of sleep.

I quickly sit up and scan the room. Everything looks in order at first glance. Fear creeps into me as I get up and tread carefully into the hallway. Everything is quiet.

Wait – everything is not quiet. There is a strange noise outside.

What now?

I am hyper-aware that I don't have my phone with me. I rush to my bedside and feel around on the carpet for my backup plan – a plane of wood from an old broken easel.

I feel utterly unprepared, even with it in hand, but I don't dare put it down.

Tentatively, I move over to the window and peer down at the dark yard. My blurry eyes can hardly take in anything but dark shapes, much less what is causing the abrupt rustling noise.

What the hell is it?

As my eyes adjust, I know I have correctly identified the sound – it is coming from behind one of my bins. I can see a dark shape moving around in the semi-darkness.

I exhale sharply as the wind picks at the corners of the object. The mass of a dark plastic sheet has been stuffed behind my large commercial bin. It flaps noisily in the wind that has picked up since I went to sleep last night.

Annoyed, I drop my feeble weapon back in its place under my bed.

It wouldn't be the first time a neighbour has dumped excess rubbish in my commercial bin. Usually though, they do a better job of concealing it. This time, however, they haven't even attempted to put it in the bin at all. They just let the wind blow it around my yard and wake me up instead – they have even left the gate wide open.

Throwing myself back into bed, I decide I will deal with it when I wake up later – if I even go back to sleep that is.

Amazingly, I do wake up later in the morning after a brief sleep. I even wake up at a normal time and without a headache. I get up promptly, shower and dress in my usual attire – smart trousers, my favourite navy blazer jacket and heels, finished with a colourful silk scarf.

My hair is neat, twisted up as before, and I apply my usual make-up with as much confidence as I can muster. I even eat a proper breakfast of muesli and toast.

Today things are going to be different. First I am going to open the gallery and tidy up, sort it all out. The next thing I will do after that is plug the phone back in and call Dave to arrange a meeting, make sure my legal rights to the property are secure.

Then, when I shut for the day, I will go into the city

and bank my backlog of takings. I will pick up something pre-prepared and healthy for dinner that I can eat on the go while travelling to the hospital to visit Andrew. It is impossible to ignore the fact I haven't been since Monday, it burns a remorseful hole in my stomach and I cringe with shame.

A deep-breath steadies me as I double-check my appearance in the mirror before going downstairs. As always, I try to avoid looking myself in the eye and look at the picture as a whole. I don't detect a single, Sophie-like thing about myself. Today I am all-Harriet. Well, apart from my regret and intense self-loathing, but that very rarely goes away anyway; only when I spend time with Andrew.

I remind myself I will see him later, and maybe the doctors will have some good news for me.

My whole day is neatly planned out.

I trot down the stairs briskly and when I reach the bottom, I discover the first sign that my day won't turn out exactly how I expect it to.

On the doormat is a sealed envelope. I am instantly reminded of the anonymous letter I received on Tuesday. This can't be another one... Not today. I really need everything to go my way for a little while – even if it is just for a short period. I just need a break.

I pick up the envelope and glance at the front. This time it is addressed to '*Harriet Harper*', rather than being blank like the other one. Unlike the first letter, this one is handwritten. I take a deep breath before I roughly tear it open. There is a single line of handwritten text inside.

GO BACK WHERE YOU BELONG, BITCH

59

I feel sick. My breath catches in my chest. I don't recognise the writing, but I don't think I have seen anything Debbie has written down. Well, maybe I did briefly when rummaging through her rubbish, but I didn't pay any attention at the time.

Does she think this is going to scare me? This letter might be more threatening than the first one – written in angry capital letters – but I am not going to let it affect my behaviour. Does she think I am going to shut down the shop and run away scared because she sends me another childish note? She can forget it; I'm tired of her games.

I am about to screw up the paper when I stop. Before I do anything else, I step outside into the street and lock the flat door. I face towards Minerva Interiors and make a big show of tearing up the paper into more pieces than is probably necessary and scrunch them up forcefully in my shaking hands. I can't see Debbie in the window, but I hope she gets the point.

Next, I gather some disgusting takeaway rubbish from in front of the shutters. Without me clearing it up daily, there is a little more than usual. Maybe I should mention it when I call Dave; it might help my case.

Once inside the gallery, I spend twenty minutes clearing the counter so I can get to the phone, and so it looks like a functional business space again. I sort out the spare papers and throw them away, before taking the small waste bin and emptying it outside.

Next, I call Judith to get an update on Andrew, my conscience berating me for not having done it sooner.

She answers almost immediately. 'Harriet! Why haven't you been answering your phone?'

The high pitched tone and frantic pace of her voice startle me and the hairs on my arms immediately stiffen. 'I-I lost it. What is it? What's happened?' *I'm not sure I want to hear the answer.*

'Oh Harriet, it is wonderful news. Andrew woke up this morning!'

'What? Oh, that's great! What time did it happen? Is he all right?'

'He hasn't been talking long. The doctors are with him now – they said they need some space to work.' She sounds stuffed-up like she has been crying. 'They won't even let the police in yet.'

'I understand. When can I come and see him?'

Judith thinks it would be best if I give the medical staff time to properly assess Andrew, so I arrange to go by after work later.

I'm suddenly re-invigorated and spend a few minutes excitedly pacing the gallery, not sure what to do with myself. I am just so happy. Andrew is awake. Maybe he could even make a full recovery.

I spend the rest of the morning happily changing the canvases in the window to make the shop look fresh, updated.

Even though I suspect it might be a bit of a bad luck charm, I hang the new piece I did on Sunday in the centre; I tell myself I am being too superstitious; just because I was painting it while Andrew was being attacked, doesn't mean that the picture is a bad omen.

My aim is to stay as busy as possible to keep my mind on track. I make a list of things I need to get to make my next window display. I don't want my happy thoughts degenerating, my consciousness slipping into

359

uncomfortable places.... Most of all, I try to avoid thinking of the latest note – as much as I try to fight it, I get a hit of panic at even the slightest thought.

At twelve o'clock, I decide to call Dave, thinking he might be free to talk before lunch. It is only when I get a 'number not in use' message that I realise I have made a mistake. For a few moments, I can't understand what I have done wrong. I even start typing in the number again more slowly – until I suddenly realise why it didn't work – Dave got a new number, and the only place I have it stored is in my lost phone.

I put my face in my hands – I had completely overlooked that – I still have no idea where my phone is. I quickly try calling it again, just in case someone has found it and switched it on, but I get the answering machine straight away.

I am so annoyed with myself. Why don't I keep a backup of my phone numbers? The answer is simple: I never considered that I might lose it.

All afternoon I glance across the street into Sally's Sandwiches. I see Sally serving customers and wonder if I could brave a visit over there. She would be sure to have Dave's phone number, he is her landlord too.

As I watch her preparing to close for the day, I formulate a plan. I will go over there and attempt to reconcile with Sally again and ask for Dave's details while I am there. It gives me a good excuse to extend an olive branch. Sally isn't as bad as Debbie, I am sure. She should respond positively – unless I have done something and just don't remember.

I roll down the shutters on the gallery windows and turn my sign around to say 'closed'. By the time I have spoken to Sally, gained the number and finished the call it should be almost closing time.

I take a deep breath and trot across the road just as Sally is tilling up, planting what I hope is an amiable look on my face as I go.

It turns out she is not in a hospitable mood. I try my best, but she is short with me no matter what I say. However, she does rummage around in the back room and jots down the information I asked for on an orange post-it note. She drops it on the counter with a cold 'Is that all right for you?' and starts mopping the floor with her broad back to me.

I pause with the paper in my hand, I even open my mouth to ask if I have done something else to offend her recently, but I decide to leave it. She obviously was always Debbie's friend more than mine; she isn't worth it.

I'm glad I did not come over here merely to make amends.

I am in such a daze as I leave the sandwich shop, that I step out into the road without looking and have to step back quickly to avoid being run over by a silver transit van.

The driver speeds past me and I am sure I can hear his female passenger shouting at me when they get further down the street. I hear the horn blare and am not sure if it is for me, or if someone else has also done something they didn't like.

With the window shutters down in the gallery, I get a little more privacy when I make my phone call, but just about enough light to see. I leave the door unlocked; the 'closed' sign should stop anyone from wandering in to browse.

I can't say I am not apprehensive about making this phone call; I have avoided Dave for too long. Now I just need to grit my teeth and do it.

As soon as I cross the threshold, I feel like someone has been in here. Or rather, I smell that someone has been in here – aftershave lingers in the air. I almost call out, but as I approach the counter, I notice something is different – a brown, leather-bound notebook has appeared beside the till.

It must belong to Dave. He had something like that when he was showing me around the place. I remember he left it on the counter as he gave me the tour.

I hurry across to the front door and open it, peering down the street, but I don't see his car anywhere.

Strange. Other than Debbie's and Sally's vehicles, there is only a red work van and a grey BMW. Maybe Dave has a new car now too, but I don't see him anywhere. Did he pop across the street while I was talking to Sally? I surely would have seen him.

I stare in every direction, but can't see any sign of my landlord. Maybe he has gone to update Debbie... delivering the news direct to her smug face that he is about to serve an eviction notice.

My stomach cramps at the thought. I shut the front door again and scurry over to the counter. A quick glance over my shoulder tells me the coast is clear before I pick up the worn, leather book. I take a brief flip through it, but it quickly becomes clear I will not find any papers or documents inside.

There only seems to be handwritten entries on each page; some quite lengthy too. My heart pounds nervously and I again glance over my shoulder at the door. I don't want Dave to catch me reading his diary. I can't seem to find anything relating to any of his properties in here, nothing business-related at all, actually. This book seems more like a journal – at least it looks that way, with some dates going back years even.

Suddenly I catch sight of my name – or rather, Harriet's – written in one of the entries.

January 18th
Monitored Harriet's old dentist this week. Her annual check is due.
Nothing. Was an unlikely possibility, but very disappointing nevertheless. I wish I hadn't bothered with this one. WASTE OF TIME!

What the hell? Has Dave been following me? I don't even have a dentist. I flick forward a few pages.

February 21st
June realises I have been watching her. So far she has shown no sign she is in touch with her daughter. But I can't be sure unless I can see what she does inside her own home 24/7!!!

Who the hell is June? Is she another woman Dave is following?

I skip to the last entry in the book, dated just yesterday.

Harriet is hiding. I know she is in there. She hasn't opened her precious little shop for days. The curtains to her flat have been drawn all day, but I know she is inside – HIDING. She doesn't know I am here though – if she did, she would have tried to run by now.

I stare at the book in my hands, feeling nauseous. I

am literally shaking with anger. Why would Dave do this? And where the hell is he? My heart starts pounding threateningly and my breath catches in my chest – but I need answers.

I move to snatch up the phone on the counter, but a sudden noise from the back startles me.

I hear a strange rustling noise coming from the yard. The back door opens and I hear a jangle of keys. It must be Dave. What the hell was he doing in the yard?

Enraged, I rush through to the back to face him at the door – ready to shout – demand answers.

'What the hell is–!' I am halfway through raising the book, ready to brandish it at the man dragging a massive sheet of plastic in through the back doorway. Still with his back to me, he locks the door behind him. But before the words have even left my tongue, and even in the dim light in the back of the shop, I realise that the man is not Dave.

As I open my mouth again in horror, the man charges at me and slams me against the doorway leading to the back of the shop.

My head hits painfully hard against the wooden door frame and I feel light-headed.

I am instantly winded, so I can't call out, but his hand is firmly pressed upon my mouth anyway.

I am still dazed, but I force my blurry eyes to focus on the man's face.

It takes me a moment before I can see straight.

Then I feel my eyes widen with recognition.

I look, wild-eyed and terrified into the eyes of Harriet Harper's husband, Dan.

60

Dan stares back at me, fierce fury turning into obvious confusion.

It is clear that I am not who he was expecting, as I'm sure the look on my face mirrors what his conveys. The only difference is his expression is missing the terror.

I feel suddenly very conscious of the way I am dressed, the way my hair is styled, even the jacket I am wearing – it's the one I actually stole from Harriet's charity collection bag. Why did I have to wear this one today? I wonder if he recognises it.

He screws up the corners of his eyes and lowers the hand covering my mouth.

'You?' he whispers in shock, looking me up and down. His eyes linger the longest on my hair and clothes. 'No – this can't...' He shakes his head angrily, disbelieving.

He looks shocked – almost as much as I am. My brain is jarring, confused, panicked. I wonder why. Why is he even here? Did he get back together with Harriet after I left Tennison Road? Did he come here to investigate some suspicious financial activity on her behalf?

How did he even find me?

My foggy mind can't come up with a plausible reason why he is standing in my shop, so I just stare at him stupidly and wait for him to make the first real verbal move.

Dan remains standing very close, pressing his weight against me with a tight grip on my forearm. 'You aren't meant to be here!' he says finally. 'Where is she!'

He backs away slightly and turns his head pointlessly towards the bathroom and then the kitchen, peering in through the open doors; the two rooms are so tiny, no one could hope to hide in them without being noticed.

I'd completely forgotten what Dan looked like, but now the person in front of me looks very different to the man I now remember. That man had been more handsome, fuller in the face. This Dan looks gaunt, shadowy around the eyes and thinner too, giving his face a slightly menacing touch.

I do nothing. I just stare at him blankly, trying to plan fast, but all I can think is: *I've been caught. I'm in trouble now. I've been caught. He is going to call the police. I've been caught.*

I feel sick. My thoughts whirr so fast I am worried he can almost hear them from standing so close.

What the hell am I going to do?

He looks back to me and gives me a slight shake, trying to prompt a response. 'Why are *you* here?'

I've got no clue as to how to play this. 'I–I have just been... It isn't what it looks like...'

I cringe – it is exactly what it looks like. There is no getting out of this one. I have been caught red-handed.

How did he even find me? I have made a massive mistake somewhere – clearly. Why did I have to do this? I should have left Harriet behind in London...What was I thinking?

I could have walked away at any point before now. I'm so stupid. Now I am in serious trouble.

I struggle to breathe, my lungs burn with the effort.

I try mindfulness in an attempt to calm myself.

I look at the patchy paintwork on the ceiling where it looks like someone has touched up just one point with

366

an off-shade; I look at the shiny silver buttons on Dan's coat; I notice the way the patches of red on his cheeks spread across his unshaven jaw where a muscle twitches; I stare at the little ovals of white on his knuckles where his grip stretches the skin tight.

'Not what it looks like?' Dan repeats.

The gallery phone rings in the background, but it is so insignificant and seemingly far away that I ignore it. Dan seems as though he doesn't hear it either – he is in a world of his own. I can tell he is thinking fast too, but I have no idea what he wants from me.

Turning my head, I watch him move from the back and onto the shop floor. He paces back and forth, looking around at the paintings on the walls and shaking his head.

I realise he has let me go.

Staying upright with such little oxygen in my lungs is such hard work, that only now am I aware he has relinquished his grip on me. The muscle in my forearm tingles with relief; I rub it, trying to soothe the pain as the blood flow returns.

I move into the shop space too, feeling a little safer on more neutral ground, rather than in the back rooms where the public isn't allowed.

He comes to a stop in front of the counter. I move nearer to the middle of the room, on the pretence of continuing our engagement. I wonder if I can make it through the front door before he reaches me. But then what? I don't even have a vehicle nearby.

'I'll tell you what it looks like,' he says, breaking the silence once more. 'Or should I say, what *you* look like. You look just like my wife.' He looks at me, a look of great concentration on his face as if he is trying to retrieve a vague, insignificant detail from long ago. He points at me. 'It's Sophie, isn't it?'

I cringe at the sound of my name. I haven't heard anyone say it out loud for so long. I close my eyes and nod.

He nods, jabbing his finger at me. 'I remember you. You were our neighbour across the hall.' He frowns. 'You look just like my wife – just like Harriet. Why is that?'

I put up my hands. 'I don't know what to say. I didn't mean for any of this to happen. I'm just so sorry...'

A flicker of something passes across his face and I suspect he is going to flip and throw a punch at me. He squeezes his fists but keeps them at his sides. 'Why? What are you sorry for? Are you hiding her here?' He looks quickly up to the ceiling, as though seeing straight through it to the flat upstairs. 'Has Harriet been living with you up there all this time?'

I feel so confused. The room has been spinning as I have been struggling for air, but now I can see things a little more clearly. Something isn't right here. Dan seems almost as bewildered as I am. Has he really come here looking for his ex-wife?

What on earth makes him think she is here?

I pause. 'I... Yes. Yes, she has.' Maybe I can convince Dan that Harriet has been here with me; maybe I can convince him I wasn't impersonating her. It would allow me enough time to slip away... I will take the box I hid under the bed – the one with all of Sophie's documents – and make a run for it. Find somewhere to lie low... Find someone else to become, at least at first, until I get on my feet.

My heart sinks even as my mind formulates a plan of escape, but it seems it might be my only option now. Other than letting myself get arrested.

Dan stares at me. 'I don't understand. I didn't even know you two were friends. Why would she run off to live with you...' I see a sudden thought occur to him. 'Wait a minute – you two aren't–?'

I'm quick to correct him. 'Oh no. We are just friends.' I shrug, hoping he doesn't realise the flat upstairs has only one bedroom. 'It just made financial sense. We both wanted to leave our partners and neither of us had enough money at the time to do it, so we became room-mates.' It is so hard to sound convincing with my heart in my throat. I chance a glance at Dan's eyes – they belie a certain air of scepticism.

He isn't buying this. 'So where is Harriet?' he demands.

I go on, aware of how high-pitched and false my voice sounds. 'She has taken a little break – she went to the lake district. My boyfriend–' my voice breaks slightly, my mouth is so dry '–his parents have a little cottage out there. Harriet went to stay in it for a week or two.'

Dan exhales through his teeth and stares at the floor. 'Gone to get away from it all, has she?'

'Well, yes. She works hard here in the shop. You see she usually works the tills and serves customers and I work upstairs in the studio to keep the place stocked up.'

His head snaps up and he looks at me sharply. 'You paint the pictures?'

'Yes... Of course.'

'Just you? Harriet doesn't do any painting at all?'

I am under sharp scrutiny again. 'Um, well, she does a little sometimes. But she mainly works the tills. She is good with people, so...'

Oh damn, what did I say?

'Well, that is very strange, Sophie.' He reaches inside his jacket and produces a sheet of paper.

He unfolds it and turns it around so I can read the headline at the top of the page.

Talented Local Artist Harriet Harper Hosts Successful Exhibition

I groan inside. That damn article – that is how he found me. But how would he even come across it? It was only a relatively small publication, and only online.

But it was enough it seems. Enough to draw Dan here.

Enough to cost me everything.

61

Dan's eyes burn into me as the gallery phone starts to ring again. I avoid his gaze and stare at the news article in his hands instead. I stare, even though the paper shakes slightly and the text blurs as my eyes fill with tears.

The ringing of the phone stops but continues in my ears as a heavy silence falls once again for a minute or two.

In the end, Dan breaks the silence. 'You can see how I might be confused. Can't you, Sophie?'

'Yes.' Although, the compulsive liar in me won't be defeated yet. 'But, you see the thing is, Harriet does paint all of the pictures, but she – well she is a little shy. So I tell everyone that I paint them.'

'Is that so?' He doesn't believe a word I'm saying now, I can tell. I can't blame him. His tone is flat, bored even. 'The article gives no mention of you. Also, how on earth does Harriet find the time to paint pretty little pictures if she is standing behind this till all day long?'

'Well, she doesn't actually work the till – I do. She stays upstairs and paints.'

'But why did you tell me it was the other way around a few minutes ago?

'I don't know. I guess I just–'

I am made to jump out of my skin by the tinkling of the shop doorbell. Everything seems to happen almost in slow motion as a woman enters.

It is Mrs. Hopkins.

I feel like a bucket of ice water has been thrown over me.

'Harriet, sweetie!' she calls out as she always does.

She bustles over to me in the centre of the shop floor, although I can already see her usual wide smile is notably absent.

I sense Dan move slightly beside the counter, listening intently.

'There you are, Harriet! I've missed you. I feel like you have been hiding away from me!' Ignoring Dan, she glances expectantly behind the counter and around at the canvases hung on the walls. 'So where is it then?'

'Where is what?' I say, my mouth desperately dry.

What little left of her enthusiasm fades instantly. She closes her eyes and sighs, irritated. 'My painting. You said it would be ready for me to pick up today!'

'Oh, that. Right. Um, I'm sorry Mrs. Hopkins. It won't be ready until tomorrow.'

She shakes her head frantically, her eyes wide as if she was expecting this answer already. 'You have been telling me that for weeks! I think I have been more than lenient with you, Harriet. I really do.'

'I know. I've-I've just had a lot going on. I have been working on it, I swear. Can you give me just one more night to get it finished? Then I promise you will get it.'

She huffs. 'No. I have been fobbed off with excuses for too long now, sweetie. I want my money back.'

'Oh, please Mrs. Hopkins – I'm so close to getting it finished. It is upstairs on my easel – I just need to add the finishing touches. It looks great so far.' I don't want to tell her it isn't a patch on the lost original. That it is dull and I would be anxious to even see her reaction to it. She seems intent to spare me, however.

'No really, I must insist on a full refund now, if you will. Let us not drag this farce out any further–'

'But I'm so close, I promise you! Just one more day and–'

'If I may interject?' Dan steps towards me, and puts his arm around my shoulders, pulling me tight towards him. I am hit with the faint smell of stale sweat underneath a strong dose of aftershave.

Mrs. Hopkins looks at him for the first time. I watch her watery eyes take in his rugged good looks and her face instantly softens a little.

I look up at the side of Dan's face I can see, and get a genuine shock. His whole demeanour has changed. He seems far less imposing, far less dangerous than he did two minutes ago. I feel like I imagined the violent way he greeted me. He looks just like the Dan I remember.

His voice takes on a soft tone with a dash of simper. 'I'm not sure if you are aware, but – well – Harriet here has been through a terrible time this past week. There has been a death in the family, you see. And although she has been working on your picture very diligently, despite everything that has been happening, she hasn't been able to get it finished quite in time.'

'Oh really? Oh Harriet, you poor thing. You should have said!' She pauses and I watch her sway, balanced on the edge of a decision. 'Well, perhaps I can wait just another day or two.'

Dan keeps his arm around me, his fingertips digging painfully tight into my shoulder. I keep my face as fixed and neutral as I can. The pressure of holding the same fake expression makes it ache.

'That is most generous of you,' Dan says, inclining his head politely. 'If only more people were like you, the world would be a much more thoughtful place.'

My immediate impression is that he is being too over the top, but then I hear Mrs. Hopkins giggle. I feel disgusted that I can see a vague tinge of pink underneath her thick layer of make-up.

Then she leaves, the bell tinkling ominously behind her in the tense silence of the gallery.

We did it; Dan and I – partners in crime. He managed to charm Mrs. Hopkins into leaving me alone for another day. I can't understand why he didn't just spill the beans, tell her what I have done.

Now that she has gone, I am not sure I actually wanted her to leave. I think I would have liked her to stay, shout at me or call the police even. Anything, rather than leave me alone here in the semi-darkness with an angry Dan.

But the thought of her calling the police makes my insides clench up horribly. I can't face the law, can't have any more contact with them. If they took a second to look any closer, everything would unravel. My fingerprints will still be in their system from my idiotic phase of acting out when I was in college. I was living in a five-bedroomed house in Richmond, Surrey. I didn't need to shoplift. I needed help. Why didn't anyone see that?

Dan waits to make sure Mrs. Hopkins is well and truly gone and moves swiftly over to the front door, pulling keys out of his pocket – my keys – and locks the door securely.

The impression of his fingertips still throbs in my upper arm, stopping me from believing for a second that he has my best interests at heart.

The phone rings again, making me jump.

This time, Dan rushes over to it and snatches the cord irritatedly out of the wall.

Something isn't adding up about his behaviour. Why is he still searching for his wife all this time later? Did she really leave without telling him where she went?

If she hasn't let him know where she is by now, then

I don't think she wants him to. Isn't that obvious to him? It is not like he can force her to take him back.

He walks back over to me, dropping my keys back into his coat pocket.

'Thanks,' I say, feeling pathetic, as limp as if my skeleton had dissolved. 'Thank you for not saying anything to her.'

I hate him being in control. He has my fate in his hands. He will call the police any minute, I know he will – when the penny finally drops. And as soon as he does, my life will be over.

62

Dan's eyes gleam with contempt, and something else; Pity? Fury? 'What was I supposed to say to her, Sophie? Should I have said: This isn't really Harriet Harper? The woman next to me has been conning you all along?'

I need to play for time. At this point, I need to come up with something brilliant. 'I don't know what you mean. You have got this all wrong.'

'Don't act dumb. I can tell you aren't that stupid.'

But I am. That is how I am in this situation in the first place.

'So why did that woman keep calling you "Harriet"!' he roars, some spit flying from his mouth.

'I pretend to be Harriet for the customers – people like to think they are talking to the real artist. Like I said, she is shy, but she keeps her name on the art. I deal with the customers for her, let people believe she is me and she just signs her name on each piece. She doesn't look for recognition or fame or anything, she is happy with our arrangement.' *Can he see the sheen on my forehead in the dim light?*

'Is she happy with you wearing her clothes?' Dan snaps back, quickly moving over to me. 'I bought her that jacket!' He snatches at the lapel, his fingers grazing my chest before he tosses it back again.

I am unnerved by how physically aggressive he is. This isn't the Dan I remember. He was always so polite and charming. I know I am in the wrong here, but he really should keep his hands to himself.

'Yes, it is all part of me being her. So customers get a

376

sense of who the artist is.' God, I've never heard such rubbish, even from myself before. I have never known the gallery to feel so tiny and claustrophobic, either.

Dan is like a dog with a bone. I wish he would relent or I think I might just crack and call the police myself just to get away from him.

He stares at me, and I marvel at how little he blinks. 'But that is going a bit far, don't you think?' he asks. 'Actually *wearing* her clothes?'

Not for me, I want to tell him. Not when the only way I can get through the day is to pretend to be someone else. An individual who isn't broken. Someone who isn't the shame of the family for killing a member of it. Someone who is a real person, not just a pathetic excuse for one.

But I don't tell him any of this. I know he won't understand. 'It was her idea, not mine. I just went along with it. Everything has been fine following her plan.'

Everything *was* fine; before Andrew got attacked; before Debbie started a relentless hate campaign against me; before someone tried to break into my home.

Before I started losing my mind.

He folds his arms and stares intently at me. His gaze hovers over my clothes. Quickly, he snaps without warning, making me jump. 'I have had ENOUGH of this silly little game! Why don't we just stop with the bullshit, right now? You know what, Sophie? I know when I am being lied to. Harriet could have told you that – if you knew her, that is.'

I start to protest, but he cuts across me.

'–I think you have no idea where my wife is. You are just pretending to be her and she is oblivious. She has no idea what you are doing – you have stolen her life –

377

her identity. But I am convinced you don't know her at all. In fact, I would be astounded if she ever said more than two words to someone like you.'

I shake my head, but can't think of a line of defence – my perpetual river of lies has finally run dry.

Dan smirks to himself. 'I know you don't know Harriet. I should have realised sooner. If you did, she would have told you all about me. And if she had done that, there is no way you would still be standing here talking to me.'

I shiver involuntarily. 'What do you mean?'

Dan glances towards the back door where he dropped the plastic sheet when he came in, then back at me. I glance at it too. *What was he doing with that anyway?*

He picks up the leather-bound journal from the counter and thrusts it at me. 'Why don't you read it? You might find it enlightening.'

I had forgotten about the little book. Was Dan the one who wrote all those entries? Why has he been following women – following me – and writing about it afterwards? He must be touched in the head to have done such a thing.

I take the book from him automatically, even though I really don't want to touch it. 'I don't want to read it,' I say quietly.

'Suit yourself. It makes no difference to me.'

He draws himself up and sighs. 'So, you have been here, pretending to be Harriet Harper all this time?'

I can't bring myself to admit it, still. I stare at the floor instead.

'Wait a minute – have you done all this with her money?' He gestures around him at the gallery.

'No!' I say, embarrassed by the amount of earnest in

378

my voice. Caught in the act, and I still don't want Dan to think ill of me. 'No, it isn't with her actual money. It is just... well, I got credit in her name. But I'm-I'm paying it all back... when I can...'

He scoffs and looks at me with disgust. Then something clicks into place behind his furious eyes. 'Back in Tennison Road, I got a statement for a bank account I didn't set up. It said I was two-grand overdue. Did you do that too?'

I shake my head frantically. 'No! No that was Nick. He was my boyfriend – back then. The whole system was his idea, but I left him. I hated what he was doing to you and other people too. I really hated it.'

'But you didn't hate it when you were spending money in my wife's name, did you?'

My voice drops to a shamed mutter. 'I didn't want to take the money. It was just the only way I could get out – leave Nick behind and start a proper life.'

'Well that has worked out well for you hasn't it?'

My eyes sting with tears and my bottom lip trembles.

'Spare me!' Dan hisses, avoiding looking at me. He paces back and forth again.

'So that man – Andrew – he was *your* boyfriend, not my wife's?'

'Yes.'

He laughs to himself, closing his eyes and nodding his head.

I hesitate. 'H-How do you know about Andrew? He hasn't been here all week. He was att–'

A sudden realisation drops into my stomach like a block of ice. Oh, God. I think of how much damage was done to Andrew; then I think of the large plastic sheet Dan brought in with him and realise the biggest danger is not just being arrested.

379

I need to get away from this man.

63

Dan shrugs, as though we are simply neighbours again discussing how clumsy his wife is. 'Sorry about your boyfriend. I thought he was sleeping with my wife – he isn't the first I have suspected. What was I supposed to do, Sophie? Just let him GET AWAY WITH IT!?'

I flinch at his sudden outburst.

This can't be right. Harriet was married to this man. Beautiful, elegant, perfect Harriet – this was her husband. She was married to him for years. She ran away from him in the middle of the night...

I now see I should have used Mrs. Hopkins's interruption as a way to get out. Her arrival was a blessing I did not decipher in time. I should have got out then. It was the perfect opportunity – my last chance.

Another mistake.

I think of the back door. Did Dan lock it when he came in? He was dragging the plastic in when I met him... I feel thoroughly sick when I imagine what he brought it in here for; my blood runs cold as I imagine him wrapping my dead body in it.

I will my brain to think. Yes, I am quite certain he locked the door behind him. I remember him doing it. He has the keys, but even if he didn't, I would never get the door unlocked in time after making a bolt for it. He would catch up with me in about two seconds. Nowhere near long enough.

I still have the diary in my hands. My fingertips are damp on its leathery surface and I come up with the best plan I have, or rather, the only plan I have.

With my heart in my throat, I get ready. I glance up to make sure Dan is still facing me head on.

Then I make my move – I quickly throw the book right in his face.

My aim is for his eyes, but I don't stop to look if I hit my target. My brain receives a brief snapshot of Dan flinching as he instinctively puts his hands up to his face.

I run.

I race straight for the bathroom in the back of the shop, dodging the plastic on the floor.

Slamming the door behind me, I click the lock shut fast and throw my weight against it, just as Dan does on the other side. The impact sends a jarring impact through my neck and I feel the bones at the base of my head grind.

He roars with rage and shouts. Repeatedly he throws his shoulder against the door over and over again.

I glance down at the flimsy lock. I can hear the wood fibres of the cheap door creaking and straining. It won't hold long.

Any minute now he will break through. And I have no doubt that he is going to kill me.

64

Harriet

I didn't have much luck trying to find the other Harriet yesterday. Her shop was shut and there was no one in the flat upstairs. Today, as I pull up at the end of the road and switch off the engine I think I will be greeted with the same scene again.

I see the red shutters of Stony Studios and think it is still closed, but then I notice that the metal guard doesn't extend over the front door today.

Before I have the chance to do anything else, I see the door open and hear the faint tinkling of a bell, before a woman emerges.

Yes! Finally. But then I see the woman properly as she crosses the road. She disappears into the sandwich shop and I find myself staring with my mouth open, bewildered.

She is styled *exactly* how I used to be. Is that another strange coincidence?

The likenesses don't just stop with the same name, age and dream career – she also dresses just like me too? Seeing her breeze by like that was like having a bizarre, out-of-body experience, as though I was watching myself from the perspective of another. But it was like looking into the past – I don't look like that any more.

That was the way I used to look, under Dan's rule. Now I mainly wear jeans and a lot of dark colours, hoping maybe I can shrink into the background. I dyed my hair dark brown too, let it grow long the way I always wanted, but Dan would never let me.

I am unnerved by how she looked – I wasn't prepared for that. There wasn't a photograph of her with the news story...

I wait, tapping my fingers on the steering wheel, unsure of what to do. The sandwich shop looks half-closed. What is she doing in there? I want her to come out again where I can see her, so I can decide what to do next.

I crane my neck trying to see into the window of Sally's Sandwiches, but the light is too reflective on the glass. Perhaps I can take a casual walk past and glance in as I walk by?

I reach across to the passenger seat for my handbag and move my hand to open my door.

Then I freeze in horror, my fingers still gripping the door handle.

It's Dan.

I feel suddenly very sick. My heart pounds noisily as I watch through the windscreen as Dan gets out of a grey BMW further down the street. He takes a quick glance over his shoulder at Sally's Sandwiches, before he slips into Stony Studios.

I sit frozen in my seat; I am suddenly aware that I am pressed firmly back into it.

He didn't look this way, I tell myself. He didn't see me. He couldn't have – he would have marched straight over here. Has he only just arrived? I was here yesterday.

Did I really get here before him?

What the hell do I do? I need to warn this other Harriet, but she hasn't emerged yet. Can I make it into the sandwich shop without Dan noticing me?

I don't dare risk it.

384

I pull my phone out of my handbag and scroll through my call history to find Harriet's mobile number and try calling it again.

It is switched off.

I swear. Why is her phone *still* off? So far I have only got the answering machine. Why does she never switch it on?

I glance up from my phone screen just in time to see Harriet slip out of the shop. She hurries across the road and has to step back quickly to avoid a transit van coming this way.

Throwing caution to the wind, I shout out of the window to her. But I don't think she hears me over the sound of the van's engine.

She steps out into the road again. There is something oddly familiar about her, but I can't conclude what it is.

Without thinking, I open my door but immediately pull it back again when the transit van beeps loudly at me. The driver gestures angrily at me, while his partner gives me a filthy look. They can't be in that much of a hurry that they couldn't let me get out!

I wait for them to pass, my hand on the door. I rush out across the street and onto the pavement, but before I make it I already know it is too late.

The other Harriet is gone.

What do I do now?

I hover uncertainly on the uneven pavement.

Maybe it will be all right. Maybe Dan will realise she isn't who he is expecting. Maybe he will just talk to her a little and just let her go…

My heart sinks. Unless Dan has undergone an amazing transformation over the last couple of years, he is unlikely to do any such thing. He always presented himself as a model citizen around others, but now I am sure he will have worked himself into such a state that he would be incapable of remaining placid, no matter who he is faced with. Like the time we were out at a pub together once. Our evening ended abruptly when he accused me of making eye contact with the bartender.

As soon as we were outside in the dark, he started shoving me towards the car, thinking there was no one else around. A man passing by saw us, tried to intervene. Dan didn't give the guy any warning, he just starting hitting him until the man was on his side in the road, his arms crossed defensively over his face. Even in the dark, I could see the blood dripping onto the asphalt.

That night we walked away and I never heard anything more of it.

Now in broad daylight, I take a few steps closer to Stony Studios, but even before I draw level with the interior design shop, I know I won't go any further. I am unable to move another yard – I am rooted to the ground in fear.

I know I should intervene, step in and make an appearance, but I cannot face Dan.

I walk back over to my car and sit back inside, but I'm not planning to simply leave.

I pick up my phone again.

My hands shake as I search for Harriet's landline number. I am about to press call, when I remember that the phone seems to have been inactive since Wednesday.

I tap the call icon anyway because I am grateful for something to do. Suddenly I am aware I am holding my breath.

It rings. Yes.

Come on, I beg. Come on. Please answer.

I don't know what I'll do if Dan answers; I decide to just end the call without saying anything if he does.

I keep my eyes trained on the front of the shop for any activity, but there isn't any. All seems quiet on the outside. I have no idea what is going on in that building. I dread to think.

The phone continues to ring until I reach the answering machine.

65

Harriet

What do I do now? My insides are writhing with nerves and I feel like I might actually be sick. My phone slips in my damp palms.

I feel like I am married to Dan again. This horrible case of nerves is one I have experienced so many times before. Waiting for the attack. That is the worst part.

If I didn't know better, I would have said that being beaten was the worst, but I know from extensive experience that isn't true. It was almost a relief when the first blow came. Dan would always be on his best behaviour afterwards and I knew I would be safe for a while before he erupted again.

The agonising period from when I knew something had riled Dan, until the moment he made his first physical move was the worst by far.

It is happening again this very moment. Only now it is far worse because I have no idea when – or even if – his first move has been made.

I rock back and forth slightly in my seat. *Should I try the landline again?* I need her to just answer so I can subtly tell her to leave. Or failing that, I want her to pick up the phone so I can tell her to run back out the door into the street. As long as she is in public view, she will be fine again.

If I call too many times, Dan might suspect something. The last thing I need is for him to get wind of the fact that I am nearby.

I'm not sure how much time has passed, but I think it

has been long enough now.

The blood surges in my ears and I strain to listen to each ring, but I hear the answering machine message loud and clear.

Why isn't she answering the phone? Maybe she can't... But why hasn't Dan come back out again? What could he possibly be messing around at?

I am suddenly filled with panic over what might happen when Dan does eventually emerge. I don't want to be here when he does. I hover with my hand over the keys in the ignition, when I see another car pull up close to the gallery.

A woman gets out of a red Range Rover and marches purposefully towards the gallery, pushing in through the door.

Maybe this is a good time. I could go in now and invent an excuse to get Harriet out of there. Dan won't like multiple witnesses. This is my chance...

But I am again paralysed with fear. I don't want to see Dan. Since I left him, I have felt stronger being on my own. But now my stomach turns at the thought of even being in the same room as him.

Maybe Dan will take this as his cue to leave. He has been interrupted. Maybe he will let Harriet go, along with the newcomer.

It isn't possible to talk to Dan when he is angry and believe he is sane. His aggressive disposition is apparent even before he gets physical. If this Harriet has any sense, she will be out of there like a shot at this opportunity.

I see the new arrival leave again after a few minutes – alone.

'No!' I whisper out loud. *'No, why didn't you go with her? What is wrong with you?'*

I try to analyse the woman's expression as she drives past. She looks happy. She has the vestiges of a strange smile on her face.

What is that all about?

I glance back to the gallery door and see Dan through the glass, see his hand move part way up the door in what is unmistakably a locking motion.

He is locking himself in there with her.

I quickly redial the gallery again. I tap my foot on the idle brake desperately. Willing someone to answer the phone.

I hear a break in the ring and inhale sharply thinking that someone has picked up.

Then I hear nothing and the call ends. Someone has unplugged the phone again.

Only this time, I know it isn't her.

What do I do now? I think desperately.

But I know what I need to do. There is nothing else for it. I would never be able to live with myself if I did not take any action while it still matters. I just hope my procrastination hasn't cost a woman her life.

I lift my phone again and am shaking violently when I do what I should have done years ago. I tap in the number and press call.

66

It's funny how when a person's life is stripped back to nothing just how clear everything becomes. Now that I have had the time to think about it, I actually think what happened was for the best. For the first time in a long time, I am not hiding.

The real Harriet showed up that day – the day everything ended. She appeared after the police arrested Dan and put him in the back of their car. It turns out she was just at the end of the road when her ex-husband paid me a visit. Quite lucky really. I'm quite certain I would have been dead now if she hadn't seen that silly little news article.

She came to see me a few weeks ago. I saw her during Dan's arrest, of course, but there was so much going on I couldn't take her in properly; she didn't say much to me that day either. I think she was in shock too. And then, of course, I saw her on another day after that, but I didn't get to speak to her then either.

I have to say I was surprised to see how she looks now. If I'm honest, I liked her better before, when she was elegant, beautiful Harriet. Dan's Harriet. The look she wears now is a much different version of her. I don't know if she has styled herself like that because it is how she feels comfortable, or if she just changed her appearance to help her hide from Dan.

Either way, it turns out *I* looked more like her than she did for a long time. Looking back, I like to think I preserved her, but as hard as I wish against it, any echoes of Harriet are fading from me.

My natural hair colour erupts at the roots,

threatening to take over again; my nail-varnish is chipped, as are my nails, not filed and neat as they were before; I haven't applied any make-up now since I left Stonegravel Street. I would love to prolong Harriet – preserve her further – but I can't, not in this place.

I like to think I did some good though. Thanks to me, the real Harriet won't have to worry about Dan for a good while. He has been sent away for a lot longer than I have. When the police arrested him, they found the journal he had religiously kept, detailing violent incidents with Harriet, as well as his monitoring of her family, friends – dentist. The log goes back years and I am told he admitted everything – GBH, stalking, harassment – he was compliant. He didn't admit to sending the notes though, but that is no surprise to me. I already know who was behind that...

It surprised me how cooperative I was when the police arrested me. I didn't even try to run. It was almost a relief, in the end, to be caught.

It meant it was finally over.

I know Harriet is pleased with me. She didn't exactly say it, but I know that is what she was thinking. Of course, she was annoyed with me at first when she found out what I had done – she had every right to be. But because of everything that happened, she can finally sleep soundly at night knowing Dan isn't out there somewhere.

Until he gets out she can live without fear, and I, for one, know that is worth its weight in gold. I did that for Harriet. Unwittingly, I have to say, but it was because of me. I have done her a favour and she knows it.

What kind of half-life was she living in hiding, anyway? I know better than anyone how hard that can be. *It really takes its toll after a while.*

My barrister tells me we did well in court. She told the judge there were mitigating circumstances, that I had a difficult childhood, with no support from my family and untreated PTSD. She got me a fourteen-month sentence officially, but she says if I behave myself I can get out sooner.

I don't mind this place that much now. I *hated* it at first. What upset me the most though was not being able to see Andrew again. He apparently made a full recovery, even though he only remembers bits and pieces of the day of the attack.

One of my biggest regrets is that I drew Dan towards Andrew. Dan went after him because of me, and Andrew suffered because of my mistakes.

I felt such a connection with Andrew. My heart aches every time I think of him. I almost told him the truth so many times, but I never had the courage. Maybe in time, I would have told him everything, but I guess I will never know now. I didn't want to risk losing him. Ironic now, I know, but that is the truth. He has no idea how honoured he should feel – I don't tell the truth to anyone, not even myself sometimes.

I was just disappointed that I couldn't be there to see Andrew recover, to visit his bedside, for him to know that I was there.

But I don't want to see him now – or rather – I don't want him to see me. The real me. That isn't who he was attracted to. He might have even been in love with Harriet.

He has tried to visit me so many times, but I always deny his requests. I have received so many letters from him too, but I don't have the courage to open them. I just threw them all away.

I think he must be angry with me. Why else would

he still try so determinedly to get in contact now he knows what I have done? Who I really am.

He probably only writes to tell me how disgusted he is with me, how much he hates me, how dare I, and all that. I have heard it all from my mother over the years, I don't want to hear it from Andrew too – it would hurt too much.

Dave popped in for a brief visit when I was awaiting trial. We had some business to take care of and he didn't exactly come bearing good news. He informed me that someone had broken into the gallery in my absence and stolen the cash left in the till, along with some canvases from the window display. The culprit didn't get far though; he was caught elsewhere in the neighbourhood. Apparently, he was a homeless man, who had been stealing food and electricals from the properties on Stonegravel Street for a long while.

Dave seemed nervous during his visit. I think he was glad to have something to witter on about while I signed some forms. Either that, or he really thought I would sleep easier at night when I found out what had happened to my kettle and the missing packet of biscuits.

As my landlord, he was tasked with sorting out the contents of the flat. He found my phone in my bedroom, lodged between the mattress and the side of the bed frame. I could have kicked myself when I heard. Still, I don't need it now.

Dave was quite nice about everything really, considering the circumstances. He even offered to put my things into storage for me. I told him not to bother. I won't need any of that when I leave this place.

The first thing I will do when I get out of here is to get some new clothes – some that aren't like Harriet's. I never really liked that blazer of hers that much anyway. I felt I could never really relax when I wore it. Now I can see why Harriet tried to get rid of it in the first place.

I go to see the prison councillor now for my PTSD. She isn't very good; not at all warm and patient like Julia was. This woman plants a half-hearted smile on her face and goes through the motions, jotting down things here and there, filling in her nice little forms. I have learned what to say to get some ticks in the right places and some positive comments on my record. Telling the truth seemed to get me extra sessions, and I didn't want that. In this place, I already feel like I have been stripped bare. Like everyone can see the real me.

I don't like it.

But I can regrow my skin when I get out of here. Build a new protective layer to hide behind.

Reinvent myself.

Life is about reinvention. A change is as good as a rest. What I really need to do when I get out is to start again. Get a fresh start somewhere new where no one knows me. A clean break.

I might be plain old, abhorrent, useless Sophie again for now.

But who knows who I will be in two years time.

I might even be a whole new person.

Author's Note

Thank you so much for reading *In Her Footsteps*. If you enjoyed it, then I would love to hear what you think.

As a first-time author, I am incredibly humbled to contemplate the thought of people reading this story, since it was merely an idea for many years.

I drew a lot of inspiration for this story from my own experiences. Having lived through an abusive marriage to my own "Dan" for over six years, I found his character naturally seeped out and into the pages of the book. Whilst no scene with him in the novel is an exact replica of what happened, they are a very close mirror-image.

In my early twenties, I was victim to identity theft in the same way that Harriet was – through an insecure communal post-box in the building where I lived at the time. Although I must admit, the consequences for me weren't as exciting as the events in the story. Identity theft is currently a silent epidemic and most people remain unaware it has even happened to them.

If you have any comments on my book, you can contact me on Twitter, Goodreads or via my website www.RuthHarrow.com where you can also sign up for free giveaways and exclusive updates on my next book which I am currently working on.

I would love to hear from you, and thanks again for choosing my book.